Honor Thy Father and Thy Mother

a novel

by
Richard Edward Noble

First Edition

ISBN 978-0-9798085-2-4

Published in the United States of America
by
Noble Publishing, 889 C. C. Land Rd., Eastpoint, Fl. 32328.

Cover layout and design by
Graphic Designer, Diane Beauvais Dyal

A Note from the Author

This is my third published work. I was raised and educated in Lawrence, Massachusetts. Lawrence was an industrial mill town. A few of the old redbrick textile mills and shoe shops still line Broadway and Canal Street and meander along the local waterways.

Once you start reading this book you will quickly become aware that this is not a fantasy or a product of my imagination. Like many works of fiction, this novel contains more fact than fiction - but it is fiction.

Keeping all that in mind, I advise you to go ahead and read. If there is any real benefit to be gained from this book it will come to you as you read the book. So, as is so often said but maybe not with this intent, this book is a "must read." I do hope that the reader will find this work to be more than just entertainment.

Dedication

My wife, Carol, is first on my list for thanks and appreciation. She has worked very hard to help me make this book a success. She has done layout, editing, proof reading and more than I could ever have expected with our computer. Her good friend Diane Dyal provided her expertise in graphic design and cover art. Dawn Evans Radford a friend and author of *Oyster Flats* tackled reviewing and editing. Ruth Morrill, a friend and neighbor struggled with Carol and me through the initial reading, editing, cutting and revisions. The very first preview was accepted by my old friend Richard Anderson Sr. Dick offered numerous compliments and an equal number of criticisms - all of which have been included and not included as suggested. I hope all my friends and assistants will be satisfied with the results.

I greatly appreciate everyone's help, assistance and suggestions. I thank you all sincerely.

1 The Goodbye Kiss

"RICHARD! RICHARD!"

He heard his mother calling. He looked and saw her standing there on the wooden porch. She was all dressed up. She had makeup on, and a hat. It was midday. He ran towards her. He flipped the latch on the gate to the chainlink fence with a stick that he had been playing with. He ran and leaped up the four wooden steps that led to the porch. His mother was worried. She was very worried.

He was a little preschooler with blond hair and big blue, Tweety Bird eyes. He was one of those kids who always looked worried and lost. One look at the wonder and confusion in his eyes always made his grandmother laugh and want to hug him and pinch his cheeks. He never resisted.

His mother squatted down in her high heels and fancy dress. She looked like a new person to him, with her lips bright and red, and her cheeks an artificial rose. She embraced the cheeks of his face with the palms of her hands. She stared into his confusion—her eyes misty with the fogginess of possible tears.

"Now you'll be a good boy, won't you?"

He nodded his head as he trembled inside. What was happening? Where? Where was she going? Why was she so nervous, so frightened? She was staring into his eyes, but she wasn't seeing him. She was talking, but not to him.

"Mommy has to go to work, now. Daddy can't make enough money, so Mommy has to go to work too." Her lips trembled. This was very serious, he thought to himself. He had never seen his mother in this state before. She had never before been so tender. She never looked helpless. Never, ever before did she look as though she needed his help. She had never, ever touched his face so softly. Now suddenly she was hugging him to her body. She was squeezing him strongly. This was a new experience. He didn't know what to do with his arms. He didn't know how he was expected to react. So he didn't react. He stood with his arms dangling at his sides and his body limp.

She smelled of a strong perfume - lilacs or flowers. This was all very strange. She never wore perfume. She never dressed up in high heels. She never hugged him, or touched his face tenderly with her hand. What did she want from him?

"I can't be here with you like a good mother should because now I have to go to work. This is not what I want to do, but we don't have enough money, so I have to." She pushed him from her embrace by grasping his shoulders with her strong hands. She peered intently into his eyes, which were now moist with their own tears. "You know, if I could, I would stay here taking care of you, don't you?" she sobbed with her voice cracking. He nodded his head. "But I can't. I have to go to work. I can't keep begging from my brothers and sisters just because my husband can't provide for his family."

She was still peering into his eyes, but yet not talking to him. But who was she talking to? "But I am going to do it. Just like when I was fourteen and I took care of my brothers and sisters. They've forgotten it all now, but it was me who paid for their school clothes. It was me who quit school and went to work and paid for their little shoes and their little dresses. No! They have forgotten all of that. They don't remember now, but I haven't forgotten. You are going to have to be good." Now, she was speaking to him. "Stay around the house. I don't want no trouble. Do you understand?" She was not asking a question, but he answered yes anyway. "I'll be back. I'll be home for supper." Then suddenly, she kissed him and on the LIPS. She leaned her head back and took a good look at his confused face, and struggled a smile. She hugged him again quickly, and then pulled away. She stood up, straightened her dress, took a deep breath and started down the porch steps. As she flipped the latch on the gate, she admonished him once again. "You'll be good now won't you?"

"Yes, I'll be good. You won't have to worry."

"Okay? You promised. I'm off. Bye, bye."

"Bye."

He watched his mother walk away. He went down the steps and out the gate. He watched her walk all of the way to the end of the street. Then she turned to the right, and was gone.

He sat down on the curb. With his stick, he swished around the dirt and a paper gum wrapper in the gutter. His mother's worried face lingered in his mind's eye. She was truly worried about him. He would have to be very good. This would be very important. She had called him over just to kiss him and say goodbye. It felt funny to be kissed. Her lips were moist and sticky from the paste she had on them. They were cold. Her hands were cold also. His mother didn't kiss often, and never on the lips. She didn't hug often either. His grandmother always hugged him and kissed him, and that's why he often went up to her apartment. He would lie on his grandmother's carpet and listen to her old, floor radio play Polish polkas. His grandmother spoke no English and he no Polish, but he knew that she loved him. They would sit in the same room without a word, and feel comfortable together.

He went to his grandmother's often. She always had soup cooking on the back of her old-fashioned stove. She sometimes had chocolate pudding with milk on it for him. He really didn't care for the milk but the chocolate pudding made it worthwhile.

His grandmother lived in the tenement house with him and his family. Some of his aunts and uncles lived there also. It was an old building in a blue-collar, New England mill town. His grandmother had always been old. She had gray hair and hobbled about with one weary, wrinkled hand bracing a hip. She looked old, tired and worn. But whenever little Richard appeared, her tender eyes would sparkle with joy and her grooved and wrinkled face would beam and blossom. She would smile. She would tweak his cheeks. She would laugh and make funny, little, sing-song noises. Sometimes it would hurt when she would tweak his cheeks, but he liked to be touched by his grandmother. His mother's touching was another story.

Why all of this touching today? Why a kiss; and a kiss on his lips? What was this all about?

The next day it was the same treatment.

"RICHARD! RICHARD!"

He came running. He flipped the latch and ran up the stairs. She hugged him. She admonished him to be good. She smelled once again of lilacs. She had tears in her eyes. She smiled. To see his mother smiling was not wonderment; it was a miracle.

"Be good," she said.

"Yes."

"No trouble?"

"No trouble."

"Okay."

A final hug and then another kiss.

There was something important going on here. He didn't know why, but it was important. It was very, very important.

As the days went by, it seemed to get more and more important. Certainly it became more and more important to Richard. For some unexplained mystery, at a particular time each day, his mother needed him. She had never needed him before. In the past he was always in the way, under her feet, in her hair. Now, suddenly she needed him. She needed him very, very badly. She needed him so badly, that it made her cry. She cried each day, every time. She was frightened. He understood being frightened. It was very important that he be there so she could kiss him goodbye. That kiss was giving her strength. It was giving her courage. It was very, very important that she kissed him goodbye. It made her smile. When she smiled, her eyes sparkled. For that moment, somehow, things were better. When she kissed him and then smiled, somehow a great burden was lifted. A cloud had just been removed from the sky; there was a new star in the heavens above; the sun had gained one extra ray of warmth. This kissing and hugging business was important. Oh my, yes! It was very, very important.

Wherever Richard was in the morning, he was sure to be there at the appointed time when his mother would make her appearance on that porch. And each time the experience got better and better. Sometimes she would even smile just to see him running towards her from the street. Her lips were always cold and paste-like. Her hug was nervous and frightened; her eyes always moist and watery; her cheeks red and rouged; her odor floral and overpowering. The smile was fleeting, but yet a peek at his mother's soul. That look was a startling flash, a ray of light, a moment of sunshine, a bit of truth. What was it? He didn't know. But it was important. It was very, very important. It was more important than anything that he had ever imagined. It was something between him and his mother. At a certain time, Monday through Friday, his mother needed him. Out of some unknown, unspoken necessity, his mother must hold him at this time. This act meant something to her. It was important for her to kiss him. As the weeks went by, he just knew that as long as he was there for her at that precise time, available for her hug and her kiss, everything would be all right. It was very easy to do; be there, on time; let her hold you; let her kiss you. Then she would be protected, and all would be right with the world.

One day, he was playing on the next block in woods on the corner. He was in the clubhouse that he and his little buddies had made from discarded wooden crates. He and his friends were trying to build a second story on their clubhouse. It was fun. They were trying to build a tenement, just like their real house. The time had passed, and somehow he had forgotten about his mother and their new ritual. A picture of her worried face flashed before him. The appointed time had passed and he knew it.

He leaped to the ground and went running up through the woods, then through the alleyway between the white-shingled house and the yellow wooden house. He then squeezed through the yellow-slatted, wooden fence that guarded the big yellow tenement and the pole of the adjoining chainlink fence of the white-shingled house. From his position there on that sidewalk he could see his front porch.

His mother was not standing there waiting for him. He was already out of breath. He ran between the parked cars and crossed the street. From that sidewalk he could see to the far corner. He saw a woman rounding that corner, and to the right. It was her! It had to be her.

He would catch her. He would run up behind her and catch her. He would pull on her skirt. She would turn and look down at him with that worried look in her eye. She would see him standing there and then everything would be safe.

He ran. He spanked his side as he ran. The spanking was for his horse - that invisible horse that all children his age rode so well. He had a fast horse. He would catch his mother. But by the time he had gotten to the corner, she was gone.

The view from this corner was much greater. He had never been all the way to this corner by himself. He had only been this way once, and he had his mother’s hand to hold at that time. They had turned at the very next corner. But, there in the distance, far ahead - wasn’t that a figure walking up there? Yes ... yes ... it had to be! That must be his mother.

He cupped his hands to the sides of his mouth and yelled, "Maaaaaahhhhh! Maaaaahhhhhhh!" But she was too far off into the distance. She could not hear him. He screamed once more, but the figure in the distance just kept walking. There was only one thing to do. He would have to catch up to her. He would put his head down and speed as fast as he could. He would catch her. There would be no doubt about it. Richard and his faithful horse with no name could run like the wind when they wanted to.

As he ran, he kept his eye fixed on the figure in the distance. He had never, ever been this far from his house by himself. He had never been all the way to the end of this street. There were more cars on this street than on his home street.

He could see the redbrick wall of a big mill at the far end of this road. He could see his mother. She had stopped and was waiting to cross the street that passed before the great, redbrick mill. There were lots of cars passing in both directions before her. He was worried for her safety. His eyes were tearing up from the wind and the speed of his running, and the terrible anxiety that was swelling inside of him. What horrors could befall his mother if she were not to be protected on this day by the mystery of his hug and the comfort from his kiss? She would be so worried and filled with fear from his absence that something horrible would happen. It would be all his fault, for he would have let her down. He would have failed in his duty. The protective shield that blanketed her and brought her to smile and gave her courage would not be with her on this day. It would be all his fault. It was inevitable. Now something terrible would happen. His eyes were now so filled with tears that all the buildings and all the cars were distorted and blurred. The buildings moved and swayed as though viewed through a fishbowl. The sidewalk began to roll in front of him. He began falling and stumbling, and when he looked up and into the distance, his mother was gone. Her black dress had completely disappeared.

He rose and rubbed his eyes with his sleeves. Miracle of miracles, she was there once again. He would not even blink now for fear that she might once again disappear. He screamed to her for a third time. She was still waiting there in the distance, but she didn't turn. He would stare at her back and send soundless, invisible messages that would act like rays.

She would feel them poking at her back. She would then turn and see him coming to save her.

She didn't turn. The light changed and she crossed to the other side of the street. He screamed, "Mother!" over and over again. It was to no avail. Why couldn't she hear him? He could see her now. She wasn't all that far away. There were lots of cars and lots of noises and lots of reasons.

Finally he was at that distant corner. He was on the sidewalk before the whizzing traffic. She was right there across the street. She was entering into the mill by way of a huge, green door, which was a tiny part of an even greater, wooden, green wall. The huge, green wall was made of slats. They were like the slats on a picket fence. The green wall was a gate in itself - a giant, wooden gate that separated the redbrick walls of this grand castle. It was a castle just like in the story books. It had peaks and towers and walls and pathways and gangplanks that stretched between the buildings and floated in the air. Crowds of women were walking on the pathways going from one building to another.

The buildings were massive structures. They stretched in both directions as far as the eye could see. They were six and seven stories high. They had long, huge windows but the windows were covered with dirt. You could see nothing that might exist on the inside of them. Suddenly all of the cars stopped racing in front of him. People began to pass from one side of the street to the other. He grabbed onto a woman's coat, quietly, and ran behind her to get to the opposite sidewalk. She didn't even notice. He ran to the fence and peeked through the slats. He saw his mother turn and enter through a door and into the redbrick building to the left. He pulled on the door that had been cut into the huge, green gate but he could not get it to open. He returned to the slatted, green wall, stuck his face between two of the slats and stared at the door through which his mother had entered into the red-brick building.

He tried to crawl under the fence but the bottoms of the slats were just slightly too close to the ground. He could get his arm under the fence, and his leg, but his chest and his head would just not make the squeeze. But he tried.

This was the worst thing that had happened to him in his entire life. He had abandoned his mother and now, undoubtedly, something terrible would happen to her. And it would all be because she was not protected by his small hug and mysterious kiss.

He began to cry as he rose once again and pushed his face between the slats of the big green wall. He stared at the space in the wall through which his mother had disappeared. His tears were now beyond his control. He crumbled to the ground. He sat with his elbows braced on his legs which were crossed beneath him. He buried his face into the palms of his hands and cried as he rocked back and forth there on the sidewalk before the giant, imposing, and impenetrable green monster that separated him from his mother.

"Hey, hey, what is a big boy like you doing here crying?" A strange man was squatting down next to him and rubbing him on the back with his huge hand. "It can't be that bad, can it?" Richard didn't know what to do, so he just kept rocking and crying. He wouldn't remove his face from his hands. He was ashamed to be crying. "You're not hurt, are you? Did you fall down?" The man explored the boy's legs and ankles for broken bones or tender places. "I don't feel anything broken. Come on now. Can you stand up?"

Richard stood, but he kept his face in his hands and continued to sob. "It is all right to cry. Everybody cries. It is all right to cry, as long as a man has a reason. I am sure that a big boy like you has a reason to cry, and I'll bet that it is a good one, isn't it?" Richard nodded his head up and down with his face still wrapped in his hands. "Okay," the man proclaimed as he pried a hand free from Richard's face. "Let's go inside and see what we can do about this situation."

The man led Richard over to the green door that was cut into the huge, green fence wall. He pushed the door open, then lifted Richard up into one of his arms and carried the boy inside. He took a bright, red handkerchief from his back pocket and proceeded to wipe the tears from Richard's eyes. "Okay now, tell the old man here what the problem is?" Richard tried to explain, but gulps of tears and gasps for breath kept getting in the way. Yet he told the story as best he could under the circumstances. The man laughed. "Oh really?" he said. "That's exactly what I thought. I knew that it had to be something very, very serious. Well, I'm going to tell you something. This is a problem that I can handle. I can't handle too many problems, and to tell you the truth, sometimes I would just like to sit down and cry too. But, nevertheless, I've got you covered with this here problem of yours, buck-y-boy. We are going to go over here and we are going to talk to the big boss about this whole situation."

They entered a little building just beyond the gate. There was a man inside sitting behind a desk. When the man saw his buddy come through the door with Richard sitting on one arm, he leaned back in his swivel chair and smiled.

"Well, well?" he said, looking at Richard's tear drenched cheeks and raw eyes. "This looks very serious ... very serious indeed. What's the problem here, Jack?"

"Well, I'll tell you boss, we got a big problem. As I understand the complaint, this young man's mother has run off without kissing him goodbye. If he doesn't find her and give her his goodbye kiss, as he does everyday, there is going to be a very serious catastrophic consequence. So, did I tell that right, son?" the man asked, while searching Richard's eyes with a face gravely serious.

Richard nodded, positively. Both men laughed. Richard suddenly felt foolish and he buried his face into his hands and began once more to cry.

"No, no, no. Hold on here, son. We're not laughing at you. Are we, Jack?"

"No sir!"

"No sir is right! I'll tell you what I'm laughing at. I'm laughing because it wasn't too long ago that the very same thing happened to me."

Richard uncovered his face and stared at the man who was now up and out of his swivel chair and sitting on the edge of his desk. "That's right," he said, appealing to the child and winking to Jack with a grin. "But it wasn't my mother who left me with not so much as a kiss, but my once lovely and dear bride." Richard was interested. "Yes indeed, one day she just walked out the door. I thought she was going grocery shopping. She didn't go grocery shopping. Do you know where she went?" Richard, sitting high in Jack's muscular arm, shook his head negatively. "She went to the damn bank and drew out all of my money." Jack laughed. "And when I went down to the bank a week later and found out how much money she had taken, I sat down on the carpet, right in front of the teller's window, and bawled my eyes out." Both men laughed. Richard looked into Jack's eyes for corroboration.

"That's right! That's the truth. I saw him, myself. Look at the size of him, will you? Can you imagine a grown man like him, sitting on the floor of the bank, crying his eyes out?" Richard looked, dubiously, from Jack to the boss.

"Darn right and I was embarrassed. It's one thing for a little tyke like you to cry, but can you imagine a big lug like me sitting in the middle of a bank lobby, crying his eyes out?"

Richard examined the boss. He was a large man, with stubble on his face. He had workman-like muscular arms. He would look strange sitting on a floor crying. He smiled at the thought. The men laughed.

"Did she ever come back with your money?" Richard asked.

"No, she didn't, but your mother is coming back, and we are going to find her. What's your mother's name?"

"Mama."

"Right, mama, I should have known that. Did you ever call her anything else besides mama?

"Mother."

"Anything else?"

"Ma."

"Do you know your mother's last name?" The boy stared, blankly.

"What did your mother call you?"

"Richard."

"Okay Richard, and what is your last name? Richard what? My first name is Bob and my last name is Ross. Your first name is Richard, and your last name is what?" Richard was perplexed. He had no idea that he had any other name. If his mother had a last name he had never heard it mentioned. "What does your father call your mother?"

"Mary."

"Mary, ah ha! Do you know any Marys, Jack?"

"Oh maybe a couple of hundred; this is Roman Catholic country. Marys are everywhere. My little girl is Mary. My sister is Mary."

"Well, let me go over to the office and check with Marilyn, anyway."

Jack put Richard over in a corner in a big chair. "Don't worry son. The boss will find your mother."

Richard wasn't worried. He felt safe with Jack and "Boss." He was in their hands. They had told him not to worry. They were grownup men, like his dad.

He kicked his heels on the rungs of the chair and looked around the room. Everything was old and dark-brown. The room was smoky. The desk was covered with papers.

It was scary not to know your "last" name. What was a last name? If you don't know your last name people don't know who you are or who you belong to. What if these men are unable to find his mother? What if that image that he had chased all the way over here wasn't even his mother? What if she had gone in another direction? How would he get back home? How had he gotten here? What would these men do with him, if they couldn't find his mother?

"I want my mother?" Richard cried out from his large chair. "I want my mother."

"Hey, hey, hey, don't get rambunctious over there. Your mother is going to be here in two minutes. Don't you worry. Do I look like the kind of a guy who would lie?"

"No."

"Well then, just take it easy. Let us worry about everything from now on, okay?"

"Okay."

Jack ruffled the boy's hair as he walked away and returned to what he had been doing. Richard's Uncle Ray used to ruffle his hair like that all the time. His Uncle Joe did too. His Uncle Joe had a gold tooth. He liked it when Uncle Joe smiled.

Jack and the boss brought Richard a soda and some potato chips. They asked him questions. His answers often made them laugh. Richard liked the two men. They were like his father. His father was always "away." He worked on a ship.

A large clock on the wall was the biggest clock that Richard had ever seen. Richard waited in the room with Jack and the boss for a long, long time. Jack and the boss were tracking down "Marys" all morning, but never the right one. They decided to just babysit until the shift ended. At that time the big gate would be opened and they could stand out in the forefront and petition all of the mothers.

Both men liked Richard. He was a cute, little guy. He spoke only when spoken to and he did whatever he was told. He had those big eyes of wonderment. Whenever either of them looked at the boy, he was looking at them. He was a people kid. His eyes soaked in everything. They could look into those intense eyes and see the wheels turning. He was very busy thinking and figuring. He was not the type of kid who would just sit there counting the fingers on his own hands or playing with his shoelaces.

The room was a wonderment and these men were a curiosity to him. They explained to him whatever they were doing. The boy wasn't a bother. He was attentive, obedient and quiet.

Five o'clock was the change of shift. A minute or so before the shift buzzer sounded, they went out and opened the big gate. They brought Richard out with them. As the ladies piled out of the redbrick buildings, the two men began shouting.

"Look here ladies! Look here ladies! We've got something here that belongs to one of you! Look here ladies!" they yelled.

Richard's big eyes leaped from one woman's face to another. The men continued screaming, but most of the women were chatting and talking. They didn't seem to notice. Jack then placed Richard up onto his shoulder, and both men began pulling women's sleeves and pointing up to the boy. There were hundreds and hundreds of women exiting the building. Finally a woman emerged from out of the crowd. The blur of faces was suddenly just one. It was his mother. Jack placed Richard onto the ground and he immediately ran over and wrapped himself about his mother's leg.

"That little tyke has been here all day," they informed the lady, cheerfully. The woman wasn't smiling. She wasn't smiling at all. Her face just seemed to get redder and redder by the instant. "Ahh, don't get me wrong," Jack interjected in a sort of defense. "He wasn't any trouble."

"No, no," Bob joined in the chorus. "He's a heck of a good kid. It was fun having him around for awhile. He was absolutely no trouble at all." The woman was not hearing a word. Her face was crimson with embarrassment and outrage.

"Yes, yes, thank-you, I'll take care of everything. I'm very sorry. It will never happen again; I assure you."

She was not about to discuss this situation with strangers. She was embarrassed. What did these men think of her? What kind of mother did they think that she was? Why wasn't a boy his age being kept somewhere, maybe with a relative or something? What was he doing out and wandering the streets of Lawrence by himself? She didn't know what to say, or how to defend herself. What possible excuse could she offer? There was no excuse. She wanted to just disappear. She could die. She wanted to cover her face and hide.

It was too late. The damage had been done. Now she just wanted to escape, to get away from these men and their inquiring eyes as quickly as possible. She couldn't even look them in the eye. She hung her head, and began busying herself with the task of untangling the frightened boy from her side. He didn't want to let her go, but she un-peeled him.

"Hold my hand," she directed the boy. "Thank-you, thank-you very much, this will never, ever happen again," she told the two men.

"Oh, that's okay. No problem. He was very well-behaved."

"Yes ma'am, he is a fine little boy." They were both well aware of the mother's anger and nervousness. They could see that junior was in trouble and they were prompting for a reprieve. "He did everything that he was told to do. I wish my two at home had a little of Richard's temperament."

"Don't be too rough on him, ma'am. He was well intentioned and everything worked out just fine."

"Yes, yes, thank-you." And Mary scurried off dragging Richard by the arm. She was rushing so fast and holding Richard's arm up so high, that the boy's feet were barely hitting the ground. He kept losing his step and falling to his knees, but she would snatch him up quickly to a standing position. He tried running to keep up with her, but she was going too fast. They crossed the highway with him half flying through the air and half dragging on the ground.

Richard was excited. He kept waving to his new friends, Jack and Boss, over his shoulder as he bounced along his way. He wanted to tell his mother everything about his day. It had all been so exciting. But the traffic was so loud, and there were hundreds of women talking and laughing. He was so happy to have found his mother. It was a miracle that nothing had befallen her. She was safe and she hadn't even received his goodbye kiss. It was probably his presence so nearby that had saved her from any disaster. He had done the right thing. Everything had turned out fine. They had found one another, and his mother was safe.

For some strange reason his mother was nearly yanking his arm out of its socket. It hurt. She was in such a rush that she just didn't realize what she was doing, he thought. He tried to tell her that she was hurting him. She paid no attention. He tried pulling his hand from hers but it was not possible.

When they finally got across the street, his mother quickly ducked into an alley dragging him behind.

"You're hurting my arm Mama. You're hurting me."

"What do you think you are up to?" she yelled.

"I ... I ..."

"Are you trying to make a damn fool out of me?"

"No ... I ... I ..."

"What were you doing over there?" she screamed. Her scream was so intense, it startled Richard.

He looked up into her enraged face. He didn't understand. Why was she so angry? Jack and Boss had told her how good he had been. He wanted to tell her that she had left without kissing him goodbye and that he was worried about her.

Before he had a chance to explain adequately, her right hand cracked against the side of his head. It was a hard blow and it made the boy stagger to one side. He was quickly straightened up when her left hand caught him forcefully on his opposite cheek. He was stunned and wobbling. What had he done? His ears were ringing. He covered his ears with his hands and began to cry. This is what he had always done at these times. She was yelling and he was staring into her horrid, screaming, hellish face. Her face was so ugly and filled with hate. He had thought that something had changed with all this kissing and hugging business. She began to strike him harder and more ferociously. He covered his head with his arms and fell to his knees and screamed pleadingly as she continued to beat him.

The blows stopped momentarily. He peeked up and into his mother's eyes. A number of women were standing at the edge of the alley. They were yelling things at his mother. His ears were still ringing and he couldn't understand what they were screaming. His mother yelled back at them. She told them that it was none of their business. She grabbed onto his hand and yanked him from the ground. She pushed and shoved her way through the crowd of women bundling at the alley's edge.

She dragged him home, sometimes just yanking him through the air. He had stumbled several times and had ripped holes in the knees of his pants from banging onto the sidewalk. He had cuts on his knees and he could feel blood running down his legs. He didn't speak. He was much too frightened. His mother had lost her mind again! Was this horrid person still his real mother, he questioned? Her face had changed completely. It was now hateful and ugly. It was full of meanness. He dare not speak. He dare not cry. What would she do once they were home? What would this strange, ugly person do to him? How would he protect himself? He was too small. He could run, but where could he run to?

Once home, she flung him into his room and slammed the door shut. He scurried under the bed and into the farthest corner. He hugged his knees up to his chin and rocked back and forth while he cried. His mother was pacing up and down the kitchen ranting and raving. She had lost her mind. She was acting crazy! She was another person.

"Trying to make a fool out of me, I should break every bone in your body! You little fool! What in hell do you think I am? Everybody looking at me! What kind of mother do they think I am?" She was pacing back and forth in the kitchen and screaming to the heavens. The bedroom door would open momentarily and he would shiver and shake with fear. His heart would jump. "What kind of mother do they all think that I am now!" He cringed at the thought that she would come for him under the bed to beat him once again. When the door would shut, he would feel safe for a moment. Finally there was quiet. He would nevertheless remain under the bed.

His older sister arrived home from her day at school. His mother then screamed the whole day's events to her in detail. She screamed and screamed and screamed! Richard feared that at any moment she would send herself off into another rage and bust into his bedroom. The door flung open.

"And if you ever do that again I'll knock your damn teeth out! Let me tell you buster, I will knock some sense into that dumb skull of yours! You can bet on that, little man! If you forget this time, you can be sure that you will not forget the next time!"

And so the little boy had truly learned his lesson. He would never do that again. He would never, ever do that again.

He would not make the same mistake twice.

He would never again feel sorry for his mother.

He would never, ever again worry about her.

He would not be so foolish as to be swayed by her apparent need for his kiss, or his hug.

No no no ... never again ... never, ever again would he hug his mother.

No no no ... never again ... never, ever again would he kiss his mother.

No, not under any circumstance would he be so foolish again ... not EVER.

2 First Day of School

"Well, what are you doing here?"

Richard was sitting on the curb. He had a note pad and a pencil. He was scratching squiggly lines onto the pad with his pencil. The postman was standing behind him with his sack of mail over his shoulder. He was reviewing a number of letters that he had bunched up in his hand. Richard looked up into the man's smiling face.

"I'm writing."

"Oh, you are? That's good. What are you writing?"

"I'm writing a book."

"Oh really? You're too little to know how to write."

"No sah ... I can write." He held his note pad up for the man to see.

"I don't see any words there, son. All that I see is some squiggly lines."

"No, no, these are words. Listen." He put his book onto his lap and began to read. "Tomorrow, I am going to school. See?" he said looking up at the man.

"Yes, now I see. Write some more?"

Richard began composing once again. As he squiggled lines onto his pad, he read the squiggles to the postman.

"And I am going to be very happy, and the nuns will like me very much. They will not want to hit me or knock my block off."

The postman laughed. "Oh it is going to be your first day at school, is it? Well I am sure you will do just fine. The nuns will probably like you because you already know how to read and write. I shouldn't think that they will knock your block off."

"And I can spell too."

"You can? Let me hear you spell cat?"

"D - f - r - n – p."

“That’s right! Hey, you are pretty good. Well, you take care. Good luck tomorrow.”

School would be an experience. His mother had been priming him for it for months now.

“You are going to be in for quite a surprise my little boy. Wait until those nuns get their hands onto you. You’re going to find out how easy you’ve had it around here. The nuns won’t take any of your guff, let me tell you. You look at one of them cross-eyed or give them that stupid look of yours and bamb! They’ll knock your block off.”

“Oh, the nuns aren’t that bad,” his sister Carol, interrupted. “You keep telling him all that stuff Ma, and he ain’t going to want to go to school at all.”

“He needs to be told. I’m just giving him a fair warning.”

“Oh don’t pay any attention to her, Richard. She has never even seen a nun.”

“Oh yeah? I’ve seen plenty of nuns. I knew nuns before you were even born there, sister. You’ve been going to school for a couple of years now and you already think that you know everything. Well, don’t get too big for your britches, little girl, because I can put that smart little smile right on the other side of your face.”

Carol quietly left the breakfast table. She knew when to walk away and keep her mouth shut. Get a little too mouthy and she could be getting “a crack in the teeth,” and she knew it. Dealing with their mother was always like walking on eggs. Tread lightly, “Mumma” was always about to crack.

Richard ate his cereal quietly. He was all spic and span. His hair was slicked down, his shoes shined, his blue pants pressed and he was sporting a bright, new, yellow tie. The tie choked him around the neck. He didn’t like wearing a tie. His new shoes were his favorite thing. They were Buster Brown saddle shoes. He liked Buster Brown and the idea of living in a shoe with his dog “Tige.” “Hi, I’m Buster Brown. I live in a shoe. This is my dog Tige. He lives in there too.” There was also an old lady who lived in a shoe. She had so many kids that she didn’t know what to do.

At the shoe store the man measured his foot. Shoes were obviously important. His mother always bought a size bigger than whatever the man measured, anyway. He was growing so fast, she always said. She bought everything too big. Who cared? He liked the smell of his new shoes. They had a picture of Buster Brown with his dog Tige on the inside. He got a new pair of shoes once every year. Richard also liked Cheerios and not Corn Flakes. His older brother and sister did not have to attend school on this day. Today was just for the little ones.

He walked with his mother to the school. On this day lots of mothers were walking their kids to the neighborhood schools. Richard would be going to St. Rita's Catholic school. The little girls wore blue skirts with white blouses and a red bow. They all had black shoes with white socks. The boys wore blue pants with a white shirt. Their shoes, socks and ties were of random colors. The schoolhouse had a six-foot high, chainlink fence surrounding it. The play yard around the school was asphalt. Hundreds of mothers and children crowded into the schoolyard.

Richard was very nervous, very excited, and very frightened. His mother had seen to it that he would be. There were others in the schoolyard who looked just as frightened as he. Many of the children were crying. The majority were clinging to their mothers. A few were off on their own, playing.

The front of the building looked like a sacrificial altar at an Inca or Aztec temple. A long flight of cement stairs led up to it on three different sides. A clutch of nuns in their ancient, cultish robes, were gathered on the main altar. A huge wooden canopy extended out and over the sacrificial slab.

Richard had never seen a nun before, but from what he could see, he felt that his mother had been telling the truth. They were scary. They dressed strangely. They wore long black gowns. Long, black shawls covered their heads and draped down over their shoulders. They had large, white cardboard bibs that covered their chests. Their foreheads and faces were wrapped in white. Their eyes, noses and mouths peeked out from their black and white camouflage. Nothing showed but this small bit of their faces and their hands. They had beads hung around their necks and dangling from their waists and from the bead-chains hung wooden crosses. They wore black boots fit for men. The boots were laced and extended up around their calves. Their black gowns dragged the ground and looked cumbersome, hot and heavy.

The majority of them had their hands tucked away in pouches on the front of their gowns. Nuns were threatening, black and white statues with eyebrows and chins. One of the nuns up on the "altar" began ringing a big, brass bell. Another began slapping wooden blocks together. They were calling the crowd to attention.

The mothers were instructed to bring their children forward. Just behind the altar, two large doors led into a spacious hall. A nun sat at a desk just inside the hall. Each mother enrolled her child. The child was then taken from the mother and led into one of the classrooms that bordered the hall. She was then told to return at three o'clock.

Richard had no previous religious training. He had been exposed to rosary beads and crucifixes. His grandmother had crucifixes on her walls. He had none in his apartment. His sister and brother had brought home holy implements from school. They were both five and six years older than he.

The crucifixes had the image or the replica of a semi-naked man stretched out and nailed to it. Spots of blood were depicted in each of his palms. His feet were placed on top of one another and they too were spiked to the cross and splashed with blood.

Richard's older brother and sister went to church every Sunday but his mother and father did not. Sometimes his mother would go, but never his father. Richard was too small to attend, he was told.

There was a huge cross hanging on the wall inside the hall. It was as big as life ... or death. The image nailed and hanging on the cross looked like a real man. There was blood at his hands and feet and also dripping from one of his sides and streaming down his forehead and face. Richard had never seen anything so imposing, so horrid, so pitiable. The crosses hanging from the gowns and around the necks of the various nuns were exact miniatures of that huge cross hanging on the wall.

The boys went to a classroom to the left and the girls to a classroom to the right. Inside the classroom there was a large picture of a man with long, brown hair, the length of a woman's hair. He was wearing a red gown. He had spread the gown open with his hands, exposing what should have been his chest. But instead of his chest, you saw his heart. His heart had a knife piercing through it. Drops of blood were dripping from the tip of the blade.

Everything about this school business was stern, bloody and fearful. Richard did not like being left here by himself; no one was laughing or smiling, neither the nuns nor the students. Each child was directed to a chair, told to sit and not to speak; eyes straight forward, hands folded on your desk and feet together on the floor.

There was a desk on a platform at the front of the room. A nun was sitting at the desk. Her position demonstrated the proper pose; eyes forward, hands folded, and feet together on the floor.

The nun, who had sat Richard at his desk and instructed him on the proper position, placed her index finger under her nose and perpendicular to her lips. "Shushhh ... no talking," she instructed. If anyone in the room spoke, the nun sitting up at the desk at the front of the room would say sternly but in a hushed tone. "Shushhh! Eyes forward! Hands folded! Feet together! No talking!"

Richard sat in one of the rows to the right of the nun who was stationed at the big desk. Both the right and the left walls of the room contained large windows. The windows to the right looked out onto the street. The windows to the left looked out onto an empty pit which was bordered on all four sides by the adjoining walls of other school buildings. All that could be seen through these particular windows were more walls and more windows.

Richard was looking straight ahead with his hands folded and his feet together; but, from out the corner of his eye, he could see a little boy to the left of him who was sniffling and crying. The boy was sniffling and trying not to cry, but what remained were coughs and sputters and little, baby sounds of one nature or another. The nun, up at the big desk, shushhhed at him sternly. The sputtering boy tried to stifle his sobbing but just couldn't. The sister at the front of the class was trying to speak but the little boy was slightly too distracting and disruptive. A huge nun suddenly appeared just behind the boy. She had obviously entered the room through the back door.

"Stop that sniffling, Robert!" she demanded, having read the name tag on the boy's shirt pocket. Robert tried, but was not successful. He made two or three gulping, hiccup like attempts to swallow up his tears, but then just gave up totally and fell into a full fit of crying. He let his head fall to his desk and began stamping his feet upon the floor. “What is wrong with this boy, Sister Mary?” the big nun behind the boy demanded.

“I don’t know Sister Edward.”

“Maybe he is in the wrong room. Maybe he isn’t a little boy at all. Maybe he is one of our little girls. Could that be the problem, Sister Mary?”

“I suppose that could be possible, Sister Edward.”

Sister Edward grabbed Robert by a handful of hair and wrenched his head back so she could look down into his face.

“Stop that crying this instant!” she screamed. The boy gave it a good try, but yet continued to sputter. “Didn’t you hear what I said!” she demanded in an even harsher tone. “I said stop that sniffling!” He managed to stop for a second or two by holding his breath, but when his need for air returned, he blurted into sputtering once again. The big nun grabbed him by his shirt and tie and shook him in his seat. “Stop! Stop that this instant! Do you hear me?” They were now nose to nose as she bent at the waist to scream down into Robert’s face.

The large nun’s screaming startled Richard as well as Robert. Richard felt that he had bounced at least a foot out of his seat. Mentally, he was under his bed. This nun was his mother. Richard would remain quiet and still. Hopefully the big nun would not be distracted from her initial prey and would contain her hostility to Robert, as was the case quite often at home between his mother and his sister, Carol. He had learned at home that the utmost attention must be given to quiet and an apparent state of invisibleness, or “beating” had the tendency to grow and spread. He felt pity for Robert, but yet thankful that it was Carol at home and Robert here in this classroom, rather than he. Even here, he knew all too well that he was within a simple arm’s reach from a sharp backhand to the teeth from Sister Edward. He was not about to provide her with one of those stupid, cross-eyed opportunities that his mother had been warning him about for all these months.

Sister Edward released Robert and straightened to a full upright position. She made herself even more menacing by folding her arms across her chest. “I guess what we need here, Sister Mary, is one of your little pink bows. All little girls like to wear little pink bows in their hair. Don’t they Roberta?” Some of the other children began to snicker and giggle. “Do you hear your classmates, Roberta? Do you hear them laughing at you? Do you want to wear a little pink bow and look like a little girl? We have a cute little pink dress up there in that closet behind you Sister Mary, don't we? ... But bring me that pink bow for the moment Sister Mary." Robert protested but continued to cry.

Sister Mary brought Sister Edward the pink bow. Sister Edward pulled a tuft of Robert's hair up between her fingers and quickly laced the bow into the boy's hair. Robert's classmates roared with laughter as the two nuns stepped back to admire their work and beamed with amused delight at their accomplishment.

Robert had resisted the bow tying embarrassment momentarily, but when he was told that his resistance would ultimately lead to his being tied or strapped to his seat, he relented.

"Stand up, Roberta. Stand up so that your classmates can see what a cute little girl you make." Robert's head fell once again to his desk, and the boy returned to his bawling. "UP!" Sister Edward screamed, bending at the waist and placing her lips to the little boy's ear in order to gain a fuller effect. "UP! UP!"

Richard was no fool. He understood this type behavior all too clearly. He remained seated in his chair, with his hands folded on his desk and his feet together, eyes straight ahead. He was not fooled by the nuns' petitioning and encouraging the other students to participate in the abuse of Robert. As with his mother, the slightest appearance of joy could lead to your turn. The abuser retains the absolute right to abuse any and all. So if you don't want to become a member of the club, just shut up; keep your eyes straight ahead, your hands folded, and your feet together. Do whatever the "big people" direct. Do not speak. Do not protest. Do not run. All such behavior only leads to more intense abuse. Sister Edward, he could plainly perceive, would be more than willing to slap a smile to the other side of his face, or turn a colorful amused eye into a sore and swollen blackened one, "faster than you can say, Jackie Robinson, buster!"

The trick was to become invisible. Don't make a move and they won't be able to see you. Be like a frog on the window or a roach caught in the light. Sit tight; don't move. Blank your face; be expressionless. Stop seeing; stop hearing; stop feeling

- if you can. Become a part of the scenery. Show no fear even if your heart is pounding. Show no love. Show no hate. Become an indifferent part of an indifferent world. If you are good at it, the world might go away, or maybe it won't notice you. Maybe it will forget that you are alive. Maybe ... maybe it will leave you be. Sister Edward and all the mothers of the world near or far might disappear and maybe you will be free. If not free, at least forgotten or overlooked.

Maybe "they" will leave you be. Who are "they"? They are the big people, of course. They are those animals that live in the same house with you; those horrid things that keep screaming at one another; those beasts who are always yelling and screaming and fighting - his mother and his father.

He and his older brother would sit up in bed and listen to them scream at one another. Richard would slide his hand into his brother's and they would sit holding hands, and feel their hearts leap as the screams burst like exploding rockets in a fourth of July sky. BOOM!

"I'm not going to ask for another nickel!" the mother squeals. That's your damn job. You're supposed to be the man! You're supposed to support the family. I am supposed to have the babies and care for the home. You are supposed to get a job; earn the money. You and your hotsy-totsy, big-shot brothers and sisters up on the Hill - they can't help out their big brother?"

"I can't go to them for God's sakes, Mary. You know that," the father groans.

"Oh sure? But Mary can go crawling on her hands and knees to her brothers and sisters ... 'Ray can I borrow five dollars? Ernie STILL can't find a job, and the kids need food to eat?'... How do you think that I feel? Do you think that it makes me feel good to do that? Do you think that it makes me feel proud? ... Oh sure ... that's it - pop open another beer; that will solve everything."

"What, now I can't have a beer, once in a while?"

And on, and on ... and on.

Sometimes Richard's brother Ernie would get sick to his stomach and he would be forced to leave his anonymous, invisible position in their dark bedroom and make his way out into the battleground and to the bathroom, where he could puke.

When their bedroom door would open, the room would become quiet. The yelling would stop until young Ernie returned to his bed. Then it would resume as if the bedroom door led into a soundproof vault that rejected all the screams and hate. Ernie would even puke quietly.

No one wanted to be sick. Being sick meant giving up one's invisibleness. Being sick meant attracting attention; being sick meant doctors. Doctors meant money. Money meant trouble.

"What do you mean you feel sick? Are you trying to put one over on me, or are you just trying to aggravate me? I'll bet you have a cold, don't you? How many times have I told you to button up your jacket? How many times have I told you to take off those wet socks? But no, no, you're too damn smart. You just do whatever it is that you right well please. Your mother doesn't know anything. She's just stupid. She's an idiot. That's what you think, don't you? You think that I'm stupid, don't you? You think that you can play little games with me. I think that you are about as sick as that wall over there, and not much smarter. You had better just get out of my sight before I really make you sick. Go play someplace. Get lost. Just get out of this house. I don't want to look at you any more. Go! ... GO NOW!"

No, no, don't say that you are sick. Take good care of yourself. The cure may be worse than the disease.

If you are sick, you had better be really, really, sick. If she calls the Doctor, and you are not knock-down, dragged-out sick you are in big trouble.

Listen from your room to the Doctor talking to your mother:

"Richard is all right, Mrs. Noble. He won't die."

(Oh no! Richard is all right, the Doctor said. How can he say that I am all right? I'm not all right. I'm all sweaty; my throat hurts; I can't talk. I cough and spit up stuff. What does he mean? Is he trying to get me killed?)

"Are you telling me that he is faking, Doctor?"

"Oh no Ma'am; I'm not saying that. The boy is very sick. He should not be sent to school for the rest of this week. Not until that coughing and phlegm clears out of his lungs. I want you to give him plenty of hot fluids and keep a check on his temperature."

(Phew, that was close! Lucky thing! That Doctor must like you. If he had said that you weren't really that sick, you would have hell to pay, little boy. But for now you can relax in your bed. The Doctor has granted you permission to be sick. She will believe the Doctor and not be mean ... won't she?)

The rest of the class could laugh at Robert, but not Richard. No, no. He would not be one to laugh. He knew better. He had already been through basic training. He was prepared. He would sit straight in his chair with his eyes forward; his hands folded; his feet together; his face without expression; his heart without emotion. He would be ready, and if the back of a hand struck the side of his head, he knew that it was "just one for good measure, buck-o." If he were knocked to the floor, he would pull his knees up to his chest and cover his head with his arms until the blows stopped. He knew it all. He was a boy at war, and he was trained.

Robert would not rise from his seat, and he would not stop crying. Sister Edward turned to the window behind her; grabbed the latches at the base, and husked it open. She turned back to Robert. With one hand she grasped his shirt collar and with the other she grabbed up his belt and pants at the rear. In the flash of an instant she wrenched little Robert from his seat and stuck him out through the open window.

"You stop that crying or I'll drop you right now."

Robert stopped crying immediately. Richard was very surprised. It didn't seem that Robert had the ability to stop crying. He didn't appear to be faking. How was he able to just stop?

In Richard's experience, crying was not something that could just be turned on and off. Once a person let it start, it just continued until the tears came to an end. But then again, Richard had never been jutted out a window, face down. He was never just hanging at another human's discretion, staring down at the pavement. It was a good distance to the ground, but even if Sister Edward threw Robert out the window, Richard didn't think that Robert would die. One of Richard's little friends had jumped from a fire-escape in an attempt to fly like Superman. Nothing happened. He received more serious injury when his mother found out why he had jumped. If Sister Edward threw Robert out the window, Richard felt that Robert would probably jump right up and then run all the way home. Clearly Robert did not project a similar conclusion.

Being that Robert had stopped crying, Sister Edward pulled him back from outside the window, and plunked him down into his seat. His butt no sooner hit the seat than he began wailing once again. Richard thought for sure that Robert would now get his opportunity to see if he could fly like Superman. Maybe he could; but Sister Edward chickened out. The fact that Sister Edward had not picked Robert up a second time to throw him out the window, Richard felt was an act of cowardice on Sister Edward's part. She had just lost the power struggle. She threatened and then didn't follow through. Robert had won. He, at least, had the upper hand now.

"Well, Sister Mary, I guess that we need that pretty little pink dress."

All the children remained in their seats with their hands folded, and their feet together; but all their wide, little eyes were on Robert and Sister Edward.

Sister Mary carried the dress from out of the closet behind her desk. She proceeded slowly up the aisle, her leather heels clicking on the hardwood floor. She held it up before Sister Edward and fluffed it about. She then handed it to Sister Edward.

"Very pretty," exclaimed Sister Edward, "very, very pretty." She bunched the dress up and then quickly pulled it down over Robert's head. She then reached in through the arms of the sleeves and pulled out each of his arms. Robert looked very amusing. The dress, now draped over his shoulders, bunched up around him at the butt. The pink bow was still tied in his hair, and sitting atop his head. The class became a rumble of giggles. Even sister Mary was forced to cover her lips with her fingers, not to show her smile.

"So look at the lovely Roberta," began Sister Edward, ready to heap more ridicule upon the ridiculousness of Robert, when suddenly Robert bolted from his seat like a cloud of dust. He was "on his horse" and gone. He was heading for the front door at full speed. Sister Mary sped to the front and headed him off. Robert hung a quick right. Robert, now having both nuns occupied, had broken the rigid decorum. All the other children had broken from their hands folded, feet together, eyes front positions; most remained in their seats. Some had their hands over their eyes or their mouths; others were bouncing up and down in their seats; some were clapping their hands or stamping their feet.

Sister Edward had blown it, just as Richard had predicted. She should have thrown Robert out the window. A threat is only a few words, but a slam to the pavement below would have spoken volumes.

Robert now had the two of them on the run. Robert was going every-which-way. Both nuns had their skirts heaped up in their hands, so that they could pursue the prey at a gallop if necessary. Even with their dresses heaped up to their waists, they had copious other black paraphernalia draping about their legs and down to the tops of their black, laced up, trooper boots. They were really no match for little Robert. He was very fast and very good at making quick turns. Sister Mary was obviously younger than Sister Edward. Sister Mary was laughing. Sister Edward was panting.

Robert was, at one moment, to the front of the room; and at another moment, to the back. He was clearly trying to get to an unguarded door. The two nuns were running and leaping about like gazelles. Who would ever have thought that nuns could jump like that? Sister Mary actually leaped right over an empty desk. Sister Edward slammed into a wall once or twice, but she was a pretty good runner nevertheless. Both nuns were exhibiting signs of fatigue. Sister Mary was quite flushed and Sister Edward's face was as red as a beet.

Robert, on the other hand, seemed to be showing no visible signs of wear or tear. It appeared that he could run forever. His little pink dress, now hanging by one shoulder, seemed no handicap whatsoever.

Robert was leaping over chairs in a single bound, scurrying under desks without missing a lick. He was more than up to speed, and an equal match for any two nuns. Round and round they went: up and down the aisles, under desks, over chairs - first this way, then that way.

Richard was still sitting with his hands folded, eyes front and feet together. He had the very strong feeling that even though Robert was winning at the moment, he was in big trouble. Richard had been well informed about the nuns by his mother. So far, everything was going as he would have expected. No one could have predicted Robert's behavior, but the basic insanity of life in the human jungle was much the same here, as it was at his home. School was a little better though. Here at school the insane and power crazed adults had more victims to choose from. Richard stood the very good opportunity of forever maintaining an invisible state.

Women were all raving lunatics. It mattered little of what their attire might consist. Crazy was endemic to their nature, he had already learned. They were to be avoided as much as possible. One moment they are smiling, the next moment they are cracking you in the teeth.

To be little was a big part of the problem. In a few years he could be like his big brother and just stay away as much as possible. One day he could be like his father and go out somewhere and drink beer. Here in school women tried to humiliate little boys and then chased them about like raving lunatics. Richard would just sit with his eyes straight ahead, his hands folded, his feet together and wait until the day would come that he would be able to disappear for real and forever. This would be his dream for years to come.

Robert had finally outwitted his pursuers. He had lost both tired nuns with a quick turn and at long last had his little hands planted onto a doorknob. But the Sisters of Terror were headed for him heatedly. Robert fumbled with the knob. His hands slipped and fumbled, but finally he had it within his power. He looked over his shoulder as Fiddle and Faddle came galloping towards him. He flung the door aside and dashed headlong into the crotch of a third nun who had suddenly appeared on the other side of Robert's door to freedom. Freedom is certainly an elusive quantity.

Sister Mary, witnessing the capture, folded over at the waist in exhaustion and laughter. Sister Edward was irate.

"And what have we here?" the third nun said with a bemused grin on her face. Both of the pursuing nuns were opened mouthed and panting. But between pants they were smiling. The third nun looked down at Robert. His little pink dress was all in tatters and the remains of his pink bow was dangling, askew, over one ear. He was still fit and ready to go - the nuns were not. Sister Mary went over to Robert and pulled his dress up over his head. She tapped Robert atop the head gently, then took his hand and escorted him back to his seat. She sat him down and removed the ribbon from his hair. She folded his hands, put his feet in place, and gave to him the gesture for silence.

As Sister Mary was walking from Robert's desk towards the front of the class, the door at the front of the room popped open. Another nun poked her head in. "Sister Mary, I just stopped by to inform you that the spanking machine is back in working order."

"It is! Well, that is wonderful, Sister Priska."

"Yes. And the body of the bad little boy who got caught in the machine and was spanked to death ...?"

"Yes? That was very unfortunate."

"Yes, but accidents do happen, Sister Mary. In any case, that child's body has been removed and the spanking machine is once again in working order."

"What did they do with the bad little boy's body, Sister Priska?"

"Well, I'm not entirely sure, but I think that Bill, Mr. Fitzgibbons ...?"

"Yes?"

"I think that he threw it into the furnace."

"Do the bad little boy's parents know what happened to him?"

"Oh yes, Sister Mary. They said that if he was being bad, then he got exactly what he deserved. So Sister Mary, if any of these boys here cause you any problems, you just let me know. Sister Priska and her handy spanking machine will solve any problems."

"That is very comforting to know, Sister. If I have any problem, I will most assuredly let you know."

"Well, don't hesitate Sister." Sister Priska then closed the door, but then opened it once again quickly. "You are absolutely sure, Sister Mary, that you don't have any bad little boys in this room at this very minute?"

Sister Mary turned and slowly examined the faces of each of the little boys in her class. The room was extremely quiet. All eyes were straight ahead, all hands folded and all feet together. Everyone was quite sure that Robert's number had just been called. Robert was still sniffling. He had clearly been a very bad little boy. Certainly Sister Mary would turn Robert over to the spanking machine nun. She would take him down into the cellar to where the spanking machine was kept. Robert would then be spanked to death and his dead body thrown into the furnace by Mr. Fitzgibbons, the janitor, and nobody would care. Not even Robert's mother and father, because being spanked to death and thrown into the furnace was deserving punishment for any bad little boy.

"No Sister, I have only good little boys here in this class."

Richard was confused. Sister Mary had lied. Why did she lie? Everyone knew that Robert was a bad little boy. He had cried and run all about the classroom. He made both Sisters chase after him. If that wasn't being bad, then what was?

Sister Mary was protecting Robert. Why?

Maybe it was because she was a younger nun. Maybe she was more like Richard's real sister at home. Sometimes Richard's real sister would lie to protect him from their mother. Maybe Sister Mary was afraid of what Sister Priska might really do to Robert if she got hold of him? Maybe Sister Mary understood that Robert was really not a bad boy, but only frightened? Maybe Sister Mary was a nice person? Or maybe she was, at least, not as mean and crazy as all the rest? Who knows?

On his way home from school that day, Richard thought about Robert dangling out the window at the end of Sister Edward's arms. Robert was really frightened. When it was all over Robert had sat in his seat and wet his pants. Richard had wet his bed once, but it had been an accident. He was sleeping when it happened. Robert was wide awake and he did it right in the middle of the first grade classroom. There was something definitely wrong with Robert. He peed in his pants. He faked crying. He ran all over the classroom and he nearly got stuffed into Sister Priska's spanking machine. Wow!

"And so, how was your first day at school?" his mother asked on their walk home.

"Fine."

"Did you cause the nuns any problems?"

"No, no, I didn't."

"Well, you had better not."

"I won't ... never. Not me."

"Good."

3 The Note

Richard learned many things in the first grade at St. Rita's grammar school. He learned the alphabet and how to sound all the letters: Ah, Ba, Ca, Da. He learned that one times one is one and two times one is two. He was given cards to memorize addition, subtraction and multiplication. One card went up as high as 12 x 12. He learned to count off numbers to one thousand. He learned to write by the Palmer Method. He had an inkwell and a pen right on his desk. He felt important to be trusted with such things. He learned to do push-pulls and ovals with his pen and ink. It was hard not to make blots. When he made a blot, he had to sop it up with his blotter. Even when a blot was sopped up with a blotter it looked bad. The goal in learning to write with a pen and ink was to learn how to do it without making blots.

He learned how to print. After he learned how to print, he learned how to write. Richard did not understand why they had taught him to print, if they then wanted him to forget about printing and learn how to write. If they wanted him to write, why didn't they teach him to write first? If he sometimes forgot and printed a letter when he was then learning to write, Sister Mary would get angry. Nevertheless, he eventually learned how to print and how to write. He learned to write his name in "his best Palmer Method." The nuns always spoke like that: "Now children, in your best Palmer Method, write such and such."

He learned to spell many words, like cat, rat, sat, pat, fat, and bat. One day when his father was home from the sea he told his dad that he could spell and showed him his spelling card. His dad looked at the card and asked him to spell the first word on the list.

"Okay, spell cat," he said.

"Cat ..." Richard repeated the word aloud as he was taught. "r - a - t ... cat." His father roared with laughter. Richard loved to hear his father laugh. Richard loved to see his father - period. Richard loved his father, period. His father never, ever struck him. To Richard, his father was mysterious and wonderful. Whenever his father was home from the sea, Richard would never leave his side. He would sit at the foot of his father's chair as he told of his adventures. His dad would tell about all of the foreign countries that he had been to. He would describe all of the sad, poor people that he had seen all over the world. He would tell about the treacherous seas and the terrible waves. He would tell about the cook with his big belly and how all the hungry children would laugh as he lifted his shirt and shook his big belly up and down. He would tell how the cook would save him all of the turkey skin at Christmas time. His dad always ate the skin, the neck, and the tail of the turkey. He said that they were the best parts. Richard always wanted those parts when his father was not there at Christmas.

Richard loved his dad, and his wavy, black hair and his brown eyes, and his wire-rimmed glasses, and his tobacco smoking pipes, and his Pall Mall cigarettes, and his Pabst Blue Ribbon beer.

His dad's breath always smelled of cigarettes and beer. Richard liked his dad the best when he was drinking beer. At those times he talked and he was funny and he always talked to Richard. He talked to Richard as if he were a little man, not as if he were a child or a baby.

Richard loved his dad. He missed him when he was away. He often cried just thinking about his dad lost out in the sea with all the frightening waves. He always feared that his dad might never return. After the nuns taught Richard how to pray, he prayed every day and every night for his dad's safety.

Richard learned all about the Baby Jesus and Saint Joseph, and Jesus' Holy Mother, the Blessed Virgin Mary. At Christmas time the nuns and the students constructed a living manger. Richard was an angel. His mother laughed aloud when she heard that Richard was an angel. His mother very rarely laughed aloud. She made constant mockery that anyone could ever think, for even a second, that Richard was an angel. Nevertheless, Richard was an angel at school and he had a set of wings. He liked having wings. He wished that he could fly, and often had dreams in which he soared above the clouds. He never actually tried to fly as his friend had done; imitating Superman and jumping off the Arlington Street School fire escape. But he dreamed of it and often imitated Superman as he ran along the sidewalks with his arms outstretched.

He learned about the man on the cross. The man on the cross was the Baby Jesus all grown up. Jesus was God. There were really three Gods. There was God the Father who was the Creator of all things. He lived in Heaven. There was Jesus who became a man and lived a human life here on earth. Then there was the Holy Ghost. Richard liked the Holy Ghost best of all. He was kind of like Casper the friendly ghost. He floated all around and could appear or disappear whenever he liked. The nuns were emphatic about the notion that all three of these Gods were really one God. They told a story about St. Patrick and a shamrock.

Richard learned to bless himself and to kneel on his chair. Kneeling on one's chair was uncomfortable. It hurt. He learned the Predge-a-lee-gents: "I predgealeegents to the flag ..."

He also learned about Santa Claus and his elves.

At Christmas time, little elves were sneaking about all of the corridors at St. Rita's school. One knew that they were there, because they rang little bells just outside the classroom doors. Santa's little elves were really alive. They were about the size of a leprechaun, but they didn't have any pots of gold like leprechauns. But if a person caught one of Santa's elves, he would have to grant that person a wish, just like the leprechauns had to give up their pot of gold. The whole school was filled with all sorts of mysterious and funny looking little creatures. Everything was mostly invisible: God, Jesus, the Holy Ghost, Santa, his little elves, leprechauns, angels, tooth fairies, the Easter Bunny, the Devil.

Every person in the world had a little devil sitting on one of his shoulders and a little angel sitting on the other. God assigned everyone a guardian angel. Your guardian angel whispered in your ear and tried to get you to do good things, instead of listening to the Devil who was always whispering in your other ear trying to get you to do bad things. The little devils and the guardian angels were in a constant battle for everybody's souls.

Your soul was that invisible part of you that was just like the Holy Ghost. One day your soul would get free of your body and it would soar to heaven - if you had been good.

Heaven was a place up in the sky that nobody could see until they were dead. God was very much like Santa Claus. Santa Claus was also called Saint Nicholas. So he also had something to do with God and angels because he was a Saint. Saints also were invisible and lived in heaven. All Saints were once people. But all people don't become Saints.

If you were bad, you got no presents at Christmas time and just like Santa, if you were bad during your life you got no heaven from God after you died.

The Devil was all red, had horns growing out of his head and carried a pitchfork. The Devil and a bunch of his friends had started a revolution in heaven. God and the good angels won the war over heaven and the Devil got kicked out of heaven and sent into hell.

At Christmas time all the children tried to catch an elf. If you heard a bell ring at the door of your classroom, you would leap from your chair and run to that door. Richard never confronted an elf upon opening the door. But oftentimes he would see Mr. Fitzgibbons, the janitor.

As the janitor, Mr. Fitzgibbons swept floors, emptied garbage cans and removed the dead bodies of bad children from the spanking machine and threw them into the furnace. Richard had never seen the spanking machine but he did see the furnace. Often times he would ask Mr. Fitzgibbons if he had seen any elves. But Mr. Fitzgibbons always said no.

Richard learned where he came from and why he was put here on earth.

Question: Who made me?

Answer: God made me.

Question: Why did God make me?

Answer: God made me to know, love and serve him in this world and in the next.

He had been given a book called a Catechism. The Catechism had all the questions and answers about God and life and death.

God made Richard. This was a good thing to know. God loved him, and it was Richard's duty to love God with his whole heart, his whole mind and his whole soul. His soul was his spirit, and his spirit was like a ghost. His body would one day die but his soul would live on, invisibly, in the invisible world of God and heaven for eternity.

Eternity was a long time. It was forever. Both God and the Holy Ghost had no body. Jesus was the only God who had a body. Now Jesus was in heaven and he had no body either.

Jesus, God and the Holy Ghost were three persons in one God. Like Superman, Super Boy and Clark Kent. Superman, Super Boy and Clark Kent were three different people but they were all Superman. Superman must have had something to do with God also. He could fly and leap tall buildings in a single bound and lift the whole world up onto his shoulder. He was also faster than a speeding bullet.

Jesus couldn't fly and he wasn't strong like Superman. But he could make "miracles." He could raise people from the dead and cure sick people without any medicine or an operation. He wasn't very good at fighting though. Everybody beat him up. Finally all the bullies tortured him to death and nailed him to two telephone poles up on a hill in the middle of the town.

Richard learned about ghosts and spirits and souls and Gods and elves and stars that floated across the heavens and kings and castles up in the sky. He also learned about an inferno that was in the center of the earth or underneath the earth.

Whenever Richard was in the street at night in the dark, he made sure never to step into any potholes. He was sure that the Devil could reach up through a pothole and grab onto his foot and pull him down into hell. Richard always jumped over potholes. Hell was filled with fire and this is where the Devil and his buddies lived. The Devil had two names. He was also called Lucifer. Lucifer was once an angel. But then he started that revolution up in heaven.

Heaven was the place where everybody is happy, but Lucifer was the kind that nobody could make happy. Even when he laughed he was mean and ugly. God and Michael the "ark" angel beat up Lucifer and threw him out of heaven. Noah also had an ark but it was not the same as Michael's "ark." Why didn't God just kill the Devil, or make him disappear forever? Because the Devil was like God, Himself; he was also very, very, very powerful. He was only a smidgen less powerful than God. And it is a lucky thing too, or we would all be going to hell and not just Protestants, Jews and pagans.

The sin of the Devil was that he wanted to be as smart as God. But God was just smarter.

One day a little boy in Richard's class swallowed a chicken bone at lunch period. He had to be taken to the hospital. The next day a priest came to their classroom. He had a little priest that came with him. The little priest was only about twelve years old. All of the children were told to kneel on their chairs. They were told that the priest was going to bless their throats. Getting their throats blessed would involve the Holy Ghost. The Holy Ghost would enter into their bodies and from then on, He would keep them from getting bones stuck in their throats.

The priest had two candles and he had them stuck into a golden candleholder. It was a funny candleholder and it made the candles cross over one another to form an "X." The priest, and his helper and Sister Mary walked up and down the rows of kneeling children. They were all kneeling on their chairs. They stopped at each child, and the priest placed the crossed candles at the throat of each child. Then he sing-sang words from a foreign language. The priest started at the other end of the room and it took a very long time for him to get to Richard. All the boys at Richard's end of the class were squirming in their kneeling positions. Finally the priest arrived.

"Patres, et Domini, et Felium Sanctum."

"Patres, et Domini, et Felium Sanctum."

The priest repeated these same words upon reaching each child and placing the crossed and lit candles under their chin and next to their Adam's apple. Richard was too excited to even look at the priest. When the priest placed the crossed, burning candles to his throat, Richard closed his eyes. The candles touched the skin at his neck. When they did, something inside of him jumped and he felt a tingling sensation that ran all the way down to the tips of his toes.

"Patres, et Domini, et Felium Sanctum."

Et Felium Sanctum reminded Richard of the Inner Sanctum. The Inner Sanctum was a radio program with a creaking door and a guy who laughed sinisterly.

Richard and his brother listened to the Inner Sanctum while they lay in their bed just before going to sleep at night. The Inner Sanctum also sent cold chills down his body. This was a wondrous and mysterious feeling. The tingling sensation must have been the Holy Ghost going into his body.

After the priest and his little helper left, Sister Mary asked the class if any of them felt the Holy Spirit enter their body. Every little arm shot up into the air. All the little children had felt the same mysterious tingling sensation. Richard believed in the Holy Ghost.

Yes, Richard learned many things at school that first year. Yet, he did not like school. He was afraid of most of the nuns.

One day, Sister Mary called Richard to the front of the class. As all the children exited to go home, she pinned a note on his shirt pocket.

"Now don't take this note off until you get home, and be sure that your mother reads it."

"Yes, Sister Mary."

"Now, what are you going to do with the note?"

"I am not going to take it off until I get home. And I am going to make sure that my mother reads it."

"That's right. Now go on before you miss your route."

Richard went home in route number two. Everyone went home by way of some route. Each route had patrol leaders. They wore white belts that went across their chests and around their waists. Each belt had a badge pinned to it at the chest. Everyone had to do as the patrol leader said. Mostly the patrol leaders just kept everyone in line. When you passed your home street, you told your patrol leader. He or she made sure that there were no cars coming when you crossed the street.

The note that Richard had pinned to his pocket made him excited. He had never brought home a note from school. It must be important. He felt very, very special and proud. Sister Mary had smiled at him as she pinned it to his shirt. Sometimes in school when he gave a correct answer, Sister Mary would put a star on his forehead. And sometimes, if he was very good, he would get a gold star.

The more that he thought about the note, the more excited he got. He began running down Chelmsford Street to his home. He lived at 32 Chelmsford Street. When he burst into the kitchen, he was out of breath. His mother was standing by the stove. He pulled the note off his shirt, and handed it to his mother. She looked at him confused and inquiring. She took the outstretched note into her hand.

"Sister Mary pinned the note onto me. She said to make sure that you read it." He just knew that it had to be something wonderful by the way that she smiled as she pinned it to his pocket. His face was beaming as he stood in anticipation of his mother's response. His sister Carol was sitting in a chair on the opposite side of the stove. He watched as his mother's eyes moved along each word on the note.

"What does it say, Mama?" He could wait no longer. Before the last word fell from his lips his mother's arm came whirling from her side and her hand struck Richard a severe blow to the face. It was such a powerful blow that it knocked Richard to the floor, and sent him sliding all the way across the kitchen floor and into the washing machine at the far end of the kitchen. Richard's books and papers went flying into the air. He couldn't believe what had happened. He was stunned.

He lifted himself and turned to face his mother. She was already there waiting. He was struck again by another blow which tumbled him once again to the floor. This time she had swung her other hand and struck him on the opposite side of his face. This blow slid him across the width of the floor and into the wall next to the old refrigerator.

He couldn't think. He wanted to ask what he had done, but he had no opportunity. He was on his hands and knees, struggling to get up once again when a blow struck the back of his head. This blow knocked his face down into the floor. When he lifted his face from the floor and his eyes regained their focus, he saw blood dripping to the floor. His nose felt numb. When he wiped it with his hand, his hand was covered with blood. Seeing his blood frightened him. He began screaming.

"What did I do, Mama? What did I do?" He was on his hands and knees looking at his mother looming above him. She appeared like a giant, outraged with fury. Her face was twisted and ugly. She was flailing at him, her hands striking in rapid succession. Suddenly a blow struck him in the mouth. This blow tumbled him over backwards. When he hit the floor, the back of his head struck the linoleum covered floor with such force that a cracking sound resounded throughout the room.

Richard's sister thought that his head had burst. She jumped up from her chair. She wanted to scream. Instead she covered her mouth with her hands. This was a wise thing to do. If she had screamed such an action could have brought her mother down upon her. Though she was frightened and terrified for Richard, her instincts for herself were even stronger.

Richard's mother was now straddling Richard's body lying on the floor. She had one foot on either side of him and was bent over at the waist flailing at him with her arms flying and the blows coming in rapid succession.

Richard's one thought was to escape. The back of his skull was throbbing. There was blood all over his white shirt. He flipped over and began crawling away on his hands and knees. He felt himself to be clawing at a pace of a mile a minute. His little hands and knees were pumping like pistons. He was heading for the kitchen table, his mother flailing at him all the while. She struck multiple blows to his ears, head and shoulders. She wasn't aiming. She was just swinging. The blows landed anywhere. Every time that he would squirm half of his body under the kitchen table she would grab him by both feet and pull him out. Then she would beat him until he crawled away once again. Finally he crawled halfway under the table, flipped over quickly and began kicking wildly with his feet while pulling himself backwards with his hands.

He scurried to the wall under the table and tried to hide among the wooden, chair legs. He kept his back to the wall so as to be able to kick with his feet. His mother began grabbing chairs and flinging them across the room. She was yelling. He could not hear the sound of her voice over the noise from his own screams.

"I didn't do anything, Mama! I didn't do anything. Don't hit me! Don't hit me! I didn't do it! Please Mama? Please Mama, don't hit me. I didn't do it!"

He was crying and screaming at the same time. She was pulling the chairs out in rapid succession. They were banging off the walls around and behind her. He knew that when the chairs were all gone, his protection would be gone and she would be able to reach under the table and grab him. He grabbed onto the rungs of the last chair. He pulled with all of his might. He could feel her yanking the chair as he held onto it for dear life.

It was no use. She gave it a good pull and his fingers let loose. He pushed back up against the wall and wailed in desperation even before her gruesome face appeared under the table. Her lips were pressed together in hateful anger. Her hair was flopping in her eyes. He was crying and screaming and yelling. But mostly, he was begging.

"Don't hit me Mama! Don't hit me! I didn't do anything! I've been good. I didn't do anything wrong. Sister Mary was smiling, Mama. She was smiling! Please stop hitting me!"

Richard's sister was standing, unmoved, next to the stove at the far end of the kitchen table with her hands still over her face. She was crying. Tears were pouring down her face. Her nose was running. What could she do? Her mother was going insane. She had never before seen her so mad. She wouldn't stop. She had pulled Richard from underneath the table and flung him across the kitchen floor. He scooted into a corner between the washing machine and the sink.

His mother, in all of her ugliness, rushed towards him. She pummeled him again and again, and again and again. Richard finally gave up his resistance. He scrunched himself up. He pulled his knees to his chest. He buried his head between his knees and put his hands and arms up and over his ears and head. Most of the blows were now hitting on his legs and his arms. But then she grabbed him by the hair and started banging his head against the wall. When his sister heard the sound of his head cracking against the wall, she could stand it no more. She screamed.

"STOP! STOP! For God's sake, you are going to kill him." She screamed the last "stop" and held the word like a blearing siren. She continued to yell at her mother from across the room, hysterically. She knew what would happen but she didn't care. She didn't care even about herself anymore. Her mother was going to kill her little brother. She could not just stand there and watch the murder.

Her mother heard the screams and stopped pummeling Richard. Her eyes were in a blind rage. She turned and looked at Carol.

"SHUT UP!" she screamed at Carol. Carol wouldn't stop screaming. Her mother rushed towards her. Carol fell into the chair by the stove. She pulled her knees up to her chest and covered her head with her arms in learned anticipation of what she knew she was about to experience. Richard could see his sister, Carol. He could see her blond hair flopping every which way from all of the blows. But, fortunately, his mother was getting tired. The pitch of her yelling was lessening. Her voice and her body were losing their fury.

Richard wanted her to stop hurting his sister but he didn't want her back on him either. He hunkered between the washing machine and the sink and he watched as his sister received her beating. He could see the red marks on her smooth girlish face as her mother held her head back by the hair and slapped her across her face. He could actually see the imprint of his mother's hand, as if her fingers were now embedded into his sister's soft cheek.

The tears rolled from her eyes, but she didn't yell or scream. She tried as best she could to protect herself. She took her beating. He was now crying for her. He could feel every blow that she received. He would never forget this picture of his sister being beaten in his place. She was very brave. There was no yelling. His mother became more and more methodical as she tired. She wanted to make every slap count. She kept pulling Carol's head back by her hair and then fishing for some open flesh. His sister puffed and sputtered, as the blows struck. Richard would forever hear the cracking of his mother's palms, slapping against the soft fleshy cheeks of his little friend and protector. Whack! ... Whack whack whack whack whack.

Even though he had stopped crying, Richard felt very bad. Somehow the tears had disappeared. But now he watched as his mother, in her blue flower-printed dress, buried his sister in blows. He watched as Carol's head was slammed from one side to the other. And now his tears began to flow once again, but not because he was hurting or in pain. His pain was gone. He felt only numbness. He cried because he was afraid; because he was so small and helpless. He cried because he wanted to help and to protect his sister. He wanted to help his sister as she had helped and protected him. But he couldn't. He loved his sister.

He didn't wipe his eyes or his nose as he stared, and shortly he could see nothing but a blur through his tears. He didn't blink his eyes. He wanted it all to disappear. He wanted his mother and his sister, and the kitchen table, and the chairs, and the refrigerator, and the stove, and the clock above the refrigerator and everything and everyone to disappear.

He succeeded. He made it all disappear in a vale of unblinking tears. He vowed that if he could ever stop crying this time, he would never cry again no matter how much it hurt, or how hard he was hit. Not his mother or anyone in this world would ever see him cry again ... NOT EVER!

4 The Apology

That evening Richard's mother nursed him and bathed him. She didn't nurse him gently. She pushed and shoved him about. In the bathroom he resented having to stand before her, naked. When she dried his hair with the towel, she dug her fingers into his scalp. It hurt when she hit the sore spots and pulled on the scabs that had already formed on his scalp.

He didn't complain. He didn't dare to complain. She dried his back and his butt and the back of his legs. She then twisted him around forcefully, digging her bony red fingers into his shoulders. She rushed a towel over his front and then down between his legs.

Next, she got out the big powder puff and began patting him with powder. Pat, pat pat ... pat, pat pat. Slowly the pats became more and more forceful. There were no words being spoken. She pushed him this way - whack, whack. The powder puff stung somewhat but not badly. She pushed him that way - whack, whack, whack. She hit him on his bare butt. It hurt.

He knew that to hurt him was her intention. She found satisfaction in hurting him. She spun him around. She dipped the puff into the powder and began slapping him with it again. He didn't look at her. Looking in her eyes might provoke her. He looked away as she swatted him. She hit him on his penis. It stung. It made him jump, slightly.

What she was doing was hurting him. He didn't move, nor did he flinch. He swallowed up the stinging and controlled his natural reaction to flinch from the spark-like pain. He looked up, hesitantly, at her face. Her face was twisted once again with that ugliness that was a part of her. He didn't understand, but it was hurting too much not to move.

He covered his crotch with both of his hands and turned his head away from her. He stared silently down at the floor. This action snapped her from her mission. Then, she began dressing him. After she had him into his pajamas, she brought him into the living room. She told him to lie down on the couch. She went to the kitchen and wrapped some ice cubes in a facecloth.

"Here, hold this on your eye."

He had a swelling on the side of his left eye. His mouth and lips felt funny also. His lips had been slapped into his teeth and the inside of his mouth, behind his lips felt funny; like pieces of skin and stuff were dangling in there. His upper lip felt twice as big as it normally did. His head felt lopsided and numb. His shoulders and sides hurt. He had black and blue marks on his arms and ribs and thighs. Some of the spots were an ugly mustard yellow. They were very, very sore to touch.

His mother sat in a chair across the room. She took out her crocheting. The faster she talked, the faster she crocheted. He didn't hear what she was saying. He was nervous that she was working herself up to another frenzy.

"Can I go to bed, please? I'm sleepy," he purposely whined. He didn't want to make any request boldly or seem demanding in any way. He purposefully made his request with an artificial whine or whimper. Like a very small child or a "baby" would do. Much like he would have done a week ago without pretending - as he would have done when he was once a baby. This day he was no longer a baby. He knew it. He was a child no longer.

His eye, with the ice cube on it, was partially closed. He could feel it and the tightness of his swollen skin. No, he was no baby. He was just ... small.

"Go ahead, get out of my damn sight," she huffed.

He went to his room and climbed up into his crib. His bed was still a crib, but with the sides removed and a larger mattress inserted.

Once in the private security of his bed, he began to examine his wounds. His eye really felt funny. When he felt it, he was startled. There was a lump just aside the bone around his eye. The lump was so big that it felt exactly like he had an entire hard-boiled egg under the skin. His thigh also felt sore. He pulled down his pajamas. He sat up and looked at his thigh. His whole upper right thigh, it seemed, was a mass of black, blue and yellow. He felt gently around the whole area. He pressed softly with his fingers here and there. At the center,

WOW! That is where it really hurt. He pulled up his shirt. His ribs on his right side looked pretty much the same. He laid back down and pulled up his pajamas. He felt around his skull. There was a huge swelling. It was sore. At the center of the swelling he could feel a scab. There were other little knots here and there and one other, good sized one, behind his left ear.

Every time he closed his eyes, he saw his mother in all of her ugliness. He saw her huge, distorted, grotesque face peering at him as he attempted to hide underneath the kitchen table. He saw her twisted back and her black hair as she leaned over his sister and "belted" her to the face. He saw his sister's hair flying this way and that, as she cowered in her chair.

Suddenly his bedroom door opened a crack and his sister's tiny face peeked in. He was five. His sister was eleven. His big brother was twelve. His brother was already over six feet tall. His brother had already made it a point to be at home as infrequently as possible. He showed up for meals and at bed time. Richard didn't see him very much.

His sister's face was smiling. She looked over her shoulder then sneaked into his room. She came over to his bed. She cringed when she looked at his eye.

"Are you okay?" she asked gently.

"Are you?" he responded in kind.

"Oh sure, she didn't hurt me. She hit me mostly on the arms." She showed him her black and blue spots. He pulled up his shirt and showed her the one on his ribs. It was almost as if they were displaying to one another their badges of courage. She touched his wounded area with extreme care and caution.

"I thought that she was going to kill you this time," she whispered with her eyes widening and welling up with tears.

"Me too," he said smiling. They both began laughing, quietly. He saw the tears in her eyes and he sat up and hugged her. She cried on his shoulder. He didn't cry.

After she had slipped from the room, he lay on his back, staring at the ceiling. He thought about tears. As he thought, he gently massaged the huge bruise on his thigh. If he were never ever to shed another tear, it would take more than just hate. He had a sufficiency of hate, but he would need more than hate.

He pressed on his thigh with his fingertips at the center of his wound. A sharp pain shot through his limb, then rushed about his body. He would have to be able to endure pain. Pain makes people cry. He pressed at the center of his wound again. It wasn't necessary to press hard. Slight pressure sent chilling pain in multiple directions. He closed his eyes and as he lay on his back, he inflicted himself with pain until he nearly screamed as his body chilled and sweated. He must understand pain if he were to survive in this home - in this house.

The next morning was Saturday. When Richard got up, his brother was already gone. His sister was sitting in her pink wool pajamas in the chair next to the stove, drinking her morning cup of hot tea. His mother was stomping around, already giving orders.

"Get in the bathroom. Do your business and get dressed. Let's get this crap over with."

He didn't know what crap she was talking about. He was not about to ask any questions.

"Put on your school clothes."

He was going to school? It was Saturday? What had Sister Mary said in that note? Why had she been smiling when she pinned it to his pocket? His mother nearly killed him because of the words that she wrote on that piece of paper. Sister Mary had smiled.

"Make sure that your mother reads this," she said.

Yes, make sure she reads it. He made sure that she read it, and his mother went nuts - like bombs exploding, like stars falling from the sky. BOOM! BOOM! How could Sister Mary trick him that way? Why did she want to see him get hurt? He never bothered her. He was always good. He kept his hands folded, his back straight, his feet together, his eyes forward. He said the predge-a-lee-gents to the flag. He never made a peep. Why? She had such a gentle face, too. Don't trust gentle faces, Richard. Don't trust women's faces.

Well, they were on their way. It was just like crossing the street at the mill when he forgot to kiss her goodbye. Yanking, pulling, pushing, and rushing up the street. They were on a mission. His mother was going to storm the schoolhouse. She would attack. She would throw desks out the window, break chairs, scream and yell. But yell and scream about what? Yell and scream at whom? What had he done?

"I didn't do anything," he mumbled almost inaudibly. "I've been good."

“What?” his mother barked.

“Nothing,” he whispered.

“It better be nothing, buster. You just better believe this better be nothing. Last night will just be a taste of the medicine that’s in store for you. You just better believe it.”

Richard spoke no more. For the remainder of the journey, there was silence. He just couldn’t understand it all. He had been good. Yes, he certainly had been good. He didn’t deserve to be punished. His mother called what she had done to him - medicine. On another occasion she had called it a licking; on another instance a spanking. It was something much, much worse than all of those things, and it certainly wasn’t medicine.

When they walked into the first-grade classroom, Sister Mary was busy at her desk. The school always had that certain smell about it. Not a smell that he could describe, but one that he recognized every time that he went into the building. Maybe it was the wood, or the varnish, or the wax on the hardwood floors. Maybe it was just a feeling caused by the high ceilings or the big empty spaces.

The building echoed, and the clomping of their shoes could be heard from one end of the building to the other. The big entrance door slamming behind Richard and his mother rang up and down the corridors. It was like a huge wooden castle. Inside, were not statues of men in armor, but statues of shepherds, and women with haloes above their heads, and poor half-dead bodies were hanging everywhere. Richard thought that he and Jesus looked very much alike at the moment. They both had very sad, weary, bruised and battered faces.

Sister Mary heard the footsteps approaching her desk. She looked up from her papers with an exceptionally broad smile. She rose from her chair to greet the woman who was approaching her. She then looked down at the child so that she would know whose mother this was.

When she saw Richard’s face she was stopped in her tracks. She looked baffled and confused. She was told when she was sent here what kind of a neighborhood this was. She knew from all of the stories told to her by Sister Francis and the old time nuns who had been here for many years that this was a tough, poor, blue-collar mill town. It was Catholic, but it was rough and tumble. These children, she had often been told, were better handled with a stick than a glove.

Sister Edward, the strong nun who had held the little boy out the window, demanded that Bill, the janitor, and four of her largest eighth graders remain with her on Wednesday afternoons, when the boys from the undisciplined, "more violent" public schools came over for their weekly religious training. She was frightened.

Sister Mary's first reaction was to comfort Richard. She stopped herself. It suddenly occurred to her that it could be possible that Richard hadn't, in reality, been run over by a bus, but merely disciplined by this woman. The woman was right here before her, standing boldly and unashamed, with her child in hand. This woman looked terribly angry. She looked outrageously upset. Sister Mary steadied herself. This was a part of this neighborhood. This was poverty. To minister to these people was her reason for being. She was a nun.

"Well, how do you do?" she said stepping off her platform and rushing up to meet Mrs. Noble. She must be gracious. She must get to the bottom of this. She extended her hand. "You must be Mrs. Noble? I'm Sister Mary."

"Yeah," Mrs. Noble said disinterestedly, as she turned directly to the question at hand. "What is this crap about Richard being kept back? If he wasn't keeping up, why didn't you tell me? I know how to teach him to keep up. He'll keep up from now on, I'll tell you. You have nothing to worry about."

Richard was totally shocked. Sister Mary wanted him to stay back. Why? She never said one word to him all that year about anything. He knew his "one times one" and his "one times two". He could count all the way to a thousand. Not once even, had he ever caused Sister Mary to scold him. He had been good. If he wasn't good, he would get his block knocked off.

"Well, I certainly hope that I didn't mislead you with that little note that I sent home with Richard." Sister Mary was nervous. She could see the look in Mrs. Noble's face. Mrs. Noble looked angry enough to fight.

"If Richard wasn't doing his work why didn't you inform me during the year? I would have put him on the right track and quick. Richard is no dummy. He is just as smart as his brother and sister. If he is not passing, it is because he is not trying. All that you had to do was tell me. Why did you wait until the last week of school and then send me this cutesy little note? 'Please come down and see me, Mrs. Noble.' like we're chums or something," she mimicked, and mocked. "If Richard gives you any trouble, you don't have to call me. You just give him a crack in the teeth and watch how fast he straightens up."

Richard was standing a foot or so from his mother's side, staring at the floor beneath his Buster Brown shoes. He loved those shoes; just looking at them made him feel special. Sister Mary stepped toward Richard and forced a small smile and laugh. She put her arm across his back and over his shoulder. She gently pulled him to her side and away from his mother's.

"Oh, no no no no no, Mrs. Noble, you have this all wrong. I am so terribly sorry for all this confusion. Richard is one of my brightest, quickest students. Actually, it is probably quite selfish of me to want to keep him in my class for another year." She laughed quite artificially. Mrs. Noble wasn't laughing. She was peering at Sister Mary with a good deal of suspicion. Sister Mary felt the necessity to continue with her explanation. All the while that she spoke, her hand roamed across Richard's back, and around his shoulder, then up along his neck, and along his face. "You see Mrs. Noble a new rule has come down through the dioceses. As Father Carney explained it to me, it has been discovered that if children start their schooling at too early an age..."

"He's five, just like he is supposed to be," Mrs. Noble blurted out.

"Yes, yes, I understand that, but he is a young five. When is his birthday, Mrs. Noble?" she asked. Sister Mary's hand was now roaming gently about the top of the boy's head. Her fingers then came upon the lump behind his left ear. She continued to talk as her long, soft fingers caressed the lump very lightly and with tender concern.

"He's born in June."

"You see, even if he is to stay back, he will only be six in the first grade, even next year. Most children start when they are five. They very quickly turn to age six. Richard won't be six until June." Sister Mary was doing well. She wasn't accustomed to lying. She found the other knot at the back of Richard's head. She was rubbing it softly as she spoke. "So, you see Mrs. Noble, this has nothing to do with intelligence. This is simply a social adjustment. We thought that it might be better for

Richard to be with children more his own age." Her fingers were now gently stroking the lump above his right eye. "Richard is not only extremely bright, but one of the most behaved children in my class. I only suggest his staying back to you because we feel that he might be just slightly behind in his degree of social maturity. Another year in the first grade certainly won't harm him and it may bring a great deal to his development in the future."

Richard didn't know what Sister Mary was talking about, but she seemed sincere. Richard's mother didn't believe a word of it. But then, on the other hand, what the hell did she know about "development" and "social adjustment."

"You mean if I want him to go to the second grade, he can go?"

"He most definitely may, if that is what you choose. But my recommendation is that he remains here with me for another year." She pulled him up close to her side. Richard could feel her leg beneath her black robes. He always thought that nuns had legs, but he had never seen one. They could have been like a spirit or a ghost. They were holy people too. It felt strange to be leaning up against a nun's leg. It felt strange to be seeing a nun in his mind's eye with legs. They always seemed to float around. He felt it was better that nuns had legs though. It was like Jesus having a body. Kind of makes them all, one of us.

She was pressing his head into her side. He could feel the curvature of her hip. There was a body under there. There was a whole body with legs and hips. This was intriguing. Like the statues. In his mind, statues were long robes with feet. They had a head but between the head and the feet was a ghost. Sister Mary having a body was somewhat of a strange discovery.

Sister Mary was searching Mrs. Noble's eyes. Sister Mary had never met a person like Mrs. Noble ever before in her life. She knew that such people existed but she had never actually met one face to face. She wondered what kind of person could beat a child, a small child, a child whose head barely reached the top of her hip.

Sister Mary was smaller than Mrs. Noble. She looked up into her eyes. She searched the eyes, looking for a soul. To Sister Mary, a soul was that part of a human that made a human, human. The soul was what separated mankind from a rock or a tree. A human being was an entity capable of compassion. A human being could shed a tear. A human being could understand the pain of another human being. A human being could understand.

Could Mrs. Noble understand? Did she feel this child's pain? Did she feel this child's pain when she struck it? Was she a human being or a creature? What was going on behind those cold, hard eyes that were glaring at her? She saw anger. She saw hate. She saw vindictiveness. She saw confusion. She saw some kind of thought taking place. Was it a thought process that could understand her words? Or was it a thought process comparable to Blake's "Tiger, Tiger, burning bright, in the forest of the night. What immortal hand or eye could have framed thy fearful symmetry?"

One pair of eyes burned while the other searched. Then suddenly both were searching.

"So you see Mrs. Noble, there really is no problem. It is more or less up to you." Sister Mary stopped and looked hopefully. There was a long silence. Mrs. Noble pondered the alternatives. Was this nun trying to trick her? Was she trying to pull the wool over her eyes? What was she up to? What was she trying to pull here? Could she be serious?

She looked down at Richard snuggled up against this strange woman's side. This woman was patting him on the side of the head much like one might stroke a dog or a cat.

Had she miscalculated this situation? Richard kept his eyes down. He continued to stare at the floor, awkwardly. These two adult minds were conniving over his future well-being. What was being decided and judged here meant something - to get beaten or not to get beaten again.

For some strange reason he felt that Sister Mary was defending him. She was fighting for him. She was touching him. She was touching him, kindly. Her fingers now didn't feel as cold as he had remembered. He wanted to stay with her. She really cared about him. Maybe it would all be for the best?

"Well you're the teacher. You are the one who is supposed to know what she is doing."

"Yes, I am, Mrs. Noble, and I do," she answered, authoritatively.

"Well ... fine."

They all just stood there in silence for another moment.

"I suppose that we will go home now?"

"Yes, certainly." Sister Mary crouched down. "And what about you Richard? Are you opposed to spending another year with me?" She put the long, thin fingers of her right hand under the boy's chin and lifted his head until they made eye contact. He shook his head, negatively. Sister Mary smiled. Then she held him by the shoulders. "You are a good boy and a strong one too." As she spoke and gazed into the boy's eyes she ran her hands up and down the lengths of the boy's arms. Her hands went along his shoulders, biceps, elbows, forearms and wrists as if she were searching for something. She kept looking up at the mother, curiously. "And aren't these wonderful corduroy pants your wearing?" And suddenly her hands were sliding down his legs. He stared at her curiously, and so too the mother. "Well, that will be fine, then." Sister Mary said as she raised herself up from her squatting position.

"Yes," Mrs. Noble repeated as she focused on the nun suspiciously. "That will be fine."

Sister Mary returned to her desk and then watched from the corner of her eye as they exited the room.

The boy and his mother exited the school. The walk home was very quiet. She held him by the hand, but without excess pressure. There was no yanking, or pulling, or pushing.

Richard stared at the sidewalk. He was watching the ants and the small bugs that were scurrying about trying to avoid being trampled by his new Buster Brown shoes. He took some big steps and some little steps in an attempt to avoid killing them. His mother was just stepping on them left and right. She was paying no attention to them. Sometimes he would look back over his shoulder to see just how many she had trampled. But even though she stepped indiscriminately on bunches of them, they all just seemed to go about their business. He couldn't believe that he could see no dead ones. He kept jerking and turning back to look over his shoulder at the ground behind him. His mother paid no attention to him or the ants, or his erratic stepping. She was thinking.

She was thinking; "What the hell was that nun up to? What was all that crap about social "development"? Mary had once been to grammar school herself. She had completed the whole eight grades. Nobody ever talked to her mother about any damn social development. This was really something. Modern times! It's not "a b c d" it's social development.

All the while that she walked home with her boy and talked to herself, pictures of yesterday's events flashed through her mind. She pictured her son scurrying beneath the kitchen table. She saw a vision of her own enraged face. Now she had seen Sister Mary face. The nun had a "look" on her face. That look! Mary had seen "that look" before. That look says; "Is this woman crazy?" Oh yes! Mary Noble had seen that look before. At first, it is a look that searches and wonders; a dumb, stupid befuddled look. But then once they - those others - decide that you really ARE crazy, then the look changes. Then it becomes blank and patronizing. "Yes, Mrs. Noble. Oh sure Mrs. Noble. We understand Mrs. Noble." That phony, hypocritical nonsense! They understand all right? They understand a hat full of crap. That's what they understand. "Come with us Mrs. Noble. It is time for your pills, Mrs. Noble. Oh yes, yes Mrs. Noble. We understand perfectly well." They understand? HA! They weren't even listening. Once you're crazy, nobody listens anymore. They just sing-song and lah-di-dah you to death. The DAMN fools!

That nun back there, she had that look. That nun was wondering if Mary Noble was crazy. And what the hell was Sister Mary looking for? Searching up and down the boy's damn body with her hands? What did she think that he had walked down there with a body full of broken bones?

That damn nun! She's the one who's crazy. Why had Mary Noble even gone down there? They are all a bunch of damn fools! Why couldn't Mary just stay in her apartment and not have to suffer all of these fools. Nervous breakdown, bull crap! He - her husband - he was making a fool of her. She knew what he was up to. She knew every minute. He wasn't kidding anybody with his cutesy little excuses. He wanted to run off and leave her. She never wanted any kids. It was all so humiliating. He didn't know what love was. He would have left in a moment, if she hadn't pretended to be crazy.

She pretended too well - too well indeed. Everyone believed that she was crazy. Before she knew it, they had her locked up in a booby hatch with a bunch of really crazy buggers. Then she had to prove that she wasn't crazy. They wouldn't listen. They wouldn't believe her. "So tell us about your childhood, Mrs.

Noble. What was your mother like, Mrs. Noble? What was your father like? Did you have a doggie?" What the hell did those fools care if she had a doggie or not?

But what had Richard to do with all of this? Was she punishing Richard for what all these fools had done to her? Look at him? What in God's name is that boy doing right now? He's staring at his shoes, and jumping over the cracks in the sidewalk. My god!

Her children were her only outlet. Mary had always been the bottom of the pile. If she complained, they would lock her up once again in the booby hatch. She couldn't talk to her mother. Her mother never even liked her. Her mother liked Mary's little brother, cute little "Ray-ray." Then, of course, there were all of her spoiled little sisters. On top of all that, you had all the neighborhood fools.

Sister Mary had that look in her eye. It was just that kind of a look that had put Mary Noble away in the past. Mary had lost her temper. She had a bad temper. She had beaten Richard badly. How badly? He wasn't dead. He had no broken bones. He had a little bump here and there. It was Ernie, her husband's fault. He was away so much. She didn't like being alone. She didn't like having all the responsibility. Kids, she had her fill of kids. She was lonely – that silly, stupid nun. What was with that note?

Dear Mrs. Noble,

I would like to talk with you about your son, Richard. I think that he should remain in the first grade for another year.

Sincerely,

Sister Mary

What the hell was that all about?

"Richard?" his mother said when they finally arrived at the corner of Chelmsford Street, after numerous city blocks of silence. "I'm Sorry." Richard was shocked. He never expected his mother to apologize. "I'll never do that again."

She would never do what again? She would never hit him again? She would never hit him so much, again? She would never disbelieve him again? She would never go to the school house again? What would she never do again? He didn't really know, but suddenly he felt stronger inside. She was wrong about something and she had admitted it. He hadn't lied. He didn't do anything. Now she knew that it was true. She knew that he had told the truth. He was right and she was wrong.

He didn't want to be holding her hand. He tugged slightly and she let it go. He didn't want to be her friend. He didn't want to like her. He didn't love her. He never loved her.

Now they walked side by side, but not hand-in-hand. It felt good not to be forced to hold her hand. He would never hold her hand again. He would never, ever hold her hand again.

His mother was a farmer. She had planted the seeds of hate. She had broken his skin and embedded the seeds of her hatred into his fertile blood. She packed them down with her flailing palms. Huddled between the washing machine and the kitchen sink he watered those hate filled seeds with his tears. They were nourished and sunned by the glow of his poor sister's burning cheeks as he watched as she took blows in his stead.

He hated this woman who called herself his mother. His painful beating would one day be but a memory, but that day would never die. The seeds of hate and anger and rage would sprout and grow in the sunless soil behind his heart and within the fertile tissues of his battered, bruised and bewildered brain.

5 His Dad

Richard was lying on the living room floor. He and his sister were listening to the *Inner Sanctum* on the radio. "Welcome to the Inner Sanctum ... Ha ha ha ha ha." Then the mysterious door creaked open. Their mother was in the room; then out of the room; then in the kitchen; then out on the front porch. Her husband, Ernie, wasn't home yet. It was already after dark.

He had recently returned home after a number of months at sea. He had left early that morning to pace the streets of Lawrence in hopes of finding a job close to home. Since World War II had ended, there were few jobs in Lawrence. The textile mills had gradually been closed down. Most of them had gone south or to greener labor pastures overseas.

One day a man had advertised for a helper at his small grocery store and a line of applicants formed in the street several blocks long. Seeing the line that morning, the man refused to even open his doors. Fighting broke out in the street. The grocer was interviewed by the local newspaper and he admitted to acting foolishly. He should never have had entered an ad in the newspaper in a town with so great a number of unemployed. From that time onward he would simply spread the word among present employees or friends and relatives.

That's the way it was after World War II in Lawrence, Massachusetts. No, it wasn't the Great Depression. It was just a mini-depression - the type of depression that just seems to pop up like a boil here and there and everywhere, no matter how prosperous the world at large happens to be.

It isn't really that hard to create a mini-depression. Simply close down a mill, or a plant, or a factory of some sort - a factory that employs tens of thousands in a town of hundreds of thousands, or a mill that employs hundreds in a town of tens of hundreds, or a small business that is the main business of a small community. This is enough. Just like magic you have a mini-depression. Truthfully, any individual without a means of income lives in a mini-depression. It doesn't matter if the whole world around him is employed and driving a Rolls Royce. If he is unemployed, it's a depression. If there is a family to support, it is a deeper depression. If no one cares whether this person is ever employed or not, the depression becomes even deeper yet. If ten such individuals are similarly unemployed, the depression gets a little deeper.

In Lowell, Lawrence and Haverhill Massachusetts, between 1948 and 1958, there were tens of thousands of unemployed. It seemed that for every man who had a job there were two that didn't.

From Richard's point of view, Lawrence was always in a state of depression. His dad had been looking for a job all of Richard's life. His dad had finally joined the Merchant Marines. He had served in the Merchant Marines during the war. He was too old to serve in the regular army and suffered from what was called hypertension. Whenever he was home from the sea, searching for a job was a part of his daily routine. His dad had kept up his membership in the A.F. of L. and was damn glad that he had done so.

No, this wasn't the Stock Market Crash of 1929, but it was a depression; and a depression, is a depression, is a depression. In Lawrence during these years there were very few alternatives to the textile mills. Those giant redbrick buildings stretched for miles throughout the city.

Lawrence was a city founded in 1845, for the explicit purpose of establishing a textile industry. Its foundations, its reason for being, its genesis was that of the industrial mill town and participation in the industrial revolution that had changed the world, and brought about the new notion of capitalism.

Lawrence was designed as an ideal community. Robert Owen, a self-made man, entrepreneur and utopian idealist had revolutionized the humanitarian spirit of the human race with his New Lanark in Scotland. He had actually built a factory which employed the hopeless dregs of that society and turned them into educated, socially responsible, well fed, decent, human beings. He created a prosperous, well-kept village that became a showplace for the world. Industrialists and moral thinkers came from countries far and wide to witness the miracle first hand and speak with its creator.

Lawrence was originally a dream of like proportion. But after years of intense competition the dream had deteriorated into a disaster. The legacy now was of huge, almost indestructible, redbrick buildings that stretched for miles. Every main thoroughfare in Lawrence led to a sprawling, redbrick Goliath, containing ten thousand window panes of broken glass and a shattered memory of the hopes and prosperity of better days.

Richard's dad once had an important position at the Arlington Mills on Broadway. He was a foreman. Family legend proclaimed his grandfather to have been a "big shot" also at the Arlington Mills. Richard never met this grandfather. He died before Richard was born. Richard had never known his dad when he was a somebody either. Neighbors and old mill workers had told Richard of his father's once late and great status. But for Richard his dad was always one of the poor and unhappy unemployed of the greater Lawrence area.

"Richard? Richard?" he heard his mother calling from the front porch. He jumped up and ran to put on his shoes. He dashed out to the front porch. He knew what was coming. His father must have appeared at the end of Chelmsford Street. His mother would want him to rush to help. His dad would be drunk. But drunkenness didn't matter to Richard. He liked his father the best when he was drunk. When his dad was drunk he smiled. When his dad was drunk he laughed and joked. When his dad was drunk he cried. When his dad was sober he never talked. When his dad was sober he never smiled. When his dad was sober he paced the floor like a caged lion. He only stopped pacing, occasionally, to peer out through the Venetian blinds or to light his cigarette or his pipe. When his dad was drunk he would let Richard light his cigarettes or his pipe with his matches or his cigarette lighter. Sometimes when he was drunk, his dad would play Doctor Jekyll and Mr. Hyde. Richard would get so excited, he would scream and run. Everyone in the family would laugh at him. It was the best time ever, playing Doctor Jekyll and Mr. Hyde.

Richard put on his jacket and his homemade knit cap. He ran out onto the front porch. His mother was staring down towards the corner. She was straining to make out a shadow in the darkness. They both stood there on the porch staring at the shadow. Suddenly the shadow tumbled to the ground.

"That's him, Richard," his mother said, pursing her lips and shaking her head. His mother was not happy when his dad was drunk. One never knew what he was going to say or what he would do. "Why don't you run down there and help him, Rich? He looks really bad tonight," she said, pathetically. There were moments when Richard actually thought that his mother loved his father. These moments were fleeting.

He did look bad. Usually he was able to hang onto the chainlink fences or to one of the rungs on a wooded slat fence. Tonight he went right down to the ground with a bang. He was still lying on the ground by the time Richard leaped down the steps to the sidewalk. Richard loved helping his dad. When his dad was drunk, he needed Richard. Otherwise, he never needed Richard. He never seemed to need anybody. Ever since the very first time that he saw his dad cry, Richard knew that his dad needed him.

Auntie Anna and Uncle Howard had come to visit one Christmas from the farm. His mother was so excited. When she saw their old, green Chevy pull up, she couldn't believe her eyes. She hadn't seen her youngest sister for a number of years. They had both been busy having babies and doing whatever else it is that keeps people and families apart. His Uncle Howard was a big, strong looking fellow. He had hard, rough hands. He wore thick wire-rimmed glasses. Richard was somewhat cautious about his Uncle Howard. He looked like he could be mean. He didn't like the city. He never had anything much to say. His glasses were so thick that they distorted his eyes and made him look spooky.

"I think that's Anna, Ernie." Mary shrieked and ran out onto the porch. "It was Anna," she explained upon returning from the porch. "She's going upstairs to see Ma and Ray first. Then she will be in to see us."

Mary got busy preparing sandwiches. She made a whole platter full of cold turkey sandwiches. Some were made with Polish rye bread, some with Polish light rye, and then others, for the kids, with Wonder Bread. She put on a pot of coffee and a big kettle for tea. When this was all completed, she tried to relax sitting in the living room. She put on her glasses and started crocheting lace trim onto a white handkerchief. She made simple white handkerchiefs very pretty this way. At Christmas time she gave them as presents. Everyone said that they loved them. It was nice to get something handmade rather than store bought, everyone claimed. Richard always thought that they were lying. He felt that people were just trying to be nice and make compensation for the fact that his mom and dad didn't have enough money to buy Christmas presents. Instead they did what poor people did. They made them.

Mary couldn't stay put. She was simply too nervous. Every minute she was up and peeking out the kitchen door checking the stairs leading to the apartment upstairs, or the corridor leading to her apartment.

"Mary," Ernie said lighting up his pipe, "sit down, for god's sake. Anna promised. She said that she would be in to see you. Now just wait your turn."

"Well, I'm just a little nervous." Mary was always just a little nervous. The reality was that she was always quite nervous, and on this occasion she was exceptionally nervous.

The evening was passing rapidly and still Anna, Howard and the kids hadn't been in to see them.

"Maybe we should go upstairs to Ma's and Ray's and visit with everybody up there." They lived in a single building containing four different apartments. Uncle Ray and "Grammy" lived upstairs on one side of the building. Uncle Clayton and Aunt Amelia lived in the apartment directly above. Mary and Ernie lived on the first floor. Bill, the carpenter, lived across the way.

"I think that I hear them upstairs. They are probably visiting Clayton and Amelia. They're making the rounds. They will be in here to see us next. So relax, Mary."

"I suppose that you are right."

"Sure I'm right. Just relax; sit and crotchet."

That was like asking a spider not to make a web or a bee not to make honey. It just couldn't happen. Every two minutes Mary would put down her needle and handkerchief and slip up to the kitchen door to peek out.

"But why didn't they come in to see us before they went upstairs? Anna said that she was going up to see Ma, and then she would be down to see us. And after visiting us she would go and see Amelia. Why would she go to Amelia's first? She said she would see us first. That's what she said."

"Well, maybe she changed her mind. Maybe they just slipped over by way of the upstairs porch. What difference does it make?"

"Well, I've made all of these sandwiches."

"If nobody's hungry by the time that they get in here, I'm sure that they won't go to waste. They will be good for lunch tomorrow, don't worry."

To Richard's way of thinking, that platter full of sandwiches was beginning to look mighty lonely sitting on that big kitchen table. His mother had inserted two extra leaves into the center of the table. The table now seemed to sprawl all over the kitchen. Chairs that were usually hidden in the bedrooms had been pulled out and were added to the setting. Every chair had a glass, a plate and a napkin sitting before it.

The evening had now pretty much passed. It was quite late. Mary had stopped crocheting. She was sitting nervously, fidgeting at the table. It all seemed rather strange. Everyone was wondering. The whole Noble family liked Howard, Anna and the kids. Anna seemed to be very much like Mary. Mary had a protective attachment to her little sister. Mary cared for Anna when they were children. Even Richard's father was now looking concerned. He had become pensive sitting in his overstuffed chair, sipping on his can of Pabst Blue Ribbon. Richard always liked that particular beer can. It had a bow on it, a big blue bow. His dad always looked cool, calm and collected; his mother was always nervous, jittery and jumpy. She looked weak, frightened and helpless. She wasn't. His dad looked strong, confident and courageous. He wasn't.

Would his mother's sister really forget to stop in and see them? This would be something. Ernie's family never visited them either. Ernie had somehow become the "black sheep" of his clan. Richard knew that to be a black sheep was something bad, but yet, he took pride in the concept. He would picture one black sheep in a crowded pasture full of white sheep. That one black sheep among the thousands of white sheep was his dad. Being the only black sheep was unique. You weren't just another of the never ending monotony of white sheep. He had heard black wool mentioned also. If you had a blanket that was stuffed with black wool it was more valuable than one that was stuffed with white wool. If you were a black sheep you were something special. You were different. That was his dad, all right. He was, at least in Richard's eyes, someone very special and very different.

Just like the black sheep, his dad had shiny, curly black hair. He never used a comb. He had special brushes that he used. The brushes were made of some kind of fancy wood that looked like mahogany or something. He had a set of two brushes and he used them simultaneously, one in each hand. Before he started grooming his hair, he always massaged his scalp with this hair cream which boasted of lanolin. Lanolin came from sheep. His dad was a beautiful black sheep with wonderful, black wavy wool that shined with glossy lanolin. When Richard grew up, he would be a black sheep too. Even if it meant that the whole world would be jealous of him - just as his dad's brothers and sisters were jealous of him.

His dad was the favorite son of his father. He was the smartest and the oldest. He was the strongest and the best fighter. He was the hardest worker and his dad wanted him right there by his side down at the Arlington Mill. All of his dad's five brothers and sisters were jealous of him. They lived up on the "hill" - Oakside Ave. That was where the rich people lived. His father's mother owned a big fancy house up on the hill. Richard and his sister Carol had been up the hill to grandma's house. They used to sneak up there by themselves. His grandmother and uncles and aunts liked to play what was called penny-ante poker. Richard always seemed to win. He was always thrilled and excited to win. The relatives always laughed. Richard always went home with his pockets bulging with pennies. He liked playing penny-ante poker with his father's relatives. They were nice to him and his sister. But why didn't they like his father? They should have liked him. He was their big brother. Richard liked his big brother. Why didn't they like theirs?

Richard's mother told him that they all disliked his dad because his dad was better looking than the rest of them.

Suddenly there was a rumbling on the stairwell in the hall. Mary leaped from her seat at the kitchen table, and his dad smiled and breathed a sigh of relief as he pulled another Pabst from the ancient Fridgerdare refrigerator. Mary ran to the kitchen door.

“Well, gee whiz! We never thought that you would get finished with your visiting up there. Come on in. Are you hungry? I’ve got plenty of nice turkey sandwiches here.”

“Well, not really, Mary,” bellowed Uncle Howard. “I’m afraid we won’t be coming in. We’re already late. We over stayed our visit with Ray and Amelia. We’ve got a long ride home now, and it’s already dark. We had better just be hitting the road.”

“Oh, ahhh ... well can’t you just come in for a second or two? Let me wrap up some of these sandwiches for you. You can eat them on the way home.”

“Well thank you, Mary, but honestly, we’d best just be getting on our way.”

Richard’s father was at the counter by the kitchen sink, getting out his beer can opener. Richard was sitting at the kitchen table, staring at the platter of turkey sandwiches. His dad cocked his ear towards the conversation in the hall. His face turned serious.

“Did I hear right, Richard? Did Howard say that he wasn’t coming in here?” Richard nodded his head. His dad shook his head in disgust. He punched open his can of beer. First punching a hole on one side and then on the other: a big hole to drink from and a small hole to let in air. He was still shaking his head as he walked past the kitchen door and returned to his stuffed chair in the living room. Mary wouldn’t take no for an answer. She kept bribing and begging.

“Well, come on? You’ve got one minute? You can’t be in that much of a hurry? You come all this way and we never get to see you. This is a beautiful turkey. Nice Polish bread, too.” She began to smack her lips as she always did when she talked about food. She could make anybody hungry just talking about eating. “Fresh Polish rye bread, real butter, slow cooked tender, juicy turkey. How about you kids? Aren’t any of you kids hungry? How about you Chicky and you Ray-ray? You boys must be hungry by this time? I know that little Cheryl would like a sandwich, wouldn’t you honey?”

“Oh for Criss sake, let ‘em go, Mary!” his dad shouted from his parlor chair. No one seemed to hear him but Richard. Was his dad right? Was his mother a black sheep too? It certainly didn’t look like Howard and Anna and the kids were going to come in. There they were, right in the hall. They hadn’t been here for years. They would just walk by the door and leave. His mother continued her begging and coaxing. It was peculiar. They couldn't stick around for another second but they could argue about it for five minutes. Was this just like his dad's relatives? These folks just didn't like their sister and her family?

His father suddenly bounced from his parlor chair and rushed to the doorway.

"Now you listen to me. For god's sake, come in here and sit down. This poor woman has been running around here all night. Look at this over here." He gestured with a wave of his arm to the kitchen table. "She has got enough food there to feed an army." He paused for a response.

"We sure do appreciate it, Ernie, but I've got to be up at five tomorrow morning. You know how us farm boys are."

"Yeah, I know ..." His dad took a long pause. He rubbed on his chin. Then he scratched his head and shuffled his feet a bit. He started to turn from the door and walk into the kitchen. He stopped, turned back to the crowd in the hall. "Yes Howard and I know bullcrap when I hear it too. What kind of a man are you anyway?"

There was silence. There was a deathly silence. This was "man" talk. Howard was a tough farm boy. What was his dad up to? Were they going to fight over this?

"Just what kind of a man is it who will keep two sisters who love one another apart?" Ernie's voice cracked. Richard couldn't believe it, but his dad then began to cry. "For criss sake," he said with tears flooding his voice. "And here it is Christmas time." Just hearing the tears in her father's voice made Richard's sister start crying. Richard had never seen or heard his dad cry ever before. Tears started to swell from inside of Richard, but he took a deep breath, blinked his eyes and stopped them before they could get started. He would not cry. He would never cry.

"I can't believe this. Christmas time is for family. Christmas time is for brothers and sisters to get together. For God's sake Howard, be a MAN."

His dad then turned from the kitchen door. Richard could see the tears dripping down from his father's eyes. They bumped their way about the rough black stubble that was forever present on his dad's cheeks. His dad could shave twice a day if he wanted.

The Johnson family stood in the hallway and stared at one another. Richard saw at that moment, through his dad's tears, what he had been looking for. He understood. His dad was standing up for his wife. But really, he was talking to his own brothers and sisters. He was yelling in defense of his wife, but he was crying for himself. He missed his own family. It hurt him to be a black sheep. Inside he was suffering. Richard saw in his dad then and there what he had never seen before in anyone else. He saw compassion. He saw feeling and tenderness. He saw concern and caring. He saw a strong man cry. Probably the strongest man who ever lived was standing there crying before his very eyes.

His dad was suffering and had a big pain inside of him. It hurt him so badly that he even cried in front of other people. Richard knew right then what he wanted most in life. He wanted his father to love him as much as he had loved his own brothers and sisters. He wanted a piece of that softness, a slice of that love, a few of those tears. There! There was the kind of love Richard wanted.

His own eyes were watery and filled with moisture, but he would resist their flow. Tears meant love, but no tears meant strength. His dad needed Richard's strength. His dad wasn't as strong as he. He would protect his dad. He would be his father's strength. His father was older, bigger and stronger, but he was weak. He would need Richard in the future to protect him. He wouldn't let people hurt his dad. He would swallow his dad up in the strength of his love and be his father's shield against the world; against everybody. A man like his dad needed a son like him.

He went into the parlor and sat down on the carpet in front of his dad's chair. He didn't look at his dad. He didn't want to embarrass him or make him angry. He just wanted to be near him. He sat on the floor and stared at the kitchen door. No one spoke.

Anna looked up at Howard, and then without a word they all came into the apartment and sat down. In a few moments everyone was visiting, and things were good.

After that Christmas, Richard liked his Uncle Howard. He liked him because he came in and sat down. If he were really a mean man, he would have just left or maybe started a fight. But he didn't. He came in and sat down. He joked and ate turkey sandwiches. Mary and Anna had a chance to visit. Everyone had a chance to visit. That was important.

When Richard flipped the latch on the gate, he could see that his dad was still down on the ground and fumbling around on his hands and knees. He ran up the street towards him as fast as he possibly could. He gave no thought to the dark, or the potholes or the glow from the streetlights. No, he ran right through the dark and the light and even the broken lights along the way. He hoped that his dad would still be down when he arrived at the scene. Then he could help him up. He would be even more important then.

His wish came true. Upon his arrival, the man was still there on his hands and knees and engaged in a deep conversation with the sidewalk.

"Holy molely!" Strangely enough, his dad rarely used foul language. He said "crap in your hat" and "goddamn" or "for criss sake" but even those he used rarely. "What happened here and who are you?" he mumbled down at the sidewalk.

"Hey dad, what are you doin'?"

"Who the heck are you?"

"It's me, Richard." His dad laughed and then rolled over onto his back. Richard laughed too. "What's so funny, Dad?"

"It's Richard! Who the heck is it? It's Richard!" He laughed and laughed. It was so much fun to hear his father laugh.

"Don't worry Dad. I've come to help you." His dad stopped laughing. He lifted his head up from the pavement. He looked at Richard; then started laughing once again. "What's so funny Dad? What are you laughing at?"

"This is Ricked. Imhum goin' to hap ya." He roared with laughter. Richard didn't understand. What was funny about that?

"Give me your hand, Dad. I'll pull you up." He stuck his hand down towards his dad laying there on his back laughing.

His dad stopped laughing. He looked up at his "big" boy, with those serious blue eyes.

"Well ... okay. You goin' to help your old man up, are you?"

"Yes."

"Give me your hand then."

"It's right here Dad; right in front of you."

He grabbed onto the boy's hand.

"Okay son, pull me up." When he said pull, he yanked on the boy's hand. The boy tumbled down on top of him, like a leaf in the breeze. He hugged the boy to him and rolled to and fro on the ground, laughing. "You're going to help your old man, are you?" He hugged Richard tighter and tighter as he laughed and laughed. His rough beard scratched against Richard's smooth baby cheeks. Richard could smell the strong smell of beer and cigarettes on his father's breath. He loved those smells. "It's Witchard. It's Witchard! I'm here to help ya. Spell cat! Cat ... R ... A ... T ... cat."

Richard was happy to be in his father's arms. It didn't matter that his dad was drunk and rolling in the gutter. But as much as the little boy loved being in his father's arms, and the manly smell of cigarettes and beer, he knew what he had to do. He had to get his dad to the house before somebody called the cops. The cops would just throw his dad in the can. He put his hands to his dad's chest and pushed back, hard. His dad stopped laughing and looked at his boy with a shocked, pretend face. His dad always wanted to play when he was drunk. He was like another person. Richard looked down into his eyes, sternly.

"Come on Dad? No foolin' around. Ma's waitin' on us."

"Ouuu. Ma's waitin' on us. And is she worried about me? Or is she worried about the neighbors? Shhhhh!" He put his finger across his lips. "Shhhhhush! Come on. Ma's waitin'," he whispered. "And we don't want all the neighbors to see old drunky, dunky daddy, do we?"

"I don't care about no neighbors, Dad. I care about you."

The father stared into the son's eyes. He pulled him down on top of him once again. He hugged him and hugged him tightly. He squeezed Richard so hard, it hurt. He actually took the boy's breath away. Richard didn't resist or complain. He waited until his father was finished. Then he pulled away and sat up on his father's stomach. He put his hands onto his hips and looked down at his dad with a very serious expression.

"Okay Dad, let's get serious here." His father roared into laughter once again. "DAD!" Richard yelled scolding.

"Quiet, quiet, quiet," his dad whispered. "My goodness, boy, do you want to wake up the whole neighborhood?" His dad's face was serious but Richard knew that it was just a put-on serious. "Well, are you going to help me up, or what?"

Richard stood, and put out his hand once again. "Ohhhh no, don't hand me that. I ain't falling for that one again." His dad rolled over to his hands and knees. The ground swayed before him. He felt dizzy. He wasn't going anywhere and he knew it. He fell flat to his face and began laughing again.

Richard placed his hands on his hips once again and started tapping his foot, impatiently. His dad dragged himself over to the curbing. "All right boy. You are right. This is ridiculous." He pushed back up to his hands and knees. Then he sat back on his haunches. "Wow! I'm going to tell you, son. I am really and truly drunk this time. I mean no foolin' around. I can't even see straight."

Richard tried pushing here and pulling there but it was no go. Finally his dad crawled on his hands and knees across the sidewalk and over to a chainlink fence. From there the two of them huffed and puffed and pulled and clawed until dad was finally in a standing position. He was sweating like a pig.

"Well, Dickie boy, we've done it," his father proclaimed.

Richard felt very proud, and very satisfied. He had given it his all. "Now let's just stand here for a minute or two and let these buildings stop running around. How can you just stand there, son, in a sea like this? You are going to make quite a sailor, Dickie my boy," he sputtered, but then tightened up. "No more laughin' here. We've got to get serious." He put one hand to his hip, leaned his head back and started tapping his foot, mocking his boy's attempt at grown-up posturing. He couldn't tap his foot very well. "Tap that foot for me, son. You do it better than I do." Richard put his hands to his hips, put that stern look on, like Sister Mary, and began tapping his foot. The boy began to smile. "Wha, uh...no laughing now. No laughin'. This is serious business, here." Then he pretended to whisper, but his whisper was as loud as his yell. "We don't want to wake up no neighbors! Shuuuuush." His eyes then got all big and round and his head wobbled slightly forward. "Wright, Wrichard?"

"Right Dad."

"Wwright! That's an affirmative, Captain. All hands to the poop deck ... poop poop, poop poop." He laughed, but only for a second. He looked around him and surveyed the neighborhood. His head bobbed back and forth slightly as he attempted to look at his surroundings in a confident manner.

He shook his head and then blew out a big breath of air. "Let's both lay down again, and we'll backstroke it home." He bent towards the ground. Richard jumped in and pushed him up against the fence.

"Oh, no you don't."

"Oh, no I don't. Oh, no I don't," his father mocked. "And what if I do? Huh? What if I do?" He looked at Richard with an angry face. Richard stepped back quickly. "Ohhh oh? And now you're afraid of your old man, are ya? Like I just beat you up all the time, do I?"

"No. You don't."

"No. I don't. And how many times in your whole life did I ever lay a hand on you?" The boy was quiet. "Come on? How many times? Huh? How many times?"

"Never."

"Never. Never! That's right. Never! And I'll tell you what, boy. If I ever do, you can put a damn gun to my head and blow my stupid brains out." He looked at the boy and then pointed a finger at him very sternly. Then he began to cry. "You know that's true, don't ya?" The boy didn't answer. "Well, don't you?" The boy nodded his head up and down, but tentatively. "Okay then. Don't you ever step back from me with fear in your eyes," he said weeping. "You know," he said, choking up his tears. "My old man used to beat the hell out of me." Richard looked at his father with surprise. His dad saw the boy's surprise and raised his eyebrows and bobbed his head. "That's right. That's right. But do you know what? I loved him to death, anyway. I wish that he was still here to beat me right now. Maybe he could knock some sense into this hard head of mine. Do you think that it would do me any good?" The boy shook his head negatively. "You don't?" His dad smiled. "Well, you are right. You are one hundred percent right. My old man beat me just to make my mother happy. My mother was always complaining. Ernie did this, she would say; Vinnie did that, she would say; Davie did this. So Dad solved the whole problem. Every night as soon as he walked in the door, he took off his belt. We all lined up and each of us took our licks. That way he didn't have to listen to two hours of her complaining after a hard day at work. What do you think about that?"

"I don't like it."

His dad nodded his head in agreement. "Me either."

They stood there for a few moments while his dad regained his composure. He clung to the fence while he ran his other hand through his hair. His hair never seemed to get out of place, but right now it looked a little duller than usual.

"So, are you going to help me or not?" He held out his free arm and smiled. The boy pushed himself up against his dad, and slid one arm around his waist. His head was just slightly above his dad's belt buckle. The boy was really too small to do much, but he had a powerful confidence. They started to walk. His dad held to the fence with one hand and leaned on his boy with the other. They made slow progress. When his hand on occasion would miss the fence, he would shift his full weight to the boy and they would both go tumbling off the curb and into the gutter. They probably would have made more actual progress if the father had just chosen to crawl all the way home. In which case, the son's pride would not have been so greatly enhanced.

Each time that his father was capable of returning to a standing position with Richard's assistance, Richard's heart swelled with heroism. He could have been accomplishing no greater act of gallantry. What greater act could a son perform for his dad than to carry him on his back, to lift him from the ground, to bring him home to safety?

On the first occasion that his dad had slipped away from the fence and Richard felt his entire weight, the boy was shocked. In his imagination, he believed that he could sustain his father. The reality, though, was a complete collapse into the gutter. This only proved that his dad needed him all the more. The boy developed a technique. He watched his dad and the fences. When his father missed his grasp at a fence, the boy would tighten his jaw and turn both of his shoulders into his dad's side and knock him back into the fence. This blocking technique, when it worked, kept them both standing. The first time that he accomplished this feat, his dad looked down at his son with a quite surprised look on his face. He smiled. He had a tough little boy at his side.

It was a joint effort. It was team work at its best. Soon they were only two streetlights from the house. His dad needed to take a break. They both looked ahead to see how far off the house was. When they looked up, they saw Mary standing there on the porch.

“Whoops, there she is, the Virgin Mother. No, no, no, no. I didn’t mean that. I’m sorry son.” He looked down at the boy to see if he had been offended. Richard had no notions of virgins or what a virgin was. He knew about the Virgin Mary, Mother of God. She was a good thing. Nevertheless, his father continued as he stared up at the shadow of his bride standing up there with her arms folded across her chest. “You know Ritchie, when I married your mother, I thought that no man could have possibly loved any woman more than I did at that moment. Now, year after year, I’ve watched as that love has slowly turned to hate.” It was very easy for Richard to understand how his father could hate that shadowy creature on that porch. She was ugly mean and cruel, but then sometimes, she was okay. The commandment said; “Love Thy Father and Thy Mother.” It was wrong for a boy to hate his mother. But if it was all right for his father to admit to hating Richard’s mother, maybe it was okay for Richard also. He would never say that he did. His dad was drunk. That’s why he could talk like that, but when he was sober he would never say such things. It was just that when he was drunk, he told the truth. When he was drunk, that was when his real self came out. This drunken father was the father that Richard loved best. This drunken father was the father who treated him like a man. That’s what he was, a man. He was just little. He was a little man. His mother had knocked the little boy out of him long, long ago. He understood his father when he was drunk.

“How did you know?”

“How did I know what?”

“How did you know that you were in love with my mother?”

His dad smiled, as he stared down into the boy’s eyes. That was a smart boy there. He didn’t say all that much, but when he asked a question it was a good one. Richard wanted to know how a smart, good man like his dad had been tricked. It must have been a trick. His mother must have set some kind of a trap for his dad. Richard never, ever wanted to fall into one of those traps. He knew that it must have been a tricky one, because his dad was the smartest man in the world - that was for sure.

“How did I know that I was in love? That’s a good one. I don’t know if I have the answer, but for one thing the whole world changed. I mean, the world that I used to see disappeared. There was suddenly a new world there in front of me. Every time your mother smiled, my heart jumped." Richard understood, because every time that his dad smiled, his heart jumped. "And I thought that if I could have this woman, or if she would have me, the world would always be a beautiful place." He looked up at the woman on the porch, and Richard's eyes followed. His dad smiled. As he hung onto the fence with one hand, he waved to the woman standing there with the other. She turned in a huff and went into the house. "And there she goes - God's gift to man. Thank you Jesus! Oh thank you so much ... Don't listen to me, son. Your mother is a wonderful woman. She's changed my life." He snickered. "No, no, no ... I really mean that. She changed my life." He pulled the boy up against his side and straightened up. "Are you ready, son?"

"Ready."

The father took one step forward and lost his grip. It happened too fast. They began tripping over one another's feet. As his dad fell, he pushed the boy into the street. Richard went sliding into the road. He got himself up and brushed himself off. His dad was now sprawled out on his back with his arm around a fire hydrant.

"Jesus Christ!" his father groaned. There was blood all over his face. Richard's heart was leaping. His stomach was knotting up inside. He was feeling actual pain in his stomach. He folded his arms about his stomach and tried to rock the pain away. His dad began to move, slowly. The boy could feel the pain in his father's face. He took off his shirt and began wiping the blood from his father's face. The father watched the boy, and then he laughed. "I thought that you were helping me, son?"

"I was ... but ... but ... I slipped ... and ... and ..."

"I know. I know. I slipped too. Don't worry about a damn thing. I got this whole thing under control. Who the heck hit me anyway?"

"Nobody hit you. You hit your head on the hydrant."

Just telling his dad how he had hurt his head, shot pains back into the boy's stomach. He began squeezing his sides with his elbows. In his imagination, he could see his dad's head hitting the hydrant. He could feel the impact himself. It was as if his head was hitting the hydrant. Looking at the blood on his dad's face made it even worse. He grabbed his own head. He wanted to scream. Why had he let go of his father? Why? Why?

“What’s the matter, Richie? Did you hurt yourself too?”

“No. I think that I just have to go to the bathroom.”

His dad snickered.

“Me too. Let’s get this show on the road.” He pulled himself over to the fence and then dragged himself up to a standing position. Richard tucked in once again at his side. Suddenly his dad was much better. He wasn’t so wobbly. He didn’t put so much pressure onto Richard’s shoulders. By the time that they reached the latch on the front gate, he was almost walking on his own power. “I got it now, son. I got it. You get the doors opened.”

Richard let go of his dad, then ran up the stairs. He swung the porch door out and pushed the hall door open. His dad pulled himself along. He fell up against the front door frame and hung there. Richard released the porch door, slipped under one of his dad’s arms, ran down the hall and swung open the kitchen door. Light from the kitchen filled the hallway. His dad meandered down the hall pushing off one wall and then off the other. When Mary saw him, she screamed, and then ran to the sink. Ernie laughed.

“I’m all right. I’m all right. Don’t worry.” Mary rushed to him from the sink and began wiping his face with a damp rag. “I got to go to bed,” Ernie blubbered. Mary put her arm about him and started to help. “No, no, no. I got me a helper. Where’s that boy of mine?”

“Right here, Dad.”

“Give me a hand, son. Come on, you started this. Now let’s finish it.” Richard positioned himself under his dad’s arm and they both went staggering through the kitchen. Richard had never been so proud in all of his life. He had brought his father to the door. He was now carrying him through the kitchen, passed his frightened mother and sister. He was his dad’s favorite - at least when his dad was drunk.

When they reached the back bedroom, his dad just flopped from his arms and onto the bed. He was out like a light.

Richard returned to the kitchen like a conquering hero. He had brought his dad home. He was slightly the worse for wear, but all in one piece. He was a special little boy. He could read the admiration in his sister’s eyes - his mother’s also. He was a very important little hero. He would be a hero, at least, until morning.

In the morning, his father would be up and last night would be forgotten. He would never mention it. He would never say thank-you. He would never hug the boy to him, as he had when they were tumbling about the road. He would not pat him on the head. He would not look into his eyes. He would not seek his compassion or understanding. He would barely recognize the boy's existence. He would wash his face slowly and methodically at the sink. He did everything slowly and methodically. He ate slowly. Sometimes it would take him two hours to eat his supper. He would just sit there and chew, and chew, and chew. He would cut his meat, set down his knife and fork, and slowly chew. One time his sister wouldn't eat her green beans. He made her sit there until she finished every last one. It took her hours. Even after she finally finished, he was still sitting there chewing.

One time he demanded that Richard eat spinach. Richard said that he couldn't, because eating spinach made him sick.

"Nonsense! Eat it!" his father demanded. Richard took a forkful and put it into his mouth. Everybody at the table watched in silence. When his sister was forced to eat her green beans, she cried all the while. She sniffled and sputtered with each and every green bean. Richard didn't cry. Richard wouldn't cry. When the spinach entered his mouth, it was cold and damp. It looked like grass, boiled grass, straight from the back yard. It was too distasteful to even chew. It was watery, cold, bitter, soft and mushy. He held it in his mouth without chewing it. The thought of swallowing it made his stomach turn. The whole family knew that he was just holding it in his mouth. They were all smiling slightly at the corners of their mouths. His dad was smiling, but shaking his head in disgust also.

"Swallow it!" he demanded. Richard tried to swallow, but when he did, he gagged. Richard's swallowing and gagging was making everyone's stomach turn. "Oh, for god's sake, just swallow it, Richard." So he closed his eyes and swallowed. It no sooner got past his Adam's Apple, when it and everything else in his stomach decided to exit. Blurrrp ... blurrrp ... He puked all over his own plate and when he saw all of that green stuff and all those bits and pieces of puke, he puked some more. That was the only time that he ever saw his father leave the table early.

No? In the morning, Richard wouldn't be a hero anymore. It would be back to all of those stern, quiet, admonishing glances. "Take that apple out to the kitchen, son. Haven't you got something better to do than sit around here staring at me, boy? Go out and play. Don't come back until supper time."

No, without the addition of alcohol his dad was one cool cucumber. Without the alcohol, his eyes were covered with a dull glaze rather than sparkling with brilliance. Without the alcohol, there were no free flowing quips; no humorous remarks; no bright smile; no raucous laughter. Without the alcohol his dad was a quiet, sulking, authoritative, brooding lump. He would stand, staring out through the Venetian blinds forever. He very rarely would even speak. His smile didn't beam. His eyes didn't sparkle. His teeth were yellow from too much tobacco. His eyes were a dull lifeless brown. He was really rather small in stature. Maybe he weighed one hundred forty pounds, soaking wet. He coughed all the time, rather violently. He always had a handkerchief tucked into the cushion in his chair. He would spit the congested brown stained mucus from his smoke and mill-dust clogged lungs into the hanky.

Richard wouldn't worry about the morning. No, the sober morning didn't really matter. He would play quietly by himself and wait. He would just wait. He knew it would be only a matter of days, and sometimes just hours before his dad would once again be drunk. It was just a simple matter of waiting. Mr. Hyde would once again disappear and the wonderful Doctor Jekyll would be back to play, to smile, to hug and to love. Or was it Doctor Jekyll who would disappear and Mr. Hyde who played and laughed? What did it matter? It was all good, and it was all evil. Richard would just wait. He would wait to play with the good, or the evil. It mattered not.

6 Grandma Is Coming

Every Christmas, for as long as Richard could remember, the month before the holiday was spent in dread and anticipation. His dad's relatives would most likely be coming. Nobody knew for sure, but as with the rising of the sun each day, their visit had been a reality every previous year. Why would it not happen this year? One could only hope that maybe this year it would be different. One debate always centered around whether they had come last year at Christmas or nearer to New Year's day. Trying to foresee the exact day of their "surprise" visit always brought his mother into a state of aggravated anticipation. The acceptance, accommodation, and approval of Ernie's family were extremely important to his mother. Richard didn't care when or if they ever arrived. He longed for the day when he would be as big as his older brother and would be allowed to leave the house whenever the company would begin to arrive.

"Well, I've got to be going; party tonight," his brother would announce. He always had a party to go to, or a date, or a job. He always had an excuse but Richard was too young. He had to stay at home with his sister and his mother. He would have to stay and meet the relatives even if his father wasn't there. Richard's sister had no choice. She was a girl.

His dad's relatives came, never knowing whether Ernie would be there or not. Sometimes Ernie would be off to sea. Sometimes he would volunteer at work, if he were employed. Other times he would just remain on his stool at a local tavern. Their visit was a family tradition, but it was a tradition that neither side of the family enjoyed. It was never a good time for anyone. They came and stared awkwardly at one another. They pretended. They pretended to be friends. They embraced when they met. They laughed. They talked about the good old days.

They slapped each other on the back. But there existed the air of mistrust, suspicion and jealousy. There were unresolved issues that floated around the room like messengers from Dickens' ghosts of a Christmas past. No probing questions were asked, no political discussions, no philosophical inquiries. It was always the same ritual.

"How whyya, Mary?" said Uncle Joe, in his distinctive nasal tone. Uncle Joe was married to the very attractive and seemingly sweet, Auntie Gerry. That would usually be it for the entire evening for Uncle Joe. He would take off his coat, hand it to Mary and then flop into a hole in the old couch in the living room. It would then be only a matter of moments before his head would fall back or forward to his chest and he would begin snoring. Auntie Gerry would give him a poke in the ribs whenever he got too loud. He would usually sputter, flutter, puff and poof, but rarely ever wake up. Visiting once a year was obviously an excess for Uncle Joe. Little Richard would do his Uncle Joe impersonation for weeks before the "joyous" celebration would arrive each year.

"How whyya, Mary?" he would mock in his deepest voice, and then follow it with a loud sonorous, snoring sound. Everyone would laugh. Richard was turning into a family clown. In bed each evening, he would do impersonations for his older brother.

"Hey!" his father would yell. "Quiet down in there!" Richard would respond with a mocking impersonation of his father - never loud enough for his father to hear, of course. This would crack his brother up. It was fun making people laugh, but this Christmas stuff was really no laughing matter. Christmas was tension, confusion, anxiety and some serious pacing of the floor by Richard's old man.

His mother made sandwiches. Making sandwiches was some sort of a defense mechanism for his mother. Whenever she was nervous, she prepared sandwiches until they were tumbling from the refrigerator. She was keeping busy. Having plenty of food ready and waiting was an act of equality and well-being. She didn't realize that it only served to identify her with her lower ethnic heritage. Only poor people worry about their guest's appetites.

Mary's answer to the holiday season was to keep busy. Ernie's answer was to keep drinking.

The holidays were never pleasant. Christmas was the most unpleasant of all. Christmas was supposed to be a time for giving, but what is it when you have nothing to give? There were never very many presents under the Christmas tree. The presents that were there were usually necessities: school clothes, socks, underwear.

That wasn't so unpleasant. It was the attitudes that floated about the apartment like vultures circling a dead carcass. The attitudes were more death like than birth-like. There was a constant dread and foreboding. A nervous tension fueled by anxiety and frustration. His father drank, paced the floors and stared out through the Venetian blinds.

What did he think about? He was worried and nervous. Why? These were his brothers and sisters. What was the problem?

The problem was the humiliation of poverty. The problem was the embarrassment over his humble circumstances. The problem was old furniture and ancient appliances. The problem was no automobile. The relatives visited Ernie because they could afford an automobile. This particular Christmas these problems were even more pressing than usual. Ernie and Mary had been arguing for weeks. The money from his last trip to sea was long since spent. Mary had been borrowing money from her brother Ray, and her mother.

Uncle Ray was Richard's favorite uncle. He always bought Richard special things at Christmas. He took Richard for rides in his automobile. He always laughed and grinned broadly whenever Richard showed up on his Polish grandmother's doorstep.

"I'm not asking any of them for another penny. I've had it," Mary argued. "It's your turn. You have a mother and brothers and sisters. You go crawling for a change." His dad had no answer to this complaint. It was true. He should ask his family for help. They were much better off than Mary's. He so hated the thought of going back to sea. He wasn't proud to be a Merchant Marine. He was a wiper, the lowest job down in the belly of a tanker. He had burned his back seriously one time on one of the boilers. He still had the scar tissue to prove it. Being out to sea for months on end was not pleasant. The living conditions onboard ship were not pleasant.

Not too long ago, he had been caught out at sea in a hurricane. He was on a giant tanker. The ship actually broke in half. They were all saved because the ship had busted over a sandbar out in the middle of nowhere just as the storm subsided. It was a miracle. There was a picture of the broken tanker in the local newspaper. The U.S.S. Sea Pender had been temporarily lost at sea. Ernie was over six months at sea on that cruise. The perils of that adventure weren't over, even after he had stepped ashore.

Sailors got paid in cash in those days. Ernie never had any trouble before, but the word was out around the docks. His ship had been out for a long time. That would mean that the sailors disembarking would be carrying some big bucks. The ship docked in Boston. Ernie was heading for the bus depot when three guys jumped him. Ernie was no pushover, but three guys were too much for him. They broke his nose and three of his ribs. He was in his bed at home when Richard saw him that next morning. Both his eyes were blackened. His face, neck and shoulders were black and blue. Doctor Kurka was leaning over him and they were talking about the attack. Richard hadn't seen his father in six months. Now here he was home, but not as Richard had been praying. He was a mess. He didn't look good.

"Well, you were mighty lucky, Ernie. A bad bunch like that could have killed you," said Doctor Kurka.

"Maybe, but I think I gave them a little more than they had bargained for. They don't think us little guys know how to fight. When I was younger, I almost went pro."

"Well, that's damn good. I hope that a couple of them are hurtin' like you are this morning."

"They wanted my money, but I had put my money in the sole of my shoe, an old sailor's trick. They dragged me off into an alley after they had gotten the best of me, but they couldn't find the money. I had twenty-five hundred bucks in cash in my damn shoe. Can you believe that?"

"Wow!"

"Yeah, wow is right."

His dad was up and about that very afternoon. His sides were all taped up, and so was his head. He looked bad, but he was alive and smiling. And he was HOME.

Richard saw his dad as a hero. He was no poor slob who had just gotten the hell beat out of him. He was a man who had taken on three guys in the middle of the night on a dark and lonely Boston street. Boston was nothing but a great big sewer, a dump. It was a trash heap of broken glass and discarded newspapers. In those days it looked even worse than Lawrence. That was hard to imagine. His dad had fought, and not only come out with his life, but his money too.

His dad was a hard guy to beat. He was a tough sailor with scars and burns to prove it. He not only risked his life for his family out at sea but on land as well. He was a man to admire and look up to. He was a man any boy could love.

That afternoon his dad let him count all of the money that he had brought home from the sea: twenty-five one-hundred dollar bills. It was more money than Richard had ever seen. To get it, his dad had almost died twice. Everybody in the family got a turn at counting the money. They would probably never, ever again see that much money in one lump sum in their lives. This was a major event. Everyone sitting at the little kitchen table counting one-hundred dollar bills. His dad stood proudly behind them taped from head to waist; black, blue and yellow; two black eyes; a swollen, scabby broken nose and a huge grin. He brought home the bacon. He looked like a pig ready for the slaughter, but he had brought home the bacon.

In the weeks that followed, Mary was ecstatic. She was as wealthy as she had ever been in her life. It seemed that nearly every morning, she was up and off to catch the bus at the corner. All the kids got new clothes, and dad too, and mom also. It was exciting to be "rich." Richard and Carol had gone with her to get, of all things, a TV. They had never been able to afford a TV before. It was expensive. There weren't that many in the neighborhood. They bought a Zenith. That was the best TV that had yet been made; the man at the store had told them. They brought it home in Richard's Red Flyer wagon. They had to be really, really careful.

Things were going well. Then one morning Mary came storming in from the front porch. Grandma Essick had insulted her, she said. Mary stormed from one room to the other, ranting and raving. Ernie kept asking her what her mother had said. She refused to repeat it, but finally she relented.

"Well, we were sitting out there talking in Polish. I told her about how you had gotten beaten up and all and what a long, tough trip you had out to sea. Then I told her about how you had saved all of the money, and how we were finally able to get some of the things that we really needed. I told her about a few of the little things that I bought. How we had gotten a new TV and now we might get a new refrigerator. And do you know what she said to me? Do you know what she had the nerve to say to me? In Polish she said, 'What are you trying to do, spend all the money, so that you can send your husband back to sea as fast as you can?' Can you believe that - my own mother?"

Ernie smiled. He then took a long puff on his pipe and said, "Just forget about it, Mary."

"Forget about it! Ha! I won't forget that one for a long time."

Richard had been sitting out at the kitchen table. He overheard his mother's protests, but it sounded like the truth to him.

Grandma Essick always liked his dad. She worried about him. When Grandma Essick's husband was alive, he was very sickly. He was never able to earn very much money. He was a cobbler. He had a small shoe repair on Center Street. His heart was too big. He fixed all of the poor people's shoes for free. Everyone owed him money. Then he came down with cancer. Grandma got a job at the mill as a weaver. It was Grandma Essick who paid the mortgage, bought the shoes and paid the light bills. Grandpa helped out as best he could, but he was not healthy.

He died a slow and very painful death. He had cancer of the throat. At the end he was unable to eat. He would ask Grandma to cook apple pies, just so that he could smell them cooking. He died of cancer, but in reality, he had starved to death.

Grandma was from the old school. She knew about taking care of a man, but not much about taking advantage of one.

What Grandma had said was absolutely correct in Richard's eyes. He had been watching his mother run to the bus every morning while his dad sat and stared out the window. Looking out that window he probably saw waves breaking over the bow of his ship, or the sweaty boiler room of some old tub of a ship that was about to split at the seams on a stormy night. And there was Richard's mom, running off with a roll of hundred dollar bills in each fist. She was only buying "necessities"? Was something a necessity if you could really do without it? He didn't need any new clothes. He had plenty of clothes. His brother and sister did, too. They needed a TV like the man in the moon. The Frigidaire refrigerator was working fine. So what if his mother had received it ten or fifteen years ago as a wedding gift.

The faster the money went, the faster dad would be gone again. If it came between having a new pair of jeans and having his dad, he would much rather have his dad. If his mother put that money into the bank and spent it as carefully as possible maybe dad could be around for a long, long time. Maybe he would be able to find a job closer to home. Maybe he and his dad could become friends. Maybe they could have a life and a family like other kids had. But that was never to happen if his mother ran off every morning for the bus. Grandma wasn't being rude, and she wasn't being mean. She was speaking the truth. Richard could see by the expression on his dad's face that he agreed with Grandma. Richard's sister, Carol, knew it, and young Ernie, his brother, knew it too. His mother was a thoughtless, abusive, selfish woman. She couldn't possibly have loved his father.

Mary told that story about Grandma, day after day. She told it at the breakfast table, at the dinner table, while doing laundry, while washing the floor, while sweeping and dusting, while doing the dishes. Her mother's remark outraged her. It clawed at her insides. But it made everyone else that heard it grin. Grandma had hit pay dirt with that one. Grandma had rung mother's bell. The truth hurt. Mary didn't really know the meaning of the word sacrifice. She knew poverty, but not sacrifice. She found it very difficult to give up anything that she thought to be within her grasp.

She complained and complained about Grandma's remark, but she still bought the TV. It was a Zenith. The best TV ever made. One hundred dollars could pay bills for a month or two. The rent in the family tenement house was only five dollars a week. But they would have a TV. When Ernie's relatives came this Christmas, wouldn't they be impressed.

Unfortunately by Christmas all the money was long gone. Ernie was now standing by the window, or sitting in his chair staring at his new TV and wondering where next week's rent was going to come from. He walked the streets of Lawrence everyday looking for work, but found nothing. He was now over forty years of age. Who wanted to hire an old man? Everybody wanted young strong kids. They didn't need forty-year-old men. To tell the truth, in Lawrence, they didn't need forty-year-old men or young men either. The job market was at rock bottom. Maybe that next door would be the right one? Maybe that next pair of eyes would see him for what he was really worth? Maybe if he just had a couple of more weeks and a little more money?

Instead, the money was gone, and Mary had been borrowing again. She was right. It was his turn to hit up the relatives. He had tried it before. He saw those embarrassed, false eyes, as they turned to the floor and complained of their bills.

"Ernie, if I had it, you know that I would help you out. I'm barely getting by myself, Ern."

Sure? They were just getting by, themselves? Who was buying all those fancy clothes, and shiny shoes, and new automobiles? Sure. They would help, if they only could? His mother - surely his mother had to care? Why didn't he just go back to sea?

He had been trying. The union hall was in Boston. That meant bus fare and a place to stay. You had to be there. You didn't just put your name in and wait for somebody to come and pick you up. You had to get to the union hall with your bags packed and be ready to go. The union let the members with no place to stay sleep on the floor. But even being there, day and night, wasn't enough. You had to know somebody, or you had to get to know somebody. There weren't that many ships. A lot of politicking went on.

American ships were supposed to hire Americans. But, American ship owners were running up foreign flags. Even if they were carrying American products for American businesses and docking and unloading at American ports, they often carried foreign flags and foreign crews. With a foreign flag the ships weren't forced to do the maintenance that carrying an American flag required. They didn't have to pay the foreign crews the wages that they had to pay American crews. The Union was fighting all of this for the American sailors, but when dollars are at stake, neither patriotism nor the American flag carry a hell of a lot of weight. For the most of these ship owners, the American Flag wasn't red, white and blue. It was green and white and had pictures of dead presidents on it.

So the guys sleeping at the union hall would all chip in and buy a few loaves of bread and some peanut butter. They were all looking to be in the same boat, if they could just find one. You bumped around the union hall and you talked to everybody. That was the big thing. Find an old buddy, an ex-shipmate. Cut a deal. If you find a job, you ask for me and if I find something, I'll ask for you. Look for an old boss. Somebody you worked under on a previous cruise. Let everybody who knows you, know that you are there. Walk around the hall. Walk around the dock. Look for faces, old friends. Remember, out of sight, out of mind.

The union hall was always shoulder to shoulder - old sailors, young sailors - but no jobs. In the bathroom, above a toilet bowl, would be scrawled: Make all your contributions to the Republican Party here, or if you voted Republican last election, take a seat, you deserve it. No laborers were Republican. Farmers were Republicans. Big shots were Republicans. There were very few Republicans in Lawrence. If they were, they never mentioned it, or ran for office. The same thing went for Protestants. If you were one, you kept it to yourself.

After a week or so in Boston, Ernie would be back to the streets of Lawrence. But in Lawrence, a day of job hunting somehow always ended up with an afternoon at Cain and Bernard's, or the Parkway Cafe or the Brass Rail, or the Builder's and Trades Club, or the Polish National, or the English Social, or Local 643. Nobody had money or a job, but somehow everybody had a nickel for a beer. A man with a lot of friends could spend a whole day in a bar with a quarter.

Ernie knew everybody. Everywhere he went, somebody knew him, or remembered his father, or knew one of his brothers or sisters. There always seemed to be an extra nickel for an old friend or an old buddy. At a nickel a beer, a guy with a job could quickly earn a celebrity status. In a bar there are no time clocks, no judgmental looks, and nobody who doesn't understand.

"I know Ernie. I know how it is. I thank God that I was lucky enough to find the lousy job that I got. If anything comes up at my place, you know damn well I'm gonna bring up the name of Ernie Noble - two more beers over here, bartender?"

The truth of the matter was, if a job did come up, everybody had four brothers of their own who were looking for something. Family came before friends, friends came before acquaintances, and nearly everybody came before some drunk you just met at the bar last night.

Everybody else in a bar is a drunk and an alcoholic, except you. You're all right, but that guy next to you? He is in real trouble. Bars were filled with losers. If you were there, you were a loser and you knew it. No matter how much you tried to cover it up, no matter how much you joked and laughed. If you had no job and you were on one of those stools daily, you were a loser. So too, was that guy next to you. Every time you pushed through that door into the darkness and the sawdust floors, put your foot up on that brass rail and leaned your elbows onto that shiny mahogany bar you had failed once again. Being a drunk wasn't the problem. It was being a drunk without a job. That is what made all the difference.

Ernie knew he had to get back out to sea, but the union hall in Boston was a dead fish. He had to get to New York.

He had told himself that this time he would not wait until the money ran out. He would put some money aside. It was always the same thing though. When push came to shove, he would hold out, looking about Lawrence right down to the last penny. It was stupid, but hope springs eternal. Somehow he would have to get enough money to get to New York. New York was the largest port on the East Coast, maybe the largest port in the world. He had been to Virginia, and New Orleans, the West Coast, to the Mediterranean. He had been all over the world. New York was the place to go. This Christmas, if and when his family came, he would have to ask them for a stake.

The week before Christmas was spent building up his courage, and practicing his spiel. He ran the words over in his mind a thousand different ways.

"You won't have to worry about the loan. I'll have them take it directly out of my pay and mail it to you. I'll have them write it into my contract."

Why did he wait so long? When he got down to his last one hundred bucks, he could have just packed up and hit the road. But no, he had to wait until he was a hundred behind.

But could he really pick up a ship in New York? That was just the talk around the union hall in Boston. It could be the very same situation in New York. Everybody said that if you could get to New York, you could get a ship. But nothing was engraved in concrete. Nobody knew for sure. What if you borrowed a hundred bucks and you got stuck in New York? What choice did he have? He had waited too long, hoping. He kept hoping that something would come up in Lawrence, or at the union hall in Boston. Hoping ... hoping ... hoping. He was just like a little damn kid. The time for hoping was now over. He had to get off his ass, and make something happen. He couldn't stand to sit on another damn barstool, or listen to one more damn lie. He could bury himself no longer in that chair at home. He had to go, and he had to go now. He would stick it out until Christmas, and then he would be gone, one way or another.

And now, there they were at his door. Everyone inside heard the knock and could feel the tension rushing through the door like a wave about to crash onto the beach; the car door outside slamming with a thud; the hall door opening clumsily; Grandma Noble's leather heels clomping down the hall. The whispering in the dark hall and then the KNOCK ... KNOCK ... KNOCK. Every heart inside jumped. The executioners had arrived: Grandma Noble in her heavy black fur; Auntie Dot in her neat, comely business attire; Gerry, pretty and sweet, thoughtful yet reserved. She looked so loving, but what did she really think of her big brother, Ernie? And, of course, Uncle Joe Shapman.

"How whyya, Mary? Long time no see." Oh my god! Hold on here. He had changed the routine. What was with this long time no see business? No, no, no, no - he's got to go back outside, knock on the door once again, and do this all over. This just ain't right. Long time no see? Where did he get that from? Oh, come on, come on, and get those smiles working. It was Christmas, for pity's sake.

Big Ernie left his chair and came to the door. A few brief hugs and kisses were followed by a number of strained smiles and affected hellos. This was young Ernie's cue.

"Sorry, but I have to run. Nice seeing you all once again."

What a lucky stiff he was. One day, Richard thought, one day soon. Brother Ernie had important business, playing poker down at the Palace Theater parking lot with his buddies.

Now it was Richard's turn, but he recoiled. He pulled back behind his mother.

"Get up here, Richard," his father ordered. "Give your grandmother a kiss."

How revolting. How could he kiss this old wrinkled bag of fancy poop who dropped in once a year as if she were somebody? Who was this woman? Who were these people? Richard no longer knew these people. They were not a part of his life. How could everybody be such hypocrites?

Richard's face was hard and ugly. He had long since stopped kissing and hugging anybody. His dad never noticed because he never hugged or kissed anybody himself.

"Come on. Come on! Front and center," his dad said seriously, but with a put-on grin. Richard stepped forward. He stood silently. Everyone was waiting. Richard was supposed to reach out to his grandmother for a hug and kiss. The offer was not forthcoming. At first his father stared at him curiously. Then his look became sharp and angry.

Richard didn't care. Richard no longer feared his father. He loved his father, but he had no fear of him. Even with his dad's sour puss glaring down upon him, Richard had no intention of prostituting his love with any lying, hypocritical hugs or kisses. These were the very people who had hurt his father. The penny-ante poker days were long over. They were not worthy of Richard's hugs and kisses. His love and affection was not for sale at any price. He would not dilute his feeling with affectation. He would not pollute the purity of his love with formality, tradition, or social obligation. No way! He was kissing nobody. Little Richard's kissing days were over. Everyone stood as if mesmerized by the boy's hard glare. This was a confrontation.

Auntie Gerry was the politician. She broke the stand-off, by pushing forward. She gave the reluctant boy a hug and a small peck on the cheek, but he was as rigid as a pole and as cold as a wintry night. She pulled back and looked into his eyes. She was very pretty. She had blue eyes and a smooth young complexion. She was the prettiest of all of his aunts. She seemed warm and tender and nice. When his dad was drunk, he always spoke of her pleasantly. But, nevertheless, she was one of "them." She was a member of that group. She was a party to the plan. She was one of the conspiring. She was one of those engaged in the conspiracy to break his dad's heart. His father may have a faint, breakable heart, but not he. Richard had a heart of steel. He must, if he were ever to become the protector of the weak and wimpy. A pretty face, a lovely perfume, a gentle touch, those things might make some crumble, but not Richard the lion hearted.

Ernie watched as his young son stoically accepted Gerry's embrace. He could hardly believe what he was witnessing. It would have been so easy for Richard to relent and place a little peck on his pretty aunt's cheek. But a tensed, fearful stomach, knotted with emotion and anger was rapidly becoming the accepted norm in Richard's gut. He didn't budge or make the slightest move towards her.

Ernie looked towards Mary, bewildered. Mary just shrugged her shoulders. Gerry slumped back. She stared wonderingly at the little boy. The boy had such a cold, indifferent glare. She had never seen a child with quite that look before.

"Well, I know exactly how the boy feels," her husband blurted. "He's no little boy anymore," Joe said reaching out and patting the boy on the head. "Who wants to be messing with silly, little hugs and kisses. You're too big for that stuff, aren't you son?" Well, if one didn't want the truth that was as good a story as any. Richard smiled, and then shrugged his shoulders. Everyone laughed. Joe had broken the tension.

That must be it, his dad thought. The boy is just too big to be kissing everybody; happens to the best of us. Richard couldn't believe his father's lack of perceptiveness. Didn't his father remember all of the stories that he had told to him? Didn't his father realize? Isn't being drunk just a game of pretend? One might not want to remember, but certainly no one could really believe that someone was truly not aware of what they had said or what they had done while drunk? His father looked so seriously bewildered - was he kidding?

"Well, let's all come in, and sit down," Ernie suggested. Joe, Gerry's husband, was the stranger. He had married into the family. Dot and Vinnie weren't married. Ernie would first try to make Joe comfortable. But, nobody would really be comfortable here tonight. It had never happened before, why should it start tonight.

Everyone then took up their positions, and the games began.

"So Joe, how's things been going with you?"

"Good Ernie, good; well, more fair than good, to be truthful," he qualified, on second thought. "We're not starving, anyway." One must be careful here. One didn't want to say or give an impression that things were too good. In which case, someone could find themselves being hit up for a loan, maybe. This was a feeling-out process. "And what about yourself, Ernie?"

"Well ..." The room went quiet, as everyone listened. Knowing how Ernie was doing would determine the tone of this evening's basic conversation. "Okay, I guess. Not too bad." Ernie chickened out. He could feel the pressure in the room. Maybe he should just scrap the I-need-money program.

Mary was out in the kitchen. She heard his opening remarks. She shook her head. She was sure that he would never have the guts to ask any of them for a nickel. As usual, it would all be on her shoulders. Ever since Ernie's father had died over fifteen years ago, Ernie's relations with his family were strained. His family never liked Mary. She was from the other side of the tracks. She was that poor, little Polish girl with her crusty rye bread, and other strange foods. Her parents spoke that gibberish. You'd think that if people were lucky enough to be let into America, they would at least learn the language.

Ernie's mother had told him not to marry one of them. Mama Noble was the boss and she never forgave the boy for his disobedience. She looked like the "Big Boss" tonight with her big fur coat and that funny hat with the black lace veil. Richard thought that she looked like a Russian general or something.

She was the Queen and the rest of the family were her escorts. She sat there on their coach with her head back and her nose in the air, as she surveyed her oldest boy's state of poverty. He had disobeyed her orders. This was a fitting punishment indeed. Certainly he deserves every inch of this disaster. It wasn't necessary for her to speak. The look on her face was sufficient.

"And how's everything at the phone company, Dot?" Ernie pursued.

"Wonderful, wonderful; I'm doing very well. I'm chief operator now. I may be coming up for supervisor." Dorothy wasn't afraid to speak up for herself. Nor would she be frightened to tell her older brother exactly what she thought of him if he had the nerve to broach her on the subject of money.

Yes, she had a little bit of money saved - maybe quite a bit of money by some people's standards. Nobody gave any money to her on some golden platter. She earned every penny of it. She had no man to do her bidding.

She was in love once though. Shortly before the wedding, he had a stroke and died. It was devastating. Who worried about her? Her future was ruined. Who was worried about her feelings? "You'll find someone else." That's what they all said. As if she was such a shallow individual? As if she was not capable of true love? As if her tears were only for their amusement? Everyone else's suffering was real but hers was fleeting. She would handle it, they all said. She was tough. She was strong. She, good old Dorothy, she could handle anything.

You don't have to feel sorry for Dorothy. No, no, no. Dot needs no pity. Now what did "they" say? Yes, now it's Dot, the old maid aunt. She knew what everyone called her behind her back. She wasn't stupid. So they think that she's "old money bags." Let them all think what they like. Someone who works as hard as she does and saves every penny because she is all alone and has no one to look after her deserves every penny she's accumulated. How did she gain all this money anyway?

Did all of those nice men out there in this competitive world, just think that she was cute? Did they all just bend over backwards to help sweet little Dorothy up that ladder of success? What about all those other women at the phone company? They were just thrilled to see her become their boss, weren't they? Why, some of them would tear her eyes out if given the justification.

Who out there can appreciate her sacrifices? She has no family, no children, no loving husband to cuddle up next to on a cold lonely night - no one to love, no one. How many times had she already cried herself to sleep at night? No hands to hold, no shoulders to cry on, nobody to be weak with. If she had no money put aside for a rainy day, who would help her out? Yes, who would help "old money bags"? Who would help the "old maid"? No one, that's who! You could take that to the bank. Both Ernie and her brother Dave could barely take care of themselves. How about brother Vinnie? Sure, he would rush right over with his every dime. Right! What about Gerry? Her husband Joe never really liked Dorothy. Joe had a sharp tongue also. No, Dorothy had to take care of Dorothy. And

Dorothy knew how to do just that. Dorothy could defend herself and she could defend her right to her own hard earned money.

"A supervisor, well?"

"Maybe. There are other people in line, but I've been there the longest. I should get the promotion by all rights. I have the know-how. I have the experience. I've put in my dues. It is not easy being a woman out there, you know."

"And why don't you tell us all about it, Dot?" Joe's sharp tongue struck out, sarcastically.

"Well, you can think as you please, Joe. You'll never be in my shoes."

"And he had better not be, right Joe?" Ernie joked.

"That's right, that's right. Go ahead. Have a good laugh on Dot. She can take it. She's got big shoulders," Aunt Dot added.

"I'm not laughing, Dot," Auntie Gerry said, leaning out from her position on the couch to get a better view of her sister. "I agree. I'm a working girl too, you know. I know exactly what you're talking about and how you feel."

"Thank you, Gerry. I appreciate that."

"Well, Vinnie, how's things down at the shipyard?" Ernie offered, trying to change the subject.

"Well, up and down, Ernie." He didn't want to say good because Ernie might be looking for him to get him a job. Who wants to be down at work begging for some relative? Everybody's got an unemployed relative. The bosses don't really like it, and they all have friends and relatives themselves. Beside, he had been damn lucky to get in there himself. "I was lucky to get in there, Ernie. It was a real break for me. You remember Gary Mahoney?"

"Sure. He was one of your chums when you was just a kid. Wasn't he one of the tag-a-longs who I took to the movies with us? You remember when I used to take you and Dave down to the Warner off Essex Street?"

"Yeah, that was him. You've got a good memory, Ernie."

"Boy, those were the days. There were really no jobs then. I was running the numbers for Jimmy Flynn."

"I remember him. He was about the biggest bookie in town in those days, wasn't he?"

"You bet. That was a tough job, let me tell you. I can't remember all the backroom windows I had to jump from."

"You know, old Houlihan, the cop, knew that you were working for Flynn?"

"Oh, you're telling me. He was a mean old flatfoot too. I kept out of his way though. You know, I was making twenty-five bucks a week in those days."

"Wow! That was damn good money then."

"You better believe it. People were lucky to be making five or six bucks a week at that time."

"Whatever happened to Flynn?"

"They finally got him. In fact, I was right there when they raided the place - me and Billy Carney and Frankie Costello."

"Frankie was in on that, too?"

"Oh yeah. He ran for Flynn, just like me."

"But you never got caught?"

"Nooooo. I sure didn't. Me and Frankie were out that bathroom window in a flash. Actually Frankie got his pant leg caught on the sill and that was one of the biggest decisions of my life. There we were, the cops closing in behind us. Poor Frank is hanging there upside down from the window sill. 'Help! Help!' he's yelling at me. I can hear the cops trying to crash down the bathroom door. Should I help Frankie, or should I leave him there? Should I get away and let him get caught and go to jail, or should I go back and maybe get us both locked up? I'm proud to say, I decided to go back and unhook the poor S.O.B. Unfortunately, I dropped him right on his noodle, but dropping Frankie on his head was actually better than dropping him on his butt - if you remember old Frankie?"

Richard had never heard this particular story. He had heard many stories about the good old days. His dad must have really been some guy. This was really something. Can you believe his dad working for a bookie? Then almost getting caught by the police. And nobody doubted a word of it. It must have all been true. Wow!

Gerry suddenly cracked up laughing. She had to wipe her mouth, as she bent forward to rest her glass of muscatel on the coffee table so that she wouldn't spill it.

"You know, I dated Frankie Costello once."

"That must have been an experience," Joe offered, amused.

"You didn't!" Dorothy erupted with delight. "Not Frankie Costello? I never knew that!"

Frankie Costello must have been an unusual character, Richard thought. It was fun listening to all this back-and-forth conversation, and then trying to put all the pieces together.

"So what happened after you dropped Frankie on his head, Ernie?" Dot requested, as Gerry started to sputter once again. Visualizing Frankie what-his-name getting dropped on his head presented a humorous image to Gerry's mind. Richard was now smiling. This was almost fun, he thought. This was like family - everybody laughing and talking about old friends. These people really did know one another. They could even be like people when they tried. And in the middle of all of this, his dad was a somebody. He was the main man in this story. The story was all about him. Maybe it was true that he was a somebody, one time.

"Well, we both took off running like a couple of bats out of hell. The last thing that I heard was old Houlihan screaming, and blasting off a couple of rounds."

"Oh my god, he didn't really shoot at you, did he?"

Richard's mother was busy getting her sandwiches ready out in the kitchen. Richard was staring at his grandmother Noble from his position on the floor next to his dad's seat. What could she be thinking about all of this? She was difficult to figure. Most of the time she just shook her head, but then once in a while she smiled. Should his dad really be telling stories like this right in front of his mother? His dad was obviously a bad guy back in those days. He had the cops shooting at him and everything. What could his mother be thinking about her son being shot at by the police?

"He damn well did. I'll bet he was aiming at us too."

"You think that Houlihan would actually try and kill you guys?"

"You bet he would."

There was a Houlihan that lived right down the road on Chelmsford Street, Richard thought. His father was a cop too. His grandfather used to be a cop too. Could it have been Houlihan's grandfather that tried to shoot his dad? Wasn't this great? These were real stories. This was stuff that really happened. Who would ever believe it? This was really an experience. Big Mama and all her little cubs had finally arrived at Goldie Locks' house, and everybody was having a good time. Everybody was laughing. Grandma's flabby double chin was bouncing up and down. Dot was snickering. Gerry was slapping her knees and covering her face with her hands. Joe wasn't snoring yet. This was almost fun. Richard didn't know quite how to act. Should he like these people or shouldn't he? Were they a part of his family, or were they outsiders? These people caused his dad serious pain. Thinking of these people brought tears to his dad's eyes when Uncle Howard and family were standing on the hall steps. Did his father hate these people, or did he love them? This was difficult to figure out.

They had all had a little muscatel wine. Richard's mother always bought a bottle of muscatel for the holidays. Richard tasted it once when she wasn't looking. It was horrible. It had a peculiar smell and a strong, hot taste. It was bitter, too. It was worse tasting than even beer. Why did adults drink that terrible tasting stuff? It had something to do with being grownup and being big. It certainly didn't have anything to do with pleasure, as they all claimed.

The evening was passing affably. Grandma Noble had even slipped out of her heavy fur coat. Maybe she intended to stay? Richard ran and got beer when anyone appeared empty. His dad was most often the candidate. He was beginning to turn into the dad that Richard liked the best. He was calling him "son" and "my boy" and stuff like that.

Then believe it or not Auntie Gerry was sitting at the old upright piano, and dad had out his harmonica. "Oh, did you ever go across the sea to Ireland ..." Richard liked everybody singing the old songs the best. Nobody knew the words so everybody just stared at Auntie Gerry's lips. She had the best lips to stare at. She had the best eyes, too. Her lips were bright artificial red, and her eyes a deep marine blue. At the piano, she sparkled. She was so nice. She was so pretty. How could anyone as nice and pretty as she ever hurt his dad?

Then there was that song with all of the Irish names in it. That was a great one. Then came his dad's favorite. "And so they sprinkled it with stardust, just to make the shamrocks grow ..."

Next it was the "spoons." Richard and his dad could both play the spoons. Richard loved it. Not playing the spoons so much, but being like his dad. They played to songs on the radio. Richard would start slapping the spoons onto his thigh and everybody just roared with the joy of it. He was such a little shy type. But put on the music and put those spoons into his hands and look out. He slapped them on his thighs, on his knees, between his legs, on his elbow, under his arms, on his backside.

Then came the finale. His dad would stand behind him as he sat on the hassock. His dad would place one large spoon on the flat of Richard's head. Then he would tap it with another spoon as Richard opened and closed his mouth, thus producing various sounds. He shaped his mouth in different, strange and humorous configurations, thus producing a wide variety of metallic, echoing clunks and thuds.

This always brought the audience to the edge of their seats. This was the *Show of Shows* for Richard and his dad. Richard took it very seriously. This was like the *Ted Mack Amateur Hour*. This was Ed Sullivan and Milton Berle all rolled into one. This was the best of times. Richard loved everything about these moments: the smiles, the laughter, the affection coming from his father and everybody in the room; the look of delight on his sister's face; his mother, shaking her head with an embarrassed smirk on her lips. This was truly the best of times. This was how it should be - he and his father, a team, the nucleus of the universe. They were the ones who led the way, the ones who carried the ball, the ones who created the show and made everyone laugh. These were the best of times.

"Okay Richard, how about a solo? Sing Rudolf the Red Nosed Reindeer for everybody." Richard didn't like solos. His face turned all red. He had memorized all of the words to that song, and sung it several times for his father. He had memorized it to sing to his dad, not just to anybody.

"Come on? You know the words don't you?" his dad encouraged. The boy nodded his head. "Well then sing it, son! Let's hear it?" The boy's face cringed and turned as red as a beet. Everyone was laughing and clapping their hands. He could feel the blood pounding in his face. He wanted to sing but it was just too embarrassing sitting right there in front of everyone. Without notice, Richard jumped up and bolted from the room.

"Well, I guess it was just too much for him," someone mumbled back in the parlor.

"He sure played those spoons, though."

"He sure did."

Then quietly a small voice came seeping from the kitchen.

"Rudolf the Red Nosed Reindeer,
had a very shiny nose."

"Sushhh! It's Richard. He's singing out in the kitchen." Everyone got quiet.

"And if you ever saw it,
you would even say it glowed.
All of the other Reindeer,
used to laugh and call him names."

Ernie had been thinking all night, and this was as good a time as any. Mary, Carol and Richard were out in the kitchen. It was just he and his mother and brothers and sisters in the parlor. Nobody had to be embarrassed. Everybody was smiling and seemed to be having a good time.

"Ah ... as you guys probably know, I'm not doing all that well right at the moment ... financially speaking." The room got even quieter. "I've been all over town. My shoes are literally worn thin." He pulled one shoe off his foot to display the hole. "I've got another one just like it on this foot. I've got two more pairs in similar condition in the closet. There just ain't a job in this town. You know what I'm sayin', Vinnie?"

"I know, Ern. I know how tough things can get."

"Yeah, well I've been to the union hall in Boston. I've been there several times. I've slept there on the floor. There's nothing going out." The Nobles began to look to one another, shuffle their feet and squirm in their chairs.

"No one would let poor Rudolf,
play in any Reindeer games."

"So the word is that there are plenty of ships in New York. I'm sure that if I could just get there, I could pick one up."

"Well, why aren't you there, son?" his mother asked, abruptly, with admonition in her voice.

"Well, you're right Ma. I should have gone a long time ago. But I kept hoping to find something here at home. I don't really relish the thought of going back to sea. It is a hard life. It is even harder for a married man."

"Ah huh," his mother grunted.

"But then one foggy Christmas Eve,
Santa came to say.
Rudolf with your nose so bright ..."

"Yeah well, that was a mistake. There is no sense crying over spilled milk. I should of went earlier when I had some money."

"Yes when YOU had the money."

Ernie could see that hard look in his mother's brown eyes. Only he and she in the family had brown eyes. The mutual color in their eyes, nevertheless, didn't draw them closer. Ernie was somewhat taken back by his mother's matter-of-fact manner and her obvious hostility.

"I know Ma, but we all make mistakes, don't we?" He spoke as if he and she had a secret. If they did, she was not acknowledging it. She sat and stared silently. "I figure that I need about fifty bucks." He really thought that he needed a hundred, but with fifty he could get there. He looked at his brother Vinnie.

Vinnie looked down at his shoes.

He looked at Dorothy.

She avoided his penetrating glare by reaching to the coffee table for her glass of muscatel.

He looked at Joe and Gerry.

Gerry looked to Joe, sympathetically. Joe shrugged.

"I'll be honest with you, Ernie," Joe said. "I ain't got fifty bucks." Gerry dropped her head and turned red in the face.

"Well, I said fifty, but any little thing that anyone could spare would help." Mary's brother Ray has been helping us a little with the rent but I know he will be willing to wait. He's got a good job at the post office ..."

"You were going to borrow the money from us to pay off your wife's brother?" his mother butted.

"Well, I suppose that wasn't such a good idea. I guess ... I ahhh ..."

"Won't you guide my sleigh tonight?
And then all the Reindeers loved him...

“You seem to be full of poor ideas, son.” Ernie frowned and then took a swallow from his beer. “And what about that?” she said pointing to the beer can in his hand.

“Oh come on? Let’s not be ridiculous.”

“I don’t think that I’m being ridiculous, son. What if we do give you some money? What’s going to stop you from drinking it all up?”

Ernie was shocked. He knew that his mother was unhappy with him, but he never thought that she would stoop this low. He was no damn drunk. Sure he had a beer now and then, and maybe he got drunk once in a while, but he was no alcoholic.

“Come on Ma! I’m no more a drunk than you are. Let’s not bring that into it.”

“It doesn’t look that way to me. Every time that I see you, you have a beer in your hand. You know that I never allowed alcohol into my house. I never approved of it with your father. I think no better of it in your case.”

Dorothy and Gerry both put down their wine glasses, hesitantly. Vinnie held his beer firmly on his knee. Joe lifted his beer and took a big swig. Joe was nobody’s son, and he resented the Old Lady’s authority and influence over his own wife. He also wasn’t a member of this family, thank God. He was merely Gerry’s husband. He had no obligation to loan any of them money. So what if he had fifty bucks? He knew that Gerry would be mad with him when they got home. This guy was her drunken brother, not one of his. Let them fight it out. Gerry had her own job. She had her own money. She could speak for herself, if she chose to.

He picked up another turkey sandwich from the table. He relaxed and ate while everyone else sat very uncomfortably.

“Sure, every time you see me I have a beer in my hand. You only come here once a year at Christmas time.”

“You know where we live.”

“Oh, let’s get off it, Ma. You know that you have had it in for me ever since I married Mary. You thought that she wasn’t good enough for us. She was below us.”

“Those are your words, son, not mine.”

“Oh brother, I can see it all over your face, Mom. You always have to win, don’t you? Mother knows best.”

“I don’t intend to sit here and be insulted.”

"And they laughed and shouted out with glee."

"Okay, I'm sorry." Everyone looked at Ernie. He never apologized. He was the toughest kid on the block. He used to fight for money in the ballpark with bare knuckles. It didn't matter how big or how tough everybody said they were. Ernie was just like his father - as tough as nails.

"Did you hear me, Ma?"

"I heard you."

"I said I'm sorry." He put down his beer. He walked over to his mother's chair. He stood there for a moment and then fell to his knees. "I'M SORRY MA! I'm sorry. I never meant to hurt you. I was in love. How do you explain being in love? Does a man have to apologize to his mother for falling in love? If there is one thing that a woman should understand, it's falling in love ... isn't it?"

"Rudolf the Red Nosed Reindeer,
you'll go down in hiss - tor - ree."

Richard jumped from his chair and ran into the parlor. He saw his father kneeling before his grandmother. His father had tears on his face. He was staring, supplicatingly, into his mother's eyes. Richard stood in the door frame at the entrance to the parlor. His father looked towards him, then back to his own mother.

"If not for me, how about for them?" There was a brief moment as Richard stood waiting for his applause. His father fell from his knees and onto his butt. "Well, you did it, son. Come over here." The boy ran to his dad with a big smile. Everybody clapped their hands. His dad was not happy. His tears were flowing readily. He was hugging, and rubbing his rough cheek against Richard's face. Some of his tears fell onto Richard's lips. They tasted salty.

Grandma Noble rose from her chair and struggled with her fur. Aunt Dot rushed over and helped her slip it over her shoulders. Everybody went for their jackets which had been stacked in a pile on an empty chair. Ernie and his boy remained seated on the floor. Ernie braced himself by placing his palms on the floor behind him and locking his elbows. He watched and shook his head sadly as his mother headed for the door with her entourage.

Vinnie stopped as he passed Ernie on the floor. He took out a pack of cigarettes, removed three cigarettes from the pack, reached down and stuffed them into Ernie's shirt pocket. Then he tapped Ernie on the shoulder and wished him good luck.

"Take care and we'll see ya, Mary," Joe groaned in his indifferent monotone as he headed out the door. Richard didn't watch the relatives leaving. Instead he sat on the carpet with his dad. He stared at his dad's face. His father's eyes were still flooded with tears. He was still shaking his head as he watched them filing out the door. He was shaking his head as if he pitied them, not himself. Why would his father pity them? They made him cry. They did it all the time. How could they hate their own brother? When their footsteps could no longer be heard, his father finally broke from his trance. Sister Carol came into the room and sat down on the floor next to them. Both children stared at their dad. Carol's eyes welled up with tears. All she knew was that her father was sad. That was enough to make her cry. Richard, of course, had no tears. He was standing guard. He was the *Keeper of the Tears* at the palace of his King. He would guard his tears. He would not let them out. He would need them on the inside. He would need them to water the seeds of all of this hate that was being planted. The father looked at his two children.

"You see that?" Both kids nodded their heads. "Don't either of you ever treat each other like that." His voice began to crack.

"Richard, if Ernie or Carol ever need anything, and you have it, you give it to them." His tears gushed. "They are your sister and brother, for god's sake. And Carol ..." Carol knew what her father intended to say to her. She rushed to him and threw her arms around him.

"I will Daddy. I will. I'll never be like them, Daddy, never!"

She hugged him and they both cried. Richard watched. He watched without a tear.

7 The Flip Side

Mary watched the company leave; another cold Christmas. The kitchen door had been left ajar. Mary went to the door. She watched the backs of her husband's relatives as they fumbled down the dark hall. She held the door open so the light from the kitchen would help them on their course. When they were all gone, she shut the door, and only then looked into the parlor. There he was - her big brave husband - on the floor and bawling his eyes out once again. Carol was in his arms and Richard was huddled next to him. She just knew he hadn't broached the subject of money with them. She just knew it.

"Don't give me that look, Mary. I've had all that I can take for one evening."

Mary was disgusted and the judgmental look on her face was Ernie's mother's all over again. As Mary stared at him, he had the overwhelming compulsion to get up and leave the house. The apartment was filled with negativism, disgust and disapproval. He couldn't stand it. Mary saw that look in her husband's eyes. She knew what it meant. In a moment he would be up, pulling on his jacket and heading out the door for the nearest barstool.

"Don't bother," she ordered, throwing up her hands in disgust. "I'll leave." She stormed out the kitchen door, and slammed it behind her.

Richard watched. It was the same old story. The tension, anger, and emotional anxiety that filled the house were suffocating him. He could hardly breathe. The feeling inside him stormed, but who was to blame? Who should be hated for all of this hurt - his dad's relatives? Who were they? He didn't even know them. They were people from someplace else. They weren't a part of his life.

That woman was supposed to be his grandmother. She was nobody. Certainly she wasn't like his real grandmother - the one who pinched his cheeks every time she saw him, and fixed him chocolate pudding with milk. Her eyes beamed and sparkled whenever she saw him coming. Not the icy glare of this cold dominant woman in her big fur coat. This woman wasn't his grandmother. He only saw her once a year and that always seemed to be once too much.

What about that troop of little elves that followed behind her? Who were they? They were uncles and aunts? They were his father's brothers and sisters. Could they really be his brothers and sisters? Well, they weren't Richard's brothers and sisters. They were nothing to Richard. They were strangers. They were people from another planet. They didn't understand. They didn't understand anything.

But was this all their fault? No. They were nothing. They didn't have anything to do with this. It was his mother's fault. She made his dad ask for money. She was the one who was always putting on the pressure. Buy this ... get that. We need a new refrigerator, a new stove, a new washing machine, a TV, new clothes. She always wanted to buy something. Nothing that she ever had was good enough. Her apartment wasn't as good as the next apartment. Her children weren't as good as the ones across the street. Everything that she had was worthless trash. What did she do about it? She sat around the house and yelled at everybody.

Why didn't she go and earn some money now that his dad needed some help? Why did his dad have to earn all the money and travel all over the world and risk his life? Why didn't she ever risk a little? She always had an excuse. Like the job at the Mill. She had to quit because Richard needed to be watched and she couldn't trust her sister who lived upstairs or her mother who lived across the way. It was always some excuse why she was unable to do anything. She was just plain lazy!

Why didn't she just go jump off a bridge and kill herself? It would be better if she just wasn't there. He and his sister and brother could take care of themselves. What did she do anyway? She only made everybody unhappy. She only slapped everybody around. What did they need her for? Why couldn't she just die? Why did his dad ever marry her?

Ernie remained on the parlor floor, staring at the kitchen door. They all remained there in silence. His father finally spoke.

"Merry Christmas," he said, sarcastically, apparently to the kitchen door. The children knew that he wasn't talking to the door. No, no, he was talking to their mother, and they knew it. He sighed deeply and Richard and Carol searched his eyes for an explanation. "I'm going to tell you kids something. It's a terrible thing to say. But, if it weren't for you kids, I would have left this house a long, long time ago."

There was hate and hurt in his eyes as he spoke. His words gave verification to Richard's thoughts. It WAS his mother's fault. She was the one to blame for all this unhappiness. Why did she stay here? Why didn't she just go? Nobody liked her. Nobody needed her. She should be the one to leave, not his dad. But was it really ALL her fault?

It was Richard's fault too. His father had just said that it was. If it weren't for Richard and his sister and brother his dad could leave this woman and be happy. Instead, we all had to live like this; in this hellhole of misery and unhappiness. Why does his dad stay here? Because he loves his children and he must provide for them. He must take care of them because he is a good man who would never leave his children.

But yet, doesn't he leave them all the time? He leaves every time that he goes off to sea. But he must go to sea, because there are no jobs here in Lawrence. He must have a job because he needs money. He must have money because ... because ... because his wife wants all of these stupid things. If she wants so many things why doesn't she go get them for herself? If he and his brother and sister had never been born, then his dad wouldn't be in this fix. So, why was Richard even born?

Question - Who made me?

Answer - God made me.

Question - Why did God make me?

Answer - God made me to know, love, and serve him in this world, and the next.

God made him to know love and serve Him in this world and the next. What does all that have to do with his mother and his father? Why did God put him in their house? Why didn't He put Richard into another house - into a happy house? Was there such a thing as a happy house? Weren't all houses, just like his house?

God wants Richard to know Him? Well, where is He? He is in the Church where Richard attends Mass every Sunday. Richard goes to Church, and his brother and sister go to Church. Why don't his mother and his father go to Church? His mother doesn't even like nuns. She was ready to beat up Sister Mary on Richard's first day of school. She threw Father O'Reilly out on his butt when he came to the house to lecture to her about family planning. She opened the door and told a PRIEST to get the hell out of her house. She knew when a man was talking SEX, she told him.

His dad never, ever mentioned God. His dad never mentioned anything unless he was drunk. But even when he was drunk, he never mentioned God. If God wants Richard to know Him, why doesn't He show Himself? Because God is invisible; you can't see God. If you ever saw Him you would never be able to live in this world again. God is so beautiful and glorious that you would want to get right to heaven and never ever leave. Once you see God, you will never need anything in this world again. You will just sit in heaven and bask in His glory and His love. You won't need food. You won't need water. You won't need TVs. You won't need refrigerators. You won't need anything, or anyone, because that's what Heaven is. If his family were all in heaven, they wouldn't need any money, either.

Richard has to serve God, also. How does he serve God? He serves God by being good, by doing his homework, by not talking when the nun leaves the room, and by obeying the commandments. Thou shalt honor thy father and thy mother; that's one of the commandments.

How could God possibly want him to honor this mother? Did God know what kind of a person his mother was? Did God know how this mother He had put upon them, beat them and hurt them and was mean and hateful all of the time? God knows everything, and everything is supposed to have a reason.

Inside the parlor, they could hear noise on the steps in the hall. It was Uncle Ray and Grandma Essick. As usual, Uncle Ray was loaded down with presents - red and green packages of all sizes, with bows and strings and ribbons - and, of course,

Uncle Ray himself standing there with his grand, infectious, beaming smile.

His uncle Ray had one tooth missing about half way back on the right side of his mouth. You only saw the space when he smiled or laughed. But he smiled and laughed every time that he saw Richard. He was always smiling and laughing. Uncle Ray had a happy smile. His mother had a strained smile. His uncle Joe, Ray's brother, had a sad and suffering smile with his sparkling gold tooth. Uncle Joe and Uncle Ray had similar smiles but what was it that made Joe's sad and suffering and Ray's jubilant and gay?

It wasn't their teeth or the way their mouths were shaped. It wasn't the sounds they made when they laughed. No, it was their eyes. Uncle Ray's eyes danced and sparkled. Uncle Joe's eyes were somewhat like his mother's - they were sunken and buried deep into their cavities. Like they were trying to withdraw and fall back into their sockets and hide somewhere. The lids and the skin around his eyes were dark - darker than the skin on the rest of his face. His mother's eyes were bitter, cold, dark and piercing. But Uncle Joe's were filled with love, pity and understanding.

His mother's eyes retreated and withdrew into herself so that the hate and anger inside her would not lash out and consume everything about her. Joe's eyes retreated and withdrew for fear that all of the hate and anger about him would not consume and devour everything inside of him. Uncle Joe's eyes always seemed moist and on the verge of tears.

Uncle Joe was his dad's favorite brother-in-law. You never knew when, where, or if Uncle Joe was going to show up. Both Uncle Joe and Uncle Ray had no family of their own. Uncle Joe was a loner. Uncle Ray was a dashing man about town. He had lots of girl friends and went dancing every weekend.

Richard used to go up to his uncle's and grandmother's apartment, just to shine his Uncle Ray's shoes. All of Ray's shoes were light brown or tan and they all had long pointy toes. He always kept shoetrees in them. They were stacked neatly on a rack in his closet. He had lots of clothes and suit jackets too. He was a "sharp" dresser.

Uncle Joe had nothing very nice in the way of clothes or shoes. Nobody seemed to know even where he actually lived. They say that he drank a lot, but Richard had never ever seen him drunk. Whenever Richard asked about Uncle Joe, everyone got solemn. They would get a strange look in their eyes. They would stare off into the distance, or out a window, or at a picture on the wall or something. Then after a pause they would purse their lips, shake their heads and say, "Your Uncle Joe got malaria during the war. Ever since he came back, he was just never the same."

The war? The war had done something to Uncle Joe.

"Your uncle Joe was once a big, strapping man," his mother would say. "But, after the war? ..."

So, it was the war; whatever the war was. That was what turned Uncle Joe into a mysterious fellow; a mysterious fellow, yes, but a wondrous fellow also. No one ever talked about Uncle Joe or mentioned him in their conversation. But whenever he came walking down the street or strolling into their apartment, boy, all the bells went off. You could just see it in all their faces. Everybody loved Uncle Joe ... even Richard's mother.

Uncle Joe would never take any money for anything. He must have been like grandma Essick's husband.

Richard never knew what Uncle Joe did for a living. He seemed to be what everyone called a jack-of-all-trades. He was always around the apartment to fix the plumbing, or the furnace, or the stove, or to paint the house. Whether he was really trained or skilled in any of these areas no one seemed to know. Whenever Richard asked his mother or Uncle Ray what Uncle Joe was skilled at, they just said that your uncle Joe can do anything.

On one occasion, he was fixing the oil burner in Richard's apartment. He had newspapers all over the floor and under the stove. His hands and face and clothes were all covered with black soot.

It was exciting to have Uncle Joe in their apartment. Richard wouldn't even go out to play. He wanted to be there to watch and help Uncle Joe.

"Now you leave Uncle Joe be," his mother warned.

"That's all right, Mary. He's not bothering me."

He looked at Richard and smiled. That gold tooth of his sparkled and flashed. He winked at Richard, as if the two of them had a secret that his mother would never understand. The truth of the matter is that they did. But what was the secret:

love, compassion, understanding, pity, kindness, knowledge? They each knew something about one another, but what was it? Whatever it was, they were both aware that Mary would not understand it. Maybe that was enough of a secret to be smiling about.

Richard could see by the excitement in his mother's eyes, and her nervousness that she was overjoyed to have Uncle Joe there in her home. Richard couldn't understand why she wouldn't stop ranting, though. She paced up and down the kitchen, putzing with this or that while constantly yapping away.

"Joe can you believe it? They make me pay rent. My very own mother owns this house, and she charges me to stay here? You know how hard things are, Joe? Ernie's not working. We don't have a damn nickel. Still she expects me to pay rent. I can't believe it! But, you know how she is? Remember when you came back from the war? What did she tell you? Get out! Isn't that right? Didn't she tell you to get out if you weren't going to work and pay your rent? That was a fine how do you do, wasn't it?"

Richard had never seen his mother act in quite this manner. She always ranted and raved constantly, but this was different. This time somebody was actually listening. At least she felt that somebody was listening. She looked right at Uncle Joe when she talked. She looked directly into his eyes. He looked back in the same manner and he seemed to really be listening.

Usually when his mother ranted it was to the walls or the windows, or just to hear the sound of her own voice. But here and now, she was talking to SOMEBODY - somebody who understood. Her eyes beseeched him and burned a path into his. Sometimes she even took a pause to wait for a response from him. Like she would really be interested in what he had to say. She never did that with anybody but Uncle Joe. She always just talked and talked and talked, until everybody just left the house. With Uncle Joe she was really and truly excited. This man was clearly a person who knew what she was talking about. But did he really, Richard wondered? Could his mother possibly be saying anything that was even remotely true?

"You're right, Mary." My God when she heard Uncle Joe say that she was right ... holy cow!

"And look at this place, will you? It's a dump. Why this whole damn place isn't worth two cents. Look at this damn refrigerator? Excuse me. I didn't mean to say damn; but will you look at it? Do you know when I got this thing?"

"Well, I should. I helped carry it in."

"You did, didn't you? How many years ago was that – ten, fifteen?"

"A long time ago, Mary." He answered her but he didn't look up from his work. He kept doing what he was doing. Richard kept watching. He wasn't really learning anything, he was just watching. He was hoping his Uncle Joe would smile again, or maybe laugh. It was nice to have Uncle Joe here all to themselves. But if his mother didn't shut up, Uncle Joe would probably be leaving. She chased everything good away.

"A long time is right! Look at this neighborhood, Joe? It used to be a nice place to live. Now look at it. Look at those new people next door. They've got fourteen million kids and nobody's watching any of them. Nobody! They're playing baseball right next to my windows. Look at them! Joe, Can you believe it? How damn stupid can kids get?

"Hey? Hey you kids out there!" She tapped on the window. "Don't play ball there! Play out in the street where you are supposed to. You want to break my windows? What's the matter with you guys?

"I can't believe it, Joe. People are on top of people around here now. Kids are everywhere. They all look at you as if you are the one who's nuts. Were we like that, Joe?"

"I don't think so, Mary." This was amazing to Richard. His mother was actually having a conversation with somebody. Joe would actually answer her back every once and awhile. Usually his mother just babbled and everybody tried to get out of her way or began arguing with her. If this were his father in place of Uncle Joe, he would keep silent for as long as he could stand it. That would usually be about two or three beers. Then he would stand up.

"Mary, are you ever going to shut up?"

"Don't you tell me to shut up! Who do you think that you are? You're not the king of this castle, or even this dump. You don't even pay the rent here half the time; I do. Who do you think that you are talking to anyway, some bimbo down at Cain and Bernard's or Tubby Clark's?" His dad wouldn't answer. He would just leave. When he came back, he was usually drunk. His parents didn't talk. They argued. She yelled, and he left. Uncle Joe, he was different. He was talking. He was listening. It was almost as though he thought that she was really a human being. Nobody treated his mother as if she were really a human being.

"I don't think so either, Mary. We had respect. If we didn't, somebody would sure knock it into us, wouldn't they?" Joe chuckled.

Uncle Joe must have had respect "knocked" into him too, when he was little. Maybe getting beat up was just a normal part of every child's growing up?

Joe looked at Richard. He raised his eyebrows and nodded his head as if to say, she is really rolling now, isn't she? Richard grinned back. Maybe Uncle Joe wouldn't leave. Did his crazy mother really have something to say, or was Uncle Joe just humoring her?

"That's what some of these kids need today - somebody to knock some sense into their thick heads. They all run around with that dumb look on their face; they don't know what the hell they are doing. Who do they think they are kidding - a bunch of little brats who think they are smarter than their parents? Well, this is one parent they won't pull the wool over. I know what they are up to before they even think of it. I've been through it all. I know all of their tricks and shenanigans. They wouldn't pull any of that stuff on me. I could teach them a lesson that they would never forget. They would get more than they bargained for with me, brother. I wasn't born yesterday."

Richard was getting somewhat nervous. When his mother usually started talking like that, it was the signal for him to get lost. If he didn't, he might find himself "learning a lesson that he would never forget." He already had a number of lessons that he knew he would never forget. He didn't really want anymore. But, it was clear to him that she liked Uncle Joe. Uncle Ray was nice, but he wouldn't listen to her for long. A second or two of her kind of talk and he was gone.

Uncle Joe never visited at their apartment other than the major holidays. Nobody ever came to visit with his mother. If they stayed around too long, she could turn on them. Eventually she would be telling them what for, or how to, or to just go and crap in their hat. She liked that "crap in the hat business."

There were never any guests at Richard's house, sitting around the kitchen playing cards and spewing idle chatter as there always seemed to be at many of his friends' homes; once a year was more than enough exposure to Richard's mother for even the closest relatives. Uncle Joe was here right now but this was only for a half a day - one half a day out of Richard's entire life. He had never done it before, and probably when he left this time, he would never do it again.

Uncle Joe was the kind that you wanted to grab onto and never let go. He had what everybody wants. That is why he had to hide. Richard understood that. Right at this moment his mother had Uncle Joe captured, but shortly he would be free. One day Richard would also be free. No one would capture him either. No, no, no. He would just flap his wings and disappear. He would be like his Uncle Joe. There he would be coming down the street, and then he would be gone. Richard always wanted to run and catch onto Uncle Joe, but he knew that if he did, Uncle Joe wouldn't be able to fly. Many times he saw Uncle Joe, but he didn't even call out because ... well, because ... he didn't want to scare him off. Like one might scare a squirrel in the park, or a cat in the street, or a sparrow nipping at a crust of bread. One must be content with just watching. Some beautiful things are just to be observed. Grabbing onto them only spoils things.

Sometimes you might see Uncle Joe waving to somebody, or stooping down to pet a dog. But whatever, it was always now you see him, now you don't. He was a mystical, magic act. He had something inside, but there was a wall around it. He lived in a castle, surrounded by a moat in the middle of a dense forest. No one could come to the castle because there was no path. Sometime you could get a glimpse of the castle, though. You had to be lucky and very careful.

One time Richard saw Uncle Joe standing out in front of Dolan's bar on Center Street. Dolan's bar was just up the street and around the corner. That's what was so amazing. There was Uncle Joe and he was so close. Like some rare bird sitting right on your windowsill drinking raindrops or something. Richard was heading that way, so he had an excuse to say hello if Uncle Joe was still there by the time he arrived at the spot. He would probably disappear into Dolan's bar, or around the corner, or into an alley or a hall. Catching him was like trying to catch an elf at Christmas time in a St. Rita's corridor.

Richard approached and, on this particular occasion, the elf didn't disappear. He was talking with a man and suddenly there was Richard right behind him. What should Richard do? He shouldn't act too excited. That might frighten Uncle Joe. He shouldn't yell, or jump up and down. Besides, maybe Uncle Joe wouldn't be excited to see him. Maybe Uncle Joe wouldn't even recognize him. Maybe Uncle Joe would rather not be disturbed.

"Hi, Uncle Joe," Richard spoke as he cavalierly passed. He spoke in a voice not much louder than a whisper. His plan was to simply say hello and keep walking. If Uncle Joe wanted to acknowledge him, he could. If he didn't, Richard could just pass by and go about his business.

"Hey! Well, will you look who's here?" Wow, Uncle Joe was not only pleased to see Richard, but even acknowledged him in public. Richard was ecstatic. "Billy, hey Billy?" Joe called the attention of another man who had been standing near by. "Do you know who this is?" The man shook his head negatively. "This is Richard, one of my sister Mary's boys." While he talked he patted Richard on the head, ruffled up his hair and slapped him on the back. The man smiled affably, but he clearly wasn't as excited with Richard as Uncle Joe.

Joe then brought Richard inside the bar. It was strange to be entering into a barroom. There were tables to the left, and a bar with tall stools to the right. There were mirrors and signs all over the walls. There were signs that flashed on and off and lit up in different colors. It was very smoky.

His uncle Joe was yelling to everybody and directing Richard this way and that. Some men were playing cards. Some men were talking and drinking at the bar. Richard met them all. Everybody shook his hand, or patted him on the back. Many of the men seemed truly glad to meet him, as if he were somebody special or important. "This is Ernie and my sister Mary's youngest boy."

"No kidding! How you doin', son? I used to work for your grandfather."

"And I used to work with your dad," said another man.

"I knew your mom, when she was no bigger than you are," boasted a third.

"I'll tell you what, son. I met your dad in the schoolyard one day and he hit me so hard I thought that my teeth were going to come out the back of my head." Everyone around the table laughed. The man was a very rough looking man, Richard thought. "He could kick like a mule. He was the toughest little son of a bitch that I ever met." Richard was confused. Did this big man like his father or not? Didn't he just call his dad a son of a bitch? "Hey, hey kido, don't get mad at me. I respect your dad." He turned back to his friends at the table. "Did you see the look on that kid? I thought he was going to smack me one. He's a chip off the old block, ain't he?" The table broke up with laughter once again.

A waitress came bustling up to the table. She had a number of full glasses of beer on a tray. The beers were all white and foamy. The foam was running over the tops of the mugs and pilsner glasses. The tray was puddled with beer and so was the table, but no one seemed to mind or even notice.

The bar had a very familiar smell. Richard couldn't place the smell, but he liked it. Then it came to him. It was the smell of his dad. It was the smell of cigarettes and beer. The barroom smelled like his dad's breath, and his dad's clothes. The smell of a bar was the smell of love - the only love that he knew anything about, anyway - the love that emanated from his dad when he was intoxicated.

The waitress scattered the beers about the table, before she even noticed Richard. When she spotted the little boy, she said; "Well, what is this?" She squatted down in front of him and brushed the hair away from his eyes. She had a number of rings on her fingers and her fingernails were painted bright red. Richard had never seen a woman with painted fingernails. She had coloring on her cheeks and her eyelids. She had big lips, and they were painted a bright red also. She was a woman who looked, talked and acted like no woman Richard had ever met before in his life. She looked up at Joe inquisitively.

"This is Richard, my sister Mary's boy."

"Well, he's a doll. I could eat him right up."

This was strange talk - strange talk indeed. Richard had never heard a woman speak like this. No one, but no one, had ever referred to him as a "doll." Why would she ever want to "eat him up"? This was funny talk. The next thing that he knew, she had his face cupped in her hands and was kissing him on the forehead. This was embarrassing. His face turned red. He could feel it reddening. He wasn't supposed to be kissing women. He had made himself a promise. He didn't kiss anybody.

This lady obviously wasn't aware that Richard didn't kiss people. She didn't give him a chance to explain his position, either. She just grabbed him and kissed him. It felt rather good. He really didn't mind all that much. She smelled quite differently also. Not flowery or like lilacs, like his mother. It was a different smell than his mother's dressed up smell, but it was along the same line and of potent quantity.

All the men were looking at his red face and laughing. But there was nothing that he could do about it. Once your face went red, you just had to wait it out. It wasn't something that you could turn on and off. The waitress stood there staring at him for the moment. Then she smiled.

"Don't mind them. They are just jealous."

"Hey, what do you say to a Fould's pork pie?" His uncle Joe exclaimed. Richard loved Fould's pork pies. His mother brought them home often. They were crunchy and crusty, yet gooey and chewy. They were a tiny, hold-in-the-hand, sized pie. Like an apple pie, but they were filled with meat. They were loaded with ground up chunky pork meat and fat. When you heated them up in the oven, the fat melted. In the crispy top crust there was a hole. That's where you poured the ketchup in. They were delicious. His uncle got himself a beer, ordered Richard a pork pie, and then sat the boy up at the bar on a stool. When the pork pie arrived, his uncle said, "Hey Cozy! We need some ketchup down here." A bottle of ketchup then came sliding down the counter. Richard climbed up into his seat and sat on his calves so that he could get into the proper position to dig into his pork pie.

"That's the way to do it, boy. Get right up here and get at it." Joe laughed as the boy poured the ketchup in through the hole in the top of the pork pie. When he bit into it, the pork juice came gushing out and ran down the sides of the boy's mouth. Pork pies were delicious. Richard picked the pie up again and prepared to take another bite. As he did he saw his uncle Joe look down at his pie. Uncle Joe looked hungry.

Richard held the pie up to his uncle for him to take a bite of it. "Oh, you gonna give me a bite?" his uncle said, laughingly.

It seemed to Richard that to have his Uncle Joe share with him would be the most wonderful thing in the world. Uncle Joe never took anything from anybody. If he would share this pie with Uncle Joe, it would be so special. Like a wild lion in the jungle allowing himself to be petted by Richard alone. Like the story of the boy who took the thorn from the foot of the lion. From then on the lion was his friend, a friend who loved and protected him. Richard didn't need to be protected, but he did want to be loved. That would be good.

Richard pushed the pie up closer to his uncle's mouth. He could see his uncle's mouth beginning to water. It was just too delicious to resist. The smell alone could drive a man crazy. "I'll just take a little one."

He took a big bite, not just a little one. That made Richard really happy inside. He smiled as he watched his uncle. Looking into Richard's big eyes made his uncle laugh and Richard could see the big piece of pork pie sitting in his uncle's mouth. They both began to laugh, and his uncle rushed to the counter in search of a napkin. Now they both had orange colored pork fat dripping from their chins.

This day was so much fun. Richard would never forget it. Uncle Joe was like his Grandma Essick and his Uncle Ray. They all had that quality that Richard so longed for. But Richard feared that he might spoil it all. He told his uncle that he must go because his mother might be looking for him.

"Okay, we don't want your mom getting mad, do we?" Uncle Joe helped the boy down from the stool and then they walked outside together. "Okay, Richie, you be good now, and we'll see you again sometime."

"Okay," Richard said with a smile. As he turned and walked away, he knew that he would never have another good time like this one. His Uncle Joe would disappear. Maybe if Richard were lucky, he would see him for a minute or two on Christmas – maybe, hopefully, but not for sure.

Uncle Joe, unlike Uncle Ray, never brought any presents at Christmas time. He never had any money. As far as Richard knew, he didn't have any money; he didn't have any job; and he didn't live anywhere. Nevertheless, everyone hoped that he would show up at the house on Christmas day, even if it were for just a minute or two.

One Christmas he did come. No one saw him put any presents under the tree. Mary went digging under the tree and gave his present to him. He sat on the couch and opened it, quietly. He looked worried. He was maybe a little embarrassed. He had brought nothing and there he sat opening his gift. It was a twenty-five cent pack of Camel cigarettes. When he saw the humble nature of the gift, he looked up to Ernie. Ernie smiled and shrugged his shoulders. They both then laughed.

It was plain that Richard's dad liked Uncle Joe the best of all the relatives. Uncle Joe was probably the only guy in the family who seemed less fortunate than he was. They both drank beer and smoked cigarettes. Joe was a good listener. His dad could really bend Uncle Joe's ear about all the real stuff in life. They were two of a kind. Richard loved them both.

Richard loved his Uncle Ray, too. Uncle Ray was different from his dad and Uncle Joe. Uncle Ray was a happy sort of fellow. You didn't talk sad, lonely, down-and-out stuff to him. You laughed and told jokes to Uncle Ray. Uncle Ray did everything for Richard. Every nice, special thing that Richard ever had was given to him by his uncle Ray. This Christmas Uncle Ray had a special present. While Richard and Carol were opening their presents and bouncing and screaming with delight, they could see Ray and their Dad standing in the archway between the parlor and the kitchen. At first they seemed to be arguing. Then, Uncle Ray reached down and snatched Ernie's hand up from his side. He stuffed something into Ernie's palm. Ernie tried to give it back but Ray wouldn't hear of it.

"How many times did you help me out when you were running the numbers? You were the guy who had the money then. None of the rest of us ever had a cent." Ernie shrugged. Somebody did remember. "And my sister, Mary, how can I ever pay her back?" He looked at Mary. "You remember that cowboy suit that you sent me from Baltimore?" He laughed. "Boy, I will never forget that. Besides ..." He looked back to Ernie. "Every dog has his day, my friend. You'll be back on top again."

"You really think so?"

"I don't think so. I know so!" Richard and Carol could see their dad's eyes tearing up again. Uncle Ray then slapped Ernie on the shoulder and joined with the kids in the living room. Ernie went off into the kitchen to hide his tears and catch his breath. He sat down at the kitchen table. He looked at his hand and slowly opened it up - five big ten dollar bills. Ray had stuffed fifty bucks into his hand. Who was Ray? His wife's brother. No kin to him. His own relatives thought that he was too much of a drunken bum to trust him with fifty dollars of their money. He showed the money to Mary who was at the stove making coffee.

"How much?" she asked.

"Fifty," he said shaking his head in disbelief.

"Well, I guess blood is thicker than water," she said.

"Not in all families," Ernie muttered.

That was a very merry Christmas. A few weeks later when the kids were taking down the Christmas tree, they found three envelopes hidden in the tree. Each of the envelopes had one of their names on it: Richard, Carol, Ernie. When they opened the envelopes, they each found a new, crisp one dollar bill inside. They searched the envelopes for a card or some clue as to the identity of the donor. There was no identification anywhere. How peculiar, they thought. Each of the children sat staring at their one dollar bill. After a moment, they looked to one another and smiled. These anonymous dollars came from Uncle Joe. No doubt about it.

Why would he do that? Why wouldn't he want his gift acknowledged? When he opened up his present, a pack of Camels, Richard and Carol sat there in front of him eager and ready to accept his thanks and hugs and kisses. That was the whole fun of giving presents. Why didn't Uncle Joe want any hugs and kisses?

Did he consider his offering to be too little? One dollar was the equivalent of four packs of Camels. Besides, who really cared what the present was? That didn't matter. What mattered was just giving something to someone else to show them that you loved them. Uncle Joe wanted to give his love, but he didn't want to receive any love in return. Why?

The most exciting part of gift giving was choosing whose name would go on the package. Richard's mother bought all of the presents for everybody, but after they were wrapped she would write on the package, From Richard, To Dad; or From Carol, To Richard. The greatest fun of all was to have someone say, Thank-you Richard for that beautiful tie or, Thank-you Carol for that wallet. It is just what I needed.

Richard's older brother didn't know how to play the game. When he would finally come home after he was sure that all the visitors had left, he would always ask, "Okay Richard, let me see what I gave you this year." That was silly to say, but it made everyone laugh. His brother Ernie just didn't get Christmas. Clearly, neither did Uncle Joe.

"Why didn't Uncle Joe put his name on the card?" Richard asked. No one answered. "Maybe it wasn't from Uncle Joe. Maybe it was from Santa Claus."

"Oh, Richard!" his sister Carol moaned in disbelief. "Don't you know that there is no such person as Santa Claus?"

"What about all the presents that I get from Santa every year?"

"Those aren't from Santa Claus, you silly. All the presents come from Ma."

"You shouldn't tell him that," Ernie said, looking at Richard's rather shocked face.

"Oh, come on. He's big enough to know better. He's no baby no more."

Richard took his envelope and went out into the kitchen.

"Ma, did you put these envelopes with one dollar in them into the Christmas tree?"

"No. I didn't."

"Then it either came from Uncle Joe or Santa Claus. Carol says that it must be from Uncle Joe because there is no Santa Claus."

Richard's mother went over to the parlor door. She stood there with her hands on her hips and stared at Carol with an admonishing look on her face. Carol looked at her mother.

"Oh, come on!" she said. "He's big enough to know better." Richard looked over to his dad, sitting at the kitchen table, still staring at his fifty bucks.

"It doesn't have any name on it?" his dad asked.

"No."

"Then my guess is that it came from Uncle Joe. Santa Claus doesn't deal in cash." Richard stared at his dad. Santa doesn't deal in cash, his father had said. His sister was obviously playing games. She was just teasing, like telling him that he was really adopted or that he wasn't really born in a hospital but found outside, under a bush. The dollar bill was from Uncle Joe, but his wind-up, spark-shooting, ray-gun was from

Santa Claus. Richard went to the parlor door, stood next to his mother and stared at his sister. His sister had a guilty smile on her face. She was clearly lying, and Richard could tell.

"Why didn't Uncle Joe put his name on it?" Richard asked his dad. His dad thought for a moment or two.

"I don't know. Why do you think that he didn't sign it?"

Richard thought about the question.

"I think that he didn't sign it because he is shy and it makes him embarrassed when everybody wants to hug and kiss him."

"I think that you are exactly right. What do you think, Mary?" His mother looked down at Richard. She nodded her head, then her face crinkled up and she began to cry. Richard had often seen his mother sitting in the parlor, alone and crying. This is the first time that he ever saw her crying for a reason. He had always assumed when he saw her crying in the past that she was crying because she didn't have a new refrigerator, or because she didn't have a new TV or stove. This is the first time that he had ever witnessed her shedding tears for a cause other than her own or her personal self. This time she was crying out of her loving feelings for her brother, Joe. She was crying because Uncle Joe was embarrassed to accept love from anybody. Could she be crying because maybe she wanted to hug Uncle Joe also? Could it be that maybe his Uncle Joe was right? Could it be that his mother was, deep down under all that calloused, brutal crust, a human being deserving of love, also?

This was the first such indication that he ever had. Maybe she was; maybe she wasn't? Maybe she just loved Uncle Joe and nobody else? Richard would watch in the future, and look for signs of his mother's humanness. Whatever, she had a long, hard row to hoe, in Richard's calculations. His bruises from her slaps, whacks, punches, and bangs had him well convinced that there was no love inside that shell for him. Her hatred for him was clear and undeniable. Nevertheless it was a discovery to find that she may have harbored feelings for somebody. This was the first indication of any such feeling that he had ever witnessed in this creature he had been trained to call mother.

8 Doctor Jekyll and Mr. Hyde

It was a merry, merry Christmas, indeed. The guests had all gone and Richard and Carol were now trying to guess what they had given their brother Ernie. After everyone had made their guesses, they would give the unopened package to Ernie and he would guess before he opened it.

Richard's dad was sitting at the kitchen table. He had just finished blowing his nose, and was wiping his eyes with a handkerchief. It was Dad's turn to guess.

"This is Ernie's present. We think that it's a wallet." His dad nodded his head, then leaned to one side and stuffed his handkerchief back into his rear pocket. He stared down at Richard with a rather peculiar, twisted look on his face. Richard stopped smiling and stood frozen in his tracks. Was his dad angry? Was he upset? Was he in pain? Was he pretending? His eyes got bigger as his father slowly raised himself from the kitchen table. He used the table as a brace, and pushed himself up by his hands. He looked up at the round florescent light that sat flat against the ceiling. As he stared at the light, his face twisted in a contorted, bewildered manner. Suddenly he slumped at the waist and made a dash for the refrigerator.

Richard's eyes got big and round and he began to tremble inside. He screamed and then began jumping up and down. He knew what was coming. It was scary and frightening but yet fun and thrilling. They were going to play Doctor Jekyll and Mr. Hyde. His dad had just remembered about the secret potion. Now he was going to the refrigerator to gather up the ingredients. He took out some eggs, a bag of carrots, some green olives, and a bottle of hot sauce. His arms were full as he dashed over to the counter by the sink.

Doctor Jekyll and Mr. Hyde was a game that he and his dad played. Everyone knew the game and how it was played. Everyone began to laugh. Richard was never quite sure if he liked this game or not. It was a scary game. It was frightening and Richard really didn't like to see his dad transformed from the kindly Doctor Jekyll to the horrid Mr. Hyde. Doctor Jekyll would drink the potion and then turn into the evil and twisted Mr. Hyde. Richard knew that it was only a game but it had a meaning for him that no one else seemed to understand.

Richard ran over to the counter and began pulling at his father's pant leg. "No, no," he screamed. "Don't! Don't!"

"Oh don't be silly, little boy," the kindly Doctor Jekyll said, doing his best Boris Karloff impersonation. "I am going to make this lovely potion that will help the whole world."

"No, no! You are going to drink it and go crazy."

"Nonsense. Nonsense, little boy; you just watch and see."

Doctor Jekyll went about his business. He peeled off a strip of bacon from the one-pound slab. Then he cracked an egg, opened it slowly and dropped it into the glass.

"Stop it! Stop it!" Richard screamed. He knew that after his dad mixed the secret potion and drank it; he would come chasing after him. He looked to his mother. She shrugged and smiled wanly. He looked to his sister. She lifted her hands, wiped her eyes and just smiled. He ran to his big brother who was already over six feet tall. He grabbed onto his sleeve. "Stop him! Stop him! He is going to drink the secret potion." His brother laughed and looked over to his father. His father winked at his oldest boy. Richard handed his big brother his present as a bribe.

"What is it?" his brother asked.

"Who cares? Who cares! Just stop him before he goes mad."

The enjoyment of this game for the family was in watching Richard. He would get uncontrollably excited. He would run from room to room screaming and looking for a good place to hide. He would hide in the closet, or behind the couch. It was almost as if he really believed that his dad was undergoing a metamorphosis. To Richard this was much more than a game. This was beyond fact or fiction. This was his father's passion play, his interpretation of life, itself. This was an act just like on Playhouse 90: the happy face, the sad face, comedy versus tragedy, love versus hate, kindness versus cruelty, and hope versus despair.

This game of Doctor Jekyll and Mr. Hyde was the stuff of life.

Didn't his mother have two faces? That ugly, evil face filled with cruelty, anger, hatred and vindictiveness - that wimpy smile and that general malaise. Those depressed sunken eyes. Then there was her other face: that active, positive, shopping, cooking, eating, lip smacking, waiting on everybody face.

What about his dad's two faces: his sober, serious, quiet, worried face; and then his father's teary, talkative, playful, emotional, drunken face? Doesn't everyone have two faces - one that can be trusted and one that can't; one for their loved ones and one for strangers; one for their own kind - for their little doggies and kitties - and that one they hold in reserve and ugliness for you and yours? Out in the world there are two faces, those that you run to, and those that you run from.

Yes, oh yes, Richard was a little boy who knew all too well the other side of a smile - the other side of her smile, his smile, and your smile. He had already learned only too well that inside of every apparent silver lined cloud there is a very rainy day. Is not the other side of light ... darkness? Good and bad? Are they not but the two different sides of the same coin? Is not happiness merely sadness upside down?

The smile is only what people use to chase away their frowns. Couldn't it be possible that his dad could drink the secret potion and remain forever the evil and horrid Mr. Hyde? Couldn't it be that the frown would win and his Father's smile would never be seen again? What causes the smile to fade and the frown to grow ... and grow ... and grow ... and then explode? Explode into horrible violence and blows and beatings. Couldn't this all be the result of a secret potion? Could it not be the result of some mysterious drink? What was it that made people happy one minute and sad the next?

Richard didn't want to see the other side of his father's smile. Both of his dad's faces he could handle. But what if this secret potion brought about a third face? A face filled with hate and brutal cruelty like his mother's second face. A face that neither laughed nor cried; a face that bit and spit fire. Wasn't it already true that his dad drank a secret potion that changed his whole personality? What was alcohol? Couldn't it be true that his dad, who was already subject and vulnerable to potions, could drink this new potion and lose himself completely? Didn't he learn at Church that the priest could change the bread and wine into the body and blood of Christ? Wasn't it also true that the priest drank this wine and ate this bread in order to become more like the dead Christ? Didn't they tell Richard that this was the actual body and blood of the once living Jesus? Didn't such a miraculous transformation happen right at his Church, every Sunday, on the hour, every hour?

Wasn't his mother already a Doctor Jekyll and Mr. Hyde? Wasn't his father already a Doctor Jekyll and Mr. Hyde? Could it be that everyone in the world was really a Doctor Jekyll and a Mr. Hyde, even Uncle Joe, Uncle Ray, and Grandma Essick? Maybe he just hadn't seen them after they drank their potion. Couldn't there really be two people inside everyone that he met or knew? Could it be true that everyone in the entire world had a Mr. Hyde inside of them that Richard was yet to discover?

Why shouldn't Richard consider this game frightening? Why shouldn't Richard seriously try to stop it from continuing?

After the bacon and the egg, a stalk of celery with all the little branches and leaves still attached was placed into the glass; he then added a whole carrot. His dad then spun around to see if Richard was still watching.

Richard had been running this way and that. He had already been everywhere looking for a good place to hide. He couldn't find one. His father, as the evil Mr. Hyde, had been to them all. Richard wanted to watch, but he didn't want to watch. He would cover his face, but then he would want to see and remove his hands. It was too scary to hide your face. He must watch so as to know where to run.

This was like when his sister took him to the Frankenstein movie. Sometimes he would jump under the seats at the scary parts. His sister would admonish him. "You're missing the best part." But it was just too scary to watch the Frankenstein monster come to life with all the sparks and lightning and Boris Karloff making all of those crazy faces and stuff. "It's alive! It's alive!" It felt better to be under the theater seat at those moments. Sometimes he would peek through the space in the theater seats in front of him. Yes, it was exciting and thrilling. But, on the other hand, it was scary and frightening.

Next his dad added a few dashes of hot sauce, and then some Worcestershire sauce, and then more hot sauce. Everybody groaned. Then he opened a large can of tomato juice. He poured a mess of that in. Next some salt and some pepper graced the concoction. He then got a potato, sliced it in half, and dropped half the potato into the brew; then came the green olives. Richard ran over to his brother once again.

"Make him stop! Make him stop! You're big, you can make him stop!" Richard always had confidence in his older brother. He was big and tall and he could take care of himself in the streets. That's what his mother had told him.

The family had come to Lawrence from Baltimore when Richard was just a baby. All the tough guys on the block picked on Ernie. One day Ernie had a fight with the toughest of them all. He hit him with one punch and knocked him right over the fence. Richard asked his big brother about that fight one time when they were in bed. His brother said that he didn't remember any such thing. He said that Ma had probably just made the whole story up.

That is what Richard liked the best about his older brother. He never bragged or made things up. He always told the truth. He never refused to hold Richard's hand at night when Richard was afraid to go to sleep. Richard trusted his big brother.

"It is only a game, Richard," his big brother said. "Dad's just playing with you. That's all." Richard looked up into his brother's eyes. He had narrow little slits with bright blue inside. They were very close together and suspicious looking, but those eyes always told the truth. They never lied and they were never fearful. They were always confident and cheerful. His brother said that it was all a game. Richard knew that it was really just a game too. His father had played this game many times before. But yet, how does one know for sure when a game is a game, or when playing is truly playing?

He believed his brother. His brother didn't lie. But when he turned and looked at his father, he knew that his father told the truth also. Richard knew what he knew. He knew what he had been taught. But he knew what he had seen with his own eyes. He knew what he had felt with his own body. Ernie didn't remember the big fight that his mother had bragged about. His dad never seemed to remember what he had said or done when he was drunk. Richard had been taught and had seen things with his own eyes that he would never forget.

"Is he really going to drink all that goop?" Carol squealed in partial disbelief. Brother Ernie shook his head with doubt. Mother watched with a smirk. Dad had topped off the concoction with a full can of beer and was, at this very moment, stirring it with a long bread knife. The potion was red and foamy and hideous looking. Richard had placed his hands on the top of his head and was bouncing nervously in anticipation.

His father turned and held the potion up to the florescent light. The celery stalk and whole carrot were sticking up above the top of the glass. The bacon strip was draped over the edge of the glass and hanging down on both the inside and the outside.

"This potion that I have mixed contains the cure for all of the ills of mankind. If I can drink it, I can save the world," his dad said, while looking goofy and making strange, pained faces up towards the round and glaring florescent light.

He put the glass to his lips and drank the beverage in one long tilt of the glass. He gulped and swallowed noisily as some of the contents of the glass entered into his mouth while an equal amount overflowed and dribbled from its sides and down onto his shirt. Everyone groaned in total disgust. Richard bounced up and down on his toes, while squinting his eyes in horror and disbelief and gritting his teeth.

What would happen now? How long would it take for the potion to take effect?

His dad held the empty glass up over his head. His right eye began to twitch. His body began to shake all over. Now it jerked and began to spasm. He stretched up to the heavens and screamed while simultaneously snatching the string that dangled from the kitchen light.

The room went dark.

Everyone laughed while Richard screamed. When the light came back on, his father had been transformed. His always perfect black, wavy hair was sticking up in random directions. His eyes were opened wide, but when he looked down towards Richard, the boy could see that they were now crossed. His lips were rolled up and his teeth were showing savagely.

"Where is that little boy? I love little boys," he said ghoulishly. He scanned the room but pretended not to see Richard who was standing right there before him. "Has anyone here seen a little boy named Richard?" His father was now bent over and tilted to one side. He looked like Charles Lawton in the Hunchback of Notre Dame. He made his way over towards his wife. His left hand was touching the floor and a deformed right leg was dragging limply behind.

"Do you know a little boy named Richard?" he inquired.

"No, I don't," his mother said protectively.

"Are you sure?" he said, ghoulishly mimicking Boris Karloff once again.

"I'm sure," she said, gesturing to Richard with her eyes wide and her eyebrows raised encouraging him to hurry and find a good place to hide. Richard caught her cue and ran quickly behind his brother. He peeked out from behind one of his brother's long legs as the evil Mr. Hyde dragged himself over towards his sister Carol.

"Have you seen a little boy with blond hair and a pushed up, funny looking nose?"

"No, I haven't. Are you sure that such a little boy lives here in this house?"

"Ohhh, I am sure. I am very, very sure," his dad said grinning fiendishly and now spotted Richard peeking out from behind his brother's pant leg. "In fact, THERE HE IS!" his father yelled.

Richard was off running and screaming. He needed a place to hide but he had to be quiet once he found it or he would get caught.

He ran into the parlor. He looked about the room. Where would he hide? He could hear Mr. Hyde dragging his crippled leg and making menacing sounds out in the kitchen.

"Where did that lit-tle boy go? I would like to be his friend. Ha, ha, ha, haaaa. Oh yes, I would like to be that little boy's friend."

Richard ran to the parlor couch. He pulled up one of the cushions, jumped into the couch, and then pulled the cushion in on top of him. When his dad entered the parlor, he laughed and motioned for the rest of the family. Everything was intact, of course, but the parlor couch. There was the center cushion on the couch, a good six inches higher than the others.

"Well, well? Where might my little friend be?" he queried in the mysterious and monstrous voice of the evil Mr. Hyde. "I don't see him. He seems to have just disappeared." As he spoke he moved closer to the couch. "Maybe I will just sit down here on this nice couch and rest for a moment."

Naturally, he sat on the raised cushion. Richard didn't squeak or make a peep. He didn't budge an inch.

"Oh, if I only knew where that little boy was. I would give him a great ... big ... hug - ha, ha haaah!"

The cushion then began to bounce slightly, and little noises could be heard seeping out.

"Well, well? What is this? Are we having an earthquake? Maybe I had better get up and look out the window."

This was Mr. Hyde's cue to Richard to run from the couch and find a new place to hide. Richard pushed the cushion up abruptly, leaped from within the couch and made a mad dash to exit the parlor.

"Well, well? There's my little friend."

His dad made a quick move and grabbed Richard before he could get to safety. When Mr. Hyde grabbed Richard, Richard went hysterical. He screamed and yelled and kicked with such fear that everyone else roared with laughter. This was the moment that they had been waiting for. Mr. Hyde was now pawing Richard and tickling him under the arms. He kept trying to squeeze Richard up to his ugly face and hug him. Finally Richard broke loose once again. This time he ran into the bathroom and hid behind the door with his head under his mother's robe.

It was only a moment before Mr. Hyde was there too. He started in, once again, pinching, and tickling and laughing fiendishly. Richard managed to escape, just as before, and ran into his parents' bedroom. Mr. Hyde was hot on his trail and with his horrible face still dripping tomato juice at the corners, he trapped Richard at the bureau.

Just as Mr. Hyde reached to snatch him, Richard leaped up onto his parent's bed and bounced across the room. He flung the door open and slammed it shut behind him.

He must find a better place. He ran to his own bedroom. There was a huge walk-in closet in that room. It was filled with jackets and overcoats and trunks and old shoe boxes.

He climbed over a big trunk and hid himself amidst the hanging overcoats and jackets at the far rear of the closet. He was only hidden there for a moment before he realized that within this closet with the door completely shut behind him, there was total darkness. He was afraid of total darkness.

In the darkness, devils and demons appeared. Evil shadows and mysterious spirits from the dead and "below" materialized and came from the depths of hell to drag helpless children back to Hell with them.

It was barely a second before he felt a furry-like animal hand on his shoulder. His heart leaped up to the top of his head. He grabbed at his shoulder frantically. Sure enough, he felt a strange furry thing sitting there. He tossed it from his shoulder and bolted from the closed closet door.

Once beyond the door, he dove to the floor and slid under his bed. It wasn't until he was huddled way back into his favorite corner - the only one with a wall on each side of him - that he realized what that strange animal in that closet might have really been. His mother had this stupid dress-up coat with some little furry animals fastened to the shoulders. It must have been one of those tiny little animals that had come to rest on his shoulder. But in the total darkness, one never really knows. The dark is filled with shadows and skeletons and devils and demons and menacing pirates with one wooden leg and black eye patches. The dark is filled with dead spirits who got lost on their way to hell or heaven and were now angry because they had no place to go. Who really knew what could have been in that closet in the total darkness? Who would take such a chance to remain there? Certainly not Richard!

Under the bed it was all dusty and dirty. The bed springs were above his head along with wooden boards and metal poles. A light from the kitchen could be seen along the floor. As long as there was light, even just a little, everything was all right. Suddenly there were his father's shoes at the foot of the bed.

"Now where is that sweet little boy? I just love sweet little children. I want to hug them and squeeze them tight."

Richard remained calm. He held his breath so as not to make any noise. His father didn't really know where the boy had disappeared to. Then he saw the closet door ajar. "Aha! Could he be in that closet?" Richard's eyes widened with glee as he almost squeaked with joy. He covered his mouth with both hands to keep any sounds from seeping out. His dad must have really thought that he was in the closet. Had he fooled his father? This would be the best thing that could ever happen.

He could hear his father in the closet mumbling his Mr. Hyde jargon. Richard sputtered and nearly burst into giggling from his safe spot under the bed. His father continued to mumble and bristle from inside the closet. Richard could hear him fumbling and the shoe boxes tumbling. It was all so very, very funny. The joke of this game was always on Richard but the tables had been turned momentarily. For this brief moment Richard was winning. This was oh so funny.

Richard could hardly keep his joy trapped inside. Periodically little puffs and sputters would burst from his ribs and rush up to his mouth. Little spewing, giggles and sputters vaporized from beneath the bed springs. He would try to grab up these sounds and force them back down inside, but it was impossible. He was like an agitated soda bottle. Even the strongest thumb could not suppress the bubbles of glee. Something had to give or the bottle would just explode.

Suddenly there was silence. Mr. Hyde had stopped his rummaging in the closet. Richard knew that he must be listening for the sound of a telltale sputter. He held his breath and tried to keep everything down. Yet little peeps and giggles kept squirting out. Had he given himself away? He must remain as silent as possible.

"Well, well? That little devil must have just disappeared. I wonder? I wonder where he could have gone? I wonder? Hummm? I wonder?"

The little boy could see his father's shoes stepping out of the dark closet. Carol, Ernie and Mother were all huddled by the bedroom door. Richard could see their shoes hovering at the threshold.

"But maybe he isn't even here in this room? Maybe he is gone? Maybe he is no longer even in this house?"

His father's feet began to shuffle and drag along the side of the bed slowly. Richard took in a big gulp of air. He covered his face with his hands to assist in the task of holding in that air. Besides, this was all just too scary to watch.

Suddenly the whole bed shook and there was a commotion. When Richard pulled his hands from his face, he saw the horrible, ugly Mr. Hyde peering at him from between the bars that stretched to the floor at the foot of the bed.

"Well, well, well? What do we have here? Is that my little chum under there?" said Mr. Hyde menacingly.

Richard began to squeal and slap on his thighs uncontrollably. Where could he go? He was trapped.

Mysteriously his father's face was suddenly transformed. It was now the angry face of his mother peering at him through the bed bars. She had come to drag him out by the heels and beat him. But then, just as suddenly, it was the evil Mr. Hyde once again. Mr. Hyde was a game. His mother was not a game. There she was, grabbing for his heels. She would pull him out from under this table. She was screaming and yelling. But it was not her screams that Richard heard. It was his screams.

His Father with his hair all a jumble was playfully grabbing at the boys ankles. Richard was now screaming and kicking hysterically. He seemed to be losing all control. He could feel his face redden as he kicked at his "mother's" hands.

"GET OUT! GET OUT! I hate you!" He reached out and scratched his father's wrists with his nails. Everybody could now hear the terrified fear in the texture of Richard's voice. His sister began to plead.

"Stop it Dad. That's enough. You're really scaring him. He thinks he's trapped."

Mr. Hyde pulled out his bloodied wrists and proceeded to examine his wounds. His father was confused. The boy had never acted like this before. He stretched down onto the floor and stared at the boy.

"What's wrong, Richard?" he asked in a calm voice.

"GET OUT! GET OUT! Don't touch me. I hate you!"

His father, still stretched on the floor beside the bed, explained softly that it was all pretend. It was just a game. But Richard would have no part of it. He screamed and screamed for his father to go away, to get out and let him be.

His dad stared at the boy's face. He could not believe what he saw. How did the boy become so horror struck? They had played this game a thousand times before. He decided that it would be best to just leave the boy alone. He got up off the floor and left the room. He paused at the door.

"I'll close this door Richard and you can be alone to calm down. Just relax."

“NOOO! Don’t close the door. Leave it open.”

“Okay, okay. I’ll leave it open. But calm down now. The game is over.”

Under the bed Richard’s thoughts were flying through his brain: his mother, his father; Doctor Jekyll, Mr. Hyde; Sister Priska, Sister Francis; the little boy being hung out the window; Jesus and the Roman soldiers; God on the Cross and the Devil; the iron bedsprings, and all the dust; his father and Mr. Hyde; his mother and her insanity. He hadn’t meant to scare everybody. He didn’t mean to. He had lost his temper. He scratched his dad. Why had he done that? He knew that his father would never hurt him. Would he?

What about that time at the beach when his dad carried him out into the deep water over his head. Richard liked to play at the shore’s edge. He didn’t like going out into the deep water. Even at the edge the water would pull at his feet and suck the sand from between his toes. The water pulled the sand from the beach. The water wanted to pull people out over their heads and drown them. The water would get rough, and you had to be careful of the “under-toe.” The under-toe could grab you by the toes and pull you out into the deep and drown you. That’s why they called it under-toe - because it grabbed your toes and pulled you under.

One day his father grabbed him from behind and carried him out into the deeper water. He clung to his father by wrapping his arms around his dad’s neck and his legs around his waist. His father carried him out, deeper and deeper. Richard clung as best he could. He dug his fingers into his father’s back. He asked his father to be careful and begged his dad not to take him out over his head. His father promised that he wouldn’t. The boy clung and trembled from the fright of the mysterious, invisible fingers of the under-toe. The fingers of the under-toe were undoubtedly attached to the hand of the Devil. His father walked deeper, and deeper, and deeper.

“Let’s stop here, Dad. It is too deep already.” But they continued deeper, and deeper, and deeper. “Don’t let me go now, Daddy. It is way too deep. Hold on to me good. Please ... please don’t let me go. I’m afraid.”

When his father finally stopped, he pried Richard loose and threw him in the deep water which was over his head. Richard went down and down and down. When his feet finally hit bottom the water was way over his head. When he tried to scream, water rushed into his mouth and now he couldn't breathe. He put his feet on the bottom and pushed up as strongly as he could. He had never imagined that his father would do anything like that to him. He loved his father and would gladly die in his father's place. He always protected his father. He picked him up when he fell down; he carried him when he couldn't walk; he felt his pain as if it were his own. How could his dad do such a thing as this?

When his head came up from under the water, he could see nothing but his father. But his father had turned his back and was rushing away. He could see that his father was laughing. When he tried to gulp in air, he swallowed mostly saltwater. Within an instant he was under water once again. Each time he went under and his feet hit the bottom, he kicked as quickly and strongly as he could. On the one hand he wanted to push himself up for air and on the other hand he wanted to escape the grasping fingers of the Devil.

The Devil was everywhere, you know. It was a great prize for the Devil to capture small children and take them to hell with him. Where was God? Why was He never about when help was needed?

Sometimes when Richard's feet hit the bottom he felt slimy things down there. That made him even more frightened. What were those things? He continued to kick and jump and splash, and reach out for his dad to save him. He kept gulping saltwater and going under the surface. He was finally close enough to his dad to reach out for him.

His father laughed and pushed him away.

Richard kept going under and gulping more water. He was drowning, he felt. He was drowning and his father was laughing. He kept gulping water and going down under the surface and kicking himself up again. He kept reaching for his father, but his dad kept pushing him off and shoving his head under the water. Sometimes he would actually grab Richard up under the arms and throw him out into the deeper water once again.

Did this man love him? Was this man trying to kill him? His mother couldn't be trusted. She had already tried to kill him. This was not funny, but his father was laughing. Maybe the next time he would let his father lay in the gutter. Who else would care enough to go and rescue a drunk like him?

Finally he grabbed his dad by the waist and crawled up his body until he had a grip over his dad's shoulders and around his neck. His dad tried to pull and push him away, but he would not let loose. Richard was almost completely out of breath. He was gasping and gulping for air. He had swallowed too much water. He couldn't catch his breath. He couldn't speak. He just kept panting and sucking in all the air he could swallow. His father kept talking about learning how to swim, and how really easy it was to swim in the saltwater. Richard didn't know how to swim. No one had ever shown him how. He had been drowning and his father was just too dumb to understand. Richard loved his dad and he thought him to be a good man, but he was clearly a stupid man.

His father finally gave up on trying to pry him loose and walked toward the shore with the boy clinging desperately to him. He kept telling Richard that the water was now shallow and he could let go. How could Richard believe that his father was now telling the truth? Why he would have to be a complete fool! His father had said that he wouldn't bring him out into the water over his head, but he did. His father had said that he wouldn't throw him in the water over his head, but he did. How could Richard ever believe anything that his father said?

"Okay, okay. I've got you. You don't have to dig your fingers in so hard."

Oh, but he did. His father didn't have him. His father never had him at all. You're safe, his father now tried to tell him. I saved you, his father told him. What his father was saying was not the truth. His father hadn't saved him at all. His father had tried to drown him. He had grabbed onto his father and saved himself. Maybe his father was too stupid to realize that Richard was drowning, but he was.

Richard had just barely saved his own life. His father was laughing. His father was a dumb human being. His father hadn't saved him. His father was merely a piece of debris in a demon-filled treacherous ocean. His father was a pole in the water. Richard had grabbed onto a pole and saved his own life. He had pulled himself up from the bottom of the ocean and saved himself.

His father? His father was a joke. Half the time, he couldn't even stand up, never mind save anybody.

He no longer trusted his father. He really didn't even like his father. He resented being forced to cling fearfully to his father's body in order to save his own life. At that moment he didn't feel very close to his father. He wanted to let loose of his father. He really didn't want to be touching anyone who seemed to hate him and deep down inside wanted to do him harm. He resented being subjected to the strength of bigger people. He resented his father for using his strength and his bigness against him when he was too weak to resist.

He would not forget this moment. One day, if he ever got big enough, he would pay his father back for this day. He would make his father suffer, just as his father had made him suffer. He would hold his father's head under the water. If his father tried to resist he would push his head down deeper. Then we would see if he would laugh. Then we would see who the little baby would be. "Don't be a little baby," his dad had admonished him. Maybe he was a baby, but nevertheless, he couldn't breathe. Every time he tried, water rushed in. This had nothing to do with being a baby. He couldn't breathe under the water, and he didn't know how to swim. His father should not have done what he did. His father should have been teaching him how to swim, not trying to drown him.

He refused to talk to his dad after that incident for days. He would punish his dad by withholding his love and affection.

His dad never even noticed. How could he notice? He never talked to anybody when he was sober. How would he notice that someone wasn't speaking to him? Why should he trust or care for his dad any more than he did for his mother? He loved his dad. It hurt that his dad did not love him.

He sat under his bed and tried to calm himself. He thought that he would never calm down, but eventually he was breathing more slowly. But why should he ever want to help his dad? He should just let him fall down and bust his head open. When his dad cried like a little child, he should simply laugh at him. Why should he care about his dad at all? Why did his dad like to scare him? It wasn't funny. It wasn't cute. Why didn't he just love him like a dad was supposed to love his son? Why did he only love Richard when he was drunk? Why should

Richard love him? Why should Richard care about him? Why should he?

But yet he did. He cared very, very much. His mother's slaps didn't hurt him nearly as much as one of his father's frowns. Why was his dad mean to him? There was nobody in the whole world who loved him as much as Richard did. Richard would protect him and care for him. He would carry him on his back if he could. He would wipe all of his tears. He would take all his pain. He would even hate for him. So why did his dad delight so in Richard's fears? Why did he laugh when Richard was suffering so?

"Hey, you still under there?" his dad asked in a soft voice. "Are you going to come out from under there?" He was now lying down on the bedroom floor and staring in at Richard. "I really didn't mean to scare you so much. I thought that we were just playing. We were just playing, weren't we?" He smiled. Richard thought about it and then smiled too. "Well then, come on out, okay?"

"Okay."

"You will?"

"Yes."

"When?"

"In a little while."

"All right, good!"

Richard didn't want to come out because he was ashamed. Why did he get so scared? Nobody else was scared. Why did being in the dark frighten him so? Why was hell always so real and heaven so very far away? He put his hands together and he prayed:

"Dear Mother of God ..." The nuns had told him to pray to the Mother of God, because if God would listen to anybody, wouldn't it be logical for Him to listen to his Mother first? "Please ask Jesus not to hate me. Please ask Him to help me to be brave. I don't like to be afraid. I don't like to be frightened. I don't want to go to hell. I want to go to heaven and be a brave angel of God. Sometimes I think that God doesn't like me. I try to be good. I can't help being afraid. Will you please ask your Son to help me to be brave? I love you all very much. Thank you." He then blessed himself.

God seemed too stern and distant. God was just like his dad when his dad was sober. Jesus had been through enough suffering. People like himself had hurt Jesus. Every time you lied, or stole, or disobeyed your mother it was just the same as sticking another thorn in the head of Christ. Every sin was another spear thrust into his side. Every hateful thought was more spit in his face. How could Jesus ever feel any compassion for people? People had tortured and abused him. They had nailed Him to a cross.

St. Joseph was the father of God, but no one ever prayed to him. He was not strong. He led the mule for Mary. What did Joseph ever do or say that mattered to anybody? He wasn't even the real father of Jesus. The Holy Ghost was Jesus' real Father. Somebody told Joseph that Mary would be wearing a flower and that he should marry her. Mary was always very important in all of the stories at school. But Joseph was a man who was barely even considered. He just did what God told him and from then on he did what Mary told him. Joseph was like Richard's father.

It was strange that Richard should be so attracted to the Virgin Mary. He didn't like his real mother. Why should he like the mother of Jesus?

She was so beautiful. She was so kind and loving. She always talked in a soft quiet voice. She was a beautiful virgin, a queen. She was the mother of God. She was chosen from all of the women of the world. She was special. If anyone would talk to Jesus for Richard, she would.

Richard crawled out from under his bed. He was ashamed and he felt guilty for spoiling all the fun. Someday though - someday it would all be fun and he would never be afraid. Someday he would never be afraid again ... maybe.

9 A Trip to the Bakery

At an appointed age Richard inherited the responsibility of going to the Polish bakery each evening. At a quarter to nine on weeknights the loaves of round Polish rye bread and the bulkies, or hard rolls, were just coming out from the huge redbrick baking ovens. The bulkies were for school lunches and the rye bread for the dinner table. All the family, including his father, loved to eat the warm crusts from the light rye, sopped with fresh-melting, real butter.

When his father was dating his mother, he was notorious for eating all the crusts off the round, hand-sliced loaves of bread. But no matter how delicious a treat this bread was, someone had to fight the elements and the perils of the night to rescue it from the Polish bakery on Exchange Street each weekday evening. Richard's sister once had the task, and his older brother performed it before she had that duty. Now it was Richard's responsibility.

Richard didn't really have all that many household tasks. He would often haul a five gallon jug down the cellar steps to get fuel oil from a big fifty gallon drum. Before that, he carried that same five gallon jug up to the gas station to have it filled with kerosene. The jug sat on the back of the kitchen stove. It had to be tipped upside down, and the spring loaded cap set into the well-type metering device. Richard's tasks were getting the fuel oil, carrying out the garbage, and doing the errands. Doing the errands included going to Walter's Variety for: four slices of American cheese, sliced very, very thin; four slices of Polish ham, sliced very, very, thin; and one can of Campbell's tomato soup.

He also went to the meat market on Hampshire Street. At the meat market the men wore red bow-ties and straw hats, and the floor of the market was always covered with sawdust.

"My mother said to get one pound of your cheapest hamburg and one pound of cubed steak." Then he would hand the man the envelope with the money and the written instructions inside.

The bakery was a neat errand also. The baker and his helpers were always kneading dough on long wooden tables stretched along both the east and west walls of the shop. At the north end were the two giant ovens. The ovens were so deep that the bakers had to use long, wooden, giant spatulas. The handles on the spatulas were fifteen to twenty feet long. The spatula itself must have been at least two-foot square. They were used to put the unbaked bread in and take the cooked bread out or to move the cooking bread from one hot spot to another. The breads were all spaced inside the oven like a checker board. The spatula could be adeptly slipped under any square and the square of breads or rolls could be shuffled around or taken out and dropped into the appropriate wooden bin, or atop some heavy-duty wooden table.

Stored about the large room were pallets heaped with crisscrossed sacks of floor and vats of sugar. There were crates of eggs and butter ready to be wheeled into a man-sized, walk-in refrigerator. It had to be a wonderful profession to be a baker. To take useless powders and tasteless grains and mold them into a wondrous concoction that had people lining up at this family's door begging them to take their money in exchange for the miracle of their creativity. Why didn't his father ever learn how to bake bread? If he had, maybe he could have been sitting safely at home instead of risking his life in hurricanes, trapped in a worthless, rusted, old tub out in the middle of some ocean.

As wondrous as the bakery was with its tasty rolls and powdery delights, getting there was another story. Unfortunately, one had to fight his way through a terror of patchy darkness and the fright of the evils of night.

It was in the darkness that all of the frightening things that had been put into his imagination came to life. The Devil liked the darkness because in the darkness no one could see him doing his dirty work. The Devil lived in hell. Though no one knew exactly where hell was, many believed that it was situated in the bowels of the earth itself, where lava flowed and flames licked with such intensity that they melted rocks. If you went to hell you would experience pain far beyond the scope of your imagination. The good nuns had told him many, many stories about hell.

If you ever burnt yourself or touched a hot stove, or put your finger above the flame of a match or the lit burner of a gas stove, you knew how hot a flame could be. You knew how your fingers bubbled and swelled when you mistakenly grabbed onto the handle of a heated frying pan. Multiply that pain you felt a million, billion times over and you have an inkling of the pain that you will experience if you end up in hell. Hell was a torture chamber. If you listened to the Devil, you would end up there. The Devil was everywhere. He was in your house. He was in your room. He was in your body. He was in your mind. The Devil was even sitting right there on your shoulder.

An angel sat on one shoulder and the Devil on the other. It was the Devil who tried to make you squirm in your seat in class. It was He, who tried to make you talk and giggle. He wanted to make you do everything bad. He wanted you to sin. If you sinned, you would one day join with Him in the tortures of hell.

In the dark, the Devil was everywhere. On windy, cold nights you could hear Him howl. He often howled right outside Richard's bedroom in the alley that separated the additions of his tenement house. The Devil lived in the darkness and God lived in the light. God was the light. God was the truth and the light. God was the "Way." The Devil was the darkness and the night. If you followed the Devil, you would become lost in the wilderness. The Devil was red, like fire. He had horns and a tail. He carried a pitchfork. He would stick you with it if you came too near. He would stick the prongs of his pitchfork into your flesh, lift you up, and toss you into his burning furnace. The Devil was the most evil, most vicious, most cruel, the most terrible thing in existence. He wanted your soul. He wanted to take your soul to hell with Him. He was miserable and unhappy, and suffering. And He wanted all of mankind to be miserable and suffer with Him.

Richard had no trouble seeing the Devil. The Devil was everywhere. The Devil was in the wind and the cold. The Devil was in the sky and the rain; he was in the thunder and lightning and all the black clouds. The Devil was in the sea. He made the sea rumble and crash with waves. He was the pulling fingers of the under-toe and the storms that crashed huge metal ships and cast them about like little toys. The Devil was in the wind and the fire. The Devil was in all the bullies who roamed his streets. The Devil was in his mother's eyes and in his father's drunken wretchedness. The Devil was in the dying leaves and the marble stones at the graveyard. The Devil was all that was evil and corrupt.

And God? God was quite scary Himself. God was "All mighty." He flooded the earth once and drowned everybody except one fellow that he liked, named Noah. He turned a nice lady into a block of salt just because she looked over her shoulder one time when He had told her not to. He threw Adam and Eve out of the Garden of Eden because they took a bite out of an apple when He said not to. He chased the Devil out of Paradise. The Devil was once God's most prized angel. He was called Lucifer. Lucifer wanted to take over heaven. God, with the help of His army of angels, tossed Lucifer out of heaven. Then God created hell. He needed a terrible place to put Lucifer into. If hell was the most evil and most terrible place in all of existence, then how much more terrible must be the one who created it? God made hell, and God would send Richard there if Richard acted badly.

Was God someone to love? Or, was God someone to fear? We are "God fearing" people. This is good? Yes, it is good to be God fearing. God had a very bad temper too. Just like Richard's mother. Sometimes Richard thought that he was being good, but his mother said that he was being bad. What if Richard thought that he was being good, but God thought that he was being bad? Would God then send Richard to hell?

Adam simply took a little bite out of Eve's apple and look how mad God got. Both Adam and Eve had only been a little bad, and God threw them from heaven and opened the gates of hell to them. He gave them pain and suffering, and disease and death; all this for just eating an apple. Richard had already done worse than that in his short life. How would God look upon him?

God had destroyed the world a couple of times. One time He made all of the people of the world speak different languages so that they couldn't help one another to escape. What about that poor lady who looked over her shoulder? Had she done such a bad thing?

One time God tortured this poor man named Job. Job seemed like a very nice, poor old man. God wanted to test Job's faith. Why?

God gave Job boils and made him sick. Why? God also sent plagues and famines to punish people. Why?

Actually God wasn't much less frightening than the Devil. What about God and Richard? One of the commandments said to honor thy father and thy mother. If you didn't it was a sin. If it was a sin to not honor your mother, what was it if you hated your mother? What was it if you sometimes wished that she would die? If his mother would die, his father would finally have peace. If his mother were dead maybe Richard could go and live with Grandma and Uncle Ray. If she were dead, maybe his dad would not need so much money. He and his brother and sister could all get a job. Maybe with the whole bunch of them working, his father could stay around home. If his mother were dead wouldn't life be much better for everyone?

If it is a sin not to honor thy mother, what kind of horror is it if you wished that she were dead? If God could turn a woman into a block of salt for simply looking over her shoulder when He told her not to; if God could throw Adam and Eve out of heaven just because they ate an apple; if God could create a horrible place like hell simply because He got mad at one of his most favorite creations; if He could drown the whole world and everything in it because some stupid people were praying to a cow or trying to build some tower so that they could climb up to heaven, then what did He have in store for poor Richard?

Richard was afraid of the Devil, but even more afraid of God. God was even more powerful than the Devil. God was the creator of all things. God had made the Devil and then put the Devil into hell. What had the poor Devil done to deserve such a horrible fate? Did he hate God and wish that God were dead, as Richard did his mother? No. In fact, the Devil admired God. He didn't hate Him. The Devil's sin was that he wanted to become more like God. He idolized God and wanted to be exactly like God.

Was that so terrible? Certainly it would have been much worse if the Devil had hated God and wished that God was dead, like Richard wished his mother to be dead. So what did God think of Richard? The Devil wanted Richard and God wanted to punish Richard. Richard knew that the Devil wanted him, and he knew that God wanted to punish him. Every night he feared that God would send the Devil to get him after he fell asleep. That is why he made his big brother hold onto his hand. That is why he prayed himself to sleep every night. Every night he said the Rosary. When he finished the Rosary he would then pray; "Oh my God, I am heartily sorry for having offended Thee..." He would say that prayer over and over until he would finally fall asleep.

Each morning when he awoke, he would thank God for sparing him during the night. He thanked Jesus and the Blessed Virgin because he knew that they must have calmed God down. God would have certainly sent the Devil to take Richard to hell if it were not for Jesus and his mother Mary. Mary was kind and understanding. Jesus was a person who understood pain and suffering. Jesus knew what Richard was going through. Jesus had been beaten and had suffered at the hands of others, also. It probably took all of their combined strength just to hold God off and keep Him from Richard. God's temper had to be a million, million times worse than even Richard's mother's. Richard was grateful and he truly loved Jesus and Mary. He always prayed to them for his safety.

He would certainly need them tonight on his trip to the bakery. He stopped on the front porch and as he stared out into the darkness he said quietly under his breath; "Jesus, Mary, and Joseph, protect me. Jesus, Mary and Joseph protect me. Jesus, Mary and Joseph protect me." He would repeat this prayer as he ran down the street and rushed through the patches of darkness and light. The Devil was the darkness and God was the light.

The light on Chelmsford Street was supplied by the power company. It hung from the telephone poles, but it was nonetheless, the light from God Himself. As long as Richard stood in the street under the glow of the streetlight bulb, he was safe and protected by the warmth of the halo of Jesus which was in this case a buzzing streetlight bulb.

It was a cold windy night and his mother had given him a twenty-dollar bill. She had never ever given him a twenty-dollar bill to go to the store. She didn't want to on this occasion. From the way his mother always griped and complained about money, Richard never thought that his mother ever possessed a twenty-dollar bill. But there it was.

She tucked it into the palm of his left hand and wrapped his fingers around it. She squeezed them tight.

"Do not lose this. Do you understand?"

"Yes."

"I mean it. That's a twenty-dollar bill. When you give it to the lady, you tell her that it is a twenty."

"Okay," he said, rushing for the door.

"Hold it! What are you going to tell the lady?" she interrogated.

"I'm going to tell her that it is a twenty-dollar bill."

"That's right! If you lose that twenty, don't bother coming home. You get me?"

"Yeah, I understand," he said, dejectedly. It hurt to think that a twenty-dollar bill was more important than he was, but he knew that it was true.

The wind was blowing and the light rain was streaking past the glow of the streetlight bulb. It was rain at the moment, but shortly it would be snow. The sidewalks were covered with snow from a previous storm. The road had been plowed. The snow from the road was piled up in the gutters. Most people had shoveled a pathway along their sidewalk. There were, of course, some who hadn't shoveled at all.

The first streetlight was directly in front of his house. It was four blocks and five streetlights to the bakery. The distance from the light in front of his house to the one on the corner, was the longest stretch of darkness of the entire journey. Across the street and draping out into the middle of the road was a huge maple tree. The trunk of the tree was so big that children could hide themselves completely behind it. Its branches stretched and reached out and around the streetlight that extended out over the center of the road. Many of the tree's limbs were blanketed in white. They looked like the giant tentacles of an octopus or a hairy spider sprawling above the light and off into the darkness.

The Donahues next-door still had their apartment lights on. The Houlihans, two apartments up, had their lights on also. The rest of the street was black and empty. His chosen path would be right up the middle of the road. He would move slowly and cautiously until he reached the edge of the Houlihans' apartment-light shadow. From that point, he would dash at top speed until he struck the circle of light at the corner and temporary safety.

He proceeded slowly past the Donahues, dawdling through the safe beams of his home streetlight. He then meandered towards the opposite side of the road and the comforting light of the Houlihans. Suddenly, without warning, the yellow fire hydrant stationed at the edge of the Donahue complex, leaped towards him. His heart jumped. He burst into a run. Then when he realized that fire hydrants couldn't move he slowed down to a skip and then returned to a walk. The real darkness began at the edge of the Houlihans chainlink fence where Georgie Fortune's house began. He would catch his breath and reserve his strength until he reached that point. Then it would be a long, full-out dash until he hit the circle of light cast on the ground by the streetlight on the corner.

BANG! A door slammed at the Houlihans. That crazy dog of theirs came rushing towards him. It leaped up and onto the fence. It leaped and jumped as if it were trying to hurdle the fence. The dog had already bit Richard once. On one occasion the dog had gotten loose when Richard was passing and it had chased him all the way to the opposite end of the street whereupon Richard leaped over a wooden fence. He was held hostage by the dog for a goodly time. Richard feared the Houlihans' dog. Richard was now stopped dead in his tracks as the dog rushed towards the chainlink fence barking, drooling, growling and snarling.

Could that stupid dog leap over that fence, he wondered? Would he run right through the fence? The dog stopped at the fence and ranted ferociously. People's dogs were often mean and chased Richard. Richard always dreamed of having his own dog, a dog that was bigger and stronger than all other dogs, a dog that would scare all of the other dogs away. Dogs were funny, but most of the time dogs were mean. Dogs always chased kids and especially Richard.

One night when Richard went to the bakery, his mother had given him an extra six cents for a raisin coffee roll. He bought his bread, buns and coffee roll at the bakery and then sat down on the bottom porch step at the apartment next to the bakery. He would eat his coffee roll there with the light from the bakery and the streetlight from the adjacent corner shining brightly. The coffee roll had cinnamon, raisins, walnuts and a delicious sweet glaze on top. It was big. It was at least a five inch square. He had taken one bite and was counting all the raisins that were then exposed on the inside of the bun. When he looked up from the roll, a huge dog was staring him directly in the face. Richard jumped with a start. Then he began to inch himself up the stairs - backwards. He didn't take his eyes from the dog. It was a St. Bernard dog. The dog stood as tall as Richard stood himself. When Richard got to the top step, he slipped back against the wall to a standing position. The dog came right up the steps and proceeded towards him. It walked up to him and stared him right in the eyes. Then it began licking him on the face.

The big dog's tongue slurping his face tickled and made Richard laugh. The dog then began to sniff at his coffee roll. "No!" Richard scolded in his best professional dog trainer's voice. "Sit!" he commanded. The dog sat down. This dog had to be the ugliest dog in the world. It had big, droopy, old eyes, and long trains of spit dribbling from the sides of its mouth. It seemed big enough to pick Richard up and carry him away. Instead it sat when Richard commanded. Then it lifted up its paw, as if it wanted to shake hands and make friends. Richard shook the big dog's paw. He patted the dog on the head, but when he did, the dog leered towards his coffee roll once again. "Are you hungry?" Richard asked the dog. The dog woofed. This dog clearly understood what he was saying, Richard felt.

Richard began talking with the dog and feeding it little pieces of his coffee roll. "Where do you live? Are you lost? You're a hungry doggie, aren't you?" Richard fed the dog and petted him on his huge head at the same time. He had never before touched such a huge and threatening animal. He petted the dog for a long while. The dog was happy to get petted. The giant dog eventually laid down and began rolling on its back and making what seemed to Richard to be sounds of pleasure. This big, giant, menacing dog liked Richard. Richard felt that he had tamed a wild beast. Certainly this dog would respond to no one else as it had responded to Richard.

Dogs were funny. They were like adults, kind of. Dogs owned things too. A dog owned his yard. Like the Houlihans' dog. If you got too close to his fence he would chase you. People in the neighborhood were like that also. If you went into Mr. Donahue's yard, he would chase you. If you were playing ball, and your ball went into Mr. Jerczick's yard, he would take it and keep it. One time Mr. Donahue chased Richard and a friend down the street and behind the big block building. Richard jumped into a garbage can that was half-filled with garbage. He flipped the lid over and held onto the handle with all his might.

Mr. Donahue chased them because they had broken two sticks out of his hedge. They had broken the sticks out of his hedge because they made the perfect sticks for a bow and arrow. They bent just right, and they had the perfect amount of spring. But when Mr. Donahue saw them getting the sticks from his hedge, he didn't ask them why they were getting those sticks. He just picked up a piece of wood and began running towards them. It was clear to Richard and his friend that Mr. Donahue had popped his cork. He was just like Houlihans' dog. People were infringing on his hedge. He would attack and hit them with a stick or bite them. Adults were always chasing after kids. They would always be yelling at them.

One time Richard was playing in front of Mrs. Houlihan's house. He was playing with Joey Kleenex. Joey hit a rubber ball with a stick. It went up onto the second floor porch of Mrs. Houlihan's house. Mrs. Houlihan then came out onto the porch. Richard asked if she would throw the ball back to them. She began to yell and scream. She said that she would never give them their ball back. She said that he and Joey were nothing but a couple of dumb Polacks.

Why was she yelling and calling them names? The boys then ran to Richard's house and told his mother what Mrs. Houlihan had said.

"What's a Polack?" asked Richard.

"Where did you hear that?" his mother asked.

"Mrs. Houlihan said that we were both just a couple of dumb Polacks."

"She did! Well, you go back over there and tell her that she is nothing but a big-mouthed, old, drunken Harp."

"A big-mouthed, drunken ... what?"

"Harp."

Joey and Richard looked at one another. This was a very strange request. Children for the most part just ran and hid when confronted by adults. But Richard's mother had told them to do it. This was like an order. They had better do it, they thought. So with great reluctance and serious inhibitions, they marched back over to Mrs. Houlihan's house. They called to her from the sidewalk. They cupped their hands to the sides of their mouth and screamed her name.

"Mrs. Houlihan! Mrs. Houlihan!" They yelled her name six to eight times before Mrs. Houlihan appeared on her porch.

"What? Don't think for a minute that you are going to get this ball back."

Joey and Richard were both quite nervous and ill at ease about this. They looked back over their shoulders. Richard's mother was standing on her porch with her arms folded across her chest. Neither of the boys was in the habit of yelling or talking back to adults. This was all kind of scary. It was kind of exciting also, and it had to be done. They cupped their hands to the sides of their mouths and simultaneous screamed.

"My mother said to tell you (Joey screamed, Mrs. Noble said to tell you) that you are a big-mouthed, drunken heart."

"What did you say?" Mrs. Houlihan said rushing up to the porch railing.

"My mother said (his mother said) that you are nothing but a big-mouthed, drunken heart."

"A big-mouthed, drunken heart?" she screamed at them questioning. The two boys looked at one another and shrugged their shoulders in agreement. "It's not heart, you stupid Polacks. It's Harp! You Polacks are so dumb that you can't even say it right."

The boys didn't know what to make of all of this. They thought for a brief second then screamed back in unison.

"Yeah, you know what you are, anyway. Don't you?" Now they could hear Mrs. Noble laughing from two doors down. They must have said something right.

On another occasion, the street kids were playing catch with a football in front of Mr. Jackson's house. The ball was tossed errantly. It bounced on his fence and tumbled into his yard. Before the boys could draw straws to see who would retrieve it, Mr. Jackson came running from his house. He snatched the ball up from the ground.

"Could we have our ball back, please, Mr. Jackson?"

"Sure," Mr. Jackson said with a grin. Then he pulled out his pocket knife and stabbed the football with it. He then tossed the deflated ball out into the street.

Adults were strange. They were similar to dogs, barking, biting, snapping and growling. It was like they owned the world. Put a little piece of grass someplace and they all rushed to build a fence around it.

Richard had some cousins who came to visit Grandma's from the country once. The thing that surprised his cousins most about the city was that everyone had a fence.

"Where we live," one of his little cousins said, "we have people who own miles and miles of land and they have no fences. Here, people own a little itsy-bitsy piece of ground and they build a great big fence around it. How come?" Richard thought that was a very good question and he had an immediate answer to it.

"They want to keep all the kids out of their yards," he told his little cousin.

"Why? Don't they like kids?"

"No sir, only their own."

One time, the street kids had nailed a peach bushel basket on a telephone pole. When one of them would miss his shot, the basketball would bounce over Mr. Solomon fence. The kids would jump over the fence to get their ball. When Mr. Solomon saw a boy straddling his fence, he would sic his two Doberman Pinschers onto him. Bobby Hannigan nearly got the seat of his pants bit off. Everybody had a fence and everybody had a dog to protect their fences.

Mr. Watson, up on the corner, had a German police dog tied up to a tree in his yard. The dog would get so angry when anybody would walk by his fence that he would nearly choke himself to death struggling to break his chain. Most of the fur around his neck was rubbed raw from pulling at the end of his chain.

Dogs and people were very much alike. They were both pretty mean and pretty selfish. Richard liked cats better than dogs. Cats were always afraid of people. Richard could understand their feelings on the matter. Cats always ran from you and not towards you. Cats knew how mean people could be. They didn't trust a one of them. Richard was good at making cats come to him. He liked to pet them. Cats climbed people's fences also. They went strolling through people's yards; people tossed things at them and chased after them just as they did with children. Cats knew that they didn't really own anything and that they had no right to go everywhere, but just like kids they roamed anywhere and did whatever they felt, anyway. When people yelled at them or chased them, well, that was all just a part of being a cat, or a child; cats and children had lots in common - neither seemed to belong anywhere. Though people fed them occasionally, nobody really seemed to want either of them.

Richard always wanted a great big dog like that St. Bernard. Then, when another dog would come running at him, he would say "Get 'em boy!" and his dog would beat up the other dog.

He encouraged the St. Bernard to follow him home that night. With that big dog with him, he felt safe. With that dog he was not afraid of the dark, and he didn't rush from streetlight to streetlight. But tonight, once again, he was without protection.

He was just stepping out of the glow of the Houlihan's kitchen light. It was at the point that he should start running, but he knew that if he did, the Houlihan's dumb dog would flip out. So, he walked for a few paces into the darkness. He slowly and cautiously slipped by Georgie Fortune's house. By the time that he reached Kenny Black's house, everything was pitch-black. Things were already beginning to appear in the darkness. There was a strange animal hiding in Mrs. Camplin's hedges. He was sure of it. He could see its evil eyes glaring at him from behind the bare, dormant sticks. He was also approaching a parked car. Parked cars were a big, big problem. Any number of Devils could be hiding behind a parked car. You wouldn't be able to see them either. They would all wait until you got real close and then they would leap out and grab you. They would then drag you over to a sewer and toss you into it. Once inside the sewer other demons would grab onto you and pull you down into hell. Parked cars were a big danger, a very big and a very serious danger.

"Clang! Clang!" A noise in the darkness rattled like the chains of a ghost. Richard's heart leaped. He put aside any thoughts of skipping and immediately burst into a full-out run. From there to the light on the corner it would be an all-out gallop for his life. He slapped himself on the thigh as he ran to make himself go faster. Just like the cowboys did to their horses in the movies. He had to hit himself because he was his own horse.

He zigged and zagged because that would be trickier: just like Crazy Legs Hersh on the football field, or John Wayne dodging the machine gun bullets as he ran to dive into a foxhole. He ran right up to the parked car. When he got to the rear bumper, he dashed off to the opposite side of the street. This action would delude the Devil. When the Devil leaped out from behind the bumper, Richard would have zigged out of his grasp. The Devil would miss and fall flat on his face, and Richard would get away.

It worked perfectly. Richard saw the Devil leap out at him. He didn't turn around to look at Him. The Devil didn't like to be tricked and he would be up in no time at all. He would be on Richard's heels.

Sure enough, there He was breathing down Richard's back. Richard switched into double speed and super zag. He slapped himself on both thighs with both hands alternately like the jockey's did to their horses coming down the stretch. Yet he had to be careful and clinch his hand even tighter around his mother's twenty-dollar bill. He could feel the Devil's breath on his neck and his evil fingers grabbing at his shoulders. He wiggled his shoulders and zigged and zagged quickly. This threw the Devil off and then with a sudden burst of speed he was into the glow and the safety of the first streetlight at the corner.

He stopped in the center of the light beam cast upon the road and spun around quickly to see if he could catch the Devil trying to encroach into the protective safety of God's divine light. But, the Devil didn't dare. The Devil hated the light like a vampire. As Richard panted, a smile came to his face. It was very, very close, but he had beaten the Devil to the corner. The Devil didn't know how fast Richard could run or how fast he could zig and zag. Now Richard would rest.

"Are you all right?" A voice jumped out at him from the darkness. Richard yelped and spun around to face the sound. An old lady was standing there next to the Arlington schoolyard fence. She was wearing a long winter coat and a kerchief about her head and ears. She was carrying a knit bag with two wooden handles, just like the one his Grandma Essick had. He looked up at the old woman's face. The glow from the streetlight cast a shadow at the woman's head. Richard saw only a kerchief with a black, empty space inside.

This was not his grandmother or even an old woman. It was the Devil and he was trying to trick Richard by pretending to look like his grandmother. Without a word Richard was off and running at full gallop. The road was lined with parked cars. He zigged and zagged and leaped and jumped. Twice the Devil had him by the neck but he pulled himself away. But suddenly the Devil reached up through a pothole and grabbed Richard by the ankle. Richard went tumbling to the ground. Even though he had twisted his ankle and it hurt terribly, he rolled over onto his back and kicked at the Devil like crazy. He then leaped back to his feet and ran off as fast as he could. He could no longer run that fast because he had twisted his ankle but he zigged and zagged extra until he got to Bruder's penny candy store and the second streetlight.

He stopped and checked around for any Devils. He looked back towards the Arlington school. There was that old lady still standing there. From this perspective he could see that she had a real face with a real nose and everything. Could it be that it was just an old lady and not really the Devil in disguise?

He stared at the old woman just to see if she would disappear. She didn't. He raised his right hand tentatively and waved to the woman. She stared for a moment and then shook her head. She then tossed a hand into the air in an obvious gesture of disgust. She turned and proceeded on her way.

Richard felt bad that he might have frightened the old woman. But how did he really know? Wasn't it better not to take the chance? She was an old lady, and she didn't seem afraid to be out in the dark. She must be crazy. There was never anybody on these streets at this time of night. She still could have been the Devil. Certainly Jesus and the Blessed Virgin wouldn't let the Devil outwit Richard. Would they?

Nevertheless, from this position to the next streetlight Richard would proceed more bravely. One must be brave. One must have faith. He would walk through the darkness. He would not skip, hop or run. He would take one step at a time. Yes it would be scary. Sure it would be frightening. But if the Devil really wanted him and Jesus and Mary didn't, couldn't the Devil just capture him lickety-split? If Jesus, Mary and Joseph really loved him, wouldn't they cluster around him and fight the Devil off even in the darkness? Of course they would.

Suddenly a bolt of terror shot up from his calf to his brain. He had positioned himself on top of a sewer cover and something was crawling up from the sewer and wrapping itself about his leg. He closed his eyes and didn't move while he braced himself to be carried off into the pits of hell and eternal damnation. "Jesus, Mary and Joseph protect me; Jesus Mary and Joseph protect me." He repeated over and over. But the demon kept circling about his calf. It must be a snake.

The devil often took the form of a snake. He had been a snake in the Garden of Eden when he tricked Adam and Eve. The devil snake was slithering about Richard's calf. He would wind himself up Richard's leg. He would coil about Richard's entire body. Then he would pull Richard down into the sewer and from the sewer into the depths of hell.

If Richard had faith, he would stand there quietly like Job, and wait for Jesus, Mary and Joseph to save him. He tried but couldn't stand to just let the snake take him over. He kicked his leg out violently and screamed. "Get away from me you Devil! Leave me alone!" He peeked down at his leg to get a glimpse of the Devil, but saw only a small, black cat cowering and dashing off for a small distance. Quickly he stooped down and called to the cat. "I'm sorry kitty, kitty," he said. "I didn't mean to kick you. I had a black kitty just like you once."

The cat came towards him cautiously. He touched the cat and it began to purr. A kitty's fur was always soft. It was something special if a stray cat liked you, because cats didn't like or trust just anyone. Cats were smart. As he petted the kitty it wound about him in circles. If he stopped petting the cat it pushed its nose up against his hand as if it wanted to be petted some more.

This cat was, more than likely, coming from the house on the corner. This house had a tall chainlink fence around it and it was called the Cat Lady's house. There was an old woman who lived beyond the chainlink fence and inside the big old wooden house. No one knew exactly what the old woman looked like. Occasionally you might see her walking on the inside of her screened-in porch. It was a big, old house but all of the paint was pealing off. Trees and shrubs had grown up all around it. She had a great big yard. Several tenement houses could have been built inside her yard. Her yard was all grown over with trees and bushes. In the summer time she just let the grass grow and grow. The whole yard would look like a field of hay. The kids all said that the Cat Woman was a crazy woman. If you went through her yard and she caught you, she would grab you and grind you up into hamburg so that she would have food for all of her cats. Richard thought that this story might be true. She had a million cats. She didn't work. Her house was all run down. She didn't take care of her property; so she was probably not rich. If she wasn't rich, where did she get the money to feed all of her cats? Human hamburger seemed very possible. He didn't know if any kids were missing from the neighborhood, but many of his neighbors had so many kids that if one or two came up missing, they probably would never have noticed.

As he stared down Arlington Street he saw now that the old woman had stopped and was peering down the street at him once again. Who was she anyway? He stared back at her, but she just stood there. Finally the old woman began shaking her head. Then she began yelling at him. He tried to figure out what she was yelling, but she was yelling in a strange language. It wasn't Polish. He knew what Polish sounded like from listening to his Grandma Essick and her Polish radio. Polish went like this: Yuk-she push-key mush-key e-dube-ski. He liked to listen to the Polish guy on his grandmother's radio. The man had a very deep voice and was very funny. He would say things like, Mush-key pa-dog-ski hot-dog. Pier-robi estrob-bia Chevrolet USA pin-kay-ya. It was funny.

The old woman would scream a little, then walk a little, then turn and scream at him once again. She had a little "push-key" in her accent but more "pa-dobna-row-bich" and "pa-dobna-ray-bich." She was probably Russian or something like that and not Polish like his grandmother. Russian people looked like Polish people though. He had seen some Russian people one Sunday coming out of the Russian Orthodox Church on Willow Street. The men parted their hair in the middle just like his Uncle Joe, and some of them had spaces between their front teeth just like Polish people did. But you could speak Polish or Russian and still be an American. Americans spoke many different languages. His Grandma Essick was an American now, but she used to live in Poland. She came here on a ship with her husband.

Richard never met his Grandma Essick's husband. He never met his father's father either. He never even saw any pictures of them, but nevertheless, he felt that he knew them. His Polish grandfather was a kind and generous man. He gave everything away and never kept anything for himself. His grandfather was like his Uncle Joe.

His Irish grandfather also seemed to be a nice person, but for some reason he came home every night and strapped his children. He did it because his wife told him to. Richard knew that his Irish grandfather was a wonderful person because if he wasn't, Richard's father would not have loved him so much.

When Richard's dad was a little boy, he was a good Catholic, too. He was an altar boy, just like Richard. When his father died he stopped going to church forever. Richard's grandfather's death hurt Richard's father so much that he took a vow never to develop such a close relationship with his own children. Richard's father did not want his children to suffer as he had.

Richard's mother told Richard that story one time when Richard asked her why it was that his dad didn't like him. He thought that his dad didn't like him because he never took him to any baseball games or fishing and because he never hugged or kissed or touched him like other kids' fathers did. Never while he was sober, anyway. Richard knew the difference between drunk and sober. When someone was drunk, they weren't acting like themselves. When his dad was drunk, he was certainly not being himself. When he was being himself, he was cold, aloof and distant, to say the least.

His dad as himself was alone. He was quiet. He never laughed. He never cried. He never spoke, other than to scold: "Get out into the kitchen and eat that apple! Don't play in here! Get out doors; Quiet down! Be still! Go to bed!"

His dad had made a personal oath not to get close to his children. He really didn't hate or even dislike Richard. It was that oath. He didn't want Richard to be hurt when he died. His dad was really a kind, thoughtful person who only kept his distance from Richard because he loved him too much to see him suffer.

But yet, the thought often occurred to Richard that if an adult didn't want to love a child why did he have a child in the first place? No one forced anyone to have children. Nuns and priests didn't have any children. Lots of people didn't have any children. His Uncle Joe didn't have any children. His dad not only had one child, he had three.

If his dad was really such a thoughtful, decent person why did he leave his children alone with a crazy person? In fact, how could he leave his children in the hands of a woman like Richard's mother? He had to know that she beat them up, didn't he? His father never hit. He didn't believe in hitting. His mother never hit the children when he was watching. Could it be that his father really didn't know what kind of a woman his wife was?

He knew. He had to know. He knew. He just didn't know what to do about it. Richard's mother had his father trapped. She had tricked him. Women were more clever than men. Richard would not be that stupid.

The old woman finally disappeared up a side street and into the darkness. She only stopped to wave her fist at him. All women were crazy.

Richard was now crouched in the middle of the street on the sewer cover, petting the friendly black cat. The cat was happy to have a friend. Richard must move on. He had completely forgotten about the twenty-dollar bill. He opened his clinched fist to see if it were still there. It was. It was all crushed up and squashed like an old piece of scrap paper, but it was there. The bakery was but two blocks away. He had better get moving. He said his good-byes to the kitty and started on his way. He would now move right into the darkest street of the whole ordeal. He proceeded slowly as he faded out of God's light and into the Devil's darkness. The same old fear returned. Instead of running he would put his fears aside and trust in the protection of Jesus and the Blessed Mother.

Two cars were parked on the left side of the street in the deepest part of the darkness. It took no genius to figure that was the most obvious place for the Devil to hide. While in the darkness it was so frightening - in the light it was bright and safe.

Why did God create the night? Why didn't He just always leave it light? Those were silly questions that he already knew the answer to. Like for Job and others, this was all a test. If you passed the test you went to heaven, and if you flunked, you went to hell. You only went to hell if you had sins on your soul.

If you had no sins on your soul when you died, you went to heaven - as long as you had previously been baptized, of course. The Catholic Church was the one true Church. All of the other churches had been made up by men. Only the Catholic Church was started by Jesus Christ Himself. I am Peter and upon this rock, I will build my Church. That is what Jesus said to Peter one day.

Every day in school they learned about the Bible. They studied their Catechism, and the nuns told stories. The nuns always quoted from the Bible. They told stories about the Light from the Bible.

Richard learned many things in school. He knew many big words: crucifixion, resurrection, confirmation, genuflection and ejaculation. When you went down on one knee before entering into your pew inside church, that was a genuflection. When you said, Jesus, Mary and Joseph, protect me - that was an ejaculation. When you got confirmed you got a scapular. A scapular was a holy picture on a string that you wore around your neck. But, nevertheless, Richard lived in constant fear. If he were to die at this very moment, he would go straight to hell. He would go straight to hell because he never ever told the priest in the confessional that he hated his mother and that very often he wished that she would die. In the confessional all he ever said was that he didn't honor his father and mother four or six or eight times. He never said any more than that. Was that good enough for God? He didn't really think so.

Honoring thy father and thy mother meant doing what you were told, going to bed when you were supposed to, and not talking back. It didn't cover hating and wishing that your poor mother was dead. How could anyone hate their own mother? It wasn't right. It was probably the worst possible sin that anyone could ever commit.

He would walk through the darkness at a normal pace. The drizzle had now turned to snow and the snow flakes were tumbling by the bulb on the streetlamp up ahead. He hoped that it would snow hard. Then, maybe, they would call off school in the morning. If there were no school, they would blow the big horn down at the fire station. It would take a lot of snow for that to happen. It would take a whole bunch of snow.

He was now approaching the two parked cars. He wanted to run. With each step that he now took towards the two parked cars he became more and more confident that the Devil was hiding between them. He wouldn't allow himself to run. He would stand up to his fears. He would face the music. He would be brave. It couldn't hurt to pray a little though. He began saying Hail Marys as fast as he could. After that he started in to whistle just like the seven little dwarfs on Walt Disney used to do. He whistled for a few paces, but then decided that whistling couldn't be nearly as good as praying. Praying made him more frightened. Maybe he could whistle and pray at the same time. He tried, but it seemed that when he was praying, he couldn't whistle; and when he was whistling, he wasn't able to pray. You had to think to pray, and you had to think to whistle. He couldn't think two different things at the same time. But then like a lightning bolt he got his best idea. He would whistle the Hail Mary.

Suddenly on the right he saw a shadow. On the right was a small sawmill. The shadow was moving about the loading dock. Maybe the shadow was the Devil and He was now on the loading dock! Maybe the cars were now a safe haven.

Sure enough, there was the Devil. He could see the Devil's shadow slinking about in the darkness. But maybe with the help of God and his whistling of the Hail Mary he could make it past the Devil unnoticed.

As he passed the two cars on the left, he searched them thoroughly. Was that something moving in that yard just beyond them? It looked like a man. The man was sneaking from one tree to another. Richard kept his eyes on the shadowy movements but all the while he continued to walk and whistle the Hail Mary. Oh no! He had forgotten about the other shadow on the sawmill loading dock. He jerked his head to see if the demon had advanced.

It was gone. There before him, not more than six paces, was the circle of light from the streetlight glow. He could dash up to it and safety. But just then he felt the breath of the Devil on his neck. The Devil had snuck right up behind him and was going to grab him up just before he reached the safety of the streetlight's glow. The Devil had only been toying with him. It was all a game. The devil had allowed him to whistle his way through the darkness, and now at the very last moment he would grab Richard up. He would laugh ghoulishly as He then dragged Richard over to the sewer and down into hell.

But if the Devil is there, the Devil is there. If it is now Richard's destiny to go to hell, he must go to hell bravely. He would not run. He WOULD NOT run. Two or three fast little steps would be okay though. And there he was, standing safely in the Divine warmth and safety of God's Light. Once in the light he spun around quickly. The Devil was gone.

Unbelievably, he had walked through the shadow of darkness and he had made it safely. He had met the challenge without running. This was a first. The snow had blanketed the ground with a light, thin covering. He could see his footprints behind him. They led up and into the light, then drifted back and into the darkness. There were no other footsteps - just his.

But, would the Devil make footsteps? Maybe not. It was peculiar, but once in the light, it seemed foolish to be worrying about the Devil. From this point on, his journey was well lit. The next two blocks were short and there was a light on each corner. He could even see the light from the glow of the baker's window.

Now he could run. Not because he was afraid but just because he wanted to. He galloped off into the streetlight glow. Galloping was different from "speeding" or just plain running. Galloping is what the big horses did. It had a rhythm to it. Like this: tha-dump, tha-dump, tha-dump, tha-dump. This was opposed to running or speeding which was, dadah dadah, dadah da-dah. Galloping was fast, but not as fast as speeding. When you galloped you hopped and bounced a little. That is what made the tha-dump sound, and not the dadah sound. He kind of jumped on the "tha" and landed on the "dump." You could even make it sound like more of a gallop if you slapped your right leg when your right foot hit the ground. In any case, he galloped his way right up to the bakery door. Once inside he stepped into the waiting line. There were not more than ten people ahead of him.

10 A Trip Home from the Bakery

It was toasty inside the bakery. It was always toasty inside the bakery. The line began in a storage area. It then led up to a door. Buzzing about at the doorway was the nice Polish lady with the gold tooth. She was always smiling and saying thank-you. Sometimes she said thank-you in Polish, jing-koo-ya, it sounded like. His grandmother often said words in Polish. "Yesh-ye-mush," she would say. He didn't know what the word or phrases meant but if he answered yes, his grandmother would grab him up, give him hugs and kisses and then something to eat. He figured that "Yesh-ye-mush" meant either, kiss my face or stuff my mouth. Either way, he always said yes.

The lady with the gold tooth was putting loaves of hot bread into brown paper bags. Richard peeked around the people ahead of him to observe the bakers with the giant spatulas. Spatulas are not like scapulars. Richard often got the two words mixed up. He once told a nun that he was wearing a spatula under his shirt. She laughed. Before long, he was next in line. He held out his hand with the twenty-dollar bill in it.

"One small, light rye, and a half a dozen bulkies, please," he said as a matter of habit. It was the memorized bakery speech. It was just like the meat market or the Walter's speech; "four slices of Polish ham - very, very thin; or one pound of your cheapest hamburg." He finished his speech with, "Put the change in the bag, please." That is what his mother always told him to say.

There was a baker all dressed in white at each oven. They were sliding in the huge spatula, taking out cooked breads, and putting in uncooked loaves. It was exciting to watch; to look right into the big ovens. To see all the breads lined up inside. The smell - oh the smell! The light rye and the bulkies were just coming out of the ovens. He had timed it perfectly. Everything would be warm and toasty. Richard liked it when the bread was coming hot out of the oven. He would unbutton his jacket, and stick the whole bag of warm bread up under his sweater. Carrying that hot bread against his tummy on a cold night was even better than sitting in front of the stove with your feet up in the oven on a freezing cold winter morning. Coming up through the sweater would be the sweet, warm aroma of the delicious, tasty, crusty smell of that oven baked Polish bread. Sometimes he would even reach down through the neck of his sweater and open the top of the bag for a moment. He would even stuff his nose right into the bag.

The bread under his sweater would keep him warm all the way home. That bread was always toasty and warm. It smelled like the bakery itself. The bakery was always clean, white, warm, and bustling with positive energy. Everybody at the bakery was happy. The bakers were always smiling and laughing. The customers were always grinning. The friendly lady with the gold tooth was always bubbling. It was a neat place to go. It was even fun to carry the bread home. The very best part was eating a crispy chunk of that hot, brown bread with a generous slab of butter on it when he finally got home.

The lady gathered up Richard's order and put it all into a big, brown bag. When she returned to where he was standing, she held the bag open so he could observe her actions.

"Now here is your change." She counted out the change while other customers looked on. When she was through, she rolled it all up and dropped it into the bag. "I put it into the bag, now. Did you see me?"

"Yes, ma'am."

"Okay. You be careful with it, and tell your mother for me that she has given too much money to a little boy to come to the store. Next time, don't bring such a large bill. Okay?"

"Okay."

The lady looked at the other customers and shook her head.

"I hate it when little children come in with so much money. If they lose it, their parents blame me. You know how it is."

The woman didn't speak English all that well. She had an accent. It could have been Polish, but it sounded like German. Richard couldn't distinguish. The lady looked Polish to him.

"I promise, I won't lose it," he told the woman.

"That's a good little boy, and you be sure that you don't." Richard did not really feel that he was still a little boy. He was clearly bigger than little.

"I'm in the third grade at Saint Rita's," he informed the lady. He was sure to say St. Rita's. He knew that everyone was aware how much more advanced St. Rita's was than the typical public school. The only children who went to the public schools were those who weren't smart enough to go to the Catholic schools. Everyone knew that. Richard knew two other boys who were at the same grade level as he but attended a public school. They didn't know half the stuff that Richard knew. They didn't seem to know anything about God and the Virgin Mary, and they didn't know lots of other stuff too.

At St. Rita's you got a much better education. You learned everything and not just some things. Telling the woman that he was in the third grade at St. Rita's would make her have a lot more confidence in him. It would let her know that he was trustworthy and responsible. Catholic children knew better. They knew right from wrong and good from bad. They weren't like the Protestants. The Protestants had churches but God did not live inside their churches. Some of them didn't even have a tabernacle for Jesus to live in. Some Protestants would sing wild songs and roll around the floor of their church. There was this group up on Center Street that called themselves the Holy Rollers. Richard and some of his friends snuck up to the door and peeked in one time. It was true. Those people were inside and rolling all over the place. They were crazy. They were like those people in Africa who danced around a fire and had blowguns and stuff like that. The only difference was that the people in Africa didn't really know any better. The people in Africa still had a chance to go to heaven because they were truly ignorant. They didn't know that the Catholic Church was the one, true church.

The Protestants and the Holy Rollers were different. They knew all about the Catholic Church, and they still wouldn't belong. They had their opportunity and they refused to take it. Unfortunately, they would all be going to hell. Richard felt sorry for all the poor Protestant children. Every time he saw one of them in the streets, he pictured them surrounded by a wall of flames. He could see them screaming in agony and in pain. It was too bad, but what could he do about it? There was a Catholic church on every corner. All that they had to do was go inside and learn the truth. But they refused to do so.

One time he was talking to Kenny Black's older sister. She was big enough to know the truth, but yet, she insisted on being a Protestant. He asked her if she knew that the Catholic Church was the one and only true church, started by God Himself. She said that what Richard had said wasn't really true. Then Richard asked her if they really had golden cows inside of her church instead of Jesus Christ. She said that she also believed in Jesus Christ. She said that she believed in the same God as he did.

"So then, why don't you go to my church?" he asked.

"What difference does it make?" she inquired.

"Because that's where God lives," he told her. She just laughed and said that God lived inside everybody's church. Richard knew that what she said wasn't true because the nuns had told him otherwise. Now he knew why Protestants were going to hell. It was because they just laughed when somebody told them the truth. If God were inside every church, why would there be any need for different churches? How could somebody finally see the light if there were no darkness? Somebody had to be right and somebody had to be wrong. Everybody can't be right. Finally he asked her if she was afraid of going to hell. She said that she wasn't going to hell.

"I'm very sorry," he told her, "but you ARE going to hell."
"Why?" she asked him.

"Because I just told you the truth about God and you won't accept it. That's why all Protestants are going to hell."

She told him that he was crazy and that she thought that all Catholics were crazy. She said that he and all other Catholics were going to hell and not her. Richard could tell that she was getting angry. She was probably afraid to have just found out that she was going to hell.

From then on, whenever Richard went by the Black's house, he felt sorry for them. Sometimes Mr. Black would be sitting out front on his porch in his T-shirt drinking a can of beer. Mr. Black would always say hello. He seemed like such a nice fellow. It was too bad that he and all of his family were going to hell. What could Richard do about it? If they wouldn't believe; they wouldn't believe.

Mr. Black was always laughing. He really didn't look any different than anybody else. But you didn't have to look funny to be going to hell. Actually both Richard's mother and father were going to hell. They never went to church on Sunday. Not going to church on Sunday was a mortal sin. If you died with a mortal sin on your soul you went to hell. Those people in Africa didn't know that the Catholic Church was the one true church. They were just ignorant. They weren't plain stupid, like Protestants. They didn't have to go to hell - because they didn't know any better. Of course, they wouldn't be going to heaven either. They couldn't go to heaven because they never got baptized. If you didn't get baptized then you still had Original Sin on your soul. Original Sin was the sin that everyone in the world was born with, because of Adam and Eve.

Actually Adam wasn't really all that bad. It was mostly Eve's fault - when Eve talked Adam into eating the apple back in the Garden of Eden that gave everybody from then on, Original Sin. In fact, that is what caused God to get mad and lock up the gates of heaven. From that time on, no human beings were allowed in.

After the gates of heaven were closed, all of the good people in the world who died went to Limbo. That is where all of the ignorant people in Africa who didn't know any better went when they died also. In fact, Limbo might be right there in Africa someplace, Richard thought. It sounded like an African place.

Limbo was packed with souls right up and until the time that Jesus suffered and died on the cross. That's why He did it. Jesus saved everybody when He died. After that, God opened up the gates of heaven for everybody once again. All the good people who had died before Jesus was killed - who had also been baptized - went into heaven. The people who hadn't been baptized stayed in Limbo - right there in the middle of Africa or someplace even worse. That's where people like them must stay forever.

Richard always thought that it was kind of peculiar that God would open up the gates of heaven to human beings because they tortured and killed His one and only Son. Certainly killing and torturing God's only son had to be an even worse thing to do than eating an apple.

Richard and his whole class were taken to St. Mary's church one afternoon to learn about the "Stations of the Cross." On all of the walls of the church there were sculptures of Jesus. The nun said that they were beautiful sculptures. But they were all about Jesus being beaten and getting killed. That didn't seem so very beautiful to Richard. One showed a Roman soldier sticking the Crown of Thorns into Jesus' head. Others showed Him being lashed with a whip. Others showed Him stumbling under the weight of His cross and falling down. Jesus fell down three times on His way up the hill. Then they showed Him hanging on the cross. There was one sculpture that showed a Roman soldier plunging a big spear into the side of Jesus. The soldiers all laughed as one of them brushed the mouth of Jesus with a sponge filled with vinegar instead of water after Jesus had asked one of them for a drink of water. Another Station of the Cross showed people in the crowd spitting on Jesus.

Doing the Stations of the Cross meant going to each sculpture and meditating in front of it. Meditating meant thinking. Richard did a lot of thinking. He was thinking all the time. Richard was always thinking. He thought every minute of every day. Sometimes he even thought at night when he was afraid to go to sleep because he knew that he had sins on his soul.

God had sent down His only Son, Jesus Christ, to save the people of the world and free all of the souls in Limbo. The people of the earth tortured, beat, and kicked Jesus. Then they stuck thorns into His head and pounded nails through the palms of His hands and His feet. Then they stuck spears into His side and gave Him vinegar to drink instead of water. Because the people of the world did this to Jesus and Jesus wanted to have these horrible things done to Him, God opened up the gates of heaven and let human beings in, once again.

Richard sometimes thought that if people did that to God's Son, God should have hated them even worse and not better. But the nuns always said that God worked His wonders in mysterious ways. God was very much like Richard's mother. You never knew what to expect from her, either. One minute she was giving you a crack in the teeth and the next minute she was baking you biscuits. One minute she was smiling and the next minute she was screaming and yelling in your face. God the Father clearly had a similar type personality. God the

Father couldn't figure out whether He liked people or He didn't like them. One minute He was carving them out of clay to His own image and likeness and the next moment He was throwing them out of heaven because they wanted to be more like Him. Well, if He was angry because they wanted to be more like Him and ate the apple from the tree of knowledge, why didn't He make them stupid in the first place - or content in being stupid, at least?

God was very, very confusing. Often times He didn't even make sense. But children should be seen and not heard, and some things a child just couldn't understand. Richard didn't understand a lot of things. One day he hoped, if he kept the faith, all of these things would become clear to him. For now, he would just have to wonder and think. He would think a lot. He didn't try to think. It just happened.

But for now, he still had to make it home through all the darkness. He took his bag over to the exit door and then stuffed it up and under his sweater. Then he buttoned his jacket up over the big, warm bulge. The bread made him feel all toasty and warm. When he opened the door to leave he saw that many of the customers were watching him. Some of them were laughing and smiling. The bread under his sweater did make him look somewhat funny. Like a little Santa, or a small boy with a grown-up beer belly. He liked to see people laugh even when they were laughing at him. Everybody looked better with a smile on their face. Sometimes he could make his brother and sister laugh. That was always fun.

The snow was beginning to pile up on the ground. Everything was now covered with a thin blanket of snow; the roads, the sidewalk, even the tops of the cars. Even the peaks of the wooden fences had a crust of snow bordering their rims. He bent to the ground and picked up some snow with one hand. It wasn't the good kind of snow. It was too light and powdery. It wouldn't stick together. Good snow was damp and heavy and it would stick together. It was good because you could make snowballs with it.

Well, off he went. He would just gallop home, non-stop. He pulled the sides of his knit cap down over his ears, buried his chin into his chest, and took off - flying. He whipped around the first corner and zoomed off into the distance. He sped by all the parked cars. He whipped, lashed and zigged and zagged.

He leaped over small piles of snow at the sides of the road. Sometimes he would run right up a snow pile and then down the other side.

The snow on the ground brightened the streets. Everything seemed just a little less dark. Within a mere zillionth of a second he was standing under the light at Bruder's penny-candy store across from the Cat Lady's house. He had whipped around the corner and was about to zoom down to Chelmsford Street. The corner at Chelmsford Street was steeped in total darkness. Somebody either busted the bulb on the streetlight with a rock, or it had burnt out.

All the kids used to bust streetlight bulbs. They made a big pop when they burst, and then they "buzzzzed" strangely. Richard could hear the light buzzing like crazy. He had been zipping and zooming, zigging and zagging; everything had been going just perfect until now.

From the corner at Chelmsford Street to his house was the longest stretch of darkness. This would make the darkness twice as long. Should he take the shortcut through the Cat Lady's fence? He always took it in the daytime. You went through the broken board in her fence and then along the fence until you came to the backyard of the large tenement house that was a tenement or two down from the dark corner on Chelmsford Street. Then you went past the garbage barrel shed and along an even bigger wooden fence. If you then scooted in behind the garbage can building and the big fence, you could slide the broken board over and crawl through. That would put you right into the backyard of "the Twins" - Adella and Adona.

The kids called the two old maid school teachers, Adella and A-donut. The Twins were two old school teachers who wore funny clothes and tied their hair up on top of their heads like a bulkie roll or some kind of a bun. All the kids thought that the Twins were weird. No one usually went into their yard. Kids only did it if they were taking the shortcut. But mostly, one only took the shortcut in the daytime. When you passed through the Twins' yard, you hopped over a little fence and there you were - right in front of Kenny Black's house. Then it would be just a quick dash past Houlihans' and the Donahues' and home sweet home.

What would he do now? From the corner of Chelmsford Street to his house was the longest stretch of darkness. That broken light on the corner, made it twice as long. Both choices were spooky and dangerous. There was something foreboding about that buzzing streetlight. It sounded like a giant bug from outer space. Richard didn't really like to go near one.

Well, if both ways were spooky and dangerous why not go the shortest way?

He scooted down along the Cat Lady's chainlink fence; then zipped into the alleyway. It was a tight squeeze and the snow there was deep because no one ever shoveled there. With each step he sank in to about his knees. Shortly he was past the edge of the building. He slipped and fell against the garbage shed. When he did, a ruckus went off. There was a cat or an animal of some kind inside the garbage can shed. It scrambled and knocked off a garbage can lid or tipped over an empty garbage can - or both. There was a banging and clanging, a cat yowling and a bunch of other crazy unexplainable noises. Then he heard a man yell,

"Hey, what the hell is going on down there?"

Richard crouched down into the deep snow behind the garbage building. He would have to be quiet and hide. He didn't like being stuck behind the garbage can building. There were always rats in the garbage. One time he went to throw out the garbage for his mother. He went inside the garbage building that they had out back at home. He lifted the lid on a garbage can and a rat, the size of a small cat, leaped out at him. It jumped on his shoulder and ran right over him. He threw the garbage that he was holding, everywhere. Then he ran away from the garbage shed and started jumping up and down. He threw off his jacket and shook all of his pant legs. He whooped and hollered in overall fear and disgust. For a month afterwards all that he had to do was think of that experience and instantly he could feel that rat on his shoulder, once again. The thought sent chills down his spine and brought goose bumps to his flesh. Now, here he was in the total darkness, kneeling behind a building that was mostly rats. Yuck! He must get out of there. He jumped up and pounced through the heaped snow.

"Hey! What are you doing down there?"

"What is it, Honey?"

"What the hell is going on down there?"

It was really too dark to see anything. Richard kept moving as fast as he could. The man would be onto him in a flash, he thought. He would be down the back porch stairs and grabbing Richard by the collar and shaking the daylights out of him. Richard began to scurry. He was finally at the break in the fence, the one with the broken board. He stepped through the tight space. His jacket got caught on a nail. It was because of the bulky bag of bread that he had tucked under his sweater. He unbuttoned his jacket quickly and tossed the bag in the snow. He tried to undue the tangle. He was too fidgety.

"Who the hell is down here?" The man was down into the backyard. The heck with it! He pulled on his jacket with both hands and it ripped loose from the nail. He pulled his other half through the hole in the fence and went clopping off through the knee-deep snow. Oh no! He had forgotten his bag of bread. He clomped back through the same holes in the deep snow that he had already made. He grabbed up the bag. He spun himself around. He lost his balance and then tumbled over backwards. The bag went flying into the air. The bag had opened and bulkie rolls were scattered about the snow. His mother would go nuts if the rolls were cold. He rushed over to the bag. He gathered up the rolls as quick as he could.

"Oh no! Oh no. Oh no," he kept repeating to himself. This was terrible. He held the last bulkie roll up to the cheek of his face. His hands were too cold to feel anything. It was a miracle. It was still warm. His mother might not even know what had happened. He stuffed the bag back under his sweater. He was off, hurdling through the deep snow heading for the Twins' backyard. Then he scurried down along their hedge. Finally he reached the old wooden gate with the piece of rope for a latch. He had been stumbling and falling down at every step, but there suddenly before him was the reasonably clear paved highway of Chelmsford Street. He put his head down and sped through the heavy falling snow towards his house. There was only one last hurdle now - the hallway.

The hallway was always pitch-black. When you came into the hallway from the street at night it was so black that you couldn't see your hand before your face. You had to feel your way along the wall. That small stretch of hallway was a battleground of demons and ghosts and creepy crawly things. It gave Richard goose bumps just to think about it.

When he got to the hall door he pushed it open violently. This was to catch any Devil who might stupidly be hiding right behind it. The door slammed against the wall and Richard dashed down the corridor. He rushed, banging and bumping, from one wall to the other, heading for the kitchen door. He fumbled all the way down the hall feeling for the kitchen doorknob. The door suddenly opened on its own. His mother had heard the commotion and opened it slightly to peek out. Richard grabbed the door and pulled it open. He pushed by his mother and dashed into the kitchen. He stood there huffing, puffing and panting. His mother closed the door and stared at the boy curiously.

"What the hell is the matter with you? You look like you've seen a ghost."

"Nothing," he answered while thoughtfully contemplating the darkness and all the ghosts he had just suffered through. Was his mother making a joke, or did she know about all the ghosts too?

"Nothing? Then why in God's name are you trying to knock down the house? Get out in that hallway and close that hall door. And if you ever slam that door open like that again, I'll crack your damn skull open."

"I can't! I can't!"

"What do you mean you can't? You had just better, my boy. If you know what's good for you."

Richard just couldn't go back out into that hall. He had all of the darkness and fear that a boy could take for one evening.

"I can't. I ... I ... have to go to the bathroom." He began bouncing from one foot to the other as if he really had to go.

"Oh for God's sake - go ahead, get in there before you pee your pants. And look at you! What, did you get run over by a truck?"

When Richard returned from the bathroom, his mother was at the kitchen table holding the brown bag upside down and shaking it.

"Where's the change, Richard?"

"It's in the bag."

She turned and looked at him with a slow, mounting, silent anger. She rushed towards him. He cowered reflexively.

"Did you put it in your pocket?"

"No. The lady put it in the bag."

"Pull your pockets out!" she screamed. She shoved her hands into all of his pockets and pulled them inside out. There was nothing. Bang! Her arm swung from her side reflexively. She struck him over the left ear, hard enough to send him to the floor. She bent over him and gave him a crack to the back of the head. "YOU DAMN FOOL!" she screamed.

Richard began to tremble from head to toe. "No, wait Ma wait," he whined. "I know where it is. I'll go back and get it." He scurried along the kitchen floor under the kitchen table. He made a mad, scrambling effort to get himself to the front door. He swung open the door and dashed back out into the night. He was going whether she said that he could or not. He wasn't going to stay in that house. He wasn't going to get his "block knocked off." He was not about to have some "damn sense knocked into his dumb skull." He had all the "medicine" that he needed to "learn a lesson that he would never forget." No way! He would go back into the night and the darkness; he would just never come home, ever again.

"You better find that money, kiddo. If you come back here without it, you can be sure that I will break every damn bone in your stupid body."

"Don't worry. Don't worry," he screamed back to her as he ran off into the street.

He had no idea where the money had gotten lost. He would simply have to trace his every step. His ear was hurting. He began to cry just thinking of his mother striking him so hard. She must really hate him. What had he ever done to fill her with such bitterness? One day he would run away and she would never, ever see him again. One day, if she didn't kill him first, he would be big enough to fight back. He would punch her with his fists. He would hit her so hard that she would fall to the floor. He would put his hands around her throat and he would squeeze until she had no breath left. He hated her. She was not his mother. She couldn't be.

He was now sobbing so hard that he could not see the ground before him. How would he find the money if he couldn't see? He must stop his crying. Did the lady really put the money into the bag? Didn't he watch her with his own eyes? She held the money right up in front of his face. She said; "See I'm putting your change into the bag."

It wasn't the Polish bakery lady's fault. His mother was angry enough to kill. She would "beat him to a pulp." He fell to his knees right there in the middle of the street. "Jesus, Mary and Joseph please help me," he wailed, with the tears streaming down his cold cheeks. "God and all the saints in heaven please help me to find this money. Help me this one time and I will never, ever bother any of you ever again."

He got to his feet and continued to pray out loud as he backtracked his every step. If it had fallen out of the bag the wind would have blown it to kingdom come by now. What did he expect, a miracle? What chance did he have of finding it? Why would God or anyone else help him? They were all grown-ups too. They were like his mother. Everyone was like his mother. He must not think like that. He must continue to pray and have hope in the Lord. "Jesus, I would have helped you," he prayed. "I would never have let anyone spit in your face. I would have helped you when the cross was too heavy. I wouldn't have denied you three times like Peter did. I would have been your best friend. I would have wiped your face with a towel like that lady from the crowd. If you help me now, I'll say a rosary every night forever."

Richard already said a rosary every night. He would have to promise more than that. His mother was angry. She had the right to be angry. He was a stupid jerk. He never did anything right. She had good reason to "knock his block off" if that is what she wanted to do. "Oh God, oh God, oh God; please oh please."

He proceeded down Chelmsford Street in this manner. He checked all the snow in front of the Twins' house very carefully. Wasn't that the spot where he had stumbled? He was in the street and out in the darkness, but he no longer cared about the Devil. He was more afraid of his own mother at this moment. But wasn't this all the work of the Devil? This is exactly what the Devil planned for him. The Devil didn't care. He was laughing. He had gotten Richard into trouble by making Richard frightened. The Devil had tricked Richard once again.

As he searched, he carefully stepped into all the same holes in the snow that he had made previously. He stepped slowly and examined every inch.

This was impossible; he would never find it. He would just have to go home and "take his medicine." This was the most foolish thing that he had ever attempted. This was insane. It was like trying to find a needle in a haystack. No, no this was much worse than that. To find a needle in a haystack, he would simply have to search through one stack of hay. He would not have to search through five blocks of snow.

It was now snowing very heavily. The falling snow would probably cover everything up. He might just as well die, or go jump off a bridge or something. He kept praying to Jesus but it just didn't feel right. He knew in his heart that Jesus wasn't listening. He prayed to St. Joseph but this brought him no more confidence.

Finally he concentrated on the Virgin Mary. All of her statues were filled with pity. She had a boy whom she loved very, very much. It hurt her to see Him suffer. If anyone could feel sorry for Richard in his present situation, it was she. "Oh Mary, Mother of God, help me to find this money. If you don't, my mother is going to kill me. She won't have any money and she won't be able to buy any groceries. So you see, I am not just asking for something for myself. I'm not being selfish. I know that it was all my fault. I shouldn't have took the shortcut. I should have went the long way - through the dark. I should have been more careful. I shouldn't have been so afraid. I should have had more faith. I should have known that you would always protect me. Oh my God, I am heartily sorry, for having offended thee ..."

He said a "good Act of Contrition." The words never before had such meaning. He said every word with true sorrow, feeling and remorse as he continued his search, his eyes darting from side to side. He was examining every inch of ground.

He was back to the spot where he had fallen. The picture of the bag flying off into the air came into his mind. Next he envisioned all the bulkies scattered into the snow. He rushed over to that area. "Mary, Mother of God, let the money be there please? I'll go to Mass every Sunday. I'll say all of my prayers. I'll never think bad thoughts again. I'll get all A's in Religion. I'll try to like the nuns more than I do. I'll do anything that you want me to. Just tell me what that is."

But he found no money. His heart sank. He thought for sure that if he would ever find it, he would have found it here. He must keep on looking. He came to the fence with the broken board. He proceeded to crawl through - when right there before him in the snow was what looked to be a roll of crunched up green paper money. He couldn't believe his eyes. Sure he had hoped to find the money, but deep, deep, deep, down inside, he knew that it was impossible. He knew that it would be impossible. He really only ran out of the house to steal some time and hope that his mother might somehow cool down.

He reached down slowly, truly expecting the small roll of green to disappear as he went to touch it. But it didn't. He picked it up and then began to unroll it slowly. He had a ten, a five and four ones. Suddenly the terror and horror were gone. Inside he felt jubilation. The whole world suddenly became bright with sunshine. A heavy weight had been bearing down on him. Now, in an instant, he was as light as a feather. But, nevertheless, he couldn't stop panting feverish sighs.

This was truly a miracle. This was a real miracle. There for the first time, he realized that it was all true. Jesus, Joseph and the Blessed Virgin were really and truly up there. They were listening and they cared. He pictured the Blessed Virgin sitting up behind a cloud in the heavens smiling down on him. "Thank you, thank-you, oh holy Mother of God I truly love you."

No one had ever done anything like this for him. Suddenly coins began to sparkle up at him from the snow. One by one he picked up the coins. No sooner would he pick up one, than Mother Mary would toss down another from the heavens. It was like magic. One moment there was nothing and the next moment there would be a quarter and then a dime and a nickel, or a penny. The Virgin Mary was now dropping the remaining coins from heaven.

He climbed out through the fence and knelt down there in the snow. He said twenty-five Hail Marys and made a promise to say a thousand more.

When you said Hail Marys or any type prayers, you got indulgences. Indulgences were like tokens or free tickets at the ski-ball at Salisbury Beach. At the end of your life, you could turn in all of the indulgences that you had saved-up to one of the angels who stood guard at the gates of Purgatory. Each indulgence might gain you a minute, a second, a day or an hour reprieve from the torturous burning fires that the poor souls in Purgatory were experiencing. Richard said many, many prayers. He said them in hopes that when he died maybe he would have enough indulgences saved-up to enable him to skip Purgatory altogether.

Richard believed in saving. He was always saving something. He knew that no mater how good you were here on earth, you still had to go to Purgatory. Everyone had to go to Purgatory before they could go to heaven.

Richard pictured Purgatory to be a big cave, situated somewhere between heaven and hell. You entered into it by way of a large culvert. Once inside, Angels guarded the exit so that nobody could get out before their time was up. Your soul had to be perfectly pure before you could get into heaven. Nobody's soul was perfectly pure after a life here on earth. Not even Fulton J. Sheen had a perfectly pure soul. Even he would have to spend some time in Purgatory. Maybe only a second or two, but nevertheless, even he would have to go there. So you shouldn't look at it as if it is a punishment or anything like that. Of course, it was a punishment, but after it was over, you went to heaven. Richard promised a thousand Hail Marys. To show his sincerity he offered up all of the indulgences gained from saying all of the Hail Marys to the poor souls who were suffering in Purgatory.

The trek home through the snow that night was the happiest that he could remember in his entire life. His whole insides were just filled with beauty and warmth. He had the new found knowledge that somebody "up there" truly cared about what happened to him. It was all a miracle. The way the money had appeared - now you see it, now you don't. Suddenly it was there, and one second before there was nothing there.

The coins? They popped up one coin at a time as if the angels in heaven were flipping them off their thumbs. They just appeared one coin at a time. It was a miracle all right. They did sparkle. Boy oh boy, did they ever sparkle. They sparkled solely for the purpose of catching his eye. There was no one else there. If that didn't mean that Mary, the Mother of God, loved him, then nothing did. That was for sure. This was probably the most important realization that he had ever had in his life. Oh, he believed what the nuns had told him about God's love.

What he didn't really believe was that God and Jesus and the Blessed Virgin and everybody else up there in heaven truly cared about him, in particular. To know that they were really and truly listening to his prayers; that they had actually answered his prayers - this is what he had always hoped for, but he never believed that he would ever know. Never did he believe that they would show him in such an obvious manner. That would be like having his real mother and father kissing him and hugging him and telling him to his face that they really loved him and were concerned about his well being, that they were happy that he had been born. Of course, he knew that would never happen. That would be asking too much of even miracles. But what did that all matter? Now that he knew how God really cared, who needed them? Mary and Joseph cared. So what if his earthly mother and father didn't? They were just temporary substitutes anyway. It was for sure that Mary cared. She really cared and she had shown him that she cared. This was all the most wondrous feeling. This was truly a miraculous evening.

When he opened the kitchen door, his mother was standing at the sink. She turned and looked intently into his eyes as she prepared herself for the coming ordeal by drying her hands on a dish towel. Richard walked up to her. He lifted his right hand up to her proudly. She put out her hand and he dropped the money into it. She eagerly peeled the bills open and then counted them. She stuffed the coins into her dress pocket. She then looked down at Richard.

He was very proud that he had found the money. He was proud of his personal miracle. He looked into her face, waiting to see her anger and hostility dissipate. He had found the money. She had to be relieved. He had felt such relief that he was nearly bursting inside. She had to be very proud of him ... didn't she? A small smile spread across his face as he looked wonderingly up into her eyes.

Instantly she struck him in the face.

There is something about being struck in the face. A whole spanking is not the equivalent of one slap in the face. He looked at her with bewilderment and confusion. So she struck him in the face once again. She had "wiped that smile off his face." He remained standing there directly in front of her. He didn't run.

"Yeah! That was for nothing," she said sarcastically. She said it as if he should really know the reason that she had just struck him. He did know. She had struck him because she didn't like to see him smile. She didn't like to see him laugh. She didn't like to see him at all. He didn't have the right to smile. Smiles meant happiness and there was nothing to be happy about in this house. It was an ugly house, and he was a part that made it ugly. This house was a dump. Just like a dump, it was filled with garbage. He was a part of that garbage. His mother didn't think so, but she was the biggest pile of garbage in that house. He hated her guts. He hated her more every day. One day he would be big enough to fight back. One day nobody would ever strike him in the face again. But that day would not be today.

Today he had been blessed. The Holy Virgin had blessed him with her love. He was thankful and he would say a thousand Hail Marys in her honor. He would start tonight. He would start this instant.

"Hail Mary full of grace; blessed art thou ..."

11 Father and Son

For most of Richard's growing-up years, Richard's father was a part of his dreams and not a part of his reality. Dad was often off to sea trying to earn a living. He was in Richard's thoughts constantly. Richard dreamed of being on the ship with his dad. He wanted to go wherever his dad was forced to go. He knew that this was impossible. Children couldn't go to sea. Even if they could, his dad probably wouldn't want Richard along anyway. His dad kept his emotions closeted inside. He had a wall built up around him, and no one could get in. Richard really didn't know whether his father loved him or if he didn't love him. Love was never mentioned or talked about by either of them - except, of course, when his father was drunk. Richard knew that those times didn't count.

The story of his dad's relationship with his own father played in Richard's mind like a fable. His dad and Richard's grandfather weren't like father and son. They were friends. Actually they were more like buddies. They worked at the same factory. On Saturday nights they bowled together on the company team. It was difficult for Richard to imagine his dad ever being that close to anyone. But according to legend, his dad did have such a relationship once. It could happen again.

These days his dad had no friends. If he did he never brought any of them home. The fact that he never brought any friends home didn't necessarily mean that he had no friends. Maybe he was like Richard. Maybe he was just ashamed to have any of his friends meet his wife, possibly his children, or maybe it was the shame of his circumstance of poverty. They never went anywhere as a family other than to a funeral. They never visited anyone's house, nor did anyone ever visit them.

No sooner had Richard learned to write than he began to compose letters to his father overseas. From his very first letter to his father, everyone in the family was excited. Richard really didn't understand why everyone was so thrilled by his letters. His mother and sister read all of his letters out loud in the kitchen. On his first letter, his mother wanted to correct all of the misspelled words, but his sister dissuaded her.

"You've got to leave it just like this, Ma. If you change anything, Dad will know that we helped Richard. This way Dad will know that Richard really wrote this himself. He'll love it."

"But your father won't understand these misspelled words."

"He'll figure them out. We did! Besides, that's half the fun. Trying to figure out what Richard is actually trying to say is what makes the real fun of it. I wouldn't change a word. This letter is just perfect."

From Richard's point of view this debate was purely academic. He knew exactly what he meant to say. His mother and sister didn't have any more trouble reading his letter than he had reading anyone else's. His mother and sister would read the letters over and over and they would laugh and laugh. Richard really didn't understand the reason for all of the laughter but he enjoyed the attention.

He never wrote anything that was intended to be funny in any of the letters. He mostly just told his dad not to worry about him and that he was praying that his ship would be safe. Then Richard told him about stuff that happened in school and while playing out in the streets. Richard told him how much he missed him. He told his dad how he wished he was old enough to get a job and then his dad would not be forced to go to sea anymore. Richard told his father about his dreams and aspirations. Like how he hoped that one day they could go fishing together.

It was strange that he had the notion he wanted to go fishing with his dad. Richard had never gone fishing in his entire life. He had never even seen people fishing anywhere. Where had he gotten the idea of going fishing? His mother and sister asked Richard about this fishing notion. He had no explanation. Yet he fantasized about him and his dad being off in a small boat together - just the two of them, alone, together. He could even picture the boat. It had oars and his dad would row the boat. His dad would wear a funny hat and be smoking his pipe. He would tell Richard stories about what the times were like when he was a child. He would tell Richard about all of the great adventures that happened to him when he was a boy. He would tell Richard about his grandfather and what a brave, successful and wonderful man he was.

His father was thrilled by that first letter. This, of course, encouraged Richard to write often. His mother never had to remind him. When his father wrote home, he said that he had read Richard's letter to nearly every one of his mates on board the ship. They all laughed and told him what a wonderful son he must have.

Richard could not believe that his father had actually said such a thing. He demanded that his mother show him, word for word, on the paper where his father had said such things. He could hardly believe that something he had done had made his father happy.

This letter business was actually better than real life. Never had he ever felt such emotional joy in real life. This was the most exciting thing that had ever happened to him. Richard was able to say things in these letters that he was unable to say in real life. For example: "I really love you very, very much. I wish that you were here with us at home where it is safe." It seemed very natural to say things like this in a letter, but yet very awkward to say the very same things in real life.

Saying these things in a letter didn't make Richard feel embarrassed or give him butterflies in his stomach. There was nothing to it. These were just plain, unadulterated statements of fact. These were things that in real life you should be able to see clearly from just looking into a person's eyes, and demonstrate openly by touching and the like. In a letter, on the other hand, you were forced to write them down. If you didn't, how would anyone know? In a letter nobody could see your eyes, or count your tears, or see your suffering. If you cared, you had to say it. If you loved somebody, you had to write it. If you felt sad, you had to explain it. That's what a letter is. If you felt things and you didn't write them, your letter would not be honest. It would not be the truth.

His dad's father had stumbled and died in a doorway on his way home from work one evening. Richard could actually see that happening in his mind's eye. He could see his grandfather grasping his heart and falling to the ground. Except in Richard's mind, his grandfather had no face. Consequently, Richard substituted the face of his father. So when he envisioned the scene of his grandfather dying, it was an enactment of his own father dying. Richard could imagine how terrible that must have been for his father to accept. He knew how awful it made him feel inside to just imagine it. How much more painful must it have been for his father? Richard could also understand how his father could come to hate God for doing such a horrible thing. Richard tried to explain God to his father. "God just wanted your father up in heaven. He needed your dad. That is why He took him. He wasn't trying to be mean to you. God doesn't hate you. God loves everybody."

It was a terrible thing for Richard's father to be mad with God. For his father not to attend Mass every Sunday only meant that he would be going to hell when he died. Richard was frightened that one day his father would end up in hell. He prayed for his dad's conversion every night. He prayed that God and all the saints in heaven would forgive his dad. He hoped that some of the saints would help his dad get into heaven. God must know, deep down inside, what a good man his father was. He told God to forgive his father because his dad was just angry and sad inside, that was all.

Richard wrote to his dad every week. His letters were building a bond between them. There was always a bond between Richard and his dad. His dad was just not aware of it.

Richard loved his dad deeply. When his dad was home from sea he never seemed to notice Richard. At those moments when Richard was able to make emotional communication, his dad was just too intoxicated to notice. Richard was proud of those occasions when he rescued his drunken father from the street corner and got him home to bed safely. But to his father these were moments of embarrassment. These were incidents that were erased from his memory in the morning.

His father never asked anyone how he had gotten home the previous evening, or how he had gotten into his bed. When Richard engaged all the perils of night to go down to the barrooms to seek out his father at his mother's request, this was not considered praiseworthy by his dad. His dad only resented the boy's nagging intervention - inspired by his mother. Was he not, a messenger from the bitch?

His dad did not turn from his barstool and beam at his little boy with pride and joy as his Uncle Joe had. He always looked down at the boy with total disgust. He was mother's little helper. He was the son from hell. He was his mother's little spy. His dad never had to say a word. Richard knew what was in his father's mind.

But Richard didn't go to Cain and Bernard's or the Parkway Cafe as his mother's little representative. Richard wasn't being his mother's little helper. He hated his mother just like his father did. He hated her even more than his father did. What Richard liked about rescuing his father from the local barrooms was the opportunity to be with his dad.

Sometimes Richard would sneak into the barroom and slip into an empty seat behind his dad. He would just sit there and watch his father drink. He would never try to stop him. Truly, he wished that his father would always be drunk. Richard wanted to be invisible. If he was invisible he could just watch over and protect his dad without getting all the dirty looks.

That was impossible though. The dirty looks came with being the son of the bitch. It was like the Original Sin. Richard had inherited Original Sin from his historical mother. It was really all her fault. Eve was the one who talked Adam into sinning. It was because of Eve that the whole human race had to live like this. That's why nuns dressed like they did, and prayed all the time, and were so ashamed of themselves, and had no children of their own. And it was because of his real mother that his father hated him. When his father looked down at Richard he saw the face of the hated bitch. Why didn't he look at Richard and see his own reflection. If he could look into Richard's mind and heart, certainly he would have seen himself.

Sometimes the bartender wouldn't even mention Richard's presence. Then other times he would tap Ernie on the shoulder and point to his son sitting there behind him. When Ernie would turn and see Richard his face would automatically crinkle up with disgust. For Richard to see that look on his father's face was more powerful and hurting than any of his mother's blows. To see the only person in this world that he loved and cared about, turn and look at him with disgust, made him want to die. With each of those looks, some part of him did die. Those parts that may have had any feeling for his mother were most vulnerable.

Richard despised seeing that look on his father's face so much that he would hang his head down and stare at the sawdust strewn floor whenever his father turned to look upon him. He could see his own horrible image embedded in that barroom floor. He could feel it run through his frame. He would sit there staring at his father's shoes and pant cuffs all the while that he knew his father's menacing gaze was upon him. That was the other side of a smile. The other side of a smile is a terrible thing. The other side of a smile turns laughter to tears and love to hate. It makes beautiful things ugly. It turns hope to despair. It turns the desire to create into the desire to destroy. It turns living into dying.

Each time his dad looked at him in that manner, the boy died. Yet, even with all the pain, he wanted to be there. He wanted to be there at his father's side. If only he weren't a little boy, but instead his father's loyal, faithful dog. If he were a dog, he could just crawl up at his father's feet at the base of his stool. He could just be there. His father wouldn't hate his faithful dog. Now and then he would reach down and pat the little dog on the head. A dog would not remind him of his wife and the home that he so hated. If he were a dog he could lead his father home safely. He could protect him from bad people and things. A man can pet and hug and love his dog.

Richard wasn't a dog. Unfortunately, Richard was his father's son. He would have to take the hate. He would just have to sit there and take the hate. Most of the time, his dad would not even acknowledge his son's presence. He would simply turn back to the bar and continue drinking. Richard would not look up until his father's feet were facing forward. Richard would just sit there and watch his dad. Sometimes he would look up at his father's face glowing in the mirror that ran along the wall behind the bar. He was sad that he had to be in such a position. Yet, he was happy to be the one assigned to bring his father back home. He knew that his dad did not like him very well at that moment, but he knew that he would like him better on the way home. He would like him better when he needed someone to lean on, or when he fell down, or when he stumbled and lost his balance. Then he would be proud to have a son like Richard.

Sometimes he even said so. Yes, sometimes when the little boy would use all of his strength to stop the man from falling flat on his drunken face, he would even tell the little boy so. "You are a good boy, Richard. You are a good boy. What would

I do without you," he would sometimes say. Richard would feel good inside to hear those words. Yes, and what would his father do without him? Lay there in some gutter? Stumble in front of some car? His father had a good point. What would he ever do without Richard? His dad did need his little boy. He needed him badly. He needed him more than even he realized. Without Richard, his father would have no one and nothing. Without Richard, his father could just die and who would really care?

Richard wrote often to his father. He expressed all his fears, hopes and protective instincts. His letters had become a combination of his dreams, wishes and personal meditations. Sometimes he wrote as if he were talking to himself.

His father was gone for what seemed to be a lifetime. Then, one day, Richard walked into the kitchen. His mother said. "Guess who's here?" She was sporting a huge grin. Richard looked down the hall and there was his father walking up into the kitchen from the back bedroom. For some strange reason Richard was not filled with joy and happiness. His dad stopped at the old refrigerator, put his hands on his hips, and beamed a huge smile.

Strangely enough, Richard did not want to rush up into his father's arms. Why should he? Such an occasion had never presented itself to him before in his life. Truly, he wanted to just turn and exit the room. His dad was smiling and looking affectionately down into Richard's eyes. It was like he was seeing Richard for a first time. In all these years his father had never really looked at him. He always looked through Richard or around him. He never looked into his eyes. It felt strange. Richard was not comfortable with the feeling. Why was his dad smiling so warmly? He wasn't even drunk. He looked like a giant standing there. He needed a shave. He always needed a shave. His father had been gone so long this time, that Richard had nearly forgotten his father's face. As he stared at his father, the images from all the old photographs disappeared. Reality took their place in just a matter of seconds. Richard just stood there staring, until his father's face became real once again.

A real face is different from an imagined face. An imagined face is often hazy and dull. It doesn't have color and animation. A real face has detail and definition. A real face is also connected to a real body. It isn't just floating there in never-never land. His dad's real face was a thousand times better than the face that appeared in Richard's dreams.

Richard had been successful once again. He had brought his father safely home. Wishing, hoping and praying his father home from the sea was really no different from carrying him home from Cain and Bernard's. The effort was just as strenuous, just as physical and just as intense. But now it was over. His father was home safe. Richard had completed his duty. Now he could go to his room or outdoors to play. Why was his father now standing there staring at him, with this huge grin as if it were he who had accomplished something?

Richard didn't move. What did his father want from him now? Why was he looking like that? Why was he standing there with his hands on his hips like some sort of conquering hero? What had he done? What had he accomplished? What the hell was he waiting for?

"Well? Don't you have a hug and a kiss for your old man?"

A hug and a kiss for his old man; was he kidding? Since when had they ever resorted to such behavior? His dad never hugged and kissed him. His dad never beamed into his eyes or stared at him with this blooming pride. What was this all about? Richard's role was always to be invisible. He was just there. He was never to be seriously noticed, and certainly not hugged and kissed. Men didn't kiss. And most certainly men didn't kiss one another. What was this new found sissy stuff?

It was the letters. That must have been it. It was those letters. What had he said that it would make his father suddenly think that he wanted to be hugged or kissed? Richard did not want to be hugged or kissed by his mother or his father, or his grandmother or anybody. These were the tactics of the weak. Richard was strong. These letters had somehow awakened in his father the notion that he had a son. Richard resented this epiphany - this new born fatherhood. Since when had Richard become an object of someone's affections? He was the keeper of the covenant. He was the guard stationed just outside the temple door. He was the confidant and comrade, the strength during his father's moments of weakness. He was the necessary but invisible shield who protected his father from the onslaughts of society, unemployment, alcohol, and his wife. Richard was a soldier in an army of one, assigned to guard the king.

Richard was stunned, shocked and immobile. He looked up into his father's eyes and he was suddenly frightened. His dad's eyes were big, bright, glowing and happy. They were filled with joy, pride and love. This could not be happening. This was a trick of some sort. Suddenly he felt resentful. Don't you have a kiss for me? How could his father do such a thing? He hadn't noticed that he never kissed Richard? How could all of these past years be suddenly forgotten in a moments notice? How does one kiss another person? Richard had stopped kissing a century ago. Did his father want to be kissed on the lips, on the cheek? Where? How? Hugging and kissing were for babies anyway. Responsible men like him didn't stoop to hugging and kissing. Besides, did his father just think that he could run off and go traipsing about the world and then pop up in their kitchen and demand hugs and kisses? Did he think that he could ignore Richard for his whole life and then show up one day with his arms outstretched and expect Richard to leap up into them? Did he actually think that Richard needed his hugs and cuddling? "OH, come over here, ga ga, goo goo, poo poo, pa pa." - BULLSHIT! That is not the way it goes. That is not the way that you earn someone's love.

What would happen if he simply refused to kiss his dad? What if he just shook hands, or just said, "Hey, how's it going?" Maybe his dad should learn what it means to be alone and to be dodging drunks and hoboes out in the streets at night. Maybe his dad should have to go down to some barroom and sit behind him and wait. Wait until Richard was damn good and ready. So Papa just strolls in and puts out his arms, and all is to be forgiven? Richard didn't think so - no, hardly.

His dad saw the boy's confusion and hesitation and his joy dissipated momentarily, but then he shook it off. "Get over here," he demanded warmly.

Richard walked up to his father slowly. His dad scooped the boy up into his arms and kissed him. He kissed the boy on the mouth. Richard felt his father's lips but had forgotten how to respond. He could smell the cigarettes on his father's breath. He could feel his dad's coarse, prickly beard rubbing against his own soft cheek. The hairs on his dad's face felt like prickers on a vine or tiny slivers on a piece of wood. Yet, once into his father's arms, all his resentments vanished. He put his arms around his father's neck and hugged him tightly.

Richard had thought of himself as so very, very big, but now in his dad's arms he felt once again like a small child. His dad was very strong. This was all a very, very strange feeling. He could remember nothing like it. Suddenly he didn't want to give his father up, or ever let him go.

12 The Merit Gas Station

Richard had started something: the letters, those crazy letters. They had said something to his dad - something that his dad had never been able to hear before. The letters had planted a seed. The seed had found a fertile spot in the hard fallow garden of his father's love. The seed had actually blossomed into a hug.

His dad had hugged him that afternoon in the kitchen on his return from the Mediterranean. It had never happened before. It would never happen again and nothing more was ever said about it. But yet, one afternoon his dad came walking into Richard's bedroom with two fishing poles and a little green metal box. He stood the poles in the corner behind the bedroom door. Richard was sitting on the bed putting on his sneakers. After his dad set down the tackle box, he turned and looked at Richard.

"Now all that I have to do is find us an old rowboat."

Richard was staring at his father's face. His dad was smiling. Richard felt that he should smile also; but should he? Sometimes he had smiled at the wrong time. Sometimes he smiled and received a crack in the teeth from his mother for his efforts. His dad was different. He didn't hit with a physical hand. He hit with the emotional fist of rejection, denial and indifference. Maybe if the boy smiled, his father would say to himself, "Hold on now. I've just made that boy too damn happy. Who is that boy to be so happy? Why, it is only Richard. Richard? Does he deserve to be that happy? Maybe I had better just pull it back a little here."

If Richard smiled and his father saw him smile, would his father then think, "There now, that's good enough. I made the kid smile. Ain't that good enough?"

No, no. There were just too many years of neglect and abandonment here to just start jumping up and down as if all of his little-boy dreams had suddenly come true. Yes, his dad had actually bought two fishing poles and a box. Did that mean that he would really, one day, get a rowboat? Come on now, how would they get this rowboat to a lake if they did in fact get one? They didn't have a car. A rowboat doesn't have any wheels. Where was there a lake around here anyway? No one ever put a boat in one of the canals here in Lawrence.

Lawrence was filled with canals. They were involved with flood control or something. They also had something to do with providing power to the textile mills once upon a time. Lawrence was in a valley. It was called Merrimack Valley. To Richard a valley meant trees and dirt roads and farm houses.

Merrimack Valley never looked like a valley to Richard. All that he ever saw were tenement houses, clothes lines, railroad tracks and garbage cans. Is New York City in a valley? Is it on top of a mountain? A valley has grass and fields of wheat swaying in the wind. Merrimack Valley was a valley without fields of corn or stalks of wheat. Merrimack Valley was a valley that spawned fields of brown, brick, mill buildings, hundred year old tenement houses and telephone poles that spun an infinite web of power lines and electric transformer nests. The sun didn't slip up over a mountain top and bask its light on a fertile crescent below. No, the sun struggled to peek its way each morning through dense clouds of gray and heavy soot. It didn't sparkle down on pristine rivers and streams or deep transparent lakes. Noooo - it hardly sparkled at all.

Instead it cast a rather dull, hazy yellow-orange glow over those woven, rubber coated, copper and steel webs that were spun in every direction by thousands of workmen spiders who flitted about the city wearing metal hats and living in complicated huge, green boxes with wheels on the bottom and ladders on the top.

That dull, orange sun glistened on a patchwork of potholes and sewer covers, wooden fences, ice-cream parlors, dime stores, barrooms, schoolhouses, mill smokestacks, empty dirt lots, gutters filled with Popsicle sticks and candy bar wrappers and canals filled with purple polluted water from centuries of dyes and chemicals left behind by the eighteenth century tanning factories and the now recently departed textile mills.

No, no, Lawrence was no place for rowboats and fishing poles. Let's not get ourselves too excited about this Richie boy. Let's not jump up and down and get all giggly. We now have two fishing poles and a green box sitting in a corner of our bedroom. This may deserve a small smile, but no Howdy Doody, whoopy-doo grin now.

He looked his dad in the eyes and watched as he left the room. There was another problem here also. Those fishing poles mentioned in his letters were a part of a dream. A dream was a picture of the way that things should be. A dream is a part of one's imagination. A dream isn't reality. If you tried to turn a dream into something real, you were taking a big chance. Real things can be broken. Real things can be destroyed. Castles in the sky on the other hand, can live forever. Real buildings will eventually topple to the ground.

Richard looked at the fishing poles in the corner but he didn't dare to touch them. No, he wouldn't just run over and spin the crank on one of those fishing reels or open up that green tackle box. Oh no, he would touch nothing; he would do nothing - no, not a thing. Not a thing until that day came when he and his dad were out in that rowboat fishing on some lake. Then the dream would be real. Two fishing poles and a little metal box in a corner does not a fishing trip make.

What if they really did go fishing though? What would they say to one another? Richard had a wild imagination but not in his most overwhelming moment could he actually picture himself and his dad strolling along with his father's arm slung casually over his shoulder and the two of them singing, "Hi ho, hi ho it's off a-fishing we go." The thought just didn't fit. It felt a little too large and a good deal ridiculous. But then, dreams do come true. Don't they?

Richard was right. This dream wasn't of the instant variety but somehow it did seem to be getting closer. Other miracles did seem to be coming into being, ever so slowly.

His dad had gone out into the dreary streets of Lawrence one fine morning and when he returned, the cobblestones were gleaming like ingots of gold. Ernie could not believe what had happened to him. An ad had appeared in the Eagle Tribune. Interviews were being conducted across from the old Arlington Mills on Broadway. The interviews would be starting at 8 a.m. Ernie was up there and standing in line at 6 a.m. As he stood there the line grew and grew and grew. Hundreds of unemployed men were lining up. Many among them were young men, in their twenties. Ernie was now in his forties.

Ernie had arrived early that morning, but not early enough to be first in line. He was far from it. His biggest hope was that he would get to be interviewed before the interviewer called it a day. By the end of the day the interviewer would certainly have talked to enough men to make a choice. There would, more than likely, be no more interviews that next morning.

Ernie did get in to see the man that day. The man conducting the interviews hired Ernie. He actually hired him right on the spot. He didn't tell him to come back tomorrow for a follow up. He outright hired him. Richard's dad returned home, flopped down into the overstuffed chair next to the piano and told the whole family the story. Richard sat on the carpet at his dad's feet. Everybody sat and listened.

His dad was a storyteller. He often told stories. They were most often about his work or his present job. They usually told about how well he had done and how much a particular boss liked him. The stories were usually coaxed out of him by a six-pack of Pabst Blue Ribbon. This evening's story was no different.

"So when I got there in the morning, it was still dark. The sun hadn't quite come up over the back of the Arlington Mill yet. There was already a long line in front of me. There were a lot of young guys too. I stood there worrying why they would hire an old fart like me? They had all of those young studs to choose from. But even before that, I wondered if I would ever get in to see this guy? I mean, how many guys is he going to hire?" As he told this most exciting, fascinating tale, he looked into the eyes of each of his children. He looked at his wife. Whichever direction he looked, the eyes said; "Yes, yes ... and then what happened? Really! Oh my God! Oh, how wonderful!"

How wonderful it was to finally get a job, a real job, after all of these years. To Richard's ears this was truly the greatest story ever told. This was the story that he had prayed and prayed to hear.

"Finally, there I am next in line," his father continued. "The guy who is giving the interviews is sitting right there in front of me - inside this little glass building. I can see his face. I'm trying to figure what does this guy want to hear? What does he want? What is he looking for? When I get into that little glass building, the first thing that I says is this. 'Sir, I know that I'm forty-two years old. That may seem old to you. But it also means that I have been around. I know how to work. My work is the most important thing in life to me. Believe me when I tell you, I can work circles around any of these young guys that you see around here.'

"He looks at me and says; 'Don't worry about your age, Mr. Noble. In fact, you are the exact age that I am looking for. I'm not looking for some young here-today gone-tomorrow little kids who don't know what they want in life. Besides, who knows, tomorrow there's another war, and off all of those kids go once again. No Mr. Noble, you are just the type that I am looking for. You are mature, dependable and responsible. You have kids and a family. That's exactly what I want.'

"I couldn't believe my ears. I didn't say another word. I just sat there while he told me what he expected. He told me about the job and what kind of a great future people who got hired there would have with this company. He talked and talked and talked. I didn't hear a word. I was still in shock. I was wondering why this guy was telling me about the company's insurance plan and its future and what they expect. Was he just talking, or did I really have a job? He didn't really say that I had the job or anything like that. I was afraid to ask for sure. So, I just sat there. I listened but everything was just going in one ear and out the other. Finally he stops talking. We both stand up and he shakes my hand. I'm going out the door and still, I really don't know what is happening. I turn around. 'Excuse me?' I say. He's writing something on my application which is sitting on his desk.

'Yes, Mr. Noble?' he says.

'Yeah, well, ahh ... does this mean that I have a job?' He looks up at me and then he laughs.

'It means, be right here this coming Monday morning at eight o'clock ready and dressed for work.'

"I can't believe my ears. The line outside the door as I was leaving was still a mile long. Everybody in the line is staring. They want to hear something - something positive. But I don't want to say nothing. I can't think about all those poor guys. I know what they are feeling, but what can I do? I still can't believe it. I just can't believe it."

What a story! His dad had the job. The whole family was just ready to burst. This was a dream come true. This was a miracle. This was Charles Dickens' "A Christmas Carol." This was Uncle Scrooge coming in the door with an arm full of presents. Richard had prayed to God, the Blessed Virgin, Jesus and all the Saints in heaven. He had hoped and hoped and hoped, but really he never believed that one day his prayers would be answered.

He had fantasized about many things, but to really believe that one day his dad would actually be working at home and live in their apartment with the rest of the family was beyond fantasy. To think that he would actually get up in the morning in the back bedroom, eat breakfast with Richard and the family in the kitchen, and then leave their apartment and walk to work; to leave their tiny apartment and walk up Chelmsford Street to a job; a job, right up on Broadway, just across the street from where Richard's father and his father's father had once been big shots at the Arlington Mills. To think that in the evening Richard's dad would be sitting there at the dinner table with Richard and his brother and sister and mother, eating. To think that now, this evening, now and forever his dad would be sitting in that stuffed chair in the parlor watching the TV.

Richard's fantasies had never gotten to such a phenomenal stage. His prayers were all rote and mechanical, like those prayers in church every Sunday for the conversion of Russia. He prayed, sure, but he never pictured any big, burly Russian leaders running around with a pair of rosary beads. This was truly a miracle.

That particular Monday, and every Monday thereafter, the miracle not only took place but it took on the actuality of every day life. No day, from that day on, would ever be "everyday life" for Richard again. He would wake up and rush to the breakfast table to see if his father would really be there. This was something that he would never get used to. It was too, too perfect. It was too wonderful.

Richard would run home from school every day at lunch time. He would have potato pancakes and Campbell's tomato soup with Ritz crackers. Those were his favorites. He would gulp it down and then grab the brown paper bag lunch that would be sitting on the sink counter. It was his dad's lunch.

One day his dad had forgotten it and his mother made Richard run it up to the gas station. Now, this had become a tradition. Richard would grab that bag and be off and running.

When he would get to the station, there would be his dad. He would be wearing that uniform. It was just like the one those guys wore on the Texaco show. "We are the men from Texaco. We stretch from Maine to Mexico." It was Milton Berle.

His dad had one of those hats. It was just like the officers in the military wore. Just like the one Ike wore. In fact, their whole outfit looked like Eisenhower's. They had that officer's cap with the shiny black rim and the silk lining, and that jacket cut at the waist with them metal buttons and those highly polished black leather shoes. The Merit gas station company gave his dad all of that neat stuff. He even had a green tie with a silver tie clasp and a green woven cotton belt with a golden, brass buckle. His dad was really "somebody" now. This was the best job ever. This was the best job his dad could ever have.

When Richard would arrive running with his dad's brown lunch bag, there his dad would be, up underneath an automobile. The automobile would be up in the air on a huge hydraulic lift. He would be doing a "grease job." That's what his father had told him - a grease job. How important it was to be doing a grease job to an automobile!

Not everybody could afford an automobile. Richard's family had never had one. It was really something to be doing a grease job to an automobile. Richard could hardy imagine ever being big enough and smart enough to perform a grease job on somebody's automobile. To think that somebody who owned an automobile would not only trust someone to do that but they would PAY them to do it was beyond Richard's knowledge.

And there, standing right beneath this big expensive automobile, was his dad in his Texaco uniform, doing grease jobs and pumping gas at the biggest, newest gas station in all of Lawrence.

Lawrence had never seen a gas station like this Merit station before. Prior to this new Super Service Merit station, all the gas stations were little, two-pump jobbers. It was usually owned by this one guy who did everything himself. Behind the two pumps, he would have a building. On one side of the building there would be an office, a cash register and a coke machine. On the adjoining side there would be a pit. People would drive their cars over the pit and the owner would get down into the pit with some flashlights and some carry-around, hook-on lamps. When a car pulled in to get some gas, this guy would crawl out of that pit. He would walk over to the car, usually cleaning his hands with a dirty, greasy rag. He would have grease and dirt all over him. He was never really that excited about pumping anybody's gas. He always seemed to have a lot of repairs to do and that is where he wanted to be. He probably made more money fixing cars than pumping gas into them.

This Merit gas station was a whole, new ballpark. It had, at minimum, ten "islands" and four to six gas pumps at each island. One was never forced to wait in a line. There were always two or three men working there, all dressed in their Milton Berle, Texaco outfits. They all had coin dispensers for making change hooked onto their belts just like the city bus drivers wore.

Each man would dash from pump to pump, sometimes filling four cars simultaneously. A gallon of gas at a Merit station was the cheapest ever - eighteen cents per gallon. This particular station took up half a block on a corner of Broadway. It was enormous. It had self-serve, FREE cleaning and service stations - you could wash your windows, put water into your battery or radiator, or vacuum your upholstery or floors all at no charge. The Merit Men performed grease jobs and changed the oil on vehicles, but that was all the mechanical type work that they would do. They did not repair cars. If you needed a repair you had to return to good old Joe, the guy up on the other corner with the pit and the greasy rag. The big question was would old Joe still repair your car if you no longer bought his gas. That was a big question but nobody really seemed that worried about it.

The Merit station was packed. Everybody wanted that eighteen-cent-a-gallon gas. That was just great as far as Richard was concerned. His father now had a job, right there, a block away from home. His dad was working at the Merit Gas on Broadway. The dream was coming true, but there was more.

It was only a month or two before his dad was offered a position as the assistant manager of Merit's second, new gas station in Haverhill. This meant that his father would have to buy an automobile of his own.

He got a 1946 yellow, four-door, Chevy sedan. The first weekend that they had it, his dad took the whole family for a ride to Hampton Beach. It was really something to be sitting in the back seat of that auto, rolling down those two lane roads, with his dad sitting behind the steering wheel. His father, an automobile, his brother and sister, his mother - and there they were, rolling down the highway like a family. Like a real family, in the normal world!

Richard was afraid to close his eyes; afraid that if he did, it might all disappear. It wasn't going to disappear though. It was really happening.

Hampton Beach was a wondrous place. There were so many people. Cars parked in long lines along the promenade directly across from the beach. For so long it had seemed to Richard that he and his family weren't a part of America. Now here they were painted right in. Their own personal car, parked along a meticulously smooth, paved road, fronting a beach - a beach that stretched for miles. There they were, gathering up blankets and towels and strolling into paradise just as if they had the right to be there.

When his father was away at sea, or even at home but without a job, the world seemed so estranged, foreign, and prohibitive. But now! Oh, but now, here they were, without shame, showing their ticket to the man and being allowed entrance to paradise. Richard felt so proud: proud to have a car; proud to be driving on the highways; proud to be at the beach; proud to have a father; proud to be a family.

His father was proud also. You could see it in his eyes and the way he walked - the look on his face when he locked up the trunk on that '46, yellow Chevy; the smile on his mother's face. She was a queen for the day.

Richard built castles in the sand and played in the surf. Then later they all went to the bandstand and listened to real people playing music on real musical instruments. This was a wondrous make-believe day. They went to the amusement center on the boardwalk. His father gave him a quarter and he and his brother and sister wandered about the massive penny arcade. There were hundreds and hundreds of machines to play for just pennies. It was even fun just watching others play the games and cheering. This whole day was like living in a story book. Hampton beach was a fairyland.

13 The Paper Route

That day at the beach was followed by others. Things at home seemed to be mushrooming into more happiness. Uncle Ray sold his dad his beautiful 1949 black Pontiac four-door sedan. His uncle bought a new Dodge, push-button drive. That next summer Richard's dad rented a cottage at Hampton Beach for two whole weeks. These were big things: cars, vacations, washing machines, new clothes, his own basketball.

He dribbled his basketball to school with him every day. But to just sit there at the dinner table across from his dad, wow! To walk down to the amusement center with the whole family, his dad puffing on his straight-necked pipe as they strolled along peacefully. To bump into a school chum and have them see you walking with your family and your father. This was the real thing. This was real life. A home without a father just wasn't a family. It wasn't a life.

Richard missed those lunch breaks with his dad at the Merit station up on Broadway now that his dad had been transferred to the station in Haverhill. It was necessary, though. To be an assistant manager was a big promotion. One day his dad would be managing a gas station all on his own. He would be the boss. That would mean more money. Money was important. Having money was making all the difference in their lives at this very moment. No money was: arguments and fighting and bitterness. Money was: a home with a father, an auto and trips to the seashore. Money was very important. Money was the difference between happiness and misery.

Now they had so much money that they would pack up all of their old clothes and other stuff and send it all overseas to a poor family that his father had met when he was in Yugoslavia. His dad told them all about Yugoslavia and all the poor and starving people that he had met there. This particular family had a little boy and a little girl who were like Richard and Carol. They were just about the same age. They had a mother but their father was gone. The police had come one day and taken him away. The poor family never saw their father again. Richard felt very sorry for that unhappy family living in such a terrible country.

Richard's father had told him all about barbed wire fences that kept the poor people contained and mud huts these people were forced to live in. He told Richard about poor women who had to sleep halfway out into the cold because there wasn't enough room inside the huts. He told him about all the little boys diving off the pier to retrieve pennies that his dad's shipmates had thrown into the water. He told Richard about how the poor people who lived behind the barbed wire fences would sneak onto the ship at night and steal the garbage out of the ships garbage lockup. Richard couldn't imagine how hungry a person would have to be to eat garbage. He asked his dad why they just didn't give the garbage to those poor people instead of guarding it day and night. His father didn't seem to know what to tell him. Finally he said that the garbage would have probably made them all sick.

Richard could not even imagine diving off a great big pier into the cold, dirty water in the harbor for a penny. Richard could see clearly in his mind's eye that fat cook his father described, shaking his big belly and making all the small children laugh. Could anyone imagine living in a country where there were no fat people? There were fat people all over Lawrence. They weren't rich either. Lots of men had beer bellies. Most of the women including his mother and grandmother were round and plump.

His father told him about the Yugoslavian police. He told of policemen carrying machine guns on their backs, and being forced to take off all of his clothes in a dark alley - they could have shot him right there. His father sneaked off the ship one night with some money and ship supplies to give to this poor woman and her children. The police didn't take his money, because they were basically just honest men who were also poor and starving. They knew that his dad was going to give the money to another poor Yugoslavian family so they didn't stop him.

God must have been protecting his father. His prayers must have been working. What else could it have been?

His dad kept repeating to them how lucky they were to be living here in America. Even though Richard had never met this family he could see all of their faces. Inside he felt that he knew each of them. He wanted to help them. He wanted to send them nice things to wear. He liked this family because his father did. Richard kept trying to put his new things into the care package and keep the old for himself. His mother would not allow that. Richard's mother wasn't as pleased as everybody else to be sending these packages off to a foreign country. She only did it because it seemed to be so important to Ernie.

His father had gotten excited when the first letter arrived from this family in Yugoslavia. He had given the woman his address before he left, but he never expected to hear from them again. His dad brought the letter to Richard's grandmother, hoping that she might be able to translate it. Yugoslavian was not like Polish. His grandmother inquired around the neighborhood until they found a man who said that he could read Yugoslavian. Richard and his mom and dad went to the man's house. The man came out from his house. He leaned over his fence while they all stood eagerly listening on the sidewalk. First he would read the words aloud in the foreign language. Then he would explain them in English as best he could.

"This letter is from a woman. The woman says that she and her children are all still alive."

After translating each sentence, the man would look up into Ernie's face to confirm the acceptance of his interpretation. His dad would look at the man and say, "Yes, yes. It is a woman, and she has two children."

Richard felt this was very strange. It seemed like talking to a fortune teller who was trying to guess at the future.

The man at the fence was heavy-set, and he was wearing his undershirt and suspenders. He had big, hairy shoulders, big arms, and a large but very hard looking belly. He seemed to have hair everywhere except on the top of his head where it belonged. He looked big, bulky and tough, but yet he had a very pleasant, conciliatory manner about him. The curious look in his eye said, I don't know why a poor Irish looking American would be concerned about some Yugoslavian woman and her children but I like a man who will help people who are not even of his own kind. It also did not seem that this man could read all that well.

"She says that - no, no, let me think - she says something here about food. It doesn't make sense to me, but she says that she is still eating your food." The man looked up at Ernie dubiously.

"Yes, that's right. Before I left, I took her to a market and we filled her closet with food. Ten dollars filled a whole closet. In America it would have been impossible."

Richard had never seen his father so happy. His dad was truly excited to be getting this news. Yet he seemed guilty somehow. When his father looked at Richard's mom, he had to explain everything to her. It seemed like he was making excuses. It was like he had to explain to her why he was spending ten dollars on strangers in some foreign country when he had a family right here at home to take care of. His mother's look questioned her husband's right to be giving away ten dollars at a time when his own kids were doing with very little themselves.

His dad went on to tell the man what a bargainer this Yugoslavian woman was. Richard's mother looked down at Richard and shrugged her shoulders. She was clearly not all that impressed with this foreign woman's conservative shopping abilities. The man continued:

"This woman says that she doesn't really know if she will ever be able to write to you again. She says that it is very dangerous to be writing to America. Some other families that she knew who had been communicating with Americans were taken away by soldiers. But, nevertheless, she prays that you will keep writing to her. She says that the soldiers may be coming no matter what anyone does. What does it matter?"

His father was clearly saddened by this news. It was plain that his father loved this family very much. Though Richard felt very sad and compassionate for this poor family, for some strange reason his father's obvious love for these people hurt Richard inside in a personal way.

He had never felt that his dad really cared for him as much as he seemed to care for this foreign woman and her little boy. On his dad's face was an expression that he had never witnessed before. It was a look of sincere concern and pain. It was a look of true feeling. It was a look of love. And, at this moment, his father was not drunk. In fact, he hadn't even had a beer yet. Richard felt himself wishing that he was the little boy of this foreign woman. This woman who was hundreds of miles away, but even from that distance she could affect his father so. The son of the woman who was right here by his side never brought such a look to his father's face.

Richard felt hurt inside. He kept staring up at his dad's face. That is what his dad's face would and should look like when he succeeded in getting his father to love him. In the mean time, it was very clear to Richard that whatever it was that his dad felt for him, it wasn't love. Or, at least, it wasn't a love as great as the love his father was feeling for this strange, invisible family who lived across the ocean in some far off country. Oh, but wasn't it terrible of Richard to be feeling this way? Wasn't it terrible of him to be jealous of some starving, persecuted family - people who lived in mud huts and had no food? To even be jealous of such poor, miserable people had to be some kind of a sin. If it wasn't a sin, certainly it was wrong. He didn't want to feel this way.

He could see that was the way his mother was feeling also. Richard certainly did not want to be thinking like his mother. If his dad loved these people, even if his dad loved that other little boy more than he did Richard, he wasn't that little boy's real father. Even if his dad did not like the woman in whom Richard had been conceived, Richard was his real son. Richard was the flesh of his flesh, the blood of his blood. Wasn't he?

Maybe he wasn't. How could a man love a strange woman's son better than he loved his own son? Maybe now, he would start loving Richard more? Now that he had a real job and now that he would be here at home. Now that he had more money, and a car, and now that things were better, maybe he would love Richard more now.

What about those fishing poles that were standing in the corner of his room? Richard would look at them every time he entered his room. The reels were green and the poles themselves were yellow. They looked like the real thing, not the toy kind. Didn't those poles mean something? His father had bought them for Richard and himself – just the two of them.

But then, maybe his father never loved Richard and Ernie or Carol. He certainly didn't love their mother. He had told Richard many times of his love turning to hate. How can a man love the children of a woman he hates? Maybe he didn't love his own children because they were the cause of all his hard work. It was to support them that he had to work so hard. If he'd never had any children, maybe things would have been better. As soon as Richard got old enough, he would get a job. Then his dad could work easier. Then his father would never have to beg his relatives for money.

If Richard had a job, he would not have to beg his mother all the time for a nickel or a dime. If he had a job, he would have his own money. If he made enough money, he could give some to his dad. Then his dad would not have to work so hard.

If his dad didn't have to work so hard for his kids all of the time, maybe he would like them better. Maybe he would like Richard better. His dad liked that little boy over in Yugoslavia because that boy was suffering. Maybe if Richard were suffering, his dad would like him better. Maybe if he had some kind of incurable disease, his dad would feel sorry for him and then like him better.

Yes, his dad did feel responsible. That is why he just didn't run off and leave the whole family. That is why he stayed on and did his duty. If he could afford to leave, Richard knew that he would. If Richard, Ernie and Carol could all take care of themselves, his dad would be gone in a minute. He told Richard so every time that he was drinking. "If it weren't for you kids, I would have left that woman a long, long time ago."

What did that all mean? He loved his kids so much, that is why he didn't leave? Or, his kids were the only thing that separated him from any real happiness? If he had no children, he could go away someplace and be happy. So wasn't it really the children's fault that he was not happy?

Richard felt that it was primarily his fault that his dad was unhappy. If he wasn't there, his dad could probably leave his mother.

Finally the hairy man on the fence looked up to Ernie and said. "And she says God bless you. And that her and her children will remember you until the day they are dead ... ah ... until the day that they die, that is. And that you will always have all of the love of her and her children with you." The man looked at Richard and then to his mother. Then he looked at Ernie. He looked at Ernie strangely - as if he were wondering why a man would have such a personal letter, with all this talk of love, read aloud in front of his wife and son. Ernie had no choice. His wife opened the mail. He couldn't say that it was a secret.

Richard had mixed feelings. He felt good and yet he felt bad. He felt good because his dad was such a nice person to be helping these poor strangers in a far off land. He felt good because now he would know some people who lived way off, across the ocean. This was a lot to feel proud about. Yet it was bad also. These people were poor and they were in trouble. They lived in a bad country where the police could come and take them away. His dad just seemed to like these people, and maybe he liked them a little too much. He definitely liked these people too much. The hairy man leaning on the fence knew it. Richard knew it. Richard's mother knew it.

His dad was too excited to be getting this letter. He was so eager to have it translated. His dad was never eager or excited - never. He was thrilled and relieved when he got his job at the Merit station. He was proud when he got his new automobile. But receiving this letter was different. He was as excited as a little kid. He nearly ran to the house of the man who would do the translating. His dad never ran. The way he talked as the hairy man translated - he was never so animated. He was apologetic and even seemed guilty. His father never apologized. He never seemed guilty. At the hairy man's fence, his dad seemed like a different man. He was vulnerable, self conscious and guilty. On the walk back to the house, none of them spoke.

After Richard's dad got his job at the Merit gas station, he stopped going out to barrooms. He didn't stop drinking, but he drank less, and he drank at home. For the most part, he didn't get drunk enough to need Richard anymore. He was usually able to make it to his bed on his own. Sometimes he stumbled a little and banged into the refrigerator or the stove, but he accomplished it on his own. This did not make Richard all that happy. Now, his dad didn't need him to carry him to bed. He didn't need him to help him down the street at night. He didn't need him to carry him home from Cain and Bernard's or the Parkway Cafe. Now Richard was even less important than he used to be. No more heart-to-heart talks about life. No more advice about picking the right woman in your life. His dad was home, but they weren't really becoming any closer. They weren't becoming buddies. Life was better though. Life was a lot better.

One time Mary gave Richard one of her surprise back-hands to the chops at the dinner table. His dad looked at his wife as if she were crazy. Richard's mother immediately defended her actions. "He's not going to sit there and look at me cross-eyed because I gave him too many potatoes or too many green beans. He will damn well eat what I put on his plate and like it."

"He'll eat what you give him, Mary. I'm sure. But there is no need to slap him in the mouth because you think that he might not. That's no good."

"Well, then you be the one to see to it. You see to it that he eats what I put on his plate."

"Why do you have to put everything on his plate, Mary? He's a big boy. I think that he could serve himself. Don't you think?"

"Oh, you want him to be serving himself do you - like he's King Farouk or somebody. I don't have no big shots around here. He can eat what I give him and damn well like it."

"Mary, just let the boy get his own. I don't want to argue about it. I would just like to have one night where I could sit and enjoy my dinner. Can we do that, please?"

So, Richard got no slaps in the mouth while dad was looking. If his dad thought that a little slap in the mouth was bad, gosh he should have been around for the last ten or twelve years. What would his dad have thought if he saw his mom knocking Richard from one end of the kitchen to the other a few years ago? Was his father kidding? He really didn't know what kind of a woman this was that he married? He didn't know what a brutal beast this was that he allowed to mother his babies? Was he really serious? Was this all some kind of a game? His father really couldn't be all that dumb, could he?

His mom and dad didn't really talk to one another though. Mary just griped; and Ernie ... drank. Every evening dad appeared at the kitchen door with his brown paper bag filled with quart bottles of beer. He would no sooner get his first glass of beer poured, when Mary would start her monologue.

"That damn school; they want more money again. They are on another "mission." They want him to fill up a card with dimes and nickels. I can't believe it. Those nuns must think that money grows on trees. Richard goes to church; I give him a dime for the collection plate. But there's three collections, he comes home and tells me. Three collections! Can you believe it? They need new heating pipes for the Rectory or something. Don't those fools know that we have heating bills too? And you know that boy of yours won't do a darn thing that I tell him to do. I must have asked him five times so far to go up to Hefferin's and get some kerosene. Talking to him is like talking to a wall. It all goes in one ear and out the other. He won't do anything I ask. He won't go to the store. He won't clean his room. He won't ..."

"You never asked me to go to the store tonight and you only asked me to go to Hefferin's once."

"Oh? Did you hear that? I only asked him once. How many times do I have to ask? Once should be more than enough. I shouldn't have to ask fourteen million times. Once, that should be all. Your father now? Oh yes, that's a different story. He just nods his head and you're halfway to the corner. You don't even know what he wants and you're off and running. But me, I've got to write it in stone. And if I ask you to get three things, you forget two of them. I have to beg for everything around here. This landlord of ours - my own brother - he's putting cabinets upstairs. Amelia, she gets new cabinets, but Mary, what does she get? She gets the same old thing for fifty years and a bucket of crap on the side. My own brother, do you think that he will do anything about this place?"

"I'm sure that he will, Mary. Just give him a chance."

"Are you kidding me? Give him a chance! Do you think that he is going to worry about me? Huh! They'll take care of everybody in the world before they get down to me."

"Maybe Amelia and Clayton are paying Ray to put in those cabinets."

"Paying? We're not paying? I don't give him his rent every week? This place was bought and paid for by my dead brother Frank so that we could all live here for free. But no, we're paying rent now."

"The rent ain't that much Mary."

"Five dollars every week? You don't think that's too bad? Let them all pay me five dollars a week and see what I end up with, buster? They have a lot of short memories around here. They don't remember when I was working out in Baltimore, paying my own food, paying my own apartment, buying my own nylons? Nylons were a dollar a pair! But I still sent them money home - money for little Amelia, and Ray and my mother. You know Ernie, I have never got a thank-you from any of them? No sir-eee. Not one word."

"Mary, how many times do we have to listen to that story? I think that I've heard that story ten million times."

"Well, it is the truth. And so what if you have to listen to my stories a thousand times. I listen to yours, don't I? What about all of those poor starving people in Yugoslavia? There they are living in all of those terrible mud huts. What the heck is so darn great about Chelmsford Street? What is this dump supposed to be - paradise? If that family of yours were over here for a year or two with these neighbors and these relatives that we've got, why I'll bet it wouldn't be long before they were wishing that they had their mud hut back. Here we are sending them clothes every month - like we are some kind of rich lah-di-dahs. We're some kind of rich, fat Americans. We can pile up dimes for the missions and ship clothes to the poor all over the world. Poor? Somebody ought to be sending us care packages. Look what I have to wear. You call this luxury? You call this fancy? Sure, this is the cream of the crop, we got here. And Richard - look at him, will you? He puts the good jeans into the box. He wears the junk with the patches on the knees. Does that make any sense?"

"The ones that I put into the box don't fit right," Richard defended. "They're too small. I like the ones with the patches. I've got them all broke in. They're the most comfortable ones that I've got."

"Stand up! Stand up! Now turn around and show your father - look! Will you look at that, Ernie! His butt is about to come out through the back of those things, but will he take them off? No, no, those are the ones that he wants to keep. And here, look at this." She ran into Richard's bedroom. "Here look at these. These, he wants to send to Yugoslavia. They're like new, but he won't wear them."

"They're not comfortable."

"Listen to that, will you? They're not comfortable."

"Richard," his father said, looking skeptically at the boy. "You wear the good ones; the old ones go into the box. You understand?"

"Oh, gee."

"Do you hear me?"

"Yes, I hear."

What was happening? Instead of Richard and his dad becoming buddies, his dad was becoming the assistant warden. His mother would tell his dad all the things that he didn't do. She would tell him everything that he did wrong. How could his father ever grow to like him under these circumstances? His mother was spoiling it all. His mother was turning Richard into a burden even in his father's eyes. Why would his dad want to go fishing with a troublesome boy like him? Why would his dad want to be with him at all? How was he ever going to love such a disappointing troublesome child?

Why did his mother hate him so? Why was she so bent on keeping him and his father apart? If he tried to please the nuns at school and fill his cards with nickels and dimes, he was a burden on the family finances. It was he and his cards for the missions and his constant begging for dimes for the Sunday collection plate that was keeping the whole family in a state of bankruptcy. If he tried to make his dad proud by putting good clothes into the care box, he was being stubborn and disobedient. He was wasting the family resources. His mother was doing everything that she knew to keep Richard and his father apart. All he wanted was a tiny bit of his father's affections, but she would not allow it. Why?

There would be no love for Richard. Even if his father was living right there in the same house, he would not be allowed to love Richard. Richard won't do this; Richard won't do that; Richard won't do anything right. He is never a good boy. Richard was more trouble than he was worth.

Richard would follow in his older brother's footsteps. He would stay away from his house as much as possible. It was very clear to Richard that he and his father were not going to be allowed to become friends. Richard's mother was not going to stand for it. Standing around the house pushing for a relationship between himself and his dad was only going to make things worse. His dad was never going to be allowed happiness. Those fishing poles would sit there in the corner of his room until they rotted. His dad was home. He wasn't out on a fearful sea. Yes, but he was not happy. He had a job and they had a car. They could afford to spend two weeks at the seashore every summer. But, his father was not happy. Dad went to work every morning. He returned home every night with his shopping bag full of beer and his cigarettes and sat in front of the TV until he drowned it all out in a cloud of smoke and an ocean of alcoholic foam.

Young Ernie and Carol were almost big enough to take care of themselves. There was a boy at school who owned a newspaper route. He wanted to sell it to somebody for twelve dollars. Richard would have to get that paper route somehow. You were supposed to be twelve years old to be a paperboy. Richard was only ten. He would just have to lie.

Richard wanted that paper route that had been for sale. He begged his dad to buy it. His dad didn't want him to have it.

"You're too young to start working Richard."

"No I'm not."

"I said that you are."

"Oh dad, please?"

"Listen son, don't make me out to be a mean old man because I won't let you go to work. You're too small to have a paper route. You're just a kid for God's sake. You should be enjoying yourself. You should be playing on the school basketball team. You should be having fun, not working. You will have the rest of your life to work, believe me."

"Sure dad, have fun? How do you have fun with no money? I can't go to the movies because it costs twelve cents. I can't go to corner store with the other guys because I don't have a nickel."

"Oh come on, don't give me that. Your mother gives you spending money."

"Yeah sure," Richard said turning to leave the room. "She gives me money if I get down on my hands and knees and beg for a week. I would rather do without than beg."

"Richard, come back here," his father said, sympathetically.

Richard returned and stood before his father. Ernie knew that the boy was right. Ernie wasn't earning all that much money. Mary didn't have extra that she could be handing out for recreation. He took out his billfold, slid out a five dollar bill and extended it towards Richard. Richard made no motion towards the money. "Take it. Go to the movies."

Five dollars was a lot of money. Richard's dad never gave him money. He gave his money to Mary and she dispensed any money to the kids. Basically, this five dollar bill that his father had extended was his private beer and cigarette money. He didn't really have any extra money himself. He worked overtime and on weekends for a few extra bucks. But once he became assistant manager he worked salary. Extra hours brought no more money.

"I don't want that, Dad."

"I thought that you wanted to go to the movies and buy potato chips and soda? That's what you said, didn't you?"

"You don't understand."

"I don't?"

"No, you don't."

"Well then, explain it to me."

Richard shrugged his shoulders and shuffled around a bit. "I want my own money. I don't want to beg from Ma, or you, or anybody. I don't want charity. I want my own."

"You're not begging, son. I want you to have it. I want you to have some fun."

"I know, but I don't want your spending money either. You work hard for your money. You deserve to have money to spend without me bugging you all the time. I want to have my own money, Dad. I want to work and I want to have money to buy what I want to buy. I don't want to be treated like a little child. Can I have a dime, oh please, please? What do you want it for? If I give it to you, will you be good? If I give it to you, will you do as I say? If, if, if. If I ask Ma for even a penny she has a list of things for me to do, a mile long. It is not worth it. Her price is too high. I would rather get a job, work and have my own money. I don't like crawling around on my knees like a dog."

"Crawling on your knees like a dog?" his dad repeated with a smile.

"Yes, that's how I feel, like a dog when I have to beg for money from her. I don't want your money either. Maybe if I had my own money, you could take more time off. Maybe you wouldn't have to work so hard, or be working all the time."

Ernie looked at the boy. The boy didn't like begging from "her." This wasn't good. The boy wanted to help out his dad.

This was good. He was only eleven years old, but he seemed so grown up. What the boy was saying was basically true. A paper route was not exactly like quitting school and going down to the mill with the men, like he had done when he was a boy. Ernie didn't want the boy to be turning out like him. He wanted Richard - all of his children - to get an education. Young Ernie and his sister Carol were doing well in school. Actually they were doing great. They were tops in their classes. Richard was another case. He passed, but just barely. He got C's, and a whole bunch of "could do much betters." He wasn't doing that well in conduct either. Maybe a job is just what the doctor ordered.

"Okay, you can get the paper route, but I don't want to hear nothing more about it. It is your responsibility. You take care of it. Neither I, nor your mother, intend to be delivering your papers for you. You got that?"

"I got it."

Richard could hardly believe his ears. This was really important. He would have his own money - his very own money to spend as he pleased. This was important. This was very, very important. Nobody would be delivering any of his papers - that was for sure. His mother delivering his papers? That would be the day! His father out delivering papers? Oh brother, that would be a sight. Richard would have his own paper route. He would have his own money. He would never beg again. God bless the child, yes sir, God bless the child who has his own.

14 The Last Letter

Dad was home, but life was not as Richard dreamed it would be. It was true that Richard and Carol were, for the moment, out from under their mother's gun-sights. Unfortunately their dad seemed to be mom's fill-in. She didn't crack her husband in the chops, or knock him about the kitchen, but she beat him up regularly. His mother needed an enemy. It didn't seem to matter who.

When her husband was off to sea, it was Richard and Carol. Now that her husband was home, dad filled her needs perfectly. Richard hated what he saw. To stand there and be forced to watch his mother destroy all his boyish hopes and dreams; to be there, right in the kitchen every evening as she made a total mockery of all his prayers. He had prayed his father home, for this? He had prayed to watch him be humiliated, badgered and abused by mother Mary, the witch from hell?

What was wrong with her? Where had she learned to turn good into bad and dreams into nightmares? Richard's dad was such a wimp. But what could he do? He would hold it in as long as he could. He wasn't much of a debater. He was more the strong, silent type, or the weak, wimpy type. It all depended on your point of view.

His dad would listen patiently, or simply try to ignore her. Sometimes he would "bubble" over and say some harsh dominating thing like, "Ah, Mary? Do you think that we could have a little quiet tonight so that maybe we could watch this TV program? Please?"

"You want quiet? I'm too noisy, I suppose? I suppose that I don't have anything important and worthwhile to say? Who wants to listen to old, stupid, unimportant me? Maybe I should just go out into the kitchen and bake some cookies, or scrub a floor or something? Or maybe I should just move out of my own house, so you could watch the TV in peace?"

Oh, what a precious thought. Richard could only dream that she would move out of their house.

Why was she doing this?

They finally had dad here at home. He had a steady job and she was doing her best to make him miserable. If only she would die, Richard sometimes thought. Whenever he had such a thought he quickly asked for God's forgiveness. But yet sometimes even in his prayers at night he asked God, politely, to take his mother up into heaven. She was clearly not happy here on this earth and it didn't look like she would ever be. Here was his father sitting right there in their living room, watching the TV like a real family does and she was trying to drive him back to the barrooms.

She nagged and complained, morning, noon and night. Richard and Carol talked about the situation. They both accepted that their mother was trying to chase their father away. He was trying to stay at home. He was trying to control his drinking. He was trying to make a stable family existence. But here was a woman who could drive any man to drink.

Richard thought of his father as the most patient man who ever lived. He was the modern day embodiment of the biblical story of Job. He had the self-control of a monk. He sat there night after night, listening to this woman babble and babble and babble. She was like an endless recording. She went on, and on, and on, and on, and on. Sometimes Richard just wanted to scream, "Why don't you just shut up. YOU ARE TRYING TO CHASE MY FATHER OUT OF HIS OWN HOME!" But, he didn't. He sat there, keeping it all inside. Just like his dad.

Sometimes as his mother ran back and forth - in and out - of the living room, his dad would look over at Richard and shake his head. Sometimes he would wink. His father knew that Richard understood. This made the tension that bubbled inside Richard subside slightly. It told Richard that his father understood his mother. His father was not going to let it get to him. He would grin and bear it all. Most important, he would not let it drive him from his home. He would not allow her to make him hate his own home, his own children, or himself. Would he?

Richard feared in the back of his mind that one day his father would just disappear. One evening he would not appear at the kitchen door with his brown bag full of tranquilizer - booze. Why couldn't his mother be the one to disappear? She didn't have to die. She could just go away. There was certainly little hope that she could ever run off with another man. No man could ever love a woman in her condition. She had trapped one sucker when she was young and beautiful, but now she was fat and ugly on both the inside and the outside.

Every Friday in the confessional Richard confessed his sins of hatred towards his mother. He didn't say, "Bless me Father, for I hate my mother and pray each evening that she will die." He said instead that he had "bad" thoughts and that he had sinned X number of times against the commandment that said that one should honor his mother and his father.

His mother would never run off with another man, but why wouldn't his father run off with another woman? Richard thought about the woman in Yugoslavia. Did his father love her and her children better than his own family? Why wouldn't he? Why wouldn't anybody? His mother was trying to drive his father out of the house and out of his mind. All the children knew it, but what could they do about it? His mother wasn't trying to hide anything. She was going to make Dad's life as miserable as she could. There were no two ways about it. Unfortunately, the more she made her husband hate her, the more he hated her children. It was obvious. It wasn't fair.

Dad didn't run away, but he did start to slowly disappear. He had the perfect excuse ... more money. He would work overtime. He would work anytime. He would work all the time. Didn't Mary want more and more and more - and more?

Nobody at the gas station wanted to work weekends. Ernie could work every weekend. What did it matter? Ernie could work holidays. Nobody wanted to work holidays. Ernie could work when other guys didn't want to work. He could work when his co-workers had emergencies, or had other appointments. He could work and he could work and he could work.

Gradually there was very little of his dad to be seen. He got up at four every morning, had breakfast and drank some coffee. He would be gone before Richard and the others got up. Then he would work overtime each evening and be home by eight or nine o'clock at night. What difference did it make? When he did get a day off, he just sat in his chair at home, listening to Mary gripe while he drank beer and gritted his teeth.

His brother Ernie was never home. Dad was never home. It seemed like the manly thing to do. Richard avoided his home also. He went to school every weekday. Richard was never too sick to go to school. He would rather die of typhoid at his desk at school than in his bed at home with "her" by his side.

After school he delivered his newspapers. He didn't rush the paper delivery either. He would return home for supper, gulp everything down and then rush out the door with his basketball. When he was little, it was the rule that he had to be home when the streetlights went on, but when his dad was away at sea, he stretched it and stretched it. Most of his friends still had to be home at dark or shortly thereafter.

Richard wouldn't get home sometimes until nine or ten o'clock. His mother never said a word. She was always too busy slapping his sister Carol around or running about the house ranting and raving.

Carol being a girl, she could not stay out in the streets until all hours of the night. Boys were different. Girls had to be home with their mothers, learning to bake brownies, do the laundry and scrub the floors. Carol was stuck. She had no rights and no privileges. She didn't even have a bedroom. She slept on a pull-out couch in the parlor. No matter what time of night Richard arrived home, he could open the hall door and hear the ranting and raving of his mother. Sometimes he would stop in the dark hall and try to think of an alternative to proceeding into that house. What could he do? Where could he go? He would stand there in the darkness and think. But there were no alternatives. There was no escape. It was for him, as it was for his father, in this life and forever, amen.

Richard was so filled with hate and frustration that he often felt that he would burst. One day he would explode and disappear into the atmosphere. One day he would be old enough to leave, but even when that day came, where could he go? How would he escape? He didn't know, but somehow he would. He certainly would. He would leave this house and he would never come back. But what about his father? What about his brother and sister? It was just her - his mother. She was the one who made everything so horrible.

Poor Carol, if he were her, he would have jumped off a bridge. She had to spend all of her free hours with that crazy lunatic. How did she keep her mind? How did she keep her sanity? How did she keep herself from just killing that woman? She had to listen and listen and listen. If Carol said anything, more than likely, she would get a slap in the teeth for her opinions. It mattered little what those opinions were. Most evenings Richard returned to the house before his dad would arrive. His sister Carol would be sitting in the corner next to the stove. She was usually being yelled at, getting lectured on something, or wiping tears from her eyes from the slap in the face that she had just received.

Each time Richard arrived home and saw his sister sitting there in that condition, a terrible anger arose inside him. It made his stomach twist into knots. Sometimes these feelings actually made him sick to his stomach. He would look at his mother and wish that she would drop dead, right there in front of the sink. If only she would just die, everybody and everything would be quiet.

"What the heck are you gawking at!" his mother would scream as he stood there in the doorjamb wishing that he were entering into someone else's home.

"Nothing," he would counter. That was the perfect answer. That is what he felt about his mother - nothing. She was a - nothing. She was absolutely nothing. He felt nothing towards her. He wished nothing for her. His love for her was less than nothing. If only he could just grab her by the throat and squeeze the air out of her, until she ... stopped. If she could just be stopped; stopped permanently - stopped for good and forever - just stopped.

"Good. I was just telling your big-shot sister over there how lucky she was. When I was a girl, I wasn't as lucky as her. At her age, I was out working a full-time job. I wasn't just lounging around the house doing a few dishes or scrubbing a floor every now and then. I had real work to do."

Richard wondered how much work his mother actually did in her life. How long did she actually work - a week, a month, a year? What did she do when she worked? Whatever it was that she did, how could it have been any harder than what millions of others had to do every damn day of their lives? She wasn't born in Russia or Yugoslavia. His mother was so full of crap she reeked from the stink of it.

"You had it real tough, Ma," he said closing the door.

"Are you being smart with me?" In "mama" language that meant, "I ain't tired of slapping people around yet. You want some of this, little boy?"

"No, I'm saying you had it real tough, that's all," he defended in a milder tone.

"You're damn right I had it tough, tougher than you'll ever know. You are another little wimp, like your sister over there. You've had it made all your life too, buster."

"I work. I have a job."

"You call a newspaper route a job. Huh! You call that work? You've got to be kidding."

"Well, it is better than nothing, ain't it? At least I'm not asking you for money every day, am I?"

"No, you're not. That's good. That's real good. Next, start making more money than what's necessary to buy a soda pop and a couple of bags of potato chips. Start making enough money to buy some school clothes and some of those fancy sneakers."

"Fancy?"

"Oh, you mean that those clothes ain't good enough for you? You poor, poor dear! Mama really feels so sorry for her little baby. I'll just run down and buy you a whole new wardrobe. I wouldn't want you to be ashamed. Are all of the other kids down at the schoolyard making fun of my poor little Richard, are they?"

Richard wasn't ashamed of his clothes, or his wardrobe. There were things that he was ashamed of though. He was ashamed to come home every night and find his sister crying in a corner. He was ashamed that he couldn't pay for all of his own needs. He was ashamed to wear sneakers that she had to pay for. He was ashamed that his dad wanted to work twenty-four hours a day so that he didn't have to be with his family. He was ashamed to have a mother like the one that was standing before him; to think that he was supposedly a part of her flesh. He was ashamed that he was not yet big enough to stand up to this woman's abuse. Did she know what "a slap in the teeth" or "a crack in the face" felt like? Some day he would teach her.

“I’m not complaining. I just said that these clothes ain’t fancy.”

“Well, let me tell you something, Buster. Those clothes that you have on your back are mighty fancy compared to what I had to wear as a kid.”

“Oh, I suppose that you were underprivileged?”

“Your damn right I was underprivileged! We had nothing fancy in our house. We made do. We didn’t complain either.”

“I’ll bet,” Richard mumbled.

“What?”

“I just said that I’ll bet you didn’t complain.”

“Do you know what happened to us if we complained?”

“No what?”

“I’ll tell you what, smart guy. We got ourselves a crack in the teeth or a big leather strap across the legs. If I ever talked to my mother the way that you guys get away with talking to me, why I’d be talking on the other side of my face. My mother wouldn’t take the guff you guys put out. We’d get knocked from here to kingdom come. You guys think you have it tough? You don’t know what tough is all about. You guys are on Easy Street. You guys are living in the lap of luxury compared to what I had, let me tell you. This place is the Taj Mah Hall compared to what I had to live in.”

“Yah, this place is the Taj Mah Hall, all right? Besides, you told me that you were born right upstairs in this very house. This house was different when you were a kid?”

“Hey Buster, don’t you get smart with me. Whenever you don’t like it here; whenever the clothes aren’t nice enough for you; whenever the food ain’t fancy enough; or just whenever you damn well feel like it, you go find yourself a job and see how far you can get.”

That was exactly what Richard had in mind. He would get himself a job and get out of this dump. When he did, he would never come back.

The letters from Yugoslavia kept coming. Each time they would go down to the fence and listen to the hairy man translate.

“She says that she received your last package. She really appreciates it. Don’t send nothing too good, she says. The soldiers open all of the boxes. They take all the good stuff for themselves. Just send old clothes, she says. She doesn’t know if you have been sending money, but don't. Money never gets to them. The soldiers search through all the pockets and they keep all the money."

The next letter:

"She says that she received your last package. She thanks you very much. Things are getting worse there. The police come every day to take somebody, a neighbor or somebody. Her and the children are very frightened."

The next letter:

"Things are very, very bad. She doesn't know if she will be able to send any more letters. The police look at her very suspiciously. They have been to her house and searched it. She doesn't know what they are looking for. Next, she thinks that they will probably come for her."

It was a couple of months before the next letter came. This letter looked different. The handwriting wasn't the same. Something was wrong. They rushed down to the hairy man's fence: "This letter is not from the same woman. This is from her little girl, her daughter. This will be the last letter that you will receive. Do not send any more packages. The police have come and taken her mother. She thinks that soon they will be coming for her and her little brother. She is very frightened. She thanks you for everything - for all of your kindness. She says that she and her brother will love you and think of you always. She knows that her mother loved you very much also. Good-bye, she closes."

Richard's father stood there at the fence frozen as cold and hard as a rock. He thanked the man, took his letter back, folded it and stuffed it into his shirt pocket.

"Thank-you," he told the man. "I appreciate what you have done."

"Me? I didn't do a thing. I was glad that I could be of help. And ... ahh ... I am sorry about your friends. I hope that they will be all right."

When they got back to the house, Mary went into the bedroom and started unpacking the last box of old clothes. She took the clothes from the box and put them back into the bureau drawers. She didn't speak, but Richard knew that she was happy. It was finally over. Mary always packed the boxes. She never liked doing it. She complained all the while. After the letter that advised not to send any good stuff, she tried to pack the box with rags. Richard and Carol would not let her do it. They told their dad and then he checked the boxes and taped them all up.

Ernie got a beer out of the fridge and went to the parlor. The house was quiet for a good hour or two. Richard could see those two poor children hiding in their apartment. How frightened they must be, he thought. They didn't even have beds to hide beneath. The only big person in their house had been taken by the police.

What did that mean? What did the police do to people in foreign countries? Mr. Houlihan was a policeman. He lived right down the street. Richard's father once told Mr. Houlihan to go crap in his hat. What were the police like in Yugoslavia?

Mary finished her unpacking and busy work. Finally she went out into the parlor. "Well, it is all probably for the best," she said sitting herself down on the couch across from Ernie. "They will probably figure out a way to do without us. They'll do all right. They'll scrimp and save like we all have to do. They will find a way to make ends meet. People always do. They'll just have to double up and pull in their belts. They'll get by."

"Mary, didn't you hear what the man said. The police have come and taken them away."

"Yes, I heard, but that doesn't mean anything. I mean police aren't going to hurt women and children. They are probably just going to send them someplace else."

"Yeah, they're going to "relocate" them, just like the Germans did with the Jews during the war."

"Not relocate. I didn't say relocate. They will probably be sent to a better place."

"Right, a place with no address; their mother went first to make the beds and put up the curtains."

"The Germans lost the war. Yugoslavians ain't Germans. They aren't going to carry them off to any concentration camps and starve them to death. Those days are past. That stuff is all over with."

"You think so? You don't think that nice Communists do things like that, I suppose."

Mary didn't know what to say. She was just trying to make things better. Her way with words didn't quite make it. Ernie sat there in his soiled, overstuffed chair smoking his pipe. He sat there staring out through the Venetian blinds, out into the darkness of the evening and drank.

Mary kept mumbling condescending platitudes. "Don't worry. Everything will be all right. People can take care of themselves."

Ernie didn't answer. He wasn't listening. He was thinking. Those people were the best thing that had ever happened to him. Now, they were dying. They could all be dead by now. Who knows how long it took that letter to get here? There would be no more letters to look forward to. There would be no more packages to send off. There would be no more dreams.

The packages and the letters were the reality that kept the dream alive. Those poor people loved him. He knew that they really cared if he lived or died. Sometimes he felt that thinking about that poor family was the only thing that made his life worthwhile.

They had come for her, the letter said. They had taken her. She would be killed or starved, or tortured, or raped, or beaten, or all of the above. What about the children? Why couldn't he have brought them all over here? Why couldn't he have smuggled the whole family aboard the ship? If he was a single man, maybe he could have married the woman or some such thing. But no - he could do nothing.

This is the way that it always was. Strangers could come and take all the things that mattered, all the things that he loved and cherished. They could take it all and just crush it. It could all be destroyed with just a flick of the finger.

His life here with Mary was the same thing. He had a wonderful, beautiful dream. It was filled with love and passion. It was a dream of wealth and gold, and castles in the sky. Mary battered it all. She bashed it and crumbled it to dust. She turned it all into an unfeeling ritual of begrudging and condescending sex and a debauchery of nickels and dimes. Their marriage was nothing but a multitude of senseless arguments, complaints and criticisms.

"Stay away," he mumbled. "Stay away from me. Just stay away from me." He sat there in his overstuffed chair, and mumbled. The world was doing it again. It was doing it all over, once again. Dreams don't come true and they die filled with hurt and pain. They die in frustration, anger and hate.

"You know," Mary bubbled brightly. "We could keep sending clothes. We could send clothes to another poor family over there. We could get the name of another family ... and ... ah, we could save clothes for them."

"OH, FOR GOD'S SAKE, JUST SHUT UP!" Ernie finally screamed.

"Don't you talk to me like that," Mary said with a tremble in her voice. "I'm just trying to help."

"Sure you are," Ernie slurred. Richard had never heard his dad speak to his mother with such harshness before. In the past he mostly pleaded for her to keep quiet. He would beg her to shut up. He sometimes raised his voice, but this time it was no polite request. He was angry. He had screamed his demand. There was a threat in his voice.

His mother didn't seem to get it. His father was about to explode. Richard could just feel it. His mother, on the other hand, seemed totally unaware. She couldn't distinguish between pleading and demanding. She didn't know the difference between annoying and hateful. She didn't shut up. She took his demanding tone of voice and his harsh words as a personal insult. Who was he to be yelling at her? Who was he to scream in such a tone, when she was simply trying to empathize with his sadness? Why was it that he always turns his problems onto her? Why does everybody blame her? It was always the same. She was the cause of everybody's unhappiness.

"Don't you tell me to shut up! These people were your friends, not mine. I gave up my things and made sacrifices for people who I never met and never even knew. What do I get for it? SHUT UP! That is what I get. When I try to help; when I try to do the right thing for you, that's all I get. Shut up! That all I ever get out of you."

"God damn it! SHUT UP! SHUT UP! SHUT UP! I can't stand it any more," he screamed, covering his ears with his hands.

Richard was lifted from his seat with fear from his father's screams; hearing his dad scream like he had never heard before sent shivers throughout his body. His dad's screaming was like a bolt of lightning cracking suddenly from a cloudless, sunny sky. He was frightened.

It was always frightening to hear his parents argue. They had argued all of his life, it seemed. How many times had he and his brother lay in their bed jumping and twitching with each burst from the kitchen? How could it just go on like this? How can two people hate one another so and continue living in the same house? Why didn't his dad just get up and walk out that door and never come back? Why did Richard never think of his mother leaving? She could never leave. She talked about when she used to work in Baltimore. She could never work. She was too crazy. She was nuts. She couldn't be with other people and get along. She hated everybody.

She got a job at the bus terminal once. The boss told her to clean the bathrooms. She quit the job on the spot. She had quit the job at the Arlington mill because of Richard. She quit though the family didn't have a nickel. She quit though her having a job could have kept her husband at home. She quit every job knowing what importance it held for her husband and her kids. What did she care? She was too good to clean bathrooms. She was too good to work. Work was for men to do. She was not a man. She was to be cared for by the man. Work was below her station in life. Well, certainly the bus station was below her station. Of course, his dad could do anything for two cents an hour, but that wasn't below his station. Why?

Why did it go without saying that this was her house and not his? Why was it understood even to Richard that if anybody left, it would have to be his father and not his mother? Why was it nothing to hear his mother yell and scream, but shocking to hear his dad raise his voice in anger? His dad had yelled and chills ran down his spine. Why? Why was his dad the caged beast in this zoo and his mother the caretaker? Why was Dad the one filled with the guilty heart and Mom the one with all the demands? Why was Dad, the big, strong man, the one with all the muscles, but yet the inferior one? Wasn't he the one who "brought home the bacon"? Wasn't he the provider?

Richard always felt that his dad lived in a cage, but the cage was of his own construction. He simply had to open the door, step outside, and walk away. He had a job now. He could always work. Why did he just sit there and allow her to make him so miserable?

She was hopeless and helpless. She could never provide even herself with a living. She was a lot of talk. She didn't have what it takes to even feed herself, never mind provide for her children. If his dad walked away from it all, what would she do? How would she survive? His dad was the one with the power. He was the one who should have been in charge of this family. He was the real boss, but he didn't act like one. He would never leave.

The children all secretly wished that he would. Richard constantly prayed that his father would leave his mother and take him and his brother and sister with him. Yet constantly his father told him that he stayed only because of him and the other children. If it weren't for them he would have left years ago. Why couldn't they all just leave? Why did any of them need this unpleasant woman? Why did they have to sit and allow this woman to destroy their lives? She made everything ugly. She made it all so miserable. Why didn't she just pack her bags and go back to hell, or wherever it was that she came from?

"I will never shut up. This is my house too. I will say whatever I please. You're not the king of this palace. Where do you get off telling me to shut up anyway? Who the hell do you think you are?"

Richard's father's face had turned crimson. The veins in his neck looked as though they would burst. His eyes were a rage. It made Richard nervous, but his mother didn't seem to notice. His dad wasn't the kind who would hurt anyone. Richard was afraid that he would end up hurting himself. He wouldn't fight back. He would run away and return drunk and battered. Richard wished that his mother would stop, or that somehow his dad could think of something to say that would make her stop. His dad didn't have that power. She couldn't be stopped. His dad would probably sit there until her batteries ran down. No she would never shut up.

His father simply sat there, staring at her in a silent rage. His face, his neck, his hands, even his forehead were blood red. He dropped his head and rubbed his rough, coarse beard with the palm of his hand. After a moment he rose from his seat, went to the bedroom and got his jacket, then exited the apartment. Mary told Richard to chase after him, but Richard refused. Everyone knew what would now happen.

It was difficult for Richard to understand his mother's thinking. Her face showed concern. She was already worried. She knew that Ernie would be going to a barroom. This woman was completely out of her mind. She literally drove this man from their home by her constant complaining, bickering, and nagging. Yet when he left, she was sad and ... concerned. What could possibly be going on inside her head?

The economic crisis of their lives was finally over. His father had a job. He liked his job and the company liked him. He was being promoted to manager. He could work all he wanted. Money was no longer the primary cause of all their misery. They had an automobile. They had a TV. They went last year for a two-week vacation to the seashore. How could things be better?

All his life Richard had prayed for this situation and now God had finally made it all possible. Why was his mother doing this? Did she like it better when his dad was somewhere out in the middle of the ocean? Did she like it better not knowing whether he was dead or alive? Why did she not treat his father kindly now that he was here where he belonged? Why must she always argue? Why must she always create tension, even when there was nothing to be tense about? Why couldn't she just agree once in a while? Couldn't she just stop talking, once - just for a few moments? Why was she constantly trying to run this man off? Why was she sad and worried once she succeeded? If she was truly concerned about this man's well being, why didn't she make any attempt to create a home that a person would want to remain in? Didn't she know what she was doing? Richard was just a child and he could see what she was accomplishing. Was she just insane? Was she mad? Did she truly belong in a nut house?

Richard went into his bedroom and got his jacket. He went out the kitchen door. Mary was now standing on the front porch. She was watching her husband disappear into the night. Richard walked passed her and down the steps. He flipped the metal latch on the gate.

"Go get him, Richard. Don't let him go off and get drunk."

"Why should I? He has the right to get drunk if he wants to. He's the one who earns all the money around here."

"Oh, is that right! You get back in here right now. Who gave you permission to go out at this hour of the night?"

"It's only six o'clock."

"I don't care what time it is. You get back into this house and go to your room." Richard kept walking. "Did you hear me?

You get back over here when I say to, or I'll teach you how to obey your mother."

Richard continued walking. He was heading in the opposite direction from his father. He couldn't talk to his father. His father didn't talk to him when he was sober.

"Well, you had better be home early then," she hollered.

Richard didn't even turn around to acknowledge his mother's last comment. He didn't care. It was interesting though, he thought. First she threatened him with violence, but when he continued to disobey, she changed her threats to requests.

He wanted to walk forever and never come back. All women were crazy and all grown men were drunks. There were barrooms on every corner in this town. They were always full, full of stupid men sitting there on a stool getting drunk. His dad had his regular haunts. Other of his friends' fathers had different places. They all drank. All the men drank and all the women bitched. Richard had been inside nearly every bar in the area, shining shoes.

His uncle had made him that shoeshine kit. Richard would wander around from bar to bar, shining shoes when his dad was off at sea. The smell of a bar reminded him of his dad. The smell of beer and cigarettes - that's what daddy means to me.

Many of the men in the barrooms had peculiar noses. Some of the fathers of his chums had funny noses - big, red, bulbous things with holes all over them. His dad didn't have a nose like that. People had told Richard that men got noses like that from drinking too much. Richard never saw a woman who had such a nose, so he believed it to be true.

When he shined shoes, some of the men in the barrooms would try to cheat him out of his dime. He learned to get his dime up front. You really didn't want to get any polish on a man's socks when you shined shoes. That was important. A lot of men got real mad at that. A good many of the men in the barrooms were just plain stupid. You had to treat them like children.

Richard just kept walking and thinking about nothing. Shoe shining was nothing; barrooms were nothing. Anything was better than thinking about his mother and father and his home. That wasn't a home. It was a zero. It was nothing.

He walked all the way up to Lawrence Street and then down past the O'Neil Playstead. The O'Neil was in Methuen. He was getting a good distance from the house. He didn't care. One day when he was more than ten or eleven years old and much bigger, he would walk away from that house and never come back. How would he take care of himself though? His dad was a smart guy, and for most of his life he couldn't find a job. He was lucky to get this job at the Merit gas station. It took nearly all of Richard's life for his dad to find this job. How would Richard ever be able to go out on his own and find a job? It wasn't that easy. Families should work together. Everybody should help one another until they were able to make it on their own. His family was a lost cause. They didn't know how to work together. They didn't know how to be a team.

Richard didn't know what time it was when he returned home. As soon as he opened the hall door, he could hear his mother's shrill voice. What was she moaning about now? There was just no end to it. She never stopped. He wanted to turn and return to the empty night streets. The streets were quiet. All the people were in their little apartments. At night the streets were quiet in Lawrence. Inside his apartment things were never quiet. As he walked about the streets, he could see people living inside their apartments: men drinking or reading the paper; women crocheting or fixing supper; families sitting in front of their TV's. How nice it would be to be a part of a real family.

He closed the hall door and headed for the apartment. He heard his father's voice. That was good. His dad had come home. His dad hadn't been bad-drunk in a long while. This might be a good sign. When he opened the kitchen door, his mother motioned him into the parlor. His mother looked nervous and somewhat frightened. She must like being in that condition, he thought. He saw his dad sitting in his overstuffed chair. He was clearly drunk and mumbling to himself.

"What ya watchin' Dad?"

"I'm not watching anything," his dad mumbled. His dad had gotten himself drunk, but at least he was safely home and sitting in his chair. That was something to be thankful for. "How's your paper route coming, son?" This was funny. His dad had never asked him once about his paper route in all the year that he owned it. Now he gets drunk, and he wants to know about paper routes. It was strange. It was really strange. This man was two different people.

"It's pretty good."

"That's good, but I still think that you should be having fun instead of working at your age."

"I'm having fun, Dad. It is easier to have fun when you have some money."

"Yeah, well, that's good. You're having fun." He paused and took a swallow from his can of beer. "I'm not having fun."

"You're not? Why's that?" Richard asked as if he were having a conversation with a two-year-old. His dad put his index finger up to his lips and motioned Richard to move closer so that they could talk more secretly. Richard scooted across the carpet, closer to his dad's chair. "Do you know why I'm not happy, son?" Richard nodded his head affirmatively. "You do?" his dad asked dubiously. Richard pointed out to the kitchen. His dad then nodded his head up and down and flopped back into his chair. He looked surprised that the boy was aware of the source of his father's discontent. Did he really think that he was keeping it concealed? One would have to be a very slow child indeed to live in this house and not know the source of discontent. "You are a wise one," his father complemented. He then pointed a finger to the side of his head. "You've really got it up here, boy. You might not be the brightest when it comes to the school books, but you got it where it counts." He then pointed to his heart. "You know what's happening inside here," he said. "That's the reason that I can talk to you. You've got it where it counts. That's where you and me are alike. You know how things feel. You don't have to get it all spelled out for you. That's why I can talk to you. Most would think that you are too young to understand these things, but you're a little man. You are a chip off the old block. Let me tell you. Did I ever tell you that before, son?"

"Yeah."

"Well good, because it is the truth. You and me son, we know what is happening around here." He slapped his palm to his chest. "We've got it in here. My brothers and sisters, they have it upstairs but they don't know what is going on down here, on the inside."

Richard loved this kind of drunken, dribble type conversation the best. This is when he and his dad were pals.

His dad wasn't treating him like a little kid, but as a grown man. These were the moments when his dad treated him like a real person and not just a piece of furniture. His father drank the secret potion and was now his other self. Even Richard's mother felt Richard to be necessary at these moments. Ernie talked with Richard, like he did with Uncle Joe. Ernie, when drunk, looked upon Richard as a friend and intellectual equal. Richard understood.

"Let me tell you something about this life son. Now you listen to me. I know you think you are smart - and you are - but you don't know everything yet. You're still young. But it won't be long before you get a little bigger and you start looking at the girls." Richard shook his head negatively. He already knew what his father was going to say. They had this conversation many times before. "Oh, yes you will. You take it from me. You just listen. This old man, he may be drunk right now, but he knows a few things. Let me tell you, and you remember ... you remember what I say. Are you listening to me?"

"I'm listening."

"You've got to be very careful son. Don't pick the wrong woman. You pick the wrong woman and she can make your life miserable. She'll make this life a hell on earth."

"But how do you know? How do you know if a woman is the right woman or the wrong woman?"

"Ahhhh! That's it. That's the 64,000 dollar question. How do you know? When I first met your mother, son, I thought that I had met the most perfect woman in the world. Really, I did - I thought that she was the best. Your mother was great back then. She was beautiful. I thought that she was the most beautiful woman in the world. I loved her. I loved her more than anything in this world. Don't you ever think that I never loved your mother. I did. Since then, I have sat here, right in this chair, and watched that love turn to hate. You would never think or believe that love could turn into hate, would you son? But, believe me when I tell you, it does."

"Why?"

"Why? That's a good question. I really don't know why. All I know is things change. Your mother changed. She got mean. She wasn't like that when I met her Richard. Do you think that I would have married her, if she was like this when I met her? Never! Never! Never in a million years. When I met her, she was quiet and sweet. She never said boo. Now you can't shut her up."

"You're talking about me, aren't you?" Richard's mother said coming to the parlor entrance. "You're telling the boy bad things about his own mother."

"Can't a man have a conversation with his own son around here?"

"Yes, go ahead and talk." She put her hands onto her hips and stood, defiant, in the doorway.

"I've been telling the boy the truth. That's all, just telling him the truth about life."

"Sure, and what's the truth?"

"The truth is that you have changed over the years. You're not the same woman that I married."

"Oh, and I suppose that you haven't changed?"

"I've changed? Okay, how have I changed?"

"Well, for one thing, when I first met you, you didn't drink. You were never drunk in those days."

"Oh really?"

"Yes, really."

"And why do you think that I drink now? Did you ever ask yourself that question?"

"Yes, a million times. I don't know. I've never been able to figure it out."

"Well, I'll tell you the answer. Would you like to know?"

"Yes."

"It's easy. It's because living with you would drive the Pope to the bottle. You would drive any man to drink, Mary."

"And I suppose that you think that living with you has been just great fun for me?"

"Oh, go away, Mary. Nobody can talk to you. I don't want to argue. I want to talk to my son."

"And tell him more of your drunken lies."

Ernie turned to Richard, ignoring his wife standing in the archway. "So where were we, son?" Richard didn't answer. "Look at her standing there. She's ready for a fight at the drop of a hat. Do you think that your old man would have married a woman like that, if he knew in the beginning what she was going to be like?"

"Don't you call me "her." I'm not "her." I'm your wife, and that boy's mother."

Ernie ignored the woman in the doorway, and continued his conversation with the boy. "Well, what do you think, son? Do you think that any man would marry a woman like that? Why it would have been smarter to tie an anchor around my neck and jump off the Merrimack Bridge."

"And being married to you has been one great, big party. I just have everything that any woman could want. Tell the boy about all the wonderful promises that you made to me. Tell him about all the great things that you were going to do. Tell him about what a big failure you have turned out to be. Tell about that, Mr. Big Shot."

Ernie continued to ignore his wife standing there. "But instead of jumping off the Merrimack Bridge, I stay here and each day I die a minute at a time. Do you know why? Do you know why I do it?" Richard nodded his head affirmatively. "Well you're right. I do it because of you. I do it because of you and your brother and your sister. I do it because I love you kids, that's why. If it weren't for Ernie, Carol and you ..." He pointed directly at Richard sitting on the floor, for emphasis. "I would have been gone a long, long time ago."

Richard wished that he could tell his dad that he could leave right then, but he knew that his dad couldn't. If his dad left, who would pay the rent; who would buy the groceries and worst of all, if his dad was gone, Richard would be back to living alone with that crazy woman and the violence. In a perverted way, his father was acting as a surrogate. As long as Dad was around, mother attacked him. If Dad were gone, Richard had no doubt that his mother would be right back into slapping him and his sister all about. If only his dad would suggest leaving and taking Richard and his brother and sister with him. What if they all just got into the car, drove away, and left her to stay behind and beat up on herself? Wouldn't that be a wonderful solution?

Richard heard all of his mother's arguments as inane and self-indulgent. She only talked of all the things that her husband was not able to provide. She talked of his promises, of love as a contract for washing machines and refrigerators. If she wanted more things, why didn't she go out and work for them? How many hours in one day could his father work? His father's arguments on the other hand spoke to the emotions. His dad just wanted to be loved, respected and appreciated. He never mentioned material things. He never mentioned money. He talked about loyalty, trust and love. His father spoke Richard's language. His mother spoke dominance and "gimme, gimme, gimme."

"So tell the boy the truth, Mr. Big Shot. Tell him ..."

"I've told him the truth," Ernie screamed.

Suddenly Richard was out of their conversation. They were at once yelling and debating with one another. Richard was a little, silent referee. "I told him how a million years ago, I used to love you."

"You did?"

"Yes I did." Mary turned and stormed back into the kitchen. Ernie paused for a moment and then slumped back into his chair. He looked down at Richard sitting there on the carpet and shook his head negatively. "What should I do, son?" he asked the boy. Richard shrugged his shoulders. "Be careful, son. Be very, very careful. That's all that I'm telling you. You can see what she is doing to me, can't you?"

"Yes."

"It is the worst thing in life to have to live with a woman like her. I never thought that I would be saying anything like this. If I had it to do all over again, I would never do it. You kids wouldn't even be alive." Richard's mother burst back into the room.

"You stop talking to him like that! Stop talking behind my back!"

"I'm not talking behind your back. I'll tell him right in front of your face." He turned and looked at Richard. "You see that woman standing right there." He pointed up to Mary standing in the doorway. He leaned forward in his chair to get closer to Richard's ear. "She has ruined my life. She was a beautiful, understanding woman when I married her. Now she has turned into a hateful, complaining shrew."

"STOP IT, ERNIE!" Mary screamed. "STOP IT! You're trying to turn my own children against me. You are trying to turn sons and daughters against their own mother. That's not right. That's not fair." She started crying.

"Is that what I'm doing son? Am I turning you against your mother?" Richard shook his head. Richard knew in his heart he was already against his mother. She had turned him against herself long ago. She had been successful in that achievement when his dad wasn't even around. She had turned Richard against her with every sadistic remark, with every cruel word. She had turned Richard against her with the cracks in the teeth, the slaps in the mouth and the brutal beatings that had knocked him from one end of the kitchen to the other. His father hadn't really done a darn thing. He was an ally. He was a supporter of the thesis. He was a grown, intelligent man who simply recognized what was going on. His mother was no innocent. She was the animal that attacked anyone and everyone within her grasp with whatever weapons she had. He was simply pointing out the facts, as everyone else knew them. He was exactly right. He was simply stating the truth.

"You're stealing my children from me. You're trying to take them away from me," she screamed.

What in the world was she talking about, Richard thought? He didn't belong to her. He wasn't one of her children. He was nobody's child. He was a creature alive and alone in a world of crazy animals. If he belonged to anybody, it certainly was not her. She was talking and acting like she cared about him and his brother and sister. "You're taking my children from me." She had said.

My children? What was she talking about?

Mary was now standing between Ernie and Richard, screaming down at her husband who was sitting in his chair. Ernie was trying to look around her, in order to speak to Richard. He was speaking directly to Richard as a way of avoiding and ignoring his wife; as if she was something that didn't exist and was simply an obstacle between him and his boy.

"Mary, get out of my way so that I can talk to my son."

"You're not talking to him. You're brain washing him. You're turning him against me. You're teaching him to hate me. You're teaching them all to hate me."

"Mary, leave us alone and get out of this room."

"You can't tell me to get out of my own house. I'll leave this room when I'm good and ready."

Richard's father rose from his chair. From Richard's position on the floor it looked like his dad towered over his mother. His father was confronting his mother physically. He had never done such a thing before. He had ordered her to leave the room. She was disobeying. Now, how would he enforce such a demand? Mary suddenly had a look of fear in her eye. Ernie moved towards her slowly. She backed up instinctively, screaming and protesting all the while. Ernie kept walking towards her and pointing towards the exit. Finally he had backed her up and out into the kitchen. Then he grabbed the parlor door and slammed it shut.

"You see what I mean, son?" he mumbled, turning his back to the door and heading back to his chair. But, before he took two steps, the parlor door was flung open.

"You don't close no doors on me in my own house," Mary screamed.

"Oh no? Watch me." He walked back to the door and slammed it.

Richard's heart was pounding. He was filled with a nervous, frightening tension, but yet he was excited and happy. Something good was happening here. His father was finally standing up for their rights. His mother was talking about losing her children. She had no children as far as Richard was concerned. Richard truly no longer cared about his mother. He could hardly remember a time when he did care. She was nobody.

After the door had been slammed for the second time, his dad headed back to his chair. He hadn't as yet sat down when once again the door was flung open.

"Don't you dare slam this door on me, in my own house!"

"In your house?"

"This is my house, too."

"OUT!" His father pointed over his wife's shoulder to the open door behind her. "OOUUTT!" he screamed even louder.

"Don't you dare raise your voice to me! Who do you think that you are talking to, some one of your bimbos down at some barroom?"

"GET OUT! NOW!" He started towards her once again. She was frightened and began backing up once more. Then she stopped.

"I'm not going anywhere," she commanded. "You are not going to frighten me."

"Oh no? You are getting out of this room, even if I have to throw you out."

"You just try it. You just try."

Ernie walked up to Mary and attempted to turn her about by hand. She slapped his hands away. He put a hand to her shoulder and she flung it from her once again. They began then, to push and shove one another. Suddenly Ernie's hand flew up and struck Mary across the face. Mary stopped. She covered her face with her hands and began crying. She stood there for a moment with her face in her hands, then turned and ran from the room.

Ernie went to the door and closed it. He then turned the skeleton key and locked the door. Then he locked the hall door. Then he went around the piano, put a shoulder to it and began sliding it towards the door. Richard rushed over and helped his dad push the huge, old, upright piano into position. His dad had tears rushing down his cheeks.

"Well, there you have it," he said in a sobbing tone. You see now, what it all comes to. I've never hit a woman before in my life. But what was I supposed to do? You tell me, Richard? What was I supposed to do? Should I just let her run me into the ground? Doesn't a man have a right to some peace in his own home?"

Mary attempted for a third time to open the door. When she couldn't she began screaming and pounding at it.

"You stop telling him lies! Stop trying to steal my children. Stop trying to take my children away from me."

"Am I stealing you?" he said looking towards the boy. Richard shook his head. "You see what I mean, Richard? That woman is crazy. I don't know what has gotten into her. I have to lock doors in my own home just so that I can have a moment of peace. What kind of a home is this? Is this a home, Richard?" The boy shook his head negatively. "Then what is it? You tell me? What do you call this place?"

"It's a nuthouse," Richard replied.

The father stood staring at the boy and nodding his head in agreement. Then he screamed to Mary who was still pounding on the other side of the door and yelling about her children being stolen from her.

"This is a nuthouse, Mary! That is what Richard thinks. The boy thinks that he lives in a nuthouse!" Richard's father shouted.

"And I think that you are right, son. This place is a damn nuthouse - a real nuthouse. That is a perfect description of this place, son. I feel exactly the same. I've tried to do my best. I work. I bring home some money. I give it all to your mother. You see me. Don't I throw the pay envelope onto that table out there every week?" The boy nodded. "You're damn right I do. And now I have slapped your mother. I can't believe it. Listen to her out there." They both stopped to listen to Mary, still pounding and screaming on the opposite side of the parlor door. "I've always thought that any man who struck a woman wasn't worth a penny. Now, here I am. It just seems that every day I watch myself turn into all of the things that I've despised and hated ever since I was a child. You think that maybe you are a little better than the next guy because you don't do this thing or that thing. The next thing that you know, you are doing all the things that you put everybody else down for. Suddenly you are no better yourself than the lowest tramp in the street. I left that bar and came home tonight because I couldn't stand looking at myself. I don't mean in that mirror behind the bar. I mean in the eyes, faces and habits of all the rest of those men down there. Suddenly they didn't look like my old pals and buddies. They all looked like a bunch of losers. I looked into all of those drunken dopey eyes, and I was staring at myself. I couldn't stand it. I had to come home. Now look what happens? I beat up my wife."

"You didn't beat her up, Dad."

"I didn't?"

"Nah."

"I hit her."

"So?"

"So, men shouldn't be hitting women."

Richard wanted to tell his father about all of the times his mother had hit him. If it were wrong for husbands to hit wives, wouldn't it be wrong for women to hit their children? His father had given his mother a little love pat on the cheek. That wasn't beating anybody. If his dad wanted to see a real beating, he should have been home the day Richard brought home the note. If it is a legitimate question to ask what kind of a man strikes his wife, it should be of equal legitimacy to ask what kind of a woman beats her own children. What kind of a mother is it that belts her child from one end of a room to the other? His dad didn't have to feel guilty about hitting her. He should have closed up his fist, and smacked her head into the wall once or twice for good measure.

Richard wanted to tell his father these things but he couldn't. Telling such a thing would be spreading his own hate. He didn't want to spread hate. He didn't want to hate even his mother. "Honor Thy Father and Thy Mother," the commandment said.

Strange, there was no commandment that said, "Thou shalt not beat thy little baby children." Neither was there a commandment that said, "Thou shalt not smack thy wife." There were a number of missing commandments. But, certainly, if his mother had broken no commandments, his father should not be torturing himself over a little "crack in the teeth." If little children deserved cracks in the teeth and slaps to knock their smiles to the other side of their faces, certainly a good man could give his wife a little "love tap" every now and then. Why was it something horrible for his father to be hitting his mother and a simple matter of daily routine for his mother to be slapping Richard and his sister?

His father was like a man from another planet. Did he not know what this woman had been doing all of these years to his children? This woman deserved to be hit, and not just a little. She deserved to get more than a little slap in the teeth.

Richard felt sorry for his father. His father was too sensitive. He was too filled with conscience and love. Richard did not feel sorry for his mother. He wished that his father had hit her harder. His mother was getting off easy, and his poor father was suffering for having done even that little bit. That woman was very lucky that Richard did not have his way. His mother would be in store for a good beating. She would know what her kitchen floor felt like. She would learn to know the taste of her own blood inside her ripped mouth. She would certainly know the taste of her tears if Richard were in charge. What she got tonight from her husband was nothing.

"You don't have the right to steal my children. It is not fair. It is not right. I'm their mother."

The woman was still screaming on the other side of the door. This woman was without doubt as crazy as a loon, Richard thought. She was putting on a show. She was trying to trick her husband. His poor father was too stupid to know the real truth, and Richard had no way to explain it to him. You cannot steal from a person what they have never had. Richard did not belong to that insane woman. She was no mother of his. Richard was his father's son. He was always his father's son and would always be his father's son – first, last, and always.

"You can't lock me up from my children. You can't steal a child from its mother. It is not natural. It is a sin. It's not fair."

Richard sat on the parlor floor, thinking. Honor Thy Father and Thy Mother ... Honor Thy Father and Thy Mother ... Bless me Father, for I have sinned. It has been all of my life since my last confession and I have sinned. I did not honor my mother - ever. I do not honor her now. I wish that she would disappear. I wish that she would go away for ever and ever. I wish that she would go and that I would never see her again. I wish that she were dead. Oh God, I wish that my mother were dead.

15 Confession

His father sat quietly in his chair. He stopped talking. Mary continued to pound on the parlor door. The door would remain closed with the huge upright piano pressed up against it. Carol was out in the kitchen with her mother, sitting in her chair at the far side of the stove, crying. Richard sat on the parlor floor staring at his father.

What sort of a man was this father of his? His dad had now been sitting for at least an hour staring in silence. His eyes blank. He was a man of strange principles. His heart was obviously broken because he had struck his wife. His confidence in himself as a man was somehow shattered. Richard could not understand. But his father had rules.

One rule was that a person was not a drunk as long as he could get up every morning and show up at work on time. This was a point of honor. Richard knew this from observation and explanation. Time after time he wondered how his father would ever manage to be up in the morning. His dad often staggered to his bedroom at night. He was doing better now that he was working at this Merit gas station, but better did not mean sober. His father had also talked about this principle. Clearly there was no commandment: thou shalt not get drunk. There was also no commandment that stated that thou shalt not miss a day at work because of a painful morning after. Nevertheless, his father had such a commandment engraved into his character. He never missed a day at work for any reason. Obviously, this was one of his dad's personal commandments. Thou shalt not beat thy wife must have been another.

His father was now sitting in that chair re-thinking his worth as a human being because he had struck his wife. This was not registering well in Richard's code of personal ethics. How could his father be so distraught over slapping a woman who had no such compunction even towards her small children? His mother hit people without a moment's thought of rightness or wrongness. His mother never sat in a chair after she had beaten him and pondered on her goodness or lack of goodness as a human being. What was going on in his father's mind? He didn't understand, but he admired his father for having such feelings, even if such feeling were totally foolish and irrational.

In Richard's fantasy when he witnessed his mother and father struggling before him in the parlor, he visualized his father knocking his mother to the floor. He saw his father grabbing his mother from beneath the kitchen table and pulling her out by the ankles as she struggled in fear to crawl away. He saw his mother's hair flying all about as his father cracked her on one side of her face and then the other. He saw his father pulling her hair up in tufts from her face so that he could get a better shot at hitting her solid, flesh against flesh, much as his mother had done to his sister time, after time, after time.

Picturing violence vividly was simple and ordinary. It was as easy to imagine as it was to witness in everyday normal life. He could see his father's foot on his mother's backside, shoving her down to the floor - sliding headlong into the refrigerator or stove. He could see his father straddling his mother as she cowered on the floor struggling to cover herself as he slapped her from one side of her face to the other. These thoughts no longer made him unhappy or feel guilty. If this is what his father had done, he would have viewed it as something befitting and appropriate. As his mother would so often reflect, "What is good for the goose is also good for the gander."

God punishes people for their wrongdoings. Sometimes He punishes them in the next life and sometimes He punishes them in this life. Whatever, He punishes them. There is no doubt about that. He burns them in Hell for eternity. He curses them with sickness and diseases. He inflicts them with pain, injury and death. To see his mother's teeth all bloody and her nose running red would be no worse than when he had seen his own face in such a condition in the mirror by his bedroom bureau. Truthfully, even fantasizing about such thoughts set his heart to rushing with excitement and anxiety. If his father had done these things, it would not be wrong. It would be the wrath of God providing justice and retribution. A child could not do such brutal things because that was against the law of God. "Thou Shalt Honor Thy Father and Thy Mother."

Obviously God thought that it was proper for children to be beaten by their parents or He would never have invented such a commandment. Why would such a command have to be stated? If parents were designed to be loving and kind to their children, no child would ever need to be commanded to honor his mother and father. It would be the natural thing to do. Clearly abuse and brutality were all a part of God's plan. It was a child's place to take his medicine.

But there is no such admonition from God with regards to adults. Adults are always beating one another in wars, in the streets, in the privacy of their living rooms. If beating is part of the law of God, then a husband should certainly have the right to beat a wife. Men are clearly greater in being than women. Women were created after men by God, and for the pleasure or comfort of men. They were a divine afterthought.

If mothers can beat children justifiably in the eyes of God, then certainly it must follow that husbands can beat wives. Why was his father then so perplexed? His father was suffering because he had laws in his mind that were of greater compassion than even the ultimate laws of God.

In this regard, his father was much like Jesus Christ the Son of God. God the Father could let His Son come to earth and be tortured, but Jesus, the Son of God, could not even bring Himself to strike out at a lowly human being. If He were struck by an enemy on the right cheek, He would turn the left cheek also. Clearly God the Father had no such attitude or scruple. Richard's mother had the power of God and his father had the conscience of Jesus. One feared God, but one loved Jesus.

Richard loved his father, and feared his mother. When his father was home he and his sister were rarely beaten. His mother had to keep up a pretense. This is what she was doing right at this moment. She was pretending to be a victim.

This man was trying to steal her children? Who was she kidding? She didn't care about her children. She was trying to impress her husband with this kind of talk. But why? What advantage did this gain her? There was some kind of a contest going on here. She was competing for something, but what? She wasn't competing for the love of her children. Richard was well aware of that. This was a battle between her and her husband - for what and towards what purpose? What did she want from Richard's father? What did she have to gain? What was she getting from all of this?

Richard could see no rational explanation. From his point of view, he saw only hate and destruction. She was a fomenter of hate. She had planted hate within Richard's heart. She was, inside herself, filled with hate and she wanted to plant this hate inside of everybody else? Why? Maybe this was simply what people do who have bad things inside of them. They don't think about it. Maybe people are just born either evil or good. If they are evil, they act in evil ways. If they are good, they act in good ways. But the good is supposed to conquer the evil. Why was his father losing this battle?

God works in mysterious ways, he had been told a thousand times. This was certainly one of God's mysteries. Richard would have to watch and learn as God played out this passion before his eyes. He would just watch and think. Maybe if he thought hard enough he would find God's message in all of this.

His father finally rose from his chair and began pushing and pulling at the piano. Richard jumped up from the floor to assist his father. When they had the piano back in its place his dad turned the key and then pulled the parlor door open. Mary came rushing from the sink where she had been washing dishes. She burst into the parlor and took up the screaming just where she had left off. Richard decided that he had had enough. He attempted to walk past his mother and out into the kitchen. His father was now positioned back into his chair, pensive and silent. The wind had left his sails.

"Where do you think that you are going?" his mother demanded, grabbing Richard by the arm.

"I'm going to my room. I'm tired of listening to your screaming."

"Oh, you can sit in here all night listening to your father's ranting and raving, but you can't listen to your mother's screaming."

"You're not my mother," Richard said standing just inches from his mother's face and staring intently into her eyes. Mary looked down at Ernie sitting in his chair.

"What did you say?" she asked in an aggressive, and at the same time, dubious tone.

"I said - You are not my mother. You are a strange insane woman who lives in this nuthouse with me, but you are not my mother."

Mary's hand came up instinctively from her side and cracked firmly against the boy's cheek. Richard looked at his father sitting in the chair. His dad's face was filled with horror and shock. Richard grinned. His dad now knew the secret of this motherly abuse. If he didn't, he should have. If his father could be so ashamed of his own actions in slapping his wife, how much more ashamed should he be to witness his wife slapping his child? Did he not witness how easily she accomplished the task? Could such proficiency have arisen spontaneously? Is not one abuse the equivalent of the other? Richard turned his gaze back into his mother's poignant, penetrating blue, vicious eyes.

"Do you think that love tap hurt me?" he asked defiantly with hate burning up from deep within. He was still grinning when her hand came up and cracked him again. Richard threw his head back and laughed, affectedly. "Maybe you better try closing your fist?" he advised.

His mother stood there captured by his audacity and the flaming hatred coming from his eyes. He was no longer afraid of this beast who called herself mother. This realization filled him with strength, confidence and courage. "Close up your fist - try it with a closed fist."

She stared.

He laughed. "You couldn't hurt me with a baseball bat. Do you know that? You could get a baseball bat and bash my head in, and I'll just laugh right in your face."

She struck him for a third time. His fists clinched at his side and he looked over at his father.

His father didn't know what to do. He looked up into the boy's eyes, as if for the first time. He saw something in the boy that he had never seen before. Earlier he had seen his own uselessness and sorry state down at the barroom in the faces of the other patrons. Now he saw what hatred in his own soul looked like in human flesh.

Mary was right. He was turning this child against her. He had turned this child against her. It frightened him. The boy's face was frightening. Mary also looked shocked. But why,

Richard thought? Did she not understand the consequences of her lifetime of abuse towards a child? Was she stupid?

"Go to your room, son," he advised in a calming, pacific voice.

"Go to his room. Is that it? Go to his room? I'll put him in his room."

She swung at Richard for a forth time, but this time Richard brought up his arm and blocked her blow. His fists were clenched. Ernie leaped up from his chair. He bumped himself between them. He looked at his son. His look was one of pity and intense guilt. He had created a monster inside this boy and he knew it. This was all his fault.

Yet, wasn't the boy expressing Ernie's own inner feelings? Couldn't Ernie have just as easily said that this woman was not his wife - that this woman was not the mother of his children? The woman that he married had disappeared a decade ago.

"Go to your room, Richard," he said again in the same controlled voice. "We will settle this in the morning."

Richard's eyes were locked with that of his mother's. Strangely enough she seemed surprised at the event now taking place. It was as if she existed in the moment. When one moment was over, she forgot the last. Life continued moment by moment, with no memory to link one moment to the next. Didn't she know how Richard felt inside?

Richard went to his bedroom. The bedroom was dark. He went to the small window in the far corner. He stood there staring out the window into the darkness. Did his mother not know how much he truly hated her? How long did she think she could beat, bully and abuse a child before the child would grow to hate her guts? It did seem that she had no contact with the consequences of her brutal actions.

Richard's heart was pounding wildly. Strangely, he felt very much elated. He had finally come to a major crossroads in his life. He no longer feared his mother. There would be no more crawling under beds. There would be no more crying, screaming and begging. It wasn't because he now had the power to dominate over her. It was the knowledge that he could withstand any thrust or attack that she might offer. He needed no weapons in this conquest. She could hit him all she wanted. She couldn't hurt him. He could walk right through her ranks. He could defeat her artillery with courage and indifference. He had never felt like this before. It was a wonderful feeling of power and control. It was much like how he had pressed his fingers into his painful bruises as a child, and endured the pain. There comes a point where one gets above the pain. He was now above his mother's tortures. She would never be able to harm him again. Her words were just words and her blows would now be painless.

His father, mother and sister were now conversing in the kitchen.

"Did you see the look in his eyes?" Mary offered to Ernie. "Haven't I been telling you? The boy is out of control. You have to do something."

Ernie sat at the kitchen table in silence. The boy was not out of control. He knew that. The boy was the product of his father's insinuations. The boy had been listening too closely to all of his father's drunken dribble. Ernie was just mumbling and moaning as he had always done. The boy had taken his father's words as truth. The boy was a true believer in his dad. Ernie was having an epiphany, a re-birth, an awakening. He was seeing the world that he had been building, unawares, through the eye of the boy. How could he change all of this?

"God, have mercy on me," he cried aloud from his seat at the table. "If ever the Creator could justifiably send a creature to hell, it's me. Did you see the look of hate in that child's eyes?"

"You're damn right I saw it. I told you. I've been telling you all along. I've been trying to explain it to you, but you haven't been listening."

"What can I do now? I could see hell right in the boy eyes. I swear. I could see hell."

Richard could not believe his ears. He thought that he had won a victory and brought his father to his side. He had exposed his mother's vicious nature. Now his dad should know who the enemy was. Didn't his father just witness his wife slapping Richard in the face three times? Was this not substantial evidence of her wickedness? Did his father think that these were the first cracks in the face that Richard had ever received? Did this not release his dad from any guilt that he might have felt for having struck his wife? Who is worse in the eyes of God, a man who is goaded into striking his wife once in his lifetime, or a mother who habitually beats her own children?

Why didn't his father rise up from his seat and slap the woman again? Why did he just sit there staring at Richard? What had Richard done wrong? Richard stated that this insane woman was not his mother. She wasn't. Richard had no part of this brutal beast inside him. This woman was a creature. This woman was a zombie. This woman was an animal of viciousness, but not apart of the inner self of Richard. He had done nothing wrong. Why was his father now so distraught? Why were they talking about the hell in Richard's eyes? Were they crazy? What about the hell that was in his mother's eyes? Didn't his father see any of that?

Carol was sitting quietly in her chair next to the stove. She hadn't done anything but cry all evening. She finally spoke.

"You could go to confession, Dad." Carol was speaking from her heart. "God forgives even the worst sinners."

"He won't forgive me, Carol. I'm too far gone." Ernie did not take his daughter's words seriously.

"That is not true. Jesus died on the cross for the sins of all mankind. He died for you too. If you ask Him, He will forgive you."

His daughter's words were simple and childlike. Yet her hope and sincerity brought tears to her father's eyes.

"Do you really think so, Carol?" he said, choking slightly.

"Yes. I think so. In fact, I know so. Jesus loves everybody. Jesus knows how good you are inside. He will forgive you in a second."

Ernie sat at the table silently. He really didn't know what to say. At that moment Richard came from out of his room.

"She's telling the truth, Dad. You are a good man and Jesus knows it. If you go to confession and tell Him that you are sorry, He will forgive you. Then you will be able to go to heaven with the rest of us."

Richard had feared for a long while that he would have to endure heaven without his father. He really didn't know if he could stand being in heaven while watching his father being punished in hell. The thought frightened him and brought him many nights of misery. Now somehow, through all of this horrible evening, God had sent a ray of hope.

Ernie looked up at his boy. The hate from hell was gone from his eyes. Ernie didn't know if he believed in God, never mind Jesus. He knew one thing for sure, though. These two children did. They believed in Jesus and they believed in their dad. The thought of this undeserved devotion brought the tears up from inside.

"I really don't think that God will want me in heaven, Rich."

"Yes, He does. I know He does. He loves you. All you have to do is go to confession and say you are sorry."

"Heaven is for everyone," Carol explained. "God made heaven for everybody. Remember that thief on the cross next to Jesus. The thief said that he was sorry for his sins, and that he believed that Jesus was truly the son of God and that was it. He was saved. If a thief can go to heaven, certainly you can. What have you ever done that is so bad?"

"Oh, you don't know girl. You don't know the half of it."

"Yes I do. I know the all of it. I know what you are inside."

"Me, too," Richard interjected. "You have got no problem with God. All that you have to do is go to Confession."

Ernie hadn't been to Confession in years. He thought about Confession: kneeling down in front of another man and confessing your sins? It was crazy. It was for children.

"I'm too big to be going to Confession. That's for children."

"It is not," Carol said. "I go to Confession every week and there are plenty of adults there."

"Yeah, all women."

"No Dad, there are plenty of men that go to Confession. I go every Friday too. The pews are full of grown men. You never grow too old for God," Richard pleaded. "Jesus was a man just like you. He will forgive you. Tomorrow is Friday. If you agree to go, I will go with you."

"I will too," Carol said.

Ernie took out his handkerchief. He wiped his eyes and blew his nose softly. He had really got himself into trouble here. He looked up at Richard. He looked into those eyes. They were filled with warmth, hope, and love. He turned and looked at his teenager, Carol. She was beaming bright and beautiful.

This was a moment here. Two moments ago this whole world was a different place. Now that these children had the opportunity to save his soul, all was bright and gay.

"So they sprinkled it with stardust, just to make the shamrocks grow."

Ernie loved that song. It always made him cry. It always made him happy. These children of his were making him very happy. He loved them. He loved them very much. He could not say no.

"Okay, we will all go to Confession, tomorrow. The three of us, now?" he added as a warning. "Now that's the three of us? We all have to go?"

Carol looked up at Richard. They both couldn't believe what they had just heard. Their father was going to go to Confession with them. It was a miracle. This was a true miracle.

Ernie sighed deeply and then sauntered to the refrigerator to get another beer. Carol ran from her chair and wrapped herself around him. Richard stood hesitantly, watching. His father looked over at his boy and then stretched out an inviting arm. The boy dropped his head and then struggled over to his father's side. His father put his strong hand behind the boy's head and pulled him to his chest.

"I love you guys. I really do."

They all stood there, huddled in front of the refrigerator. Even Mary had tears softening her cheeks as she watched and busied herself at the sink. Ernie looked over his shoulder to the woman at the sink. He stretched out his hand, smiled and winked. She shriveled up into tears, struggled over and grasped his hand. This would be an evening to remember.

"You know, I'll tell you all one commandment I haven't broke. I never take the Lord's name in vain. And I'm a sailor you know. You should of heard some of them guys on board some of those ships. But I never did. I never took the Lord's name in vain."

Carol and Richard both smiled. They knew what he was thinking. He was already getting himself prepared for the priest tomorrow night. He was nervous already. It was funny, watching your father being returned to the ranks of a child. It was funny.

"So they sprinkled it with stardust, just to make the shamrocks grow," Ernie bellowed out in baritone. No one else felt like singing. "What the heck is the rest of that song?"

"And so they called it I-ahh-land," Richard and Carol both mumbled into their dad's shirt pockets.

"That's not it, but what the heck - all together ... And they called it I-ahh-land."

They all wept.

16 Promises, Promises!

Ernie arrived home at about six o'clock that Friday evening in his Dwight Eisenhower, Texaco imitation, attendant attire. He put his greasy finger-stained officer's cap on top of the refrigerator. He emptied his brown bag of treasured beer onto a refrigerator shelf, picked himself off a cold bottle, poured it into a glass, and marched into the parlor. Carol and Richard were already seated in the parlor. They were both as neat as a pin - Richard's hair even displaying a neat, straight part on one side of his head. The brother and sister were sitting side by side on the couch, at what could only be described as a position of attention.

Ernie sat down in his chair with his glass of beer. He placed it deftly balancing on one of the hand-crocheted doilies that sat on each arm of the chair. He retrieved his pouch with tobacco, pipe and matches that was stuffed in the space between the left side of the cushion and the arm of the chair. He packed his pipe, lit it and took two or three healthy puffs. Then he coughed violently for ten or fifteen seconds. This was followed by a moment or two of gasping, hacking and spitting into his handkerchief. After which, he sat back calmly, but red faced, and stared over at the children. They were staring at him. He puffed on his pipe, as a silent cloud of smoke wafted up to envelop him.

After finishing his first glass of beer, he rose wordlessly and marched back out into the kitchen to procure a second. His wife stood by the refrigerator door as he bent at the waist and reached inside the cold-box. She leaned over the small refrigerator door and stared into Ernie's eyes.

"What?" Ernie asked curiously, looking up at Mary.

"You do remember the promise that you made to the children last night?"

"Promise? What promise?"

"You promised Richard and Carol that you would go to Confession with them tonight," she whispered. She had whispered but the kids in the other room could hear every word.

"I WHAT? Oh no, you have got to be kidding!"

"Be quiet, they can hear you." Mary continued to whisper. "They told you last night that you could still get to heaven if you went to Confession and told God that you were sorry. You agreed to go."

"That is impossible. I would never have agreed to such a thing. I'm not crazy. I don't even believe in heaven, for God's sake."

"Maybe not, but you promised your children that you would go. They have been waiting like that on the couch all afternoon for you to get home."

Ernie poured himself another glass of beer and marched, a little less confidently, back into the parlor. He reassumed his position, looking very much like Abraham Lincoln sitting in his stone easy chair at the Lincoln Memorial.

"Ah, I am not going to argue this with you children," he said, after a pause. Then he stopped. He rubbed the rough stubble on his chin with his grease stained hand, as he peeked up into their eyes. There was a long silence as Ernie tried to recall the previous evening. It was coming back to him in bits and pieces. The whole story was beginning to sound familiar. At first this morning he had thought that he had only dreamt it, a nightmare of sorts. It was now becoming more and more real. Then suddenly it was vividly clear. As the previous night's promise became more and more vivid, so too, did the color of embarrassment on his face. "Okay, I've never gone back on a promise in my life. What time do these confessions start?"

"They are going on right now," the children responded. Ernie rose slowly from his chair and left the parlor silently while shaking his head. The kids didn't really know what to think. Was he going to go or not? If he were going to go with them, where had he gone off to? Momentarily, there he was, standing in the doorway. He was dressed in a pair of gray pants and a blue Windbreaker jacket. His hair was brushed. He was holding in his hand one of his prized soft felt hats. This one was brown with a black band. Richard and Carol, on the couch, looked up at their dad and were never so proud in all their lives. They leaped from the couch and ran to the door.

"Put on your jackets," their father admonished.

The three then marched down the dark hall, out the hall door and into the street. They walked to Arlington Street. Then down to Hampshire Street and turned right at the Saint Rita's school. Saint Rita, the patron saint of lost causes loomed forebodingly there in the darkness. They were all the way to King Tut's, at the corner of Park and Hampshire, before anyone said anything.

"I'm going to tell you guys something. I'm doing this because I promised you kids - and that's all. I made a promise and I'm going to keep it. But I don't take no guff from nobody. If this priest down here starts giving me any grief, I'll tell him to go crap in his beanie, faster than either of you guys can say Jackie Robinson."

"Priests don't wear beanies, Dad. That's the pope."

"Well, I don't care what he wears. If he starts in on me about not being a good Catholic and not going to church for thirty years, I'll ..."

"You haven't been to church for thirty years, Dad?"

"Well, I was a young man when I stopped. Of course, I went when me and your mother got married, but that was it."

Listening to his dad speak, Richard couldn't help thinking that this was the best ever. His dad had only had one beer and here he was talking to them. It was as if he and his sister had suddenly come alive. They were born anew. Suddenly their father could see them.

The night was brisk and the sky above was clear and packed with sparkling stars - he, on one side, his sister on the other and their father in the middle, marching. They were actually walking together up Hampshire Street on their way to Saint Mary's church. This had to be the greatest event to yet arrive in Richard's life. The moment felt truly heroic. He knew as he looked up into the heavens that God and all the saints in heaven were smiling down upon them. They were bringing a lost soul back to Jesus.

Jesus must be so proud of them. Sure, his dad was complaining. He was afraid, that's all. It had been a long time and now he had to face Jesus. His dad is thinking that Jesus might hate him because he has been bad for so long. Richard knew that such was not the case. Jesus would forgive him. Now, no matter what other terrible things happen to them in this life, they will all one day be happy together in heaven.

Richard had pictured his father standing and burning in the horrible flames of hell many, many times. As a child the thought often made him cry. As a man, as he now thought of himself, the idea nevertheless frightened him. It was a terrible torture to know that your father would be spending his eternity in hell. There was never any way to justify such thoughts or to find consolation. Nothing in the universe could provide compensation, but now, this night, marching up Hampshire Street, he, his sister and his father, were all marching on the road to righteousness, on the road to glory, on the road to salvation. What a glorious evening! Who would ever think Hampshire Street one of God's chosen pathways to heaven?

This was a glorious evening. This was truly a glorious evening, Richard thought as they passed the gloomy specter of the old city jailhouse.

Carol was worried. She didn't want her father to tell the priest to go crap in his hat, or something worse. She had orchestrated this whole event. She had thought of this confession idea as a solution. She felt very proud. She loved and respected her dad. The thought that she could somehow be responsible for saving her father's soul and possibly bring peace to their home, filled her with joy. She and her father had never before walked anywhere, side by side. They rarely had intimate, sober moments. This was probably the closest to her father that she had ever felt. She wanted to reach over and take her father's hand, but even the thought was intimidating. She reached over, nevertheless, and entwined her arm with his. He looked down at her glowing face and smiled.

Ernie was reviewing his entire life. What would he tell this priest? He pretended to himself that he was not a believer in such things, but deep down inside he was more of an angry little boy than an atheist or agnostic. He had initially become angry with God for stealing his father away from him as a young man. After that he simply convinced himself that religion was just a lot of hooey. The idea of Priests dressed up in gowns and listening to the sins of other men was ridiculous. Why didn't they listen more to their own sins? They were all men just like him, no better and no worse. Rituals and holy masses, bells and gobbledygook were not holiness - they were foolishness. But yet, deep down inside he looked upon God as real. He could certainly go into the confessional and just lie. What the hell, what would the kids know? He could tell the priest that he told a lie once or twice and that would be the end of it. But this type of thought did not enter into his mind. He truly harbored hopes of his own salvation. He was frightened and worried - even anxious - but he was not in doubt of the existence of God. He was simply in doubt of God's willingness to forgive him, personally. He was in doubt of his own worthiness in the eyes of God. There were times when he hated God. Could God now forgive such hate?

Saint Mary's church was a beautifully designed church directly across from an equally spectacular Lawrence Public Library building. Nobody took very much notice of these buildings, but they looked like they could have been flown in directly from Europe - Rome or someplace like that. Once inside the church, Ernie looked about and recalled the days of his youth. He had been inside this church a thousand times. He had served mass as a young boy right up on that very altar. The church sparkled with purple and gold, with marble and mahogany. The windows were beautiful portraits in stained glass. There were huge sculptures of the Stations of the Cross, which depicted the sufferings of Jesus on his way to crucifixion. St. Mary's church was a solemn temple, a religious archive. The ceilings stretched upwards two or three stories high; just the sound of the huge doors slowly closing behind, made a person feel privileged.

They each daubed their fingers in the bowl of holy water at the rear of the church and blessed themselves. Ernie stopped at the back of the church. His children each grabbed a hand and pulled him gently over to a confessional to the left of the church. They genuflected and then slipped into a pew. Now was the time to kneel in the pew and contemplate one's sins. Richard had his stories all prepared and memorized. Carol then stepped off confidently as another patron exited the confessional. Once inside she performed the rituals, but then did something that she had never done before. She made a petition to the priest on a personal level.

"Father, my dad is about to enter next to confess his sins. He is a man who has not been to church since he was a child.

He is very nervous about all of this. My brother and I talked him into it. We told him that he still had a chance to go to heaven if he would come down here and confess his sins to a priest. I am asking if you will please be kind and understanding of whatever he has to tell you. My younger brother and I have gone through a lot to get him here and we don't want him to get frightened off at the last minute. He's a good man. He drinks somewhat but he doesn't swear, and he's a sailor too."

"That is very commendable, my child. I assure you, your father will be in good hands," said Father Casey.

The children watched their dad enter the confessional. That alone seemed a miracle. Richard and Carol both had given up any hope of ever witnessing such an event. It was something to witness your dad, the most powerful person in your life, proceeding humbly to a confessional. They could imagine him kneeling there inside that little box. Richard expected shortly to hear loud voices, followed by his father slamming out of that confessional. His eyes were locked onto the side of the confessional his father had entered.

Nothing happened for a long time, but eventually his father appeared. He had that look on his face that each of the children knew so very well. It was a look of pride and satisfaction with oneself. It was a look of renewed confidence. It was eyes all sparking and a complexion alive with the inner feeling of joy and blessedness. Emerging from a confessional was an invigorating experience. You only have to imagine having a personal interview with God and then arising from that interview with God's personal approval of your goodness. Like Jesus Christ, Himself, coming up to you, throwing an arm over your shoulder then rubbing his free hand into your scalp and saying with a laugh; "You are a good man Charlie Brown. We all love ya."

When the kids saw their dad's expression, both their smiles beamed and a cheer burst into their hearts. Talk about miracles!

Their father didn't return to the pew. He proceeded to the main altar. He knelt there to say his penance. When he finished his penance he went to the rack of candles under a portrait of Jesus. He put some money into the metal box and lit a candle. The kids just watched.

On the way home their father was exuberant. He explained in detail his confessional experience. Father Casey applauded him for his courage and his return to the flock of the faithful. Father Casey had recited each commandment and then asked Ernie to think if he had been offensive to it. The good priest had been very helpful and cooperative. Each time he hit upon a commandment that Ernie hadn't violated - for example, thou shall not kill - he praised Ernie for his strength and piety. Ernie was pleased with the whole situation. He felt better about himself. He truly did.

Richard was ecstatic. He kept interrupting his father at every step on their journey home, asking, "And then what did the priest say? And after that what did he say?"

Carol smiled to herself. She knew that she had done it all. She had saved her father's soul. Could there be any greater gift that she could give to show her love for her dad? Hardly!

17 All Good Things

Richard was awakened from his sleep to the sound of voices in the kitchen. The voices were not loud. They were trying to whisper. The voices were that of his father and his brother. Richard rolled over to return to his sleeping but then he heard his father say, "This is serious, Ernie. This is no indigestion."

Richard sat upright and listened attentively. Doctor Kurka had been to the house twice this week. Richard's dad had been experiencing discomfort in his chest. He had been pacing the house all week with his arms wrapped about his chest. He spoke of severe pain.

"This has got something to do with my heart," he told his oldest son. "This is exactly what happened to my father. My dad walked around the house in pain for about a week. Then bang, one day he just dropped on his way home from work. They found him sprawled out on the ground in a storefront doorway. I think this is it, Ernie."

"But didn't doctor Kurka say that this was just indigestion?"

"Yeah, that's what he said. But he's wrong. I know what indigestion feels like. This is not indigestion. In any case, I want you to promise me something, son."

"Sure Dad. What?"

"I want you to promise me that you will take care of Richard and Carol. I mean, if I'm gone, you are going to be the man of the house."

"Nothing is going to happen to you Dad. You're just worried and nervous. Just because something happened to your father, it doesn't mean that the same thing is going to happen to you. Tomorrow these pains will be all gone and everything will be back to normal."

"Maybe you're right, son. Nevertheless, I want you to promise me that you'll do what you can to look out for your little brother and your sister. I need your word on that."

"Sure. You've got it. But, I still think that you're just overreacting a little."

"You might be right, but ..."

"I understand, Dad. Don't worry."

"Well, we better turn this light out and get to bed before we wake everybody up. You go to bed, son. I'm just going to sit here and smoke my pipe for a bit."

Young Ernie didn't really know what to say to his dad. He was only nineteen. He had yet to see any death, up close and personal. In a way he thought his father was just being silly, but yet his father knew more about this sort of thing than he did. If his dad thought that he was about to die, who was he to question it? What if his father really did die? The thought frightened him. He got undressed and slipped into the bed next to Richard. He and Richard now shared the one remaining bed in their room on weekends. Ernie was off at college during the week. He had an academic scholarship to Northeastern University. He was studying chemical engineering.

"Is Dad going to die?" Richard whispered.

"I don't know, Rick. I suppose that he could. Everybody dies."

"Why doesn't he do something about it?"

"Well, he was up to the hospital and he has had Doctor Kurka over here twice. They all say that he's got indigestion."

"What's indigestion?"

"Just something simple, you don't die from indigestion. It's like a chunk of meat that didn't go down right, or is stuck someplace."

"What does Dad think?"

"He thinks that it's his heart. His father died of a heart attack, so now he thinks that he is going to have one."

"Do you think that he will?"

Ernie hesitated, and then said with a contrived confidence, "No. I don't think so."

The two brothers lay staring up at the ceiling. They were both extremely worried. Richard had a natural inclination to always believe that the worst was about to happen. In one way his father being gone would not be anything new. His father had been gone someplace most of his life. If he died, his father would now simply be gone forever.

Why would God take his father at this particular moment, though? Everything was going so well. The fishing poles were right there behind the bedroom door. They hadn't gone fishing yet, but they were there. His dad was one of the Merit gas station's top employees. He was working close to home. They had an automobile. His father had gone to church and confessed all of his sins. They were eating round steak and chopped beef and less fried baloney and canned soup. Why would God want his dad now?

Richard had the uncontrollable feeling that it was because of him. Richard had been praying for his mother's "disappearance." Life would have been perfect if she would just go away. He didn't necessarily ask God to kill her, but that was one of many acceptable alternatives. God could have taken these prayers and requests the wrong way.

Then there was the general notion that life, overall, was just a cruel game that God was playing on everybody.

Life was a test. It was a test to see just how much hurt an individual could take. God knew that taking Richard's father would be the greatest hurt that he could inflict on Richard. God was in the background of all of Richard's thoughts, but his dad was in the foreground.

Richard without his father would be like a boy without his legs, like a body without a soul. To Richard, winning the love of his father was his whole life. Without his goals in relation to his father, Richard had no goal. Without his father, forever, Richard's life would have no meaning. To win his father's love and friendship had been the only real purpose of Richard's entire life. Richard's father couldn't leave him now. He couldn't just die. If his father were going to leave, Richard wanted to leave with him. Living made no sense without his father. Richard had no explanation for such an eventuality.

Ernie was confused. If his father did die, how was he supposed to take care of his sister and brother? He told his father that he would, but doing any such thing was basically impossible. How could he possibly take care of anybody? He didn't have a job. He was still going to school. He was only nineteen. He had worked in the Arlington Mill one summer before it closed, but he couldn't do anything like that for the rest of his life. He would have to finish his schooling no matter what happened. His father wasn't going to die. Was he? Everybody thinks that bad things are going to happen to them, but that doesn't mean that they really happen.

Both boys lay there thinking, until they finally dozed off.

Their father sat at the small kitchen table smoking his pipe in the dark. He was positive that he was about to die. So what was he supposed to do about it? He couldn't go sit up at the hospital. He didn't have any money. How the hell could he ever pay a bunch of hospital bills? Even if he did have money, what the heck could they do about it?

What would it feel like to die, he asked himself. He had an idea of the pain, but would that be it; or would it be worse? He always knew that he was going to die. Everybody knows. It is different, though, when death is sitting there right in front of your face. Everything suddenly seems so unimportant. Even his job at the Merit gas station didn't seem to matter. What would hell be like?

He had gone to Confession, but certainly he was not a fit candidate for heaven. It wasn't that simple. How could hell really be any worse than all of this life? How could there really be a God with a world like this? Who gives a damn anyway? If there is a God, He is going to do whatever it is that He is going to do. What will be, will be.

Why didn't he take Richard fishing once or twice? Why did he just sit there every night drinking beer? His wife? She has been worried to death all week. She tried. In her own way, she tried. He could have tried harder, that was for sure. If somehow this all goes away, he would change everything. "Why now?" he mumbled to himself. "Why now, God?"

In the morning Richard and Ernie were jolted upright in their bed by their mother's screams. She went rushing by their half-closed bedroom door screaming for Carol.

"Carol! Carol! Help me! Do something! Carol!"

In another moment, mother and daughter, both ran by the boys' bedroom door. They were heading to the back bedroom.

"Oh my God! Oh my God!"

Richard's brother was on the outside of the bed. Richard had the side against the wall. As Ernie sat on his edge getting dressed, Richard threw the covers off and jumped off the front edge of the bed. He rushed into his trousers as he dashed into the kitchen.

His sister was now in her seat next to the stove dialing the telephone. Richard looked down the corridor to his mother and father's bedroom. The door was open. His father was lying in his bed on his back. His mouth was open and he seemed to be struggling for breath. Each time that he tried to suck in air, his chest raised right off the bed. He kept gulping and gasping and struggling. Richard had no idea what to do. He stood in the corridor staring at his father struggling for his life.

His mother was in a panic. She wasn't crying but she was screaming bloody murder.

Carol wasn't crying either. She was too frightened. She had somebody on the phone and was giving them instructions on how to get to the house. Mary suddenly bolted passed Richard. "I'm going upstairs to get Uncle Ray," she screamed to Carol. Carol began dialing the phone once again.

Richard had no idea where to go or what to do. Instinctively he began walking down the corridor towards his father's bedroom. By the time he got to his father's bedside his dad was still bolting spasmodically, as if he were being shocked electrically. His eyes were open and glaring upward. They were filled with pain and fear and lack of awareness. They weren't seeing Richard or anyone else.

"Don't die, Dad. Please don't die," Richard said, looking down at his father. His father was gasping and choking. His chest was heaving upward. "You can't die now, Dad. It isn't fair. We were just becoming friends."

Richard's only thought was what would his father do without him? Who would pick his dad up when he fell down on his way to heaven or hell? Who would his father have to lean on if Richard were not there with him?

Richard fell to his knees beside his father's bed. "God, if you take my father, take me too. I don't want to be here alone. My father needs me. He has always needed me. If he is not going to be here anymore, I do not want to be here anymore. This world will be no fun without my father. It has been too hard. It is just too hard. It is too hard trying to win love from people. If he is to die, I want to die also. I want to die. I want to die too. Don't worry Dad; I'm going with you. We will do it together. You won't be alone. I'm not afraid. I want to die. Oh God, I want to die too."

Richard could feel his father's pain inside his own chest. He knew that the second his father died he would die also. Silently, in his mind, like a prayer the words, "I want to die," kept repeating. His mind would say nothing else, but, I want to die ... I want to die ... I want to die.

Suddenly his Uncle Ray was behind him and pulling him up from his knees. Doctor Kurka was in the bedroom. He had placed his black bag on the chair. He had a huge hypodermic needle in his hand and he was crawling up onto the bed. He had his shoes on. He was climbing onto the bed and he still had his shoes on! He pulled open the top of Richard's father's pajamas and pushed the needle into the heart side of his dad's chest. Uncle Ray was dragging Richard from the room.

"You can't do anything, Richard. You have got to let the doctor do his job. Come on, we have to get out of the way."

Uncle Ray guided Richard from the bedroom and out into the kitchen. They both stood by the refrigerator, staring down the corridor.

The big needle would save his father's life. Doctor Kurka knew what he was doing. Doctors know how to fix people. It would only be a minute or two and his father would be sitting up on the edge of the bed. It would only be a minute and this nightmare would be over. Doctor Kurka threw the needle aside and put both hands onto his father's chest and began bouncing up and down. What was he doing?

A few moments went by and Doctor Kurka crawled back off the bed. He walked around the far side of the bed and then over to the bedroom door. He looked at Ray and shook his head. Then he closed the bedroom door.

Richard broke from his uncle and ran down the corridor. He pushed the door open, and then stood silently beside the bed. His uncle came up behind him.

"You can cry, Richard, if you want to. There is nothing wrong with crying at a time like this. You have the right."

"I don't want to cry. I want to die."

"Oh no no no, you don't mean that. You don't want to die."

"I want to die right now. What is he going to do without me? He needs me."

“No, no, he is with God. Your father is with all his family and friends who have already gone. He will be happy now.”

“No. He has no friends. All his family hate him. I am all that he has. I’ve got to go with him. I have to die too. I want to die; I want to die. I want to die, right now.”

“Richie, Richie, Richie,” his uncle said, his voice cracking into tears. “You can’t die, child, even if you want to. You can’t just die. That is not the way it works. Only God says who lives and who dies.”

“I want God to kill me. I want God to kill me, just as He has killed my father. I want to be with my father. I don’t care about God. I want to be with my father. I want to die now.”

Richard fell to his knees by the bed. His uncle squatted down beside the boy. He rubbed the boy’s back and then pulled him into his arms. The boy hung there in his uncle’s arms, motionless and tearless. He did not want to cry. No, no, no. He did not want to cry. The boy wanted to die. He prayed to God to end his life. He just wanted to die.

18 The Funeral

There were so many people at the wake that Richard and his sister, Carol, were stunned.

"Who are all of these people?" Richard asked.

"I don't know. They must be friends of Dad's."

"If Dad had all of these friends, how come we never saw them when he was alive?" Richard asked.

Carol had no answer.

For the entire three days of the wake, Carol and Richard sat in the room with the casket. The funeral home was actually the converted first-floor apartment of a tenement house. The living room was where the body was displayed. The kitchen was where everybody went to drink coffee and smoke cigarettes.

From their folding chairs, Carol and Richard could see their father a few feet away. He had been waked in the only suit that he ever owned. Mary bought it on sale one day. When she showed it to her husband, he commented that he would probably only have occasion to wear a suit like that at his funeral. He was right.

His cheeks were rosy. His lips were a vibrant red. His hair was black and shiny. He had rosary beads strung through his hands and fingers and a handkerchief in his breast suit coat pocket. He looked handsome. Many people commented on that fact. When Richard heard such comments he thought how much he would rather have his father drunk, ugly and alive, than handsome and dead. He voiced this opinion to several of the visitors. None of them responded. His sister told him not to say that anymore.

"Funny," Richard said to his sister in a quiet moment. "I stare at Dad laying there and I expect him to pop up, laugh and say that this is all just a joke."

"Me too; sometimes I try to will him back to life. I just keep staring at his chest telling him to breathe."

Richard thought that to be a good idea. He also began willing his father to breathe.

The casket was buried in bouquets of flowers. Richard had never before seen so many flowers. He figured that they must be on loan from the funeral home. His sister told him that they were bought by people. Richard didn't believe her. Carol took him up to several of the bouquets and read the cards that were attached. Richard was shocked. He walked around the casket and read the cards on each basket. He couldn't believe this whole thing.

When his father was alive and he needed ten dollars for groceries, he couldn't get a penny from even his own brothers and sisters. Now that he was gone, everyone showered his dead body with baskets of expensive flowers. There was a huge basket of flowers from every one of his dad's family. This seemed very strange. Clearly, Richard thought, his dad's family liked his father better dead than alive. His father should have asked his relatives, back in the days when he needed money, to give him five dollars then and forget about sending the ten or fifteen dollars worth of flowers when he was dead.

All these folks now showed up at his father's wake. Where were they all during the rest of his dad's life? They never came to the house. Richard had never seen one of these people talking to his father in the street. What were they all doing here now that he was dead? This wake business was a very peculiar happenstance.

Two of his father's sisters had even cried. What were they crying about? When his dad had asked them for fifty dollars they had left him sitting there on the parlor floor, weeping. Uncle Vinnie, his dad's brother, had put three cigarettes into his dad's shirt pocket. His dad had taken them out of his pocket and crushed them in his hand after Vinnie had left.

Richard's mother didn't cry enough to satisfy his liking. She was always blowing her nose and her eyes were red, but she never seemed to shed a real tear. The look on her face did not seem to him to be one of sadness, but of fear. She should have been more frightened when he was alive. Maybe that would have made her more understanding. Maybe she would have been a little nicer. Maybe she would have tried a little harder.

Richard was torn in his attempt to assign blame for his father's death. He knew that, ultimately, God was in charge. God could say, "Let this person live" or "Let this person die." God said let him die. Why had God allowed his father to die? Whatever God's reasons, Richard truly resented God for His decision. God was not only mean and revengeful, He was cruel. Richard decided that God was no longer worthy of his love and devotion. God was not a nice person. God was mean and abusive. God was like his mother. God was criminally insane. He yelled and screamed and destroyed whole nations and worlds full of people. Richard still loved Jesus and the Blessed Mother, though. They made more sense. They were not involved in killing and punishing people. "Father forgive them, for they know not what they do," Jesus had said.

At other moments Richard blamed himself. He had been wishing, hoping and even praying for his mother's "disappearance" for years. If only something had happened to her, everything would have been all right. God obviously resented Richard for thinking this way. As a punishment, God decided to take Richard's father instead of his mother. God was teaching Richard a lesson. God had taken Richard's father as punishment for Richard's evil and sinful thoughts.

Richard was the one to blame for his father's death. Richard had killed his own father. Honor Thy Father and Thy Mother, God had said. Richard had dishonored his mother and now had killed his own father. He didn't stab his father in the chest with a knife, but he had killed him. Certainly Richard's evil and vengeful thoughts about his mother could be the real cause of his father's death. How could he ever be forgiven for these sins? He should be dead also. God should take Richard also. But God was more vindictive than that. God would make Richard stay alive. He would make Richard stay alive so that he could suffer longer. God would punish Richard for his evil thoughts. Doing is only half the sin. Thinking, wishing and hoping for evil is equal to the evil. Richard was as guilty of killing his father as anyone else. He should be punished. He would be punished. He would be punished in this life and in the next.

Then, of course, there was Richard's mother. If she hadn't brow-beaten, abused and mentally battered his dad for all of their life together, his heart may never have gotten weak and quit beating. If she hadn't made him so miserable every waking minute of every day, maybe he would have wanted to live. Maybe he would have tried harder to stay alive. She drove the poor man crazy. She drove everybody crazy. She was crazy. She never stopped - yak, yak, yak - she went on and on. Her criticism never stopped. Her mouth never stopped. Nothing nice ever seemed to come out of her. God may have hated Richard for wishing this woman's death, but truly, this woman did not deserve to be alive. She hated life and everyone in it.

Richard had, at times, fantasized about actually physically assaulting his mother. Sometimes he thought of putting his hands around her neck and squeezing until she died. He could actually feel her struggling beneath his clutching fingers. He would hold and squeeze until he could feel the breath of life leave her body. Other times he thought of beating her to death with his fists. He would just punch and punch and punch, until her whole face would be nothing but a bloody pulp. He could feel the impact of his fist against the flesh of her face. It would be better to feel his flesh impacting her flesh for a change. Why not? Why not smack her skull against a floor or a wall? What is good for the goose is good for the gander – remember?

There was no doubt that he hated this woman. God knew of Richard's hate. God knew all his terrible feelings. God said, Honor Thy Father and Thy Mother. Richard had sinned against God's commandment. Richard was a sinner. Richard thought evil things. Richard was evil, just as his mother was evil.

This brings us to the last accomplice in this murder. Couldn't his father have tried a little harder himself to stay alive? Didn't he know how much Richard loved him? Didn't he know that Richard's love and friendship would have eventually overcome all of his mother's stupidity? Didn't he love Richard? Didn't he know how much Richard needed him? How could he just give up like that? He quit. He really didn't want to live. So he just gave up. He had no right to do such a thing. He was partly responsible for bringing Richard here into this world. He had an obligation to see it through to the end. It didn't matter that his wife was a jerk. She was always a jerk. She would be a jerk until the day that she died. What did she have to do with anything? His father was a quitter. His father drank instead of fighting back. His father was spineless and weak.

His father allowed himself to die. He did not have the right to do that.

If he were a brave man, he would have overcome the hardships. He would have concentrated on the love and not the hate. He would have been a man instead of a wimp. He would have taken Richard fishing with him. He had the fishing poles right there behind the bedroom door. Why didn't he ever follow through? They didn't need a boat. They could have just walked together up to the side of some lake. They could have gone down to the Black Rocks at Salisbury Beach. They didn't have to catch a fish. What did that matter? They didn't have to talk, really. Just being together would have been enough. Just being sober and being together. That would have been something in itself, just he and his dad, just the two of them. That would have really meant something.

What did those two fishing poles sitting behind the bedroom door really mean now? They meant that his dad had thought about loving him for a moment. His dad had thought just long enough to buy those poles. But when it actually came to spending an hour with his son, his father had decided that it just wasn't worth the effort. A Pabst Blue Ribbon was more important. Old dad could find more love in a beer can than he could in his son's eyes - in his son's heart. Sit, sulk, and slop down booze. That was his dad's whole life. A beer a day keeps the children away.

"Do you think that Dad really loved us?" he asked his sister as they sat there staring at his dad's dead body in that silk lined casket. His sister started to cry once again. She had been crying on and off ever since her father died. She jumped from her seat and ran to the back of the funeral parlor towards the lady's room. She hadn't answered Richard.

The boy knew that he loved his father, but he was not sure if the feeling was mutual. How does one judge? His father had never said, soberly, that he loved Richard. His mother had certainly never said any such thing. Actually no one had ever told Richard that they loved him. No relatives, no friends, not even his grandmother. It was like everyone was withholding their judgment until ... until when?

Did he have to do something? What? Be the fastest in a race? Win a prize at the Carnival? Get the most stars on his forehead at school? What did one have to do or accomplish to be loved in this world by somebody? It was too hard to win people's love. It was just too, too hard.

The priests and the nuns had told him that God loved him. They never said that they, themselves, loved him. It was very plain that they didn't. It was easy to claim God's love. God never showed up to verify it.

"Do you love me, sir?"

"Ah ... God loves you, son." It was all kind of a cop-out, wasn't it?

There was one guy who stayed there in the back room at the funeral home for hours, drinking coffee and telling jokes. Richard kept staring at the man. The man finally looked at the boy and said, "I don't mean any disrespect, son. I'm just trying to lighten things up a bit."

He was just trying to lighten things up? That was interesting. A man drops dead and this is the time to become Milton Berle? Maybe they should have a magic act and a couple of jugglers and an elephant or two also? What was this, a dog and pony show?

"Step right up. Step right up. Now looky here folks; I'm gonna tell you what I'm gonna do. Pick the little bean out from under the right cup and you win a prize. Throw the ring over the peg and get a balloon. Step right up folks. Step right up."

They called it a funeral, but it was a sideshow. Hundreds of dollars worth of flowers for a dead body?

There was a huge stack of envelopes on a giant silver tray. The envelopes were stacked so high they kept falling off the tray and onto the floor. Richard and Carol kept picking them up and placing them back onto the tray. Days later, Richard learned that the envelopes were from well-wishers and many of them had dollar bills inside them. When Richard learned that fact, he felt that he shouldn't have been picking the envelopes up off the floor. He thought that the people watching must have thought of him as a money grubber. There he was diving to the floor to pick up their dollars. He didn't even know that the envelopes had dollars in them.

Priests came to the wake. One evening everyone knelt on the carpeted floor and prayed the rosary. Many male friends of his father paid their respects, then went out onto the front porch and smoked cigarettes. Friends of his older brother and sister came. Many of Richard's street corner friends and school chums came. Some of his buddies were frightened of his father's dead body. They had never seen a dead body before. One of his school chums wouldn't look at the body. He said that he thought that it was spooky. Richard agreed, but not deep down inside. He tried to imagine what he might say to a friend if it were the friend's father who was lying there, dead in a box, in the middle of a room. Would he tell him that his dead father looked spooky?

Richard loved his father both dead and alive. It hurt to hear people say that his dad looked spooky, or that looking at his dead body made them feel peculiar. When Richard looked at the body in the box, he saw his father. He saw the man whom he had dreamed about most of his childhood. The body in the box was still his father. He just wasn't breathing.

Many of the old people reached out and touched the back of his father's hand. After a day or two, Richard went up to the body and reached out and touched it also.

The body was cold. He hadn't expected it to feel that way. At first touch, he pulled his hand away. After a moment he reached out and touched it again. The feel of a lifeless body was like nothing he had ever felt before. When he removed his hand from the corpse and turned, it seemed that the whole room was staring at him. There was an aura of fear in the room. It seemed that nobody knew quite what to make of death. Everyone looked, touched and sat. Everyone watched everyone else. They all seemed to be looking for some insight.

Why did they have such a thing as a wake? Why did they display a dead body, all dressed up nice, in somebody's living room? This was not really a pleasant circumstance for anyone. Some people walked in the door, took one look at the body and began to cry. Some knelt down on the kneeler before the casket. Some stood silently with their hands folded. Some said prayers. Others appeared to be just looking. Everyone was thinking. What were they thinking about? Richard didn't know. He really liked the fact that so many people came. What if there had been no one there? What if it were he and his brother and sister and their mother, and no one else?

His sister returned from her trip to the lady's room and repositioned herself in the seat next to Richard.

"Daddy loved all of us," she said. Richard looked at her dubiously. "He wasn't good at showing it, but he loved us," she went on, looking at her younger brother. Richard didn't answer. He simply turned his head and stared at the dead body before him. "Daddy could have left and just never came back." That was true. "But he didn't. He took whatever job that he could find. He did his best. Now he is in heaven. Now maybe he will have peace. There will be no one nagging him up in heaven."

Carol had gone to the lady's room to think. She obviously knew, as Richard, that their mother's nagging was the curse of their father's life. Now in heaven, he would be free from their mother. That would mean peace. His father would now have peace in heaven, but Richard would still be here with his mother, experiencing hell on earth. Hell was Richard's mother. She made it all hell. She made it hell for everybody.

They rode to the cemetery in a limousine. The people from the funeral parlor picked them up daily and took them home in a limousine. The man who drove the limousine wore gray gloves and a black tuxedo. He had a fancy gray and black tie. They all did. All of the people from the funeral home were perfect. They dressed perfectly. They acted perfectly. These men were professional death attendants. They never laughed or even smiled inappropriately. The slightest smile on their part was censored with sympathy and compassion. Richard liked these men. They took death seriously.

The general public who attended the funeral were very unprofessional. They reacted in every possible way. They were not consistent like the funeral parlor staff. Some of the random observers were overly sympathetic. Some were jovial and lighthearted. Almost all of them were confused and surprised by this circumstance of death. The undertaker, his family and assistants were perfect in their emotional positioning. They always knew what to say and how to act. They led Richard and his family always in the proper direction. When Richard did not know what to do, he simply looked up at one of them and they would immediately respond with the proper direction and attention. They were very reassuring.

The burial site at the cemetery was prepared. There was a canopy over the hole. The flowers that had surrounded the casket at the funeral parlor were now circled around the grave site. A graveyard had always been a place of mystery, ghouls, ghosts and demons to Richard. Now that his father was being lowered into a grave, the mystery disappeared. Under every headstone or monument was somebody's father, or mother, or family member. They weren't ghouls or ghosts. They were the bodies of real people. They were people who had once been alive. They had been loved by others. The graveyard wasn't really a scary place. It was a sacred place. It was a place that had been set aside to honor the dead.

Richard wondered where his mother and father had gotten the money to own a grave site. Everything costs money. His family had no money. Was it the community that provided these spaces for people to be buried - even unimportant people? On the trip home in the limousine he asked his mother. She told him that his Grandma Essick had purchased a plot for the whole family many years ago. It was his grandmother who had anticipated death. She was very wise. Everyone else just seemed to ignore it, but not his grandmother. She was very wise.

At the grave Richard was directed to toss a handful of dirt onto his father's casket which had been lowered into the ground. He refused. He did not want to participate in the burial of his father. To his mind, throwing dirt upon the casket was a symbol of forgetting. The idea that just because his father had died, he would be forgotten was not true. Richard would never forget his father. He didn't really believe in the permanency of death. There was a life after death. Jesus rose up from the dead and wandered about the streets once again.

Richard also harbored the fantasy that this whole death thing was a trick that his father had concocted. His father had to escape from his mother. He just couldn't stand it any longer. His father would somehow appear again. This death business was not a permanent thing.

In the days after the funeral, Richard became sullen. He spoke very little, and not at all to his mother. He answered any direct questions by her, but briefly and with a minimum of words. He appeared to be barren of any emotion. He went to school. On the first day that he returned to school after the funeral, his eighth-grade nun called him out into the corridor. When he stepped out of the classroom there was a bevy of nuns standing there. They clustered around him in a semi-circle. They wanted to know what had happened. Richard explained the entire morning of his father's death in vivid detail. To

Richard, recreating the event was a part of putting it all into a permanent memory. The nuns stood about ooh-ing and ahh-ing and moaning and groaning. Occasionally one of the nuns would reach out and pat him on a shoulder. They would constantly interject, "Oh, how horrible!" or, "Oh heavens! What a brave young man you are." Richard related the story coolly and without emotion. He observed the nuns as he spoke. All their faces were filled with pathos. Their gestures were animated. A hand would rush to a mouth. Fingers would press against a pair of lips. The nuns were clearly shocked by the whole event.

But why? If there were any group that should be ready for death, it should be this one. They talked of death daily. They had been teaching Richard about it since he arrived on that very first day. Why did they seem to be so frightened and shocked? They had the dead body of Jesus hanging around their necks and dangling down by their sides.

Richard felt a strange sense of superiority. He had been an eyewitness to death. He had seen death with his own eyes. It was like being one of the apostles who had witnessed the torture, persecution and death of Jesus. Now as an apostle he was explaining it all to the disciples. They were all in the state of awe. He was the littlest of heroes. He was Richard - the boy wonder.

When school was out, he stayed in the schoolyard, or walked the streets. His friends questioned him. Their reactions were much like the nuns. He wouldn't look his mother in the eye for fear that she would be able to read his mind.

His father was gone, but yet he saw him everywhere. On one occasion as he walked down Essex Street, he was so sure that a man up ahead was his dad that he ran past the man then peered up into his face in anticipation.

It was not his father. He had been so sure - the gait of the man, his hair color, his jacket. It had to be his father. This type of experience happened nearly every day. Richard would not let his father go. This whole thing could not be true. This could not be a part of life. God would not do this to his creatures. This was far too painful to be acceptable to God. God was kind and loving. He could not be this cruel.

Richard could not help thinking how much better life would be if it had been his mother who had died. He fantasized about awakening in the morning and going out into the kitchen and finding his father sitting there with his morning cup of tea. His father would smile and tell him to hurry and get ready for school. Many mornings he rushed out into the kitchen from a similar dream, only to find his mother sitting there.

Day by day he blamed his mother more and more. Certainly she was the cause of all of the unhappiness while his father was alive. She just couldn't stand to see anybody happy. She was never positive, never happy. Even those few moments when she did smile, her smile was burdened with pain and negativism. Just looking at her could wipe any smile from a person's face. He could no longer look at her. So he didn't.

Mary was in a very unpleasant state herself. She sat in the parlor fidgeting and staring out the window. Her energy level was low.

Carol did the shopping and paid the bills for her mother. Richard would accompany Carol to the grocery store on occasion. They had very little to say to one another. They just walked. To Richard's way of thinking, his mother had not cried sufficiently. She hadn't cried the day his father died. She never cried once at the funeral. He never saw her crying in these few days after the funeral. She didn't cry because she didn't really care. Even if she did cry, he would have known that she was crying for herself and not for the loss of his father. She was worried because his father was no longer there to bring home a paycheck, but she was not sad because he was dead. She was worried about how she would now survive. Richard prayed every night for his father's acceptance into heaven. Did his mother say such prayers?

One evening, in the quiet and the night, Richard awoke with a start. There in the darkness he saw his mother. She was sitting on the edge of his bed. She had been rubbing his left shin with her hand. Richard leaped to a sitting position and pulled his leg away from her touch. He stared at her shadowy image there in the darkness of his room.

"Richard," she asked. "Do you love me?" Richard did not answer. His mother stared into the boy's eyes. "Sometimes I think that you hate me. Sometimes I think that you blame me for your father's death." She paused, waiting for a response.

His mother looked into his eyes once again. She grimaced at his bitter silence. "I didn't kill your father, Richard. He died from a heart attack. I know how much you loved him, but I didn't kill him."

Richard refused to believe her. In his mind the phrase, Oh yes you did, repeated over and over. His mother's presence right here, right now, was the living proof. If she didn't kill his father why would she be here apologizing? If she were not so filled with the guilt from her actions, why would she be sitting here on the edge of his bed in the middle of the night making this appeal?

She killed him as sure as she was sitting there. She killed him with the bullets from her ugly mouth. She cut him open with the razor of her criticisms. She strangled his heart and his love with her biting hatred and constant discontent. She killed him all right. She made his life so miserable that he didn't want to live. She was a murderer. She couldn't be put in jail. She couldn't be tried in a court of law. But, she was as guilty as sin and Richard knew it.

"I loved your father too, Richard." (Bullshit!) "I wish that he was here right now." (Why? So that you could nag him back into his grave.) "Do you believe me?"

His mother sat there and sat there - waiting in the darkness. She was pathetic. She was sickeningly pathetic. The boy's bitter silence and hateful glare was her only answer. She sighed deeply. She could see that it was no use. She could look at the boy's face no longer. His hate for her was agonizing.

She rose from the edge of his bed. She hesitated there for a moment. She looked at the boy. She had no more words. What could she say? What could she do? She would leave his room. She shuffled to his bedroom door. At the door she stopped and turned to the boy one last time.

"Richard, I'm going to tell you the God's honest truth. I wish that it had been me who died and not your father. I truly do." She looked down at the boy sitting stiff and upright on his bed. This time the boy spoke.

"I do too."

Her eyes then opened wide. They expressed shock and horror, but not hate or even anger. In a moment her look mellowed.

"I know you do, son. I know you do."

19 The River Ends

With his father now gone, Richard's life went to a period of reconstruction. Everything was now changed. He had no real reason to be alive. He often stopped along the Merrimack or the Spicket River bridges and contemplated suicide. He visualized himself floating through the air and then collapsing onto the rocks and the rushing water. Suicide was not a real and pressing idea. He knew in his heart that he would not do such a thing. It was just a feeling. It was what he felt like doing.

The thought of suicide was an expression of emotional fulfillment. It was like the thoughts he harbored in wishing his father home from the sea. It was like the fantasies he had of striking back against his mother's cruelty. It was like the dreams one has of food when one is hungry. Just as one tried to taste the imagined food, Richard tried to feel the suffering and pain of death. He imagined his own death because wouldn't that truly be the only death that would satisfy these ugly feelings? How does one vent his anger against himself? How does one punish himself for being alive? How does one revolt against the will of God? How does one show his anger for life itself, for injustice? How does one challenge the very concept of reality, of existence itself?

He could strike out at others, but does punishing another thing or person satisfy any of this? Hardly. It was his experience, his life and his family. What did anyone else have to do with all of this? Besides, Richard did not have the capacity for that kind of rationalization. He had no heart for outward aggression or for blaming others.

His father did not deserve to die. Even alive and drunk every night was better than dead. Even alive and unhappy was better than dead and gone. Dead and gone leaves no hope, no wishing, no dreaming; dead means ... the end.

The Merrimack River was huge. It had a dam that was gigantic. In its time, it was a wonder of human construction. Today it was just a waterfall. As he looked down onto the water beneath the bridge, it seemed to bubble and boil. It was filled with swirls and eddies. If someone were to jump off the Merrimack Bridge, what guarantee would there be that he would die? Were there rocks down there just below the surface? One does not die from just floating through the air. Splash! You hit the water.

Then what? It's cold. The current spins you around, and off you go this way or that. You swim and you swim and you swim. Then you tire. You sink. Water rushes into your mouth as you gasp for breath. You swallow the water instead of air. You gasp and struggle. Just like his father lying on his back in his death bed. His father's color had actually changed. He was gray - then a grayish blue. Then he was still.

There must be an easier way to die than drowning? Why do people jump off bridges? Certainly shooting oneself would be easier. You could jump off a sidewalk into moving traffic. Who says that you would get killed if you did? What if you merely broke your back and you were crippled or an invalid for the rest of your life?

Then, on the other hand, what would he do with his life if he lived? Day after day he thought, but nothing came to mind.

He did a good deal of walking. He walked and walked and walked. He never wanted to go home. He didn't want to sleep in that house.

An uncle from his mother's side came to the funeral. He felt sorry for Richard. He had a boy who was Richard's age. He would come over to the house and pick Richard up in his automobile. The three of them would go to a little league game, or over to the man's home for supper. Richard didn't understand what the man was trying to accomplish. One day when the man was dropping Richard off at his house on Chelmsford Street, Richard asked the man a question.

"What are you trying to do?"

The man was confused. He looked at the boy.

"Nothing."

"You can't be my father. My father is dead. A boy only has one father, you know."

"I know."

"The father that I had is the only father that I ever want to have. I don't need a substitute."

"I'm not trying to be a substitute. I'm ..."

"You are trying to take my father's place. I don't want anyone in his place."

"I understand," the uncle said.

When the poor man left that afternoon, he never returned. Richard was not hateful of the man. It was just ... It was just that he was a one-man dog. He didn't want to wag his tail for just anybody who came along. He was a son and he once had a father. Now he was a son with no father. That's the way life is. This man was a total stranger. Who did he think that he was? What was this man thinking? What was he feeling?

It didn't matter. Richard only wanted to be left alone. He had no desire to talk to anyone. Richard would often walk along the banks of the Spicket River behind the mills. He would watch the multi-colored dyes pour out of the huge mill drain pipes at the rear of the buildings.

The Spicket River was actually a city dump. It was filled with old furniture, busted bed springs, cardboard boxes, tree limbs and old paint cans. One could walk across the river at various points by just stepping from one pile of hung-up garbage to another. Richard thought nothing of this. This discarded refuse, was what a river was for.

One pressing thought in Richard's mind was that God had created this situation to punish him. God, for some reason, didn't want Richard to be happy. Richard was placed here on this earth to be punished. That was clear. His religion said that everyone was placed here to be punished. Religion said that a person could not commit suicide. Committing suicide was cheating God of his pound of flesh. God is the one who decides when you have had enough of life. It is not up to you. You must endure. You must take His hate and consider it one less day to wait. Life was not meant to be happy. People were not meant to be happy. Life, at best, was a challenge to be endured, not something to be enjoyed. Richard had committed the most grievous sin. He had asked to be happy. Of course, being happy meant the "disappearance" of his mother along with the return of his father.

God had to know that Richard's mother was no good. God is the one who made her that way. God is responsible for all things. God made disease. God made death. God made his mother as nutty as a fruitcake. His mother didn't choose to be nutty. Richard didn't choose her to be his mother. Did God really expect that He would make a human being who beat other human beings and the beaten would harbor no hatred? Did God expect that He could torture and punish humans and they would love Him for doing so? God knows what He is doing. He has a reason for everything. What other reason could there be for this present circumstance other than God wanted to punish Richard and make him suffer.

God also knew about hatred. God knew about revenge. This God was a vengeful God, was He not? He had flooded the world. He had destroyed whole populations.

God? Everybody was always talking about love, about God's love. What love? Where was this love? Who in this life had love? Did they have it, or did they just think that they had it? Richard certainly did not have it.

He had returned home many nights to a dark hall and an equally dark kitchen. His mother would sometimes call out from her bedroom. "Is that you, Richard?" Richard would grunt some type of acknowledgment.

"What time is it?" she would ask.

"It's early," he would answer.

"Okay."

His mother slowly but surely regained her confidence. Each day she became more and more assertive and demanding. Richard ignored her. She would tell him to do something and he would just pick up his basketball and leave the house. He had decided that she no longer existed. She was simply there, like a lamp or a couch. He walked past her without speaking. He rarely answered her questions. He didn't care what she said, what she thought, or how she acted. She would often shout to the back of his head as he exited a room or the building. Sometimes as he dribbled his ball down the street, he could feel her eyes. He would turn around and there she would be, standing on the front porch staring. He would laugh. She was upset. She wasn't in control. That is all that mattered to her. He was now out of her control.

He was. He most certainly was. She had absolutely no link to the boy. He had nothing to say to her. He had no feelings for her. He did not respect her. She could laugh, cry, and stand on her head. None of it mattered to Richard. It was all dead. Whatever was supposed to be there was now all dead.

Often when he returned home in the evenings, he would hear his mother's voice in the kitchen. He hated the sound of it. On some occasions he would turn about and return to the streets. He couldn't stand her. He didn't want to look at her. Her voice alone would be enough to send chills of disgust down his spine. She did not deserve to be alive. She should have been the one to die. Whatever God had been thinking in this case, He had been wrong.

Sometimes Richard would lean up against the wall in the dark hall and just listen to her. If he could only disappear; if somehow this all could be gone?

Yak, yak, yak - she never stopped yakking. Did she not know how irritating her every word was? How could his sister sit there every night? How could she stand it? Just the sound of his mother's "living" voice was an insult to his "dead" father. She should not be here. Where she should be, he did not know. But she should not be here.

He would swallow it all up and proceed down the dark hall. He would hesitate at the door. Light from the kitchen would come through the spaces around the edges of the poorly fitted door. If there could just be silence and darkness, it would be so much better to hear nothing, to see nothing, to be nothing.

He would open the door and there would be the woman. She was always at the sink. She was always cleaning or washing something. She was always talking. He would walk through the kitchen sometimes to the bathroom. Other times he would go directly to his bedroom. Sometimes she would look at him. Sometimes she wouldn't. He had nothing to say to her and she had nothing to say to him.

One evening, a week or two after his father's death, he entered the dark hall and heard his mother and sister both screaming. The sound of their screaming voices went through his body like shrapnel. It shocked him and sent waves of anger, hate and revulsion from his head to his toes. His mother was screaming at his sister about something. His sister was screaming back, tearfully, in her own defense. This couldn't be happening he thought to himself. We weren't going to be returning to this state of madness, were we?

His mother was ranting in a heated anger. It was all too familiar. She was getting wilder and wilder. Suddenly he heard that familiar sound of flesh cracking against flesh. Crack! Crack! Crack! His sister screamed with each blow. Richard felt that he could stand no more of this.

He would leave. How could he leave? Once again he heard his mother's palms cracking against his sister's face. What could he do? Tears welled up inside of him. He could not live like this again. His father was gone. His brother was away at college. He was the only man in this family. His heart began to pound. He could feel himself flushing red. He began to tremble. He was afraid.

What could he do? He was still but a boy. Could he actually win over his mother in a fist fight? How would he stop her? She certainly wouldn't be frightened by the likes of him.

Crack! Crack! Crack! And his sister screamed and yelled in protest.

"You're not too big yet for me to teach you some manners. You don't disrespect me, little girl."

Richard wanted to turn, to exit the hall, to leave the building, to leave everything. He wanted to leave all of this behind, to go somewhere and never, ever return.

But how could he? Where could he go? He was still a child. He couldn't leave. How would he ever take care of himself? What could he do?

He could fight couldn't he! He could enter that kitchen door and challenge his mother. He could tell her to stop beating up her children.

But what if she wouldn't? What if she attacked him? What could he do, put down his head, fall to the floor and scurry under the kitchen table? She was still much bigger than he was.

Could he fight his own mother like some stranger out in the street or neighborhood? Could he close his fists and strike his mother? Could he punch her in the face? Could he hit her and knock her to the floor? Could he punch her or bang her head into the floor until she bled just as she had done to him?

What if she went crazy like she always does? What if she wouldn't stop fighting? What if they fought and she refused to give up? Could he fight and fight and fight? Could he beat his mother until she gave up – until she quit?

And if she didn't quit? And if she wouldn't give up? And what if she fought and fought and fought? Could he beat her until she could take no more? Could he beat her to death if he had to? Could he fight his mother in a battle to the death?

Richard had no idea what he would do or what he could achieve, but he must do something. He walked slowly and hesitantly down the dim corridor. He opened the door slowly. His mother was now by the sink. His sister was in her chair. Her nose was all red and the marks of her mother's slaps were visibly embedded all over her flaming cheeks. Richard took a deep breath and closed the door behind him. He took two steps further into the kitchen. He was trembling. He had never felt like this in his life. He stood there staring at his mother. She was still blustering and blabbering at her daughter. She took a quick look over her right shoulder and saw Richard standing there - staring. She ignored him and went on with her outrage. When she turned once again, Richard was still there staring.

"What the hell are you looking at?" she demanded. Richard didn't answer. "You had just better get the hell into your room and shut up before I give you a taste of this."

"This is going to stop," Richard said cautiously.

"And who is going to stop it?"

"I am."

"You're going to stop what?"

"You are not going to hit anybody in this house ever again. The hitting is going to stop."

His mother turned around and faced the boy. She put her hands on the sink behind her.

"Is that right?"

"That's right."

"You know buddy. I've had just about enough of you. You are also not too big for me to give you a piece of my mind. You're pretty brave all of a sudden, aren't you?"

"Brave enough."

"You know, I think that I am going to come over there and smack some sense into that big mouth of yours."

"I wouldn't try that if I were you."

"And why is that?"

"Because if you lay one hand on me, I am going to bust your face in with my fists. I am not going to slap. I am going to close my fists and I am going to punch your face until it is a bloody pulp," Richard said, confirming the demanded, imagined actions to himself.

Richard braced himself and clenched his fists by his sides. If she attacked, he would strike. He must! The time for thinking was over. His mother stood there staring at her child.

"Are you listening to this, Carol? What a proud mother I am. How proud your father would be to hear his son speaking like this to his mother. What a fine, fine son you are - a son who could hit his own mother. Isn't that something?"

"And what kind of a mother is it who can beat her children? What kind of a mother is it who can hit her small boy so hard that he falls to the floor? What kind of a mother is it who can beat a boy, not tall enough to even reach her waist? What kind of a mother slaps her daughter around as if she were some kind of rag doll?

"Let me explain this to you in detail, mother. You strike me or my sister ever again and I am going to knock you from one end of this house to the other. I am going to punch you with my fist for every slap that you have ever given out. I will hit you ten times for every one time that you have struck either of us. I am going to knock you to the floor. I am going to smack your face into the floor. If you try to crawl away under the kitchen table to escape my beating, I am going to grab you by the ankles and pull you out - just as you did to me when I was no more than a baby. I'm going to beat you to within an inch of your life. And if I have to, I will beat you to death."

"Oh you were never a baby," she said, casually ignoring all of Richard's hateful words, vindictive tone, and threats. "You were a bad boy. You had been bad at school."

"That's not what the nun said."

"The nun lied. She wouldn't have kept you back if you hadn't have been bad."

"Well, why did you apologize on the way home?"

"I don't know why. I should never have done it. You obviously didn't deserve an apology. Let me take that apology back right here and now."

"Well, it doesn't matter. I'm just telling you, I'm going to smack you, kick you, and punch you. I'm going to knock your head into that wall. I am going to beat you like you have never been beaten before in your life. You don't understand any other kind of language. But I know how to speak your language. You taught me. You taught me well. Now I am ready. I'm giving you your choice. You can apologize to your daughter for all of these years of abuse. You can tell her that you are sorry. Or you can try me on for size. I'm warning you ..."

"You are a fine son," she interrupted once again. "You know that? You are really special." As she spoke she dried her hands on a dish cloth. "I'm so proud that I gave birth to such a loving child. When I think of all those loving moments that I carried you inside my belly, boy! I'm so damn proud."

"You gave birth to nothing. I was never inside your body. I am no part of you whatsoever. I am not your son. You are no mother of mine. You never were and you never will be."

"You ungrateful snipe! I've heard enough out of you! I'll teach you to speak to your mother like that."

She came rushing towards Richard. The boy clenched his fists and gritted his teeth. He would give her every opportunity to stop, but the minute one of her blows struck him he would strike back. He would strike and strike and strike.

Her hand cracked against the side of his head. Suddenly she was gone. She had disappeared. She was there coming forward, getting bigger and bigger and bigger. But now, in the space in front of him, he could see only red. It was red. Everything was red. All was gone, all was dead, and all that remained was the heat, the flame, and the hate. All was red.

The End.

Dear Mom and Dad:

If you think I am not listening; think again.

If you think I didn't understand; I did.

If you think I will forget; I won't.

If you think it won't hurt; it hurts a lot.

If you think you have the right; you don't.

Love, Richard.